# WICKS END
*Salem Mysteries*

# Shadow Over Siri

## John and Vincent DiGianni

# WICKS END
*Salem Mysteries*

## Shadow Over Siri

# Acknowledgement

Writing a book is a little like building the Great Pyramid. While the primary authors in that monumental undertaking are easily credited, such as Pharaoh Khufu and his master builder, Imhotep, there were a lot of helpers that lent their comments and encouragement.

For their own endeavor, the authors would like to thank the following for all their assistance, both big as hauling sandstone blocks and small as shifting pails of sand.

My wife Lisa, with love, for her patience and editing skills
Mom and Dad
Elizabeth
Rose and Emily
Uncle Joe
Tom and Ashley
Florrie

*In the supernatural department:*

Bob
Grandma and Grandpa DiGianni
Grandma and Grandpa Wall
Aunt Margaret

# Foreword

Wicks End – Salem Mysteries: Shadow Over Siri is a work of fiction, inspired by Salem's unique atmosphere and history. Some of the places depicted in the novel are actual places, such as the Witch House, Gallows Hill, and the House of the Seven Gables. Other locations are purely fictional like the Black Ram Inn on Hardy Street. The characters in these pages that walk the streets of Wicks End and the town of Salem are fictitious, and their resemblance to any real persons is purely coincidental. Sadly, the witchcraft hysteria of 1692 that sent nineteen innocent souls to Gallows Hill, and one to pressing, is not a literary invention, but an actual historical event. Nowadays Salem balances both this tragic part of its history with its promising future as a tourism community, psychic capital, and maritime center on Boston's North Shore.

But it's time to meet Siri Braddock. Let's turn the page and drop in on her life on WICKS END.

# CHAPTER 1: Trapped in a Museum

If a fortune teller had told Siri yesterday that she'd be trapped in an eerie museum at night, fighting to escape, well, she wouldn't have given such a crazy prediction a second thought. What a difference a day makes!

"I can't believe this is happening to me!" Siri's mind whirled.

But it was happening. She couldn't talk or even scream out. She was being wrapped like a mummy as she lay on a granite slab in a dark chamber. Siri glanced down at her body bound in bandages. She wiggled like a worm, but it was no good. The sinister man with the surgeon's mask covering his face snickered. It was such a low, evil laugh. He continued his work, wrapping and wrapping. The linen roll he worked around her chin and mouth was tight, so tight Siri could feel her eyes bugging out of her head. Then a band of linen rolled over her eyes and cast her in darkness. Siri felt her body being lifted and set down within a sarcophagus. She knew the one – the one the stolen Egyptian mummy used to occupy. Siri could smell the cedar wood even through the bandages that covered her face. Then she heard the carved, wooden lid wrestled back into place on top of her. Buried alive! Not the best way for a girl to end her first week as a sophomore at Windward High School.

As Siri struggled in the bandages, she recalled how she hid in the lady's room of the Salem Museum of Antiquities that afternoon – how she waited until the lights went out at closing time. She had to go there that day. There was something she needed. The Tutankhamun exhibit on loan from the Egyptian Museum in Cairo was the sensation it promised to be. The continuous crowds kept security so busy Siri knew that all she had to do was hide and bide her time until all the exhausted staff left, performing marginal searches for strays and loiterers until the lights went out and the place was locked up. Then she could set her plan into action. But as Siri crept out into the museum's grand atrium with its soaring glass roof, she soon realized someone else was in there too, and it wasn't a night watchman. Her eyes trained on the ray of a flashlight roaming over a glass display case – one full of golden Egyptian amulets that glittered in the darkness. Siri watched the light disk move over to a crisp papyrus scroll showing the mournful pageant of a funeral boat with its large, double oars conveying a sarcophagus adorned with the likeness of Osiris down the Nile. The flashlight beam then turned upon great, regal statues carved of black granite looming out of the dark, their blank eyes fixed ahead, heedless of the probing ray. Siri ducked behind a statue of Horus, the falcon-headed Egyptian god of the sky, and watched the probing flashlight beam settle upon a row of coffins arrayed in glass cases upon the floor of the gallery. Within each reposed a mummy bound in time-yellowed wrappings. One mummy, Siri noticed, lay in a grand sarcophagus trimmed in gold, and inlaid with jasper, lapis and turquoise. The coffin lid, raised on elegant supports over the mummy, bore the recumbent image of Tutankhamun, the boy king, his crossed hands holding the striped crook and flail, his eyes open patiently awaiting eternity. Siri strained to see something of the trespasser, but the pitch dark shadows were too deep. Whoever he was, he set the flashlight down upon the glass display case that protected the famous exhibit of the boy king. Then, with a diamond cutter and suction cup, Siri watched as he went to work, incising a broad hole at the head of the mummy case. Siri knew she was witnessing a heist, one unusual in the annals of crime – the theft of Egypt's famous pharaoh, the mummy of Tutankhamun. Suddenly the flashlight beam turned upon Siri's face – blinding her. *She was discovered!*

# CHAPTER 2: Wicks End

Siri sat up so fast in her bed it was as if a spring uncoiled behind her and launched her from the mattress. Siri took one breath and then another. She realized she was in her bed. She looked around her bedroom. It had happened again. Another dream had taken her on a wild ride. Siri reclined on her pillow and tugged the covers up to her neck. The dim glow of a night-light across the room bathed her soft features. Siri Braddock had her mother's eyes. One was brown, the other blue. Her long, brown hair and fair face contrasted sharply with her tomboyish demeanor, and her small stature earned her the nickname "Sprout." Siri's pajamas were practically drenched and her heart was still beating like a tom-tom. Her dream, like others she had had recently, seemed so real. During this one she experienced what it was like to be trapped in a museum, sealed in an Egyptian sarcophagus fighting to get out. It wasn't a pleasant feeling.

Siri knew she wouldn't sleep any more that night. She was wide-awake. The hours would tick by and daylight would eventually shed its amber glow into her bedroom window. She would feel as tired as a dog, and then have to get up for school. She'd drag the entire next day. Siri hated her dreams when they got so vivid and tangible. She hated those kinds of dreams because they came true, but Siri's latest dreams have been throwing her curve balls because they didn't come true right away, despite the usual symptoms of night sweats and post insomnia. Siri was wondering what was going on. In the last month three of her dreams had come true the very next day. Siri was so sure they would happen she called the police to prevent them from occurring, and her dreams were dead-on. There was the one about the bank robber dressed up as a little old lady who held up the Salem Bank. The police were ready for him with the handcuffs when she, or rather he, pulled up to the bank's curb side with a satchel bag and a concealed snub nose revolver, plenty of probable cause. Then there was the one about the little towheaded boy who walked out on the fifth story ledge of the Hawthorne Hotel. A patrolman was dispatched to head off that incident just as the boy was about to climb out the window with his mother's umbrella, which he intended to use as a parachute. Then came the dream where Siri, standing in drenching rain on a street corner during a power outage, saw two separate funeral processions careen into each other, hearses colliding and spilling caskets onto the slick pavement. If Siri didn't make the call a patrol car wouldn't have been on the stormy scene the next day to direct traffic and prevent the terrible accident. Siri's predictions impressed the Salem Police to the extent that a call from her would send them into action. But when one of her predictions sent them out on a wild goose chase in police boats up and down the Ipswich River one day, that one miss cost Siri her credibility. Chief Detective Vincent Scarpetti had a spate of missing persons on his hands, and he didn't have time or patience for wild dreams or guesses. He thanked Siri for her civic help, but preferred her to let the police do the police work. Siri remembered how red his face was when he came to the house, like an over-ripened tomato ready to burst.

"No way am I reporting this dream," Siri thought. "Not if I know what's good for me. Maybe this time it was just an ordinary nightmare. Besides, who would want to steal a musty old mummy anyways?"

Siri got out of bed and stepped over to the window. She peered out from behind the curtain and looked out into the night at the street lamps. Her clock read 12:30 A.M. There was a spooky halo of fog around the old gas lamp-style streetlights that formed a row down her street. For weeks now, since her dreams had become so vivid and premonition-like, Siri had the strangest feeling like she was being watched. She could feel someone's eyes upon her – even to the point where she would turn and look behind herself. But no one was ever there. No one she could see, that is.

"I know I haven't been imagining it," Siri thought as she looked out into the night. "I know you're out there, somewhere. Who are you? What do you want from me?" Siri strained to see deep into the swirling vapors, but saw nothing but the lamps and fog. Siri put the shade back into place and stumbled back into bed. She lay on the mattress, her body forming a star shape as she stared up at the ceiling.

"Something's going on with me," Siri whispered to herself, "something really weird. It all started when we moved to this creepy, old town. What's going on with you, Siri? Why are your dreams so scary? And who could be watching you? What is all this leading up to?"

Siri reached over to her night stand and opened a drawer. She withdrew a folded piece of paper. It was very gray and crinkly-looking. Siri opened it and pondered some cryptic words written upon it, and as Siri thought, her mind began to wander.

Siri lived in an old Victorian house on Wicks End, a quaintly cobblestoned, dead-end lane. Wicks End wasn't very long. There were just a few ancient houses with high, peaked roofs and scraggy property bordered by black, wrought iron fences with Siri's house situated at the very end of the street. Lined with old gas lamps converted to electricity and knotty, old, spreading oaks, Wicks End was one of the oldest streets in Salem. Not many people strode the shady old lane occupied by some very peculiar residents.

There was 22 Wicks End, a yellow gambrel roofed house, where Mister Gable lived, all alone. He once had two Boston Terriers named Charlie and Chaplin. He loved them very much, and when Charlie and Chaplin died, Mister Gable boiled them down, and made two canes out of their bones, and he walked with those two canes, every night, one in each gnarled, trembling hand. You could tell it was Mister Gable because you could hear his bone canes tapping the sidewalk. *Tap! Tap! Tap!*

In 27 Wicks End Miss Emily Curtis lived. It was a run-down

saltbox-styled house with rose trellises lining the whole walkway leading to the door. Miss Curtis was widowed on the day of her wedding, September 29th, 1959, when her fiance, a railroad yard worker, got pinned between two interlocking boxcars in the wee hours of the morning. He was rushing to get off work, when he crossed the wrong set of tracks. He got hitched, but his bride-to-be didn't. She never got over his death, or her love for him, so she wears her wedding veil every day to show the world her chasteness, and prunes her roses and does her gardening, all in her lacey white veil and white wedding heels.

Siri lived at 7 Wicks End. The house wasn't in the best of shape, but her dad bought it at a decent price. The purplish dragon scale shingles were missing in places just below the dilapidated, wrought iron railing that fenced in the widow's walk. And the high, pointed, conical tower just above the master bedroom had a bent lightning rod at its apex. A beautiful stained-glass window that overlooked the hedged-in front walk was Siri's favorite part of the house. It was untouched by time and in the evening the setting sun shed a prism of colors over the dark woodwork of the staircase. Siri never forgot the day they moved into the looming old place. It was a year ago on her birthday. The day she turned fourteen. A month later her mom died. Now it was just Siri and her dad, and he was always working.

The attic was a special place for Siri. There, at the end of a steep, dark flight of creaking steps there was something that fascinated her. Her new house was over a hundred years old, and the passage she had to squeeze through was so narrow Siri wondered just how small people were way back when. What attracted Siri to the attic was an ancient trunk. It had belonged to her mom. Now it belonged to her. It was tucked away in a far corner of the attic, and was made of wooden planking and bound with studded, wrought iron bands. The interior was lined with plush, red velvet, torn and moth eaten in places. There were some old pictures in there, daguerreotypes depicting women in broad, dark, crinoline gowns, like black umbrellas, their hair done up in buns. Siri could almost see her own likeness in their smooth features. They were her ancestors, but she didn't know anything about them, not even their names. There were bunches of time-yellowed letters tied up with old ribbons, the iron gall ink faded and barely legible, like smeared, black watercolor paint, but the most interesting item of all was an old gown. Dresses weren't Siri's thing. They hadn't been for a long time. Her mom made her a dress once when she was seven. It was yellow and the most beautiful thing Siri had ever worn, but her mom was gone now, and that was the end of dresses for her. Yet, there was something about the shimmering material that attracted Siri to this dress, attracted her like a moth to a flame. One day Siri gently lifted it from the trunk. She was about to hold it up against herself, and examine her reflection in a full-length mirror festooned in cobwebs, when she discovered something. It was a little piece of paper sewn into the ruffled hem of the gown. Siri carefully sliced the stitching with her Swiss Army Knife, slipped out the paper, and read it.

*"Start at twelve, turn twice passed three, then back to nine, to open thee."*

It was a riddle or clue, Siri thought – a very old riddle judging from the grey parchment it was written on. Siri rummaged through the old trunk, but could find nothing else. As yellow rays of afternoon sunlight shown through the window slats and the floating dust specks twinkled like stardust, Siri wondered about the hidden riddle and the woman who wrote it – and why. Siri was that way. Odd little trifles could set her mind working.

.   .   .

Suddenly a creak outside the bedroom door snapped Siri from her thoughts. She quickly folded back up the little gray paper and put it back in her night stand drawer. Then she got out of bed and stood listening. Siri heard the noise again. *Creak!* Siri reached for her Louisville Slugger, a baseball bat she kept tucked under her mattress. Someone was definitely in the hall, maybe a prowler? Siri quietly approached the bedroom door and cracked it open a hair. Something tall and dark was skulking around just outside her door. Siri could see its black outline go by the narrow slit she peered through. Just as she heard the creaking approach the stairs,

Siri threw the bedroom door wide open, switched on the hall light, and shouted.

"Just where do you think you're going?"

A man in his mid-forties stood dumbfounded in the overhead glare of a light bulb. He was holding a backpack and a pair of night-vision binoculars, judging from the phosphorescent green lenses. Siri immediately recognized the tall figure with black hair and sharp features, and shouted again.

"You're not ditching me this time! Get the car started! I'll be right down!"

# CHAPTER 3: Spying Eyes

Siri gazed up at a full moon high overhead. The dispelling fog caused its pale light to cast a weird, bluish luster over the dark woods surrounding her. Siri sat alone in her dad's vintage MG convertible, a two-seat, open sports car stopped on the shoulder of a winding, tree-lined road. Crackled bursts of radio communications came from police cruisers parked alongside the white roadster. With the top down, Siri could look all around her, and as she did, the looming trees appeared to crowd in upon her. When the wind blew, it caused branches to rustle and shadows to move. The round dials of the instrument panel cast an amber glow over the bucket seats and armrests patched with duct tape. An owl hooted from above, but Siri was too busy focusing on her laptop screen to be scared. Siri loved surveillance gadgets. She had attached a tiny video camera the size of a matchbook to the front of her dad's night-vision binoculars, so whatever he saw and heard in the woods, she saw too. She managed to stick it on with a piece of chewing gum when she handed them to her dad just a few moments ago. He was too eager to notice. Several nights ago Siri dreamed of a mysterious incident near the Ipswich River twenty miles north of Boston. She was so convinced her dream would come true she called the Salem Police tip line to report it. It was then Siri got into trouble because when the police investigated they found nothing to substantiate her call. Now she was there, at the river she dreamed about, and everything she reported was coming true.

"Eat crow, Scarpetti" Siri muttered.

Siri was no stranger to crime scenes. She couldn't count how many nights she waited behind yellow perimeter tape as her dad covered a story for his newspaper, but tonight she was prepared. As blue strobes danced over her face, Siri watched transfixed as her laptop screen displayed greenish, night-vision video of a tow-truck pulling a late-nineties Honda from a winding river brightly lit by spotlights. Draped in weeds, the mid-sized car was pulled onto a nearby embankment by a heavy, silt-laden chain. Then Siri noticed someone watching her through the camera, or her dad rather, someone who considered her *persona non grata*.

"Uh, oh," Siri muttered again.

The man immediately ceased his conversation with a police officer and marched up the embankment seemingly towards her, at least that's what it looked like on Siri's laptop. Her dad's binoculars were still trained on the man until his broad, flat nose and double chin filled Siri's LCD like a big, phosphorescent, green blob.

"The Audubon Sanctuary is a mile up the road, Braddock," said the man, like he had gravel for a larynx.

There was no mistaking the pit bull features of Chief Detective Vincent Arthur Scarpetti of the Salem police department. Scarpetti was short and thickly built. His neck seemed to be lacking a few vertebrae, which gave his round head with respect to his body the appearance of a bullet in a shell casing. Siri's dad was still looking through the binoculars, judging from the auto focus straining to keep Scarpetti's green, ham-sized face from going blurry. Siri watched the detective reach out with what looked like a catcher's mitt, but it was his hand through the wide-angle lens. Then the video image shook and tilted downwards and Siri found herself looking at the dark, leaf-covered ground. The detective just confiscated the binoculars from her dad.

"Come on, Scarpetti," Siri blurted, "right at the good part!"

The detective and her dad started arguing, but their voices became all muffled due to Scarpetti unknowingly covering the camera's microphone with his hand. Still, Siri caught a few words.

"Maybe if you…taken my daughter seriously…this wouldn't have happened."

"Keep…kid of yours out of my hair…or I'll…

"You don't have hair…"

"The missing…piling up…on your watch. You need all…help you can get."

"Not from an ex-cop or…green reporter. Go scoop the Glen… Garden Club, I hear they're growing poppies."

Suddenly Siri saw the detective turn and walk briskly down the embankment, which meant her dad had the binoculars again. She watched Scarpetti talk to a lanky officer standing by a flatbed truck carrying the Honda. The officer seemed hesitant at first, but then walked up the embankment towards Siri's spy lens. It was Officer Dwight. Siri recognized him from two other occasions. He always gave her dad good tips, and her dad returned the favors – in twenties. Dwight looked like an eerie, green beanpole on Siri's LCD as she listened in. She could catch only a few words still. Now her dad's hand was covering up the microphone. There was "Onion Head," which Dwight used every time he glanced over at Scarpetti, but from what Siri gathered, the car belonged to a Salem teenager, one of four who had been missing for twenty-four hours. They were last seen at the Witchcraft Victims' Memorial on Hobart Street (a point Siri took careful note of). She also learned that an old woman discovered the half-submerged car during an evening walk. It was then Siri received what amounted to a small shock. The thing that grabbed her attention was on her laptop screen behind her dad and Officer Dwight, and only she could see it! They were two, little, green lights hovering six feet above the ground, moving in and out from behind a grove of birch trees. At first Siri thought they were two fireflies, but the little green lights weren't blinking as they typically do with fireflies. Instead, they were constant and glaring and seemed to be looking straight at her, the way staring eyes do, the kind that are at home in the dark!

# CHAPTER 4: Hysteria in Stone

Siri was so tired she couldn't stand it. Somehow she had managed to get to school and plop down at her desk at home period. It was always that way when a nagging thought gnawed at her brain, and didn't let off. Siri had spent three precious hours, those dim wee hours before dawn when sleep is the deepest and most peaceful, toggling back and forth through video footage her dad unwittingly shot with her spy camera. Now Siri was paying the price for her curiosity. She could barely keep her eyes open and her head up. Mrs. Breath, her American History teacher, was rattling off, emphasizing the important points that were bound to be on a test. Mrs. Breath was an ageless sort, sixtyish, with a mop of downy hair that kept its round, tightly curled shape even in a hurricane. A stickler for good posture, she would walk straight as a ramrod up and down between the rows of her slouching students, nudging the usual slackers in the spine with a poke of her pointer. One or two examples were enough to straighten the entire class. Siri hadn't listened to a word Mrs. Breath said. Something lurked in the background of that video she watched last night – lurked while her dad was having a talk with Officer Dwight by the river. Whatever it was hovered six feet above the ground, about the height of a man. There was no doubt about it. They were eyes looking straight at Siri's monitor, eyes that shimmered and glinted like brilliant green gems, eyes that belonged to some strange nocturnal thing that was looking directly at her!

Siri did her best to perk up at her desk. She glanced up at Mrs. Breath one second and down at her school PC the next. She made believe she was taking notes on her laptop. With a few keyboard strokes a picture of a granite memorial located on Hobart Street in nearby Danvers appeared on her screen. The monument was dedicated to victims hung for practicing witchcraft in the early days of the hysteria that gripped the region in 1692. The memorial was cleverly carved to look like a slant box parson's pulpit with open Bible. Siri read the dedication to herself.

*"In memory of those innocents who died during the Salem Village witchcraft hysteria of 1692."*

Siri had learned in her history class that the small town of Danvers, once known as Salem Village, was the epicenter of the New England witchcraft hysteria. It was also through Danvers the Ipswich River flowed on its course to the Atlantic Ocean.

Suddenly Mrs. Breath pounded her fist against a blackboard driving home the deadline she had written in white chalk so that any tardy loiterers on the road to knowledge could make no mistake that their book reports were due "Next Wednesday!"

Mrs. Breath asked everyone to log off their computers and take out their science notebooks, for she had a surprise visitor from MIT, The Massachusetts Institute of Technology. Siri's nightmare – being trapped in an ancient Egyptian sarcophagus – still stuck like fresh mud in her mind.

Mrs. Breath introduced Emil Adelman, Professor *Emeritus* of Molecular Biology and Astrophysics, to the class. He had been waiting at the threshold with charming patience. Now he entered. Adelman looked like a scientist. Siri gave him that much. He was of medium height and build, sported a trim, iron-grey beard, and wore an Irish pullover sweater. Siri noticed he carried a scuffed, leather briefcase and peered over a set of steel bow spectacles. The guest speaker gazed with smiling eyes upon the young, attentive faces arrayed in rows staring back at him.

"Have you all had your Vitamin D today?" Adelman began. "No? Ah! But I'm willing to bet you did and didn't even know it."

Then, with an air of exuberance and infectious enthusiasm, Professor Adelman launched into a lively lecture about the sun and its life-giving properties. Even Siri was captivated, despite her weariness and grave concerns of nightmares and floating green eyes. She couldn't help but watch as Adelman waved his arms, jumped up and down, and like a kid on a sugar high, dashed from one end of the blackboard to the other, drawing a diagram of the solar system with a broad circle on the blackboard as its center, slashing ray-like spokes from its circumference, and writing the words: **"SUN – OUR BESTEST FRIEND"** in the middle of his solar disk in broad, bold strokes. Some students giggled at the guest professor's manic antics. Even Mrs. Breath didn't quite know what to make of it all. She appeared quite taken by surprise. Adelman relished his audience and all of his talk of the sun. A giggle escaped Siri. At least Emil Adelman wasn't boring, Siri thought. The guy was fun to watch, if anything. Siri forgot how tired she was.

Then, as Adelman dolled out his solar theories, Siri's eyes wandered back toward her PC screen. She hadn't logged off. Siri studied the Hobart Street memorial to the witchcraft victims. There was something haunting about it – and it gnawed at Siri. She felt like she was looking at a clue in the sprawling, paneled granite, but just didn't know what to make of it. Twenty innocent men and woman lost their lives during that terrible time so long ago, but what was the significance to her now? The Witchcraft Victims' Memorial: four teenages met there and disappeared soon after. The newspapers told that much, but what was the connection? Suddenly Siri felt tired again. She couldn't get the image of the two, green glowing eyes out of her head.

# CHAPTER 5: Interrupted Journey

Windward High School was built in 1872 – a true American Gothic. Two conical clock towers rose from its east and west wings and were covered in leafy green ivy. The sprawling building was composed of grey and brown granite and its gabled slate roof bristled with chimney pots – like those old English manor houses found on desolate, mist-shrouded moors. Siri had begun her morning at Windward feeling like a wrung out dish towel. Now she was madder than a wet cat. Another note taped to her school locker set off her inner Vesuvius. Siri tore the note off the second she saw it, tape and all. She started to crumple it up, but then decided to read what was typed in Times Roman Italic 14 point type.

*"What a tale of terror, now, their turbulency tells! In the startled air of night, How they scream out their affright! Turn away from what does not concern you!"*

Siri fumed and crumpled up the note. It was the fifth note she had gotten in two weeks, each in its own poetic way telling her to mind her own business. But Siri was minding her own business. That she told herself. Wasn't she? Siri kept the notes, even after crumpling them up and stuffing them in her pocket. *"And travelers, now, within that valley, through red-litten windows see. You had better stop seeing!"* That was another one of them. Then there was *"There is a two-fold silence – sea and shore – body and soul. One dwells in lonely places. Keep to yourself!"* Not long after that appeared *"Far down in the dim*

15

*West, Where the good and the bad and the worst and the best have gone to their eternal rest. Stop interfering where you do not belong!"* Siri shrugged at that one. Then there was *"Take thy beak from out my heart, and take thy form from off my door! And call Scarpetti – NEVERMORE!!"* Yes. That one spoke volumes. Whoever wrote the notes had a problem with Siri calling Scarpetti. That much she understood, but by now the note writing thing was getting a bit much.

The school corridor was crowded and it roared with students talking and shouting to each other. Siri pushed her way through, turning sideways at times. She passed one guy and girl really smooching it up in a corner. Siri shook her head and moved on, dodging guys shoving each other or "going long" for a snatched lunch bag. Siri scanned faces coming her way and passing her on both sides, like a gauntlet. There was Buck Crabtree, the triathlete, hitting on Daisy Dooberry, the smartest girl in school. Doug Graves was kicking the candy machine again, which never worked. Valerie Pitts and Tibby Lovely were whispering into each other's ears. Two bullies, Foghorn Kelly and Growley Howard were forcing geeky Regis Toomey to stand on his head, but no one gave Siri the slightest notice as she squeezed by. Siri wondered who the culprit was. Who in all this sea of faces was the one taping notes to her locker? Finally, there was the hallway exit ahead of her, the big double doors, leading to fresh air and sanity!

Siri couldn't believe it when she walked out into the sunlight and saw her dad's MG waiting by the curb. Wow! On time, she thought. For once Siri didn't have to wait for him. She jumped into the passenger seat and plopped her backpack down by her feet. The vintage roadster sputtered and roared to life. With the iPod's signature white cord trailing along her side, Siri listened to her recent downloads – Mozart's Symphonies 39-41 and Rachmaninoff's Piano Concerto #3. Siri was an oddball when it came to music. She preferred classical, which most teenagers relegated to the Stone Age. Pachelbel's Canon was one of her favorites. As the MG roared along tree-lined Chestnut Street, an avenue of Federal Era mansions, Siri suddenly spoke.

"You need to clean the carburetor!"

"I did that yesterday."

"Did you remember to disconnect the throttle cable this time?" Siri asked.

"Uh ah," Her dad nodded.

"Must be the solar flares then," Siri remarked.

"Solar flares?"

"A man from MIT came to our science class today," Siri clarified. "He called them coronal mass ejections. They're supposed to cause all kinds of weird things here on Earth. Like you being dependable for once."

"Pizza tonight?" Siri's dad asked.

"Okay."

As the roadster wound its way past scarlet trees and quaint houses trimmed with Halloween decorations, orange pumpkins, scarecrows and cornstalks, Siri was pensive. She had a lot on her mind. Suddenly a young man straddling a Harley shot past on the left. Its gunning engine came up so fast it startled Siri. In a flash of chrome, the low-profiled motorcycle roared off down the road, disappearing around a bend. Siri felt a weird sense of *déjà vu* just then. Her stomach was growling too. She really wanted to tell her dad about the note she found on her school locker, but decided not to. Siri didn't always tell her dad everything, even though he always kept telling her *"Sprout, you can talk to your ole dad about anything, anytime, you know. So don't ever feel like you have no one to talk to. Okay?"* The nagging feeling of espionage against her coupled with the phenomenon caught on video was starting to tell on Siri's nerves. She felt it creeping up on her. Siri turned to her dad.

"Dad, be careful, okay?"

"Okay," Siri's dad replied, keeping his eyes ahead. "Can I ask what I need to be careful of?"

"Just be careful, that's all," Siri said.

"Okay, I promise to be careful," Siri's dad returned. "Hey, how's that book report coming along? 'Witches Among Us?' That's the name of it, isn't it? I hear the author is a local guy."

Siri knew what her dad was trying to do – keep her mind off what was bothering her. Siri thought her dad was an okay dad, even though he was always off chasing a story for his newspaper. Suddenly the roadster sped past "The Pizza Penguin," Siri's favorite pizza place and their destination. She turned and watched the restaurant whiz by.

"Hey!" Siri exclaimed, pulling her earpiece out. "What's the big idea?"

Her dad didn't answer.

"Fess up," Siri scowled. "I know what you're up to. The last time you pulled this stunt I waited two hours in this old junk heap."

Siri's dad smiled and drove on. Siri folded her arms across her chest and looked away. She watched the road alternate between sunshine and shadow.

"Here," Siri's dad finally said, tossing something to her. "I believe this is yours."

Siri looked at the thing – and cringed. In her palm was a miniature video camera no larger than a matchbook.

"Got anything to say?" he asked.

"I plead the Fifth."

"I thought so."

# CHAPTER 6: The Uninvited

Siri's dad stood on the stoop of a trim, white colonial house and knocked on the door. Siri stood one step below, waiting. A dragonfly whizzed by and amused her for a moment. Suddenly the door opened and a gnome of a woman with a mop of white hair, with tweezers tucked into her shirt pocket, stepped outside.

"Sorry, but I'm not buying anything," she said.

"We're not selling anything," Siri replied.

Siri's dad cast a look at Siri and turned to the homeowner. He smiled and flashed his press badge.

"I'm Collin Braddock from the Salem Times and this is my daughter, Siri. She's tagging along with me. I'd like to ask you a few questions, if you don't mind."

"A few questions?" the old woman asked. "What sort of questions?"

"I understand you found something in the river last night," Collin replied.

The woman looked at Siri and smiled. Siri smiled back.

"Please come inside," the old woman said, cordially. "My name is Angie Simmons, by the way."

Siri and her dad were admitted into a small parlor that doubled for a greenhouse. Exotic plants sprouted from every nook and cranny. Even the windowsills bristled with assorted cacti and succulents. With thin tweezers in hand, Mrs. Simmons delicately pinched a green bottle fly, lifted it from a glass jar, and inserted it into the distended, saber-leaf jaws of a Venus fly trap. The spiked leaves clamped shut like tiny prison bars, entombing the buzzing insect. Mrs. Simmons turned to Collin and Siri as they stood looking on.

"I hate doing that, but it's the only way to feed my little darlings. *Dionaea muscipula* are so hard to grow here in New England."

Mrs. Simmons looked at Siri.

"I have lady fingers in the pantry," she said. "It's just down the hall. Help yourself."

"Lady fingers?" Siri asked – a twist in her face.

"Cookies!" The old woman answered.

Siri looked at her dad. He gave her a nod and she dashed down a hall past a gauntlet of botanical prints. About halfway down, she stopped and backed against the wall next to a framed etching of a Glossy-leaved Pittosporum. Siri wanted to listen in on the conversation.

"I hear a lot at night, especially near the river," Siri overheard Mrs. Simmons say. "My hearing has become extremely acute since the passing of my husband, Gordy. That's him over there."

Siri spied a decorative Asian urn on top of a mantle.

"Poor guy," she thought. "What a way to spend eternity. Probably dusted every Sunday."

"Did you hear or see anything unusual last night?" This time it was her dad talking.

"Last night was unusually still. I told the police as much."

"Let's not over-do-it in there!" Collin shouted down the hall at Siri.

"Whatever you say, dad," Siri replied, moving into the pantry. She didn't want to be caught eavesdropping. On the counter she found a cookie jar shaped like Humpty-Dumpty. Siri opened the domed head, reached in, and crammed two ladyfingers into her mouth. The pantry Siri occupied apparently doubled as a potting shed. Empty terracotta pots and bags of potting soil were clumped together with blue mason jars and storage tins. Then, beyond the lace curtains of the pantry window, Siri saw a Gothic building with pointed towers perched on a hilltop catching the last amber rays of the setting sun.

"That's the old asylum," said Mrs. Simmons, standing in the

doorway and noticing Siri's gaze. "The Danvers State Mental Infirmary. It's been closed for many years now." Collin followed the old woman into the kitchen.

"It looks like a castle," Siri remarked.

"Not a storybook castle," Mrs. Simmons added.

"Can people go up there?" Siri asked.

"They shouldn't, Siri," Mrs. Simmons replied. "And you shouldn't either. Never ever. The whole place is condemned – all falling to pieces. Some even say it's haunted."

"Really?" Siri pressed.

"Really," the old woman replied. "One night about a year ago, I came out here to water my magnolias. That's when I heard it – a voice – a forlorn voice calling from one of the asylum towers. "WHY HAVE YOU LEFT ME BEHIND?" it shouted. "WHY MUST WE BE APART?" I've never forgotten the sound of that voice. It was so mournful, so lost. It wasn't a normal voice, the way it echoed and re-echoed through the night. Oooh, I've got goose bumps just thinking about it. Why, I've even heard music come from the towers, violin music just sobbing away up there, very melodic, and yet very sad."

Siri listened to the old woman with wide eyes. She couldn't help but look at the asylum looming beyond the window curtains.

"Have you seen or heard anything recently?" Collin asked.

"Last night I came in to water my African Violets," the old woman answered. "They're sensitive to certain dew points, you know. It was about midnight when I happened to glance towards the asylum and I could have sworn I saw a light, right up there," she pointed. "In that top left tower window. Then, when I looked again, the light was gone, just like that." The old woman snapped her fingers.

Suddenly the back door opened and a young woman stomped in.

"Mom, you won't believe what they want to do..."

The woman stopped in mid-sentence upon seeing Collin and Siri.

"This is my daughter, Emma," said Mrs. Simmons.

Emma, a striking brunette in her late twenties, tossed a denim handbag on the counter and pulled an elastic band out of her hair.

"How was your meeting at the historical society today, dear?" Mrs. Simmons inquired.

"Who are these people, mom?" Emma asked, looking annoyed.

"This is Collin Braddock from the Salem Times and his daughter, Siri."

"A reporter, huh?" Emma shrugged. "What did you do mom, shoot another kid with rock salt?"

Siri's eyes widened. The old woman's face flushed pink.

"Of course not. Apparently some young people have been reported missing. I found their car abandoned in the river not far from here."

Emma turned to Collin.

"I take it my mother already reported this to the police."

"Yes," Collin replied. "But I was hoping she might have seen or heard something else that could provide a lead."

"Or a good headline," Emma returned. "And did you, Mom?"

The old woman busied herself removing deadheads from a geranium.

"No, not really."

Siri's stomach grumbled despite the ladyfingers. It was time to go. Plus a sugar rush was giving her a headache.

"Dad, don't we have to be somewhere?"

Collin got the hint.

"Right."

He thanked Mrs. Simmons and turned to Emma. "It was nice meeting you. Something tells me we'll be bumping into each other again."

Emma said nothing. She just opened the pantry door, revealing back steps leading to a lush garden. Siri took Collin by the hand.

"Come on dad," she said. "Looks to me like we're taking the scenic route."

They both walked out the door. Emma closed it behind them. They could hear her slide back the bolt.

# CHAPTER 7: The Clue in the Attic

It was after 11:30 PM – not the best time to rummage around in an attic, but Siri had to wait until her dad dozed off before heading up there. She didn't need the questions. The attic was a spooky place after dark, like a cave. Siri half expected a horde of screeching bats to fly out of the blackness at her. She brushed aside a string of cobwebs and aimed her flashlight ahead. In the dim halo beyond lurked her mom's trunk.

Siri opened the trunk and picked through its contents. She knew the clue to the riddle had to be in there somewhere. Arrayed around her on the floorboards were fragments of the past, old photographs Siri had never seen before. There was a picture of her dad as a uniformed cadet fresh from the Boston Police Academy. Another small picture of her mom lay closest to Siri. It showed her smiling sweetly while proudly showing off a basket of mushrooms she had just picked. Siri noticed some old slate gravestones and a pond in the background, and knew just where the picture was taken – Old Burial Hill in Marblehead. Siri looked at that picture for about a minute. Then she had to put it down. It was getting painful to hold – to see her mom so full of life, when now she was gone.

Siri untied one bundle of letters. Then she opened each one systematically, and scanned the crammed penmanship of each. Then Siri opened another bundle. Some letters were in excellent condition and easy to read. Others were written in quill pen from ages past and took more effort. Siri picked up one letter, set it down, reached for another. She read letter after letter. Siri read letters from the years 1821, 1847, 1864, 1882, 1902, 1917, 1924, and 1932. Holy Mackerel! Siri thought. How her ancestors could write! No texting back then! How did they ever find the time?

Suddenly Siri read something that caught her eye. She read and reread it. She was exhausted. It was a simple letter written in 1932 by a great aunt or someone, who signed her name *"LMS."*

*"I regret the selling of our wonderful clock. You know the one, Katrina, grandmother's Highland Mantel Clock, but with William out of work and the run on the bank we needed the money. Sold it at auction for $300.00 and it was nice to know that the buyer was the Museum of Antiquities, right here in Salem."*

"So it's a clock," Siri whispered to herself. "It has to be. *Start at twelve, turn twice passed three, then back to nine, to open thee.* The turning of the hands must be like turning the dial of a safe, a secret safe. No. It can't be. That only happens in the movies. But what if it's true? People back then weren't dumb. Pirates and smugglers invented all sorts of hiding places and false drawers to fool revenue men and each other. Maybe the clock is something like that? But what could be hidden in a clock? Something pretty darn important, that's for sure. Something so important somebody thought that a regular safe was too risky." Siri could feel the wheels in her head turning. Sleep wasn't going to happen that night. She knew what she needed to get her hands on and where to get it. Siri put the letter back with the others in the trunk and thanked her prolific letter-writing ancestors for making that part of her quest easy. It was the other part that wasn't going to be so simple.

# CHAPTER 8: Night Thoughts

When Siri went to bed she couldn't get the mysterious clock out of her mind. What made it so important? Was something hidden inside it – jewelry, diamonds, or even a treasure map? That riddle she found sewn in the dress was a combination of some kind to the clock, a hidden compartment or something, in the clock. That Highland Mantel clock! It had to be!

Siri was grateful for the little side mystery she had on her hands. It was a welcome distraction from her dreadfully realistic dreams. Siri let her mind wander a little, hoping to fall asleep. For some reason she thought about the asylum she saw from Mrs. Simmons' kitchen window. She closed her eyes a little and imagined a strain of strange violin music drifting from the tower, floating down and spreading like a calm, silky sheet. She envisioned a dark outline of a man in one of the tower windows, a candle in the background. Siri felt herself falling asleep. She was surprised how calm she felt. Then came that mournful bellow. It was so forlorn and haunting as it echoed through the starry night. "WHY HAVE YOU LEFT ME BEHIND? WHY MUST WE BE APART?"

Siri sat up in bed. The digital clock read 2:30 AM. Then she heard it, the voice of a woman singing in the kitchen below. For a moment Siri sat so still she felt that even her heart had stopped. Siri recalled how her mom would sometimes hum and sing to herself, especially when she had trouble sleeping after visiting her doctor. Then Siri heard something else, footsteps in the hall outside her bedroom door.

Siri figured her dad heard the sounds too and was investigating. It happened before. Siri cautiously got up and poked her head into the hall, just in time to see her dad's shadow disappear around a corner. She quickly tiptoed down the hall after him. The darkness gave everything a grey, muted aspect. Siri quietly peeked over the railing and watched her dad cautiously approach the kitchen in his undershirt and jogging pants and bare feet, the melancholy strains of a low sung tune growing louder until he reached for the light switch and flicked it on. Then the music stopped.

The kitchen was deathly quiet. From Siri's place on the stairway all appeared just as they had left it after supper – a few dishes in the sink, and on the table a folded newspaper, a cell phone in its charger, a police scanner, and a bottle of transmission fluid. The only audible sound was the monotonous drone of the refrigerator. Siri watched her dad pull out a chair and sit at the table, collecting his thoughts. He raked a hand through his dark hair. Peaceful dreams were hard to come by for both lately it seemed. Siri turned and walked quietly back upstairs.

# CHAPTER 9: Unexpected Encounter

Siri sat on a bench in Salem's Armory Park right in the shadow of the Visitor's Center. She was perplexed. The kitchen incident still clung in her mind. Siri looked around and huffed. The armory was the headquarters for the Second Corps of Cadets, which traced its history back to the late 1700s. Siri didn't like being dropped off there. The young mothers, crying babies, and noisy tourists embarking on trolley tours drove her nuts. But she figured it was punishment enough for her latest spying stunt. Payback time, she consoled herself. At least her best friend would be meeting her there. Siri's dad told her he'd pick her up later. He didn't say where he was going, but Siri had her suspicions. She fitted an earpiece into her ear and dialed in the frequency to a little hand-held receiver. Siri's mind had many channels and frequencies too. As she tuned in, she recalled an old song her mom used to sing. It was a slow, sad melody about bringing back Bonnie from over the ocean, bringing back Bonnie to me. It was the same song Siri heard last night.

Suddenly through her earpiece Siri overheard her dad's MG as it veered onto a dirt road. Her equipment was working spot on. She recognized the groaning of the engine and the sound of her dad yanking up the handbrake through her earpiece. Siri adjusted a dial and finally found the perfect frequency.

"Someone's got to look out for him," Siri reasoned, listening in. Siri thought her dad's age was beginning to tell on him. Through her earpiece she could hear him huffing and puffing his way uphill through high grass and brambles.

"Boy, dad," she thought. "Don't have a heart attack. I'm signing you up at a gym."

Siri imagined herself on top of the great hill where she knew her dad was at that very moment, the great, massive Gothic asylum presenting itself like an abbey out of the Middle Ages. Siri heard bursts of radio communications and barking dogs amidst the sound of her dad's gasps and grunts. A criminal investigation was in the works up there with a K-9 unit! No doubt about it! Siri knew her dad well enough to know he was keeping low and undercover, surveying the police activity through his binoculars after checking it for spy-wear first probably. Siri chuckled. The tiny, radio microphone she planted on the back of his shirt collar had a four-mile range. He'll never notice it.

"Now who's that?" Siri heard her dad whisper. She wished he didn't talk to himself so much. It was a bad habit of his, and it only made him look weird, but Siri didn't mind it this time. He was giving her the play-by-play without knowing it. Siri figured someone other than grouchy Detective Scarpetti had honed into her dad's view. Siri raised the volume of her receiver and was surprised to hear a reply – in a woman's voice!

"His name is Alex Cedric."

"Emma!" Siri muttered. She could never forget that voice. It belonged to Mrs. Simmons' feisty, bad-tempered daughter. Siri shook her head. The memory of how Emma practically threw them out of the house still nettled her, but Emma had unwittingly given Siri a clue. Siri pulled out her cell phone and punched in Alex Cedric's name on a search engine. There were several Alex Cedrics out there, but only one lived locally and worked in Danvers. That Cedric was head of the Historical Society. There was a picture of him posted too. He looked friendly enough, kind of grandfatherly with white whiskers and grey eyes. "Just what the heck is going on up there?" Siri wondered.

"What are you doing here?"

Siri noted Emma's voice again as she listened in. She sounded really annoyed, like back at the house. The woman was too tightly wound, Siri thought.

"I told you we'd see each other again," Siri overheard her dad say. "Come up to go bird watching?"

"Don't hand me that," Emma replied.

"Who is he?" Siri's dad insisted, "that old fellow in tweed?"

"If you must know," Emma huffed, "Cedric is our town archivist. He also chairs the Historical Commission, and is the only one with a key to the asylum. A joint venture wants to knock the whole thing down and turn it into condos. Condos! Like the world needs more of those!"

"Well, the view will be nice," Siri's dad remarked.

"That building and this hilltop have great historical significance," Emma declared. "This land you're standing on once belonged to John Hathorne."

"John who?" Siri's dad asked.

"Gee dad," Siri muttered. "Even I know who he is."

"John Hathorne," Emma replied. "One of the presiding judges of the Salem Witchcraft Trials. Didn't they teach you anything in school?"

"Have you ever been inside?" Siri's dad asked impatiently.

"No," Emma huffed. "It's condemned. Are you always so abrupt?"

"Where can I get some blueprints?"

Siri didn't like the sound of that. It gave her a bad feeling.

"Hey, what's that?" Emma asked.

"What's what?" Siri's dad pressed.

"That thing on the back of your collar," Emma replied.

"On my collar? Get it off!" Siri's dad ordered.

"Hold still," Emma insisted. "And stop jumping around."

Siri got a sinking feeling in her stomach.

"Well, what is it?" Siri's dad asked.

"Hey, it's a microphone!" Emma exclaimed.

"A microphone?"

Suddenly Siri heard her dad's voice ring out clear as crystal in her earpiece.

**"Sprout! Now hear this! This is the last straw! When we get home…!"**

Siri pulled the earpiece from her ear and turned off her receiver.

"Busted," she grumbled.

# CHAPTER 10: The Hall of Mummies

The man who served Siri her two orders of fried dough looked down at her through two, narrow eyes. He was Mongolian – that Siri was sure of – not Chinese or even Japanese. He even had a drooping Genghis Khan mustache. Siri tried not to stare at him. He was so big – so bulbously muscled – like a wrestler. And here he was handing her two orders of fried dough and three dollars in change from this dinky, tiny cart. Siri thanked him, but he said nothing in return. He just looked at Siri and his leathery, expressionless face morphed into a Cheshire-Cat grin, exposing a wall of badly yellowed teeth. Siri smiled and walked away, hooking Mallory by the elbow and shuffling off as nonchalantly as she could. Siri could still sense the Mongolian's eyes watching her as she guided Mallory onto the crowded, cobblestone street.

Mallory Swift, Siri's closest companion and confidant, was eighteen, blonde and had supermodel looks that turned guys heads until their necks corkscrewed. At first glance, the two girls appeared to be polar opposites, Siri being tomboyish, shorter, three years younger, and quiet. Mallory was sociable and vivacious. But like an old vaudeville team they complimented each other. It was early October and Salem was in the midst of *"Haunted Times,"* an annual, month-long festival that celebrated the town's *"Witch City"* reputation, as well as its connection to the tragic hysteria of 1692. Storefronts and lamp posts along Essex Street, a cobblestone pedestrian walkway home to the Salem Museum of Antiquities and a gauntlet of occult shops, bristled with ripe cornstalks and round pumpkins, as potions and charms were peddled to the meandering crowd.

"How's the book report going?" Mallory asked, biting into her fried dough and tearing off a spongy hunk with her teeth.

"Okay," Siri replied with a shrug. Siri's mind was elsewhere.

"Mrs. Breath has singled me out," Mallory remarked. "On my last quiz she scribbled: 'Mallory. Blondes are not dumb. I know because I was a blonde once. Multiple choice means circle one choice out of the list for your answer, not the whole list. Please try harder. A mind, even a blonde's, is a terrible thing to waste.'"

Siri was barely listening. Banners outside the Salem Museum of Antiquities caught her eye.

"HALL OF MUMMIES – MET and MFA Mummies on Display: Pre-dynastic Period – New Kingdom. October 1-31."

Siri turned and headed directly for the museum entrance, tugging Mallory with her.

"Come on, Mal," Siri said.

"Where are we going?"

"You'll see," Siri replied.

Siri tugged open the glass-front doors, strode up to the admission desk, and with Mallory behind her, flashed her school I.D. to the attendant. Mallory did the same, but she didn't have a clue why they were there. Pass stickers were given to them to apply to their sweaters. It wasn't hard finding the mummy exhibit. Siri unconsciously reached out for Mallory's hand and towed her through a moderate crowd of patrons milling about in the grand atrium with its soaring glass roof. Mallory's eyes wandered about her impressive surroundings, but Siri, following a trail of strange music, like flute strains and harp pluckings, kept Mallory moving and led her around a corner. The two girls stood in the threshold of a grand gallery. Before them, spread upon the floor and arrayed in rows, were glass display cases containing ornate coffins. Inside each was a mummy in time-yellowed bandages. Some were lying in open sarcophaguses of wood. Others were reclined under glass in their wrappings like cannolis in an Italian bakery. It was a hall of mummies, with just enough space for people to walk between them. Siri could hardly believe her eyes when palm trees and hieroglyphic-carved obelisks emerged into sight, adding to the Egyptian splendor. There was even a stuffed camel reposed on a mock sand dune, the sand having been trucked in from nearby Gloucester.

Siri took Mallory by the elbow and tugged her through a row of mummy cases. As Siri scrutinized the reclining Egyptians swathed in ancient linen in one row of cases, Mallory gazed down into the others, like she was window-shopping. There was something about these human relics that the girls found fascinating. The Egyptians, in their quest for immortality, had achieved something very much like it. Preserved by the ancient art of embalming, their organs removed and stored in canopic jars, and their bodies preserved in natron for seventy days, now here they lay, objects of curiosity and wonder, three thousand years since. The siege of Troy, the rise and fall of Rome, Marco Polo and Napoleon – all have faded into oblivion, and yet, these immortals remained. Siri noticed the absence of King Tutankhamun's mummy and learned it was still safely tucked away in the Egyptian Museum in Cairo, and that put her mind at ease.

Siri reached out for Mallory, and led her across to a gallery of maritime paintings.

"You mean this isn't why we came here?" Mallory asked, looking around.

"Come on," Siri said.

The two wound their way up a stairwell. Mallory followed, pausing only briefly before a display of quirky ship figureheads. Mallory quickly joined Siri and entered a dimly lit exhibit titled *"Treasures of England 1770-1840."* Siri looked around the darkened room. A few people were shuffling in and out, but they were alone for the most part. Siri examined the space carefully. There were exquisitely painted fireboards used to block drafts from fireplaces in colonial times. Finely carved chairs and tables gleamed in the corners. And there were clocks. Lots of clocks! There were grandfather clocks, wall clocks, and mantel clocks – some gilded in gold as if they belonged to Louis the XIV of France, and some of rich, polished wood and ivory. Siri scanned the display signs of each for a clue. Mallory hung close, not quite sure of what Siri was up to.

"What are you looking for?" Mallory asked. "If you tell me, perhaps I can help?"

"I need to find a clock," Siri replied, searching the room. "An old Highland Mantel Clock. It's very important I find it. It has to be in here somewhere."

"What does a Highland Mantel Clock look like?" Mallory asked, joining the search.

"I haven't the slightest idea," Siri returned, going from clock to clock.

Suddenly Siri stopped before a clock ticking on a mantle. It was square and boxy, made of dark wood, and had a little brass handle on top. She read the little sign below it and her heart nearly skipped a beat. *"Highland Mahogany Mantel Clock – 1770, bought at auction, 1932."* Siri stared at the big clock face.

"This has to be it," she said. "It was bought by the museum in 1932, the same date mentioned in the letter."

"What letter?" Mallory pressed.

Siri just stared at the clock, muttering the ancient riddle written on parchment she had committed to memory.

*"Start at twelve, turn twice passed three, then back to nine, to open thee!"*

"Are you feeling all right?" Mallory asked, placing a hand on Siri's forehead.

"I'm fine, Mal," Siri replied, straining to see a fissure or secret compartment in the clock, but couldn't see any from where she stood.

Siri stepped closer to the mantle, but did not cross over the alarm strip on the floor. She surveyed the clock's dark wood construction carefully. It had to be the same clock mentioned in the letter, Siri thought. It just had to be. Her instincts were never wrong. It was then Siri felt eyes upon her. One look at Mallory confirmed her feelings. Mallory half turned around and faced the doorway. Siri half turned too, and saw a dark figure of a man standing in the gallery entrance. How long he had been standing there, Siri didn't know. He was silent as a statue, and appeared to be interested in something in their direction. The man took several steps to the side. Siri noticed that he was dressed entirely in black and wore dark glasses even in the dim light. His face was pale – almost chalk white, and partly covered by tangles of black hair. Siri didn't like the strange vibes he was giving her.

"Don't look now, but see that guy in the doorway?" Siri whispered, turning to Mallory.

"What guy?" Mallory whispered back discreetly turning her head.

"That guy behind us."

"There's no one there."

Siri looked once more at the doorway. The man was gone.

"There's no one there now, but he was a second ago," Siri said. "Come on, Mal. You must have seen him."

"I tell you I saw no one."

Siri looked once more at the empty doorway.

## CHAPTER 11: Uneasy Feelings

Siri pushed through the glass doors of the museum into bright, afternoon sunlight and looked up and down the busy cobblestone street. Mallory had to run to keep up.

"Do you mind telling me what's going on?" Mallory asked.

"Something strange is going on Mal," said Siri.

"You mean something involving that old clock?"

Siri didn't answer. She felt like she was being watched, but everything was normal along the thoroughfare. She glanced toward a rooftop of an old bookstore. It was an odd place to look for someone, but Siri wasn't leaving anything to chance.

**"BOO!"**

Siri almost jumped out of her skin. Two teenage boys had thrust their ghoulish, mask-covered faces into hers. One was a glaring skull and the other a grinning devil!

"Morons!" Mallory shouted. She smacked them both over the heads with her handbag. The boys laughed and dashed down the street.

"That's assault," one boy yelled back. "We're gonna report ya."

"Do that, idiot," Mallory yelled back. "See where it gets ya."

Mallory turned to Siri.

"We need to get your mind on something else," Mallory said. "The big Halloween party next Friday is just the thing. Are you going?"

"Don't know," Siri replied. She surveyed the jagged line of rooftops.

"You've got to," Mallory urged. "It won't be any fun without you."

"Sure it will," Siri quipped, her eyes still searching.

Suddenly the roar of an engine caught Siri's ear. A white MG had just turned a corner at a busy intersection. It followed a young woman driving a red Jeep. Siri recognized the driver of the roadster. It was her dad. Siri recognized the driver of the Jeep too. It was Emma!

"Come on!" Siri blurted. "We can't lose them!"

She grabbed Mallory by the arm and tugged her across the street. The two zigzagged through the crisscrossing traffic. One driver tooted his horn at Mallory. She turned and waved. On the other side of the street, the two ran through an obstacle course of pedestrians. Siri hugged the storefronts as they hurried along, taking care not to be spotted in her dad's rear-view mirror. She watched him follow the Jeep across North Street, where it circled around and parked before a brick, Federal-style building with white Doric columns. Siri and Mallory caught their breath in the doorway of an Army and Navy store. Siri watched as her dad stepped from his car and started talking with Emma. She felt a pit in her stomach when she saw him follow her into the building.

"Now why are they going in the athenaeum?" Siri muttered.

"The ath-e-what?" Mallory asked.

"Athenaeum," Siri replied. "It's a sort of private library."

"Ohhh," Mallory nodded, clueless. "One of those."

# CHAPTER 12: Blueprint to Mystery

Siri and Mallory poked their heads around the doorjamb of the Salem Athenaeum and gazed into a foyer lit by a fanlight. The coast was clear and the two slipped inside, Siri first, then Mallory. Siri backed against a wall and brought a finger to her lips, signaling for absolute quiet. She pointed to a thin, old man sitting across the way behind a wooden desk with books piled in neat stacks on both sides of him. Siri figured he was the head librarian. He was looking down with his wedge-shaped nose literally buried in a book, his hairless head shining like a light bulb. Mallory knew the plan Siri had coached her through just a minute or two before: *"Operation Under Wire."* She quickly donned her sunglasses and undid two top buttons to her blouse. Then she strolled over toward a row of books like a fashion model shimmying down a runway. Siri was keeping an eye on the librarian who lifted his gaze at Mallory's intrusion, and at the sight of her, raised an eyebrow. Mallory feigned browsing, letting out little frustrated breaths while running a finger along some book titles. She then got on her tiptoes and reached for a book high over her head. The librarian continued to watch with interest. Mallory continued to exert herself, huffing and puffing. Her intentional fumbling finally caused a book to tumble to the floor with a thud.

"Ooops," Mallory cringed. She looked helplessly towards the librarian, biting into her lower lip.

The librarian rose from his chair and stepped away from his desk. Siri saw her chance and dashed up the spiral staircase. She was on the balcony that overlooked the first floor in no time. Siri carefully leaned over the railing, and spotted her dad and Emma directly below seated at a long table. They were examining blueprints of a sprawling Gothic building bristling with turrets and pointed spires. Siri recognized the blueprints at once. They were the plans to the former state mental institution, the one she had seen on the hilltop from Mrs. Simmons' kitchen window. Siri crouched down behind the banister and did her best to listen in.

"Why are you interested in these plans?" Emma whispered.

"Your mother told me she heard someone shouting from one of the asylum towers about a year ago. That someone could still be up there. Several nights ago four teenagers were reported missing, not more than a quarter mile away. Put one and one together."

"The police searched the place top to bottom today and came up empty," Emma said. Then she leaned up against Collin. "What do you know that they don't?"

Collin didn't answer. Emma clutched him by the cuff of his jacket.

"Listen. This is a private library and you're in here on my invite. Whatever you're up to, I want in."

"I need a copy of these plans."

"I'm in or no plans," Emma whispered through her teeth.

"You're in like Flynn," Collin said. "Now get me a copy of these plans."

"You're a real charmer," Emma said. She rolled up the plans and headed for the copy room.

Siri watched her dad and Emma get up and enter a small room near the library entrance.

"Time to go!" Siri thought.

Siri scrambled to her feet and darted down the spiral staircase. At the bottom she found Mallory and the librarian. Siri could hear the drone of a copy machine nearby and her dad and Emma murmuring.

"This is my friend, Siri," Mallory announced. "Siri, meet Luther T. Dobbs, head librarian of the Salem Athe…"

"Athenaeum," Dobbs politely interjected. His eyes twinkled full of Mallory. He then went on in a droning, monotonous voice that Siri thought would bore the paint off the walls. "It's one of the oldest private libraries in the country. Your friend, Miss Swift, has expressed interest in the history of Salem, and as I am an authority on the subject, I have volunteered my time to tutor her, at her convenience of course. Did you know the Native American name for Salem is Naumkeag? Not many people here do. Are you from Salem? Your bone structure is similar to that of the woman folk of Salem's founding fathers. Their portraits hang over yonder at the Museum of Antiquities in the portrait gallery. The line of your jaw and your brow ridge are unmistakable Crowninshield traits. Did I mention that I'm also a genealogist? I'm descended from old Derby stalk. My great, great, great grandmother..."

Suddenly the groaning of the copy machine stopped.

"Nice to meet you, Mister Dobbs," Siri blurted.

Siri quickly grabbed Mallory by the arm, and ran out the door with her, leaving Dobbs standing there with his mouth open.

# CHAPTER 13: The Live Slow

The "Live Slow Café" was a quaint café on the Derby Street waterfront and a favorite hangout of students from Windward High School. Some were talking on cell phones. Others had their eyes riveted to lap tops and e-readers in little nooks decorated with artwork and photography from local artists. An 80's pop tune about *"walking like an Egyptian"* blared over the shop's speakers. The head barista, an attractive brunette, had just handed Siri and Mallory their drinks in bright orange cups.

"Great to see you guys again," the barista said cordially.

"Hey, nice top," Mallory commented.

"Thanks!" The barista replied, flattered that her "Ankh" tank top depicting the handled cross, the Egyptian hieroglyphic for eternal life, snared positive notice. Siri hardly regarded her latte art, a scarab beetle rendered in creamy, white foam.

"You know, that Mister Dobbs had nice ears," Mallory remarked, flipping through a fashion magazine, "like big muffin tops."

"He's a thousand years older than you," Siri returned. She looked out the café window, surveying the street.

"Okay, what's on your mind now?" Mallory asked.

"I don't like what my dad is getting involved in," Siri replied.

"Emma seems nice."

"I'm not talking about her."

"You mean that spooky old place on the hill?" Mallory clarified.

"I just don't want him going up there," Siri said. "Something's not right about that place. I feel it."

"There's nothing you can do about it. You're not the police. So stop worrying."

Siri turned to Mallory with a big, bright look on her face.

"Mallory," Siri exclaimed. "You're are a genius!"

"What did I say?"

# CHAPTER 14: Parent Trap

Scarpetti sat cross-legged on a yoga mat, deep breathing with his arms slightly extended, and the forefinger and thumb of each hand connected in a little circle. His eyes closed, Scarpetti looked like a classic swami in a lotus position. The plain-clothes detectives and uniformed police officers gathered around him knew better, and saw a smoldering volcano on the verge of eruption.

"There are seven missing persons to date," the detective huffed, his eyes clamped shut. He took a deep breath that inflated him. He then exhaled, his girth collapsing like a leaky balloon. "And we're no closer to solving this case than we were a month ago. Any further disappearances will result in some persons disappearing from this precinct. Do I make myself clear?"

A silver-haired policeman poked his head through Scarpetti's door. The detective could sense him even with his eyes closed.

"What is it, Mace?"

"Sorry to interrupt, chief. But there's a call for you on the tip line. It's about the old state hospital."

Scarpetti opened his eyes. He rose flushed in the face.

"Don't tell me it's that Braddock kid again. She calls me more than my wife."

He snatched up the receiver, practically taking the whole phone up with it.

"Chief Detective, Scarpetti," he barked.

Mallory stood in a phone booth near a busy street corner. She faced an open notebook that Siri had pressed against the glass from outside. Mallory held the phone to her lips and read from the page.

"Hallooo, Detective Scarpetti," said Mallory in a haughty voice. Mallory did her best to sound like high society, even gesturing in the air, but Siri thought she sounded like a floozy with a few too many gin and tonics in her.

"I hooooope you are wellllll. You boysss in bluuuue make me feel soooooo safe, esssspecially at this time of year. I know you're very busy so I'll get straight to the point. Whilsssssst I was jewelry shopping, I overheard a man and woman talking about the old state hospital, you know, that old bit of run-down real estate on the hill. They looked very suspicious and they mentioned something about blueprints. It wouldn't surprise me if they were planning to vandalize the old place. Sooooo keep a close watch up there."

"Who is this?" Scarpetti asked over the phone.

"Oh, you don't know me," Mallory continued. "I'm just a concerned citizen doing her bit for the community. I always feel that law-abiding citizens like myself should take up their share of civic duty to make society a better place for all civic-minded citizens to civilly live civilized in a civilization, and all that sort of civil thingy..."

Siri looked at her notebook. The words she wanted Mallory to read were done and Mallory was still talking, worse yet, she was ad-libbing. Not a good thing. Siri yanked the cap off a magic marker with her teeth, scrawled something, and then quickly turned the page back towards Mallory.

"HANG UP NOW!!" it read.

45

# CHAPTER 15: Night Walker

Siri liked to relax in her *"Good Girls Go To Heaven, Bad Girls Go To Salem"* T-shirt. It was past midnight and Siri was anything but relaxed. She lay on her bed, her eyes wandering about her room. An outside street lamp threw a crisscross pattern on posters hanging on Siri's bedroom wall – mostly playbill reprints of vintage mystery movies. Siri should have been working on her book report, but wasn't in the mood. Her room was a mess too. She hadn't cleaned it in weeks. Every flat surface it seemed was cluttered with tangled charging leads, microphones, digital recorders, well-thumbed mystery magazines with a few soda cans, candy wrappers, and stale pizza crusts thrown into the mix. Siri couldn't shake the feeling like she was very near the edge of something, like a cliff, but a proverbial one. She was on the crossroads and felt something pushing her toward a path from which there would be no return. A sudden creak in the hall caught Siri's attention. Siri snuck over to her bedroom door and cracked it open. Her dad was trying to sneak out again.

"I'm going too," Siri said.

"No you're not," Collin said. "Get back to bed."

Siri grabbed her coat off her bedroom door peg and her dad's keys out of his hand and was down the stairs and halfway out the front door before her dad had a chance to say another word.

"I'll warm up the car," she called out.

# CHAPTER 16: The Man in Black

The MG pulled up to the curb side. Siri's face pulsed red and blue from the strobes of first responders.

"Now stay put!" Collin said, yanking up the hand break. "Mind me for just once, will you please? For once..."

"But dad..."

"No buts," Collin said getting out of the car. "I'm the parent. You're the child. You do what I say or I'll have Scarpetti have one of his boys drive you home in a squad car."

Siri folded her arms before her and huffed. She watched her dad duck under yellow perimeter tape, snapping pictures with every step. The Salem Museum of Antiquities, normally a serene place, was a hubbub of noise and confusion. The entrance was blocked with police cruisers parked at odd angles, and detectives questioned anyone hanging around the pedestrian mall nearby. The museum's atrium was all lit up and Siri could see Scarpetti barking orders to police officers inside. His bald head and face were red as a Chinese lantern. A police officer walked by the MG and gave Siri a curious look, like she didn't belong there. It was Officer Pantano, who Siri ran into once or twice before.

"Hey Al," Siri said. "I'm with my dad tonight. What's going down?"

"Grand theft," the officer replied. "Pretty crazy if you ask me. But whoever did it was a pro. He deactivated security cameras, alarms, everything."

"What was stolen?" Siri pressed.

"Mummies," the officer replied walking away. "He stole all the mummies on exhibition. A whole museum of precious artifacts and the only thing stolen were mummies. Yup. A real coconut was at the bottom of this one. So much for another Halloween in Salem."

Siri sat for a moment, thinking. Her dream about a mummy heist was coming true – in spades. Suddenly she got that tingly feeling all over, like she was about to do something really daring. She climbed out of the car and strode towards the museum, mindless of the commotion around her. Siri remained completely calm, imagining herself invisible as she walked through the front doors, passing busy police officers and detectives snapping pictures and dusting display cases for fingerprints. Not one looked up. Siri could hear her dad arguing with Scarpetti in the grand atrium, but she didn't turn around. She just walked right passed everyone. They were too busy to notice her. Siri entered the gallery of maritime paintings and ducked into the shadows just as two officers with flashlights walked by. A series of big ship models made good cover and Siri took full advantage of them. She crawled behind the schooners and three-masted tall ships and made her way to the dark stairwell. And when she got there, she dashed up it!

The second floor was dimly lit, illumined by little round overhead lights. Siri passed a row of ship figureheads, their carved arms and heads appearing to move in the shadows. Siri gave one furtive look over her shoulder before ducking into a gallery titled *"Treasures of England 1770-1840."*

*Tick-tock-tick-tock-tick-tock* went the clocks in the darkness. *Thump, thump, thump,* went Siri's heart. She looked at the security camera above her. It stared down like a great, cyclopean eye. Siri remembered what Officer Pantano had told her and was grateful it was deactivated. She looked at the display of clocks in front of her, specifically the boxy Highland Mantel Clock, which was small enough to conceal under her coat. Siri looked at the big clock face. It looked so elegantly fashioned. She took a step towards it. It was then she heard the floor creak behind her. Siri turned and her thumping heart nearly stopped. In the doorway stood a man draped in a dark overcoat and gathered up in gloom.

"It's him," Siri thought. "It's the man in black!"

She had seen him that very afternoon in the same spot – silent as the grave! He took a step towards Siri without saying a word. Siri tried hard not to scream.

"Don't come near me," Siri said.

The man in black stepped closer, then closer – so close Siri could see his pale face sharpening into focus with every cautious step he took towards her, from a blurry mist into a sharper relief of smooth, angular features. A stray glimmer of light caught his eyes and they lit up, reflecting back the dim radiance like tiny signal mirrors. Siri didn't know what to do next. Luckily her instincts took over. She turned and lunged for the clock. The man in black sprang after her, missing her by inches.

Siri gathered the clock in her arms and dashed into another gallery, one she hadn't been in before. She could hear the man in black sprinting behind her. The room she was in was almost totally dark, lit mostly by high windows that faced the streetlights. Siri bumped into a pedestal. A vase perched on top wobbled, but didn't fall. Siri found herself ducking behind furniture and sliding under display tables, all the while dodging the desperate lunges of the man in black. Whoever he was, Siri thought, he had the agility and eyesight of a cat. Siri was pretty quick too. Her small stature together with adrenaline coursing through her muscles made her as nimble as a Ninja. Siri figured she was in some Asian gallery judging from the obstacle course of bamboo furniture, Fu Dogs, and elegant vases she dodged. At one point Siri got a good glimpse of her pursuer. He was crouched atop a mock temple roof, looking like some hideous medieval gargoyle ready to pounce. His hair was jet black, hung shoulder-length, and was evenly divided alongside each half of his face. The face itself was pale, his forehead – high and broad. His nose was thin and finely molded. His cheekbones were sharply sculpted.

Siri caught her breath behind a statue of a Samurai warrior, gathering her nerve to make the next move. Mister Silent, who Siri had now dubbed the man in black, was biding his time, scanning the darkness like a hawk on a limb looking for the slightest movement.

The way his eyes caught the dim light as he turned his head gave Siri a chill. She remembered she had seen eyes like that before – on her laptop monitor. Siri wondered who Mister Silent was and why he wanted the clock. It appeared they both took advantage of the break-in at the museum that night. Siri had the clock and she wasn't parting with it. She held it closely with one arm. Then she made her move.

Siri dashed from the gallery, down a flight stairs, and bounded out the back doors. Mister Silent sprang from his perch. He took a few mad steps and leaped after Siri, clearing the staircase in a single bound, the coat tails of his duster filling with air and spreading wide like great bat wings. He burst through the double doors. Siri hid in an alley and tucked the clock under her jacket. The cold air outside felt good as she caught her breath. She could see her dad's MG just down the narrow, cobblestoned way. Mister Silent was outside too. Siri could see him standing with indecision, wondering which way she went. Siri slunk alongside a dingy brick wall, doing her best to keep out of sight. She could see the steamy breaths puffing from Mister Silent's mouth under the ray of a street lamp. Siri quickly rounded a corner, ambled up to her dad's car, and got in, appearing like she had never left it. Her dad appeared, opened the driver's door, and sat beside her. He grumbled something about Scarpetti and then gave her a look before starting the engine.

"Are you putting on weight?"

"I've been thinking about taking up track," Siri replied, crossing her arms over her belly.

"Well at least you minded me and stayed in the car."

The MG pulled away from the curb. Siri checked the rear view mirror. There was no sign of Mister Silent – just an avenue of dark cobblestones lit by lamp light.

# CHAPTER 17: Rendezvous

"Get me through this day," Siri huffed.

Siri watched Mrs. Breath's spindly figure advance down her row with the poise of a drill instructor in the midst of raw recruits. She was busy handing out papers to her right and left, which made the room so silent you would think she was metering out death warrants. Siri hardly slept the night before, and had a terrible headache, so terrible it felt like Windward High's marching band drummer, Punk-head Ledbetter, was beating John Philip Sousa's "The Thunderer March" between her ears. When Siri received her paper she gave a short gasp and held her hand to her forehead. There was red ink all over the front page. It looked like Mrs. Breath had burst a blood vessel. Siri saw the "D-minus" and shook her head. Siri couldn't believe her grade. She looked over at Mallory in the next row. Mallory gave her a thumbs down. Siri mouthed the words "Library."

Mallory nodded.

·    ·    ·

The school library had an outdated, but adequate bank of computer terminals. Siri was sitting at a reading booth scanning the local newspaper when Mallory entered.

"What's up?" Mallory asked.

Siri pointed to an online headline. Mallory bent over Siri's shoulder and read it.

"MUMMY HEIST BAFFLE POLICE: EGYPTIAN RELICS

STOLEN FROM SALEM MUSEUM."

"I heard about the big break-in," Mallory said. "You were there with your dad, weren't you?"

"We weren't the only ones there," Siri replied. "Mister Silent was there too."

"Mister Silent?"

"The man in black," Siri clarified. "The man who has been following me."

Mallory felt Siri's forehead.

"Will you stop that? I'm fine," Siri huffed. "He even chased me through the museum."

"Why would he do that?"

"Because I have something he wants," Siri replied,

Mallory's eyes widened. Her mouth hung open.

"You stole the clock?"

"Shhhhhhhhhhhhh," Siri whispered. "Not so loud."

Mallory huddled up next to Siri and whispered.

*"You stole the clock?"*

Siri nodded.

"Where is it?"

"It's in a safe place."

"What are you going to do with it?" Mallory asked.

"Try to open it," Siri returned.

"Why?"

"Because I believe something's hidden in it."

"Hey, you two," a voice rang out.

Siri and Mallory turned. A teenage boy with dark hair and quick eyes approached them.

"Hey Christian," Mallory said. "What's goin' down?"

"The Grand Masque on Friday, of course. I'm on the planning committee. Are you two going?

"What's a Grand Masque," Siri asked.

"He means the annual Windward High Halloween Bash," Mallory interjected.

"Oh, that," Siri said. "I suppose so."

Christian Fletcher was in Siri's and Mallory's science class. He was tall, stylishly dressed in a leather jacket and jeans, and had boyish good looks that made him popular with girls. Siri heard a rumor he moved from England to live with his father after his parents divorced. He didn't have a British accent, at least one she could detect.

"Good," Christian said. He looked at Siri and smiled. Then he curled his fist around his chin and studied her for a moment, like an art critic evaluating a painting.

"What's the matter?" Siri asked. "Am I sprouting a third eye?"

"I was just thinking," said Christian, "that you'd make a great Marie Antoinette."

"Wasn't she the Queen of France who got her head chopped off?" Mallory asked.

"Yes," Christian replied, still eyeing Siri. "But it was such a pretty head."

Siri forced a grin. Christian winked at her and walked off towards the book stacks.

"He likes you," Mallory said.

"So?"

"He's the richest kid in school. Plus he's the son of the principal."

"We don't have time for that," Siri replied. "What are you doing tonight?"

"Not a thing. Why?"

Siri lowered her voice to a whisper.

"Be at my house at eight o'clock sharp. Tell no one where you're going."

# CHAPTER 18: The Attic Dark

The doorbell rang, and Siri peered into the little peephole in the front door. After satisfying her curiosity, she slid back several security chains and flipped back the dead bolt. She cracked open the door and tugged Mallory in.

"Did anyone follow you?" Siri asked.

"Of course not," Mallory replied. "Who would follow me?"

"I'd say about half the guys at school."

Siri peeked out a curtained window and surveyed the dark street outside. It was foggy. The street lamps appeared like dim little halos arrayed down one side of Wicks End.

"What's up with you?" Mallory asked.

"Come away from the door," said Siri.

She pulled Mallory into the parlor. The television was on and for a moment the screen captured Siri's attention. On the TV was a fair-haired woman cloaked in a black cape and cowl marching in a parade. Then a reporter interviewed her off to the side. She said she was on a crusade to provide better awareness to the public about the Wiccan faith. A caption read, "Kaelyn Skye, Salem's Official Witch." Suddenly another news item flashed upon the TV screen with captions announcing "VITAMIN SUPPLEMENT SMASH AND GRAB." There was a little video of a pharmacy that had been ransacked.

"Follow me," Siri said, finally moving on towards the stairwell.

Mallory followed Siri up a dimly lit staircase.

"Where's your dad?"

"He's out."

Siri led Mallory up one flight of steps, and then another and another. It seemed there was no end to the stairs. Finally, Siri led Mallory to a narrow stairwell and they both climbed that too.

Siri creaked open the tiny attic door and ducked her head in. Mallory followed, careful not to bump her own head. Siri switched on a flashlight and aimed it down a constricting passage. Mallory followed her, her large blue eyes roaming over boxes and steamer trunks with edges softened by layers of dust and veiled by gossamer cobwebs. An old shoebox fell when Mallory inadvertently brushed it with her elbow. When it landed on the floor it opened, revealing an antique porcelain doll with staring eyes. Suddenly a spider crawled out of its little pursed mouth. Siri opened a trunk, which was a little less dusty than the others, and withdrew a boxy mantel clock with a little brass handle on top. It was the Highland Mantel Clock from the museum. Mallory recognized it instantly.

"You really did take it!" she exclaimed.

"Watch," Siri said.

Before Mallory's big, blue eyes, Siri turned the minute hand of the clock around the clock's face. As she did, she recited a little rhyme.

"Start at twelve, turn twice passed three, then back to nine, to open thee."

Suddenly a compartment below the face of the clock sprang open revealing a hidey-hole. Siri reached inside and removed a simple folded piece of parchment paper. She unfolded it under the glare of her flashlight and revealed to Mallory a barely legible formula penned in antique iron gall ink common to the Eighteenth Century. It was a meticulous list of ingredients, some Siri recognized, like "a drop of oil of clove" and a "sprig of thistle." Others were completely strange to her, and all written in neat cursive penmanship. Mallory's eyes widened at the sight of it. She wore an expression of genuine awe.

"I can't believe you found this," Mallory said.

"It's a formula of some kind," Siri said. "But of what?"

Suddenly the sound of a door shutting downstairs caught Siri by surprise.

"It's your dad?" Mallory asked.

"No," replied Siri. "He's not due back yet."

Siri wore a perplexed expression. She walked down the dusty expanse of attic to where the stairwell lurked. At the top of the steps Siri peered over the rail and couldn't believe her eyes. There, at the bottom of the steps leading up to the attic, stood Mister Silent, his face covered by dark glasses. He began to climb up the steps, one at a time, with the slowness and resolve of one sure of his game. Siri's blood congealed.

"Mal!" Siri shouted. "It's HIM! HE'S HERE!"

"Who's here?" Mallory asked.

Siri ran back to where Mallory stood by the open trunk.

"Mister Silent!" Siri exclaimed. She was almost shaking, and clung to Mallory like a koala. "He's coming up the steps!"

"You're imagining it," Mallory chided. She walked back up towards the stairwell. "I'll prove it."

Siri clung onto Mallory's sleeve. She tried to tug her back.

"No, Mal!" Siri shouted. "Don't go near the stairs!"

"Don't be a big baby!" Mallory said. She freed herself from Siri and stood at the top of the stairs looking down.

"See," Mallory said, her hands on her hips. "There's nobody here. Come see for yourself."

Siri reluctantly approached the stairwell. Then she cautiously peered over the rail and looked down the stairs. Mallory was right. No one was there.

# CHAPTER 19: Listening In

Siri laid in her bed, her Louisville Slugger clutched close to her chest. She was too terrified to fall asleep. She just stared at the window or at her bedroom door. Both were securely locked. Even a chair was wedged against the doorknob. The little yellow parchment Siri discovered was tucked into the sock she wore. She was keeping it that close. Whatever the mysterious formula written on it was for, it had to be pretty important, Siri figured. It seemed that Mister Silent wanted it too – and badly. Seeing Mallory up in the attic must have scared him off. Siri wished Mallory could have remained a little longer, but Mallory said she had to get going. At least she stayed until they both searched the house.

It was late. Siri wished her dad would come home. She wanted to call him, but decided to ride out her latest brush with fright. Something deep inside told her to keep quiet about things, at least for the time being.

Suddenly a car door slammed outside. Siri jumped out of bed, parted a curtain, and peered down at the street below. Wicks End was shrouded in a curtain of fog. Siri could barely make out three dark figures standing by a Jeep under the misty halo of a street lamp. She recognized the outline of her dad and Emma, but the third figure Siri never saw before. It was a young man with a blonde buzz cut dressed in a leather jacket. Something about him seemed vaguely familiar. Siri cracked open the window and tried to hear what they were saying. It had to be something really important the way they were huddled together, but it was no good. Siri couldn't make out the words. She needed something to amplify their voices.

"How did that flatfoot Scarpetti know we were going up there tonight? He was waiting for us," Emma huffed.

"Are you sure no one overheard you enlisting the help of Mister Houdini here?" Collin pressed, turning to Mister Buzz Cut. "We were doing fine until he showed up."

"Hey, don't blame me, man," said Mister Buzz Cut. "I don't advertise picking locks. We were set up. Double crossed if you ask me! It wasn't my bright idea to break into that old nut house in the first place, remember?"

Siri could now hear every word clear as crystal. She was holding a shotgun microphone to the window screen, headphones fitted over her ears, turning the volume knob of a little black receiver box.

"What eats me is Alex Cedric was waiting up there too," said Emma. Siri saw her slim form leaning against the fender of the Jeep, her arms folded against herself. "Cedric pulls a lot of weight in this town. He wasn't bluffing about charging us with trespassing. I'll be kicked off the historical commission for sure."

"Chill out, babe," Buzz Cut said. "You and I have been in tighter spots than this." He then turned to Collin. "Someone gave us away, someone close to one of you, someone who doesn't think twice about ringing up Scarpetti and getting his boiler up to steam."

Siri watched her dad turn his gaze up towards her window. Siri quickly ducked out of sight.

# CHAPTER 20: Unexpected Thrill

A chill breeze was coming off the ocean. Siri sat in the passenger seat of the MG as her dad drove. It was a bright afternoon. Her dad had just picked her up at the usual curbside in front of Windward. Siri didn't feel like talking. She just watched the road ahead. Mallory did everything possible to get her mind off Mister Silent that day, even to the point of tugging her into the lady's room for a beauty makeover.

Mallory didn't care who was watching, but Siri did. The lady's room mirror was broad and Siri felt embarrassed as freshmen and senior girls eyed her with noticeable smirks in its reflection as they came and went. Siri sat on a stool, her face turned upwards as Mallory applied a deep, ruby-red shade of lip color to Siri's lips, which Mallory had to force by squeezing Siri's cheeks into a pucker. Siri never did get over Doug Graves telling her she was so skinny that when she stuck her tongue out, she looked like a zipper! Mallory's make-up kit was like an artist's paint box, complete with every tool of the trade and ready for immediate use. At last the portrait was complete and Mallory stepped back to better judge her creation. Siri sat on her stool and gazed into the mirror, and frowned. She looked like a ventriloquist's dummy.

Siri noticed her dad wasn't talking much either during the ride. He didn't even ask her how she did on her book report, which worked in her favor. Siri watched the Salem Custom House go by, a spacious Federal-style building topped with a golden eagle. Suddenly the smooth road turned to cobblestones. The MG took a right and slowed before a quaint, three-story gambrel situated a stone's throw from "The House of Seven Gables," a historic mansion made famous by Nathaniel Hawthorne in the novel of the same name. A large wooden signboard creaking on a post read, *"Black Ram Inn, established 1760."* The car turned onto a gravel driveway. Suddenly Siri noticed a motorcycle parked before an old carriage house that served for a garage. Its no-frills profile seemed familiar to Siri. She felt her sock-covered ankle. The parchment was safe and sound. Her dad stopped the car and yanked up the hand brake.

"Dad, I'll be just a minute. You go on inside," Siri said.

"Don't be too long," Collin replied.

Siri watched her dad enter the inn. She got out of the MG and approached the motorcycle. Its handlebars and exhaust pipes gleamed in the sunlight. Suddenly something large and powerful came bounding out of the garage straight at Siri. Before she knew it, a big Saint Bernard had pinned her to the ground.

"Simon, get off!"

A tall, young man with a blonde buzz-cut stepped from the garage. He was wearing a grease-stained sweatshirt and was wiping his hands on a rag. It was the same young man Siri saw the night before when her dad and Emma were talking outside her window.

"He doesn't bite," the young man remarked. He nudged the dog aside and offered Siri a hand getting up.

"The name's Bernie Putnam. What's yours?"

Siri brushed herself off and found she was looking into the deepest, bluest eyes she'd ever seen.

"My name's, Sprout. I mean, Siri Braddock."

"You're Collin's daughter. You like motorcycles?"

"Yeah," Siri replied, not knowing what else to say.

"Well get on."

The Saint Bernard let out an enthusiastic *"whoof"* as Siri found herself throwing a leg up and planting herself on the saddle. What she didn't expect was Bernie seating himself directly behind her. He switched on the ignition and turned the throttle. **VARROOOM!! VARROOOM!!** The motorcycle shook and vibrated beneath Siri as it roared to life.

"What do you think of her?"

"It's loud!" Siri replied.

"I'll have to mothball her for the winter soon! Hate to do it, since it shortens the life of the battery!"

"You should get a battery tender! It will keep it charged and make it last a long time!"

"I'll do that! Hey, you're alright!"

Siri sprouted a smile. If only Mallory could see her.

"Want to go for a ride?"

"Okay."

Before Siri knew it, a helmet was over her head and the motorcycle, a Harley Fat Boy, roared out of the driveway kicking up a rooster tail of stones. Siri shrieked at the unexpected thrill of the blast off.

"Hold on!" Bernie shouted.

Siri pressed herself tight in the seat and gripped the handlebars with Bernie. As they careened onto Derby Street, Bernie threw out his boot to steady his leaning machine, and once on the straightaway, opened up the throttle so that his bike screeched like a dive-bomber. Siri shrieked again, her face beaming like a Jack O'Lantern. Siri couldn't remember the last time she had so much fun. The wind in her face was exhilarating and the raw power of the bike beneath her made her want to go even faster. Salem was whizzing by on both sides of her. Siri wasn't afraid. That was the strange part.

"This is great!" Siri hollered over the roaring engine.

"Faster?"

"Open her up!"

Suddenly the Fat Boy soared down the street. It was posted 35 MPH. The speedometer read 65. Then suddenly Siri saw him. It was just a quick glimpse, but there was no mistaking those dark sunglasses. It was Mister Silent. He was standing in the shadow of the Old Custom House watching Siri as she rode past. Siri suddenly felt a pit in the middle of her stomach. The fun was gone.

"I think we better get back!" Siri shouted.

Bernie nodded and turned a corner.

# CHAPTER 21: The Eye of Horus

Siri didn't feel like doing anything much now. She wished she had stayed home. She didn't even feel like talking. Bernie kept going on about his bike, the re-built engine, and the new shocks, but Siri smiled and nodded politely. She had Mister Silent on her mind, and couldn't for the life of her, get him out. Siri's brash act – the stealing of the Highland Mantel Clock – was beginning to have real consequences. Being followed by a dark stranger with eyes that glimmered at night was a big deal. He invaded her house and now he was showing himself in broad daylight. It was not like having notes stuck to her school locker. This was big time stuff, and Siri felt like she had bitten off more than she could chew.

Siri followed Bernie inside the Black Ram Inn. The place was built during the Revolutionary War and looked it. Bernie led Siri through a quaintly appointed colonial hall, passed a great grandfather clock, and then into an elegant dining room with a beamed ceiling and a brick fireplace that ran the length of a wall. Diners were having breakfast, waited on by two elderly ladies in frilly aprons. Bernie walked Siri right up to them.

"Aunt Amy. Aunt Dody," Bernie said. "Meet Siri, my new bike partner."

Aunt Amy tipped down her bifocals and looked at Siri with a smile. Amy had a head of curly white cotton and was tall and lean as a carrot.

"Hello, dear," Amy said, her voice grandmotherly and tremulous. "Do you like lady fingers? I just pulled a fresh batch out of the oven."

"I love 'em," Siri said, smiling, though the cookies smelled of charcoal and looked like freshly roasted caterpillars.

"Oh, she would much rather prefer a slice of my cherry pie. Wouldn't you, Siri?" Aunt Dody chimed in from the side. Dody was short and plump, like a ripe pumpkin.

"She said she liked lady fingers," Amy said. "So don't butt in."

"Oh, she was just being polite," Dody interjected. "I can see it in her face. Those cookies of yours are putting her off. Bernie, take her into the kitchen and get her a slice of warm, cherry pie. I picked the cherries myself from our own tree out back."

"Lady fingers." Amy insisted.

"Cherry pie," Dody repeated, stamping her foot.

"Time out!" Bernie said, placing his hand between the two like a referee. "Come on, Siri." He led Siri into the kitchen. "I'll get you some lady fingers AND cherry pie."

Suddenly one of the dining guests, a tall man, stood and called from a table. Siri noticed he had a British accent.

"Bernard, my good fellow!" His accent was distinctly British. "What a wonderful place you have here. And your two darling aunts are just treasures."

Bernie smiled and approached the man.

"I'm glad someone thinks so."

The two engaged in a cordial handshake.

"I was hoping you'd arrive, sir," said Bernie. "I was beginning to worry."

"My flight got delayed," the man clarified.

The guest turned his gaze upon Siri

"And who is this lovely young lady? he asked.

"This is Siri," Bernie replied. "Siri, this is Dent, the president of Earth Sense, an international environmental group. They're having a big conference here in Salem."

"Hello, Mister Dent," Siri said.

"Just Dent..."

Dent reached out and shook Siri's hand. Siri smiled politely. The Englishman impressed her. He was tall, handsome, and his perfect tan set his green eyes ablaze when he looked at her. A silver pendant hanging from Dent's neck caught Siri's notice. It was shaped like a heavily mascaraed eye. Siri had seen something like it in history class.

"Do you know what symbol this is, Siri?" Dent asked, noticing Siri's gaze fastened on his pendant.

Siri nodded and replied, "The Eye of Horus."

"That's right," Dent said. "It's also called the Wedjat. It's an ancient Egyptian symbol for power and protection. The eye symbol represents the markings around a Peregrine Falcon's eye."

"How do you like Salem?" Bernie asked Dent.

"I find it all very intriguing," Dent said. "A city where real witches and ghosts make the news everyday! I can't wait to take one of those cemetery tours and learn more about it."

Something then caught Dent's eye. Siri followed his gaze. In the dining room doorway stood a bearded man with a red cylindrical hat with black tassel on his head. Siri knew the hat was called a Fez, the traditional headgear of Middle Eastern men. The man looked sternly at Dent and nodded. Dent nodded back, as if in understanding. He then shifted his gaze to Bernie.

"Well, I'll let you get on your way," Dent said. "I hope I have the pleasure of meeting you again, Siri."

Siri smiled. Bernie gave Dent a lighthearted pat on the shoulder and led Siri into the kitchen.

# CHAPTER 22: The Parchment

Siri sat at her desk in her bedroom. It was past midnight. That much she knew. She was tired, but Siri did her best thinking when all of Salem was quiet and dark. Her desk lamp flickered a bit, a loose wire. Pachelbel's Canon played on her CD player, its forlorn strains plucking chords in Siri that few musical compositions could. It always helped her concentrate. Somehow the somber melody heightened her awareness of things, lifted her out of herself. Siri needed inspiration that night – all she could get. She had been looking over the formula penned onto the old folded piece of crinkled parchment and was racking her brain trying to figure out its meaning.

*Satyrion Root – ½ parts, Yarrow – 8 parts, Meadow Sweet – ½ parts, Mandrake Root – 1 part, Wolfbane (Monkshood) – ½ part, Moonwort – 2 parts, Hawthorn Blossoms – 4 ½ parts, Sulphur – 2 parts.* That wasn't the half of it. Even the moon's phases had to be taken into account when blending certain ingredients. There was also a lengthy chant to invoke to ward off the evil eye!

"Pretty heavy stuff," Siri thought. "What did it mean?"

Siri was tired now. It was hard to fight it. Her mind began to wander. She liked Bernie. He was fun and cute. He loved his bike. It was his world to him. Siri understood that. And he loved his aunts. That made him a good person in Siri's book. Emma was a piece of work though. When Siri was in the kitchen of the Black Ram Inn sampling Aunt Amy's ladyfingers and Aunt Dody's cherry pie, she kept trying to overhear what her father and Emma were talking about. It concerned the asylum. That much Siri got. But Emma just kept going on about how riled she was about being set up. Emma needed to get over it. Siri wished she could have overheard more, but judging from the blueprints her dad and Emma were looking over on top of the bar counter, it was pretty obvious that they were planning on taking another stab at penetrating the old asylum. Siri wondered what her next move would be too.

Suddenly Siri's cell phone flashed and beeped. She picked it up and studied the LCD screen. There was an unidentified text message on it. "COME TO THE WINDOW," it read. Siri turned to the window, perplexed. She got up from her desk and made sure her door was securely locked. It was. A chair was propped up against the doorknob. Siri turned and approached the only window to her room. It wasn't Mallory who sent the text message, so who was it? Siri gently parted the curtain. She could hear the wind rattling the windowpane and howling through the tree branches, sounding like a mournful ghost. Siri peered out of the window and into the night. Wicks End was dark and silent, a few converted gas lamps dimly illuminating the cobblestones. It was then the windowpane detonated inwards showering the room in broken glass. Siri glimpsed a tree limb thrusting towards her, but when five fingers unfurled and gripped her by the wrist, Siri couldn't believe it! It wasn't a tree limb! It was a HAND! A TERRIBLE, CLUTCHING HAND!

Siri sat bolt upright from her pillow. She panted quick, shallow breaths. She looked at her bedroom window. It was unbroken. No glass shards anywhere. She looked at her wrist. No horrible finger marks. Siri glanced over at her cell phone on the night table. She reached over and picked it up. It was all a terrible dream, a nightmare. Siri checked her phone for text messages. There were none, thank goodness, not even a message telling her to "COME TO THE WINDOW." Siri checked her sock-covered ankle. The parchment was there and safe. Siri tossed the covers aside and walked towards the only window in her bedroom. She was apprehensive about that window now, and how it overlooked Wicks End. Siri parted the curtain and looked out. A pit came to her stomach. She saw what she half expected to see. There he was standing under the street lamp. Mister Silent. He was looking up at Siri, his eyes catching the lamplight and reflecting it back like a nocturnal creature. Siri just stared at him. Suddenly, to Siri's surprise, Mister Silent raised his hand and made a beckoning motion. Then he pointed at the front door.

Siri didn't know how she got there, but she was in the upstairs hallway wearing her nightshirt. She was walking passed her dad's door and heading towards the stairway. Siri gripped the banister rail as she stepped down the stairs, one after the other. She was doing it against her will and she knew it, like a sleepwalker who had no control over her movements. But Siri wasn't asleep. And she knew that too. She was going out to meet Mister Silent. She didn't want to, but she couldn't help it. Before Siri knew it, she was sliding back the chain locks one by one, her eyes wide and staring. Siri could see the dark outline of Mister Silent through the curtain. He was true to his nickname and silent as the grave. He was standing on the porch, waiting for her on the other side of the door. Siri caught a glimmer from his eyes. They were like two stars in a void and had such a weird effect on her. Siri reached for the last deadbolt. She turned it back. Siri was about to open the front door when her dad, in a hastily donned T-shirt and jeans, abruptly thrust it closed, and in the process, woke Siri from her stupor.

# CHAPTER 23: The Curse

Siri didn't like plays. Those she had seen were dull and dragged on and on. Yet, despite that, Siri didn't mind the one she had to attend. It was in a regional theatre, the Black Alley, where aspiring talent acquired stage experience. Mallory sat beside Siri in the rear balcony level, and appeared absorbed in the performance. The play was called *"Sisters on a Limb."* It was about the Salem witch trials and executions on Gallows Hill. Siri and Mallory had to write an essay about their experience attending the play. It was their penance for messing up big time on their book reports. It was the only way Mrs. Breath allowed them to make up for it. The Black Alley set was impressive, yet simple, consisting of an oxcart, ladder, and a series of nooses hanging from a gallows tree. Gathered around a furrowed, papier-mâché tree trunk stood young women in white bonnets and smock dresses beside young men in dark frock cloaks, tall hats, knickers and buckle shoes. The Black Alley auditorium was like a vast grotto with footlights illuminating great marble statues on either side of the grand stage. On one side was Dionysus, the Greek god of theater, and on the other, his companions of satyrs and nymphs, their lithe and muscled figures twisting along grape vines that formed a great arch that disappeared high into the shadows.

Siri hadn't forgotten about the night before. How could she? The way she lost control of her actions frightened her beyond belief. Mister Silent would show up again. Siri was sure of it. The way

Siri figured it, she had something he wanted – the parchment. The formula, or recipe, or whatever was written on it was important enough for a stranger with strange eyes and stranger powers to try and hypnotize Siri into giving it to him. As Siri watched the performance on the stage below she felt her sock for the fourth time that day. What it held was tucked away good. Siri figured she needed to talk to someone about the parchment, someone besides Mallory, someone who knew something about the things written on it, but who?

An actor in the footlights drew Siri's attention back to the stage. He spoke out in a high, nasally tone. He portrayed Reverend Nicholas Noyes, the famed accuser of Gallows Hill. He was cloaked in a great black cassock and a white minister's collar. Five women stood behind him arrayed upon a scaffold all noosed and ready to hang.

"Confess, Sarah Good," Noyes spoke with a dramatic sweep of his arm. "Confess! You are a witch and you know you are a witch! Confess!"

"You are a liar," cried a young woman portraying Sarah Good, a noose around her neck, her hands tied behind her.

Siri and Mallory expected her to recite the next line. They knew it by heart. It was in all the history books. *I am no more a Witch than you are a Wizard, and if you take away my life God will give you blood to drink.* But that's not what the actress declared to the audience. Instead of reciting the expected lines, the actress portraying Sarah Good suddenly quivered and trembled. Her head cocked to one side and to all who observed her she appeared to be suffering a spasm or seizure. Some actors upon the stage looked to one another, bewildered. A few members of the audience stood up out of their seats. The actress who portrayed the unfortunate Sarah Good opened her mouth wide. Then she turned her gaze in the direction of the rear balcony level where Siri and Mallory watched. The voice that boomed out of her was not that of a young woman coached for the stage, but one that belonged to someone older, a woman with a bygone accent who had seen a hard life.

71

"I am a witch, Nicholas Noyes! If that is what you believe! Let God forsake me. But as I stand in innocence, and will surely die, I plead upon the powers to forsake the young innocent who stand in witness to your crime! These children of Salem Village will know not the peace of death, but will wander like the winds from age to age, until they slake their thirst upon the philter of my kinsmen!"

"Hang her!" Noyes commanded.

Sarah Good, before all eyes, was swung to her death. Everyone in the audience started mumbling to one another. Siri turned to Mallory.

"Hey, those weren't the lines she was suppose to say."

Mallory didn't answer. She just stared ahead at the stage. Her face was white as a sheet. She looked like she had seen, or rather heard, a ghost.

# CHAPTER 24: The Costume Shop

Samantha's Costume Shop on Essex Street was the place to go in Salem for costumes. Siri didn't want to go in, but Mallory was insistent, and dragged her through the doors by one arm.

"I don't want to do this, Mal," Siri said, holding back.

"Come on," Mallory said. "This is fun. You need this to get your mind off things."

Siri decided there was no use fussing. She entered the shop and looked around at the assortment of wigs, masks, costumes, or stylish witch hats they passed as they made the rounds about the narrow aisles of the shop. Mallory had her costume all picked out. She bought it weeks before. Now the focus was on Siri.

"I don't know about this, Mal," Siri said as she passed a mannequin decked out in a suit of armor, ready for a joust. She picked through a rack of sultry cat suits and nurse uniforms. "I can't find anything I like."

"You're not trying hard enough," Mallory chided.

Finally the store clerk approached Siri and Mallory. She was dressed like an Arabian dancer eloped from a harem, her dark outlined eyes flashing through her scarlet veil.

"Can I help you two?"

73

"Yes," answered Mallory. "I'm looking for a costume for my friend here. We're looking for something elegant, but Halloweenish."

The clerk looked Siri over and nodded.

"I have just the thing," she said.

# CHAPTER 25: The Grand Masque

Windward High School's Halloween extravaganza had been planned for months. All the students talked about it in the halls and at study period – the costumes they would wear and who they were going with. Siri adjusted her wig. Her dad had dropped her off at the school where Mallory said she would meet her, but as Collin drove off, Siri was alone. The past few days were a trial for Siri. She wanted to tell her dad everything, but didn't. Siri surveyed the front of Windward High under the cloak of night. The moon was full and high and appeared to be balancing itself atop the spire of the school's gold painted cupola. Siri knew Mister Silent was out there, somewhere. Then she saw costumed revelers both entering and leaving the school under a broad, black and orange banner spelling out *"The Grand Masque"* over the concrete lintel of the school's double doors, just beyond the short flight of granite steps. Siri climbed the steps and waited outside the doors, but saw no sign of Mallory. It was time to go inside. Siri handed a ticket to a party-striped harlequin donned in a conical cap and bells. She parted the doors, entered the gym, and couldn't believe the spectacle confronting her.

As if gliding into a dream, Siri wandered into the transformed room, which now resembled a Gothic arcading of the Doge's Palace, the gravity-defying landmark overlooking a Venetian lagoon. Siri could hardly believe her own footsteps as she trod the herringbone tiles of the great piazza of Saint Mark's Square. Masqueraders cloaked in gaudy reds, royal purples and grim black writhed in this medieval Venice compressed into the space of a high school gymnasium. For music there was the lute, the lyre, and the horn, the hallmark instruments of the period. Siri strained to take all of this in, pressing through the throng of masks and hoods, attempting to recognize a voice here or a pair of masked, glinting eyes there. Lifted goblets and laughter over flowing punch told of a party in high gear. Siri could hardly believe her eyes as she beheld porticos and balustrades and the hulking shapes of three great horses, exact replicas of the bronze chargers that adorn Saint Mark's Basilica. This was stagecraft at its best and Siri was hardly prepared for the effect it had on her.

"Where have you been?"

Siri turned. It was Mallory, a golden headdress of a winged vulture adorning her head, a white robe draping her figure, her eyes outlined in mascara. The ankh scepter Mallory held along with a rubber cobra was the clue that this was Cleopatra, ruler of Egypt and lover of Mark Antony, about to do herself in.

"Sorry I'm late," said Siri. "You look great. And I can't believe what they've done to the gym."

"Never mind me," Mallory returned. "Look at you! You're absolutely stunning!"

Siri blushed in her makeup, a cute over-done mole shaped like the ace of spades on her cheek. Her blonde wig was done up in high curls and crowned in a diamond tiara, and she wore a shimmering ball gown that trailed behind her. A dripping bloodline encircling Siri's throat signaled this was Marie Antoinette, the beheaded queen of France, walking the Earth once more, severed head reattached.

Suddenly a flash effect of orange and black strobes stole Siri's attention and a loudspeaker broke over the din of chatter.

"Now to get the party really going," announced the emcee, a tall middle-aged man wearing a black eye patch and a pirate costume. "Here they are, the Idle Bones!" A deafening base note vibrated the air and shook Venice like an earthquake. A rack of purple bulbs, hints of a corner stage, shown glaringly upon four glowing skeletons, three guitarists, one drummer. They struck their cacophonous instruments again and all hell broke loose.

"Wanna dance?" asked a handsome figure of D'Artagnan of the famed Three Musketeers, brazenly placing himself between Siri and Mallory.

The cavalier's sparkling eyes behind the purple mask looked piercingly at Siri. She didn't need to guess who it was. It was Christian. The music was heavy metal mixed with 80's punk, not Siri's favorite, but the beat was fast and catchy. The lyrics of the band's signature tune, *"You Make Me Wanna Bang My Head Against a Car Door,"* blared through the loud speaker and made Siri's ears feel like they were being jammed with screwdrivers. It didn't help that the lead singer, a young man with a skull mask and spiked hair, screamed like he was having an appendectomy (sans anesthesia). But Christian caught her by surprise, led her into the dance fray, and something inside her told her to go with the flow. Then he said something to her, but Siri couldn't hear over the brain-shattering guitar blasts.

"What?"

"You're a pretty good dancer," Christian shouted.

"Thanks," Siri shouted back.

They were just hopping up and down, so Siri couldn't figure why she deserved the compliment. She smiled, and tried not to stomp on Christian's toes. Over his caped shoulder Siri noticed Constance "Sourpuss" Nash ladling out punch to partygoers. Constance was not the party type. She was fifteen going on fifty, plain-faced and dour, like she'd been weaned on a pickle. Constance, a natural hallway monitor, seemed out of place to Siri, but there she was, costumed in a Puritan-era bonnet, shawl, ankle-length homespun dress, and square-toed shoes that looked really uncomfortable. She was ladling out punch to Salem's Official Witch, Kaelyn Sky, who was sharing a laugh with Salem's mayor, Lawrence Atwill, and the principal of Windward High, Bramwell Fletcher, Christian's father. It amused Siri to see these three dignitaries keeping the party spirit. Siri had seen Kaelyn before on TV. Blonde, blue-eyed, and thirty-ish, Siri thought her quite pretty for a witch, especially with her purple hood pulled back over her long, yellow hair. The mayor, sporting red devil horns and a scarlet satin cape with crimson tights and tail, reminded her of the logo on a can of Deviled Ham – add fifty pounds. Bramwell Fletcher came dressed in a white periwig, swallow tail coat, and stocking knickers which called to mind one of the founding fathers, but whether it was George Washington or Thomas Jefferson, Siri couldn't tell. Siri smiled at Christian to keep up appearances. He smiled back. Siri shot a glance over at Mallory to see her reaction, but it was Siri who found herself staring, and with a pit in her stomach. From in between a screen of bobbing dancers Siri could see Mallory standing in a corner whispering to a scholarly, stern-faced man with an iron-gray beard. Siri had seen his face before. It was Alex Cedric, the Danvers Town Archivist. Both Mallory and Cedric shot glances at Siri while she danced with Christian. Siri pretended not to see them, but Bramwell Fletcher did. He graciously excused himself from Kaelyn and Atwill and approached Mallory and Cedric in the wings. Siri watched every move. She tried to shield herself from view behind Christian, who drank Siri up with his eyes, all in a world of his own. Siri did her best to look like she was having fun. She smiled at Christian and shouted in his ear.

"Do you know the Funky Chicken?"

"I never heard of it."

"It kinda goes like this."

Siri tucked her hands to her ribs, flapped her elbows, and turned around as she hopped.

"That's really goofy," Christian said, smiling.

Siri stole another glance over at Mallory and Cedric and realized it was Christian they were looking at, and as they did, they shared an expression of joint concern. Bramwell joined them. Something was going on, a consultation of some kind, and whatever was being said caused all of the color in Principal Fletcher's face to fly away.

None of the revelers noticed the hand, gloved in black and reaching through the throng, zeroing in on Siri as she danced. Siri didn't notice it either. She was thinking of an excuse to tell Christian so she could leave the dance floor when the gloved hand touched her shoulder, and when it did, a change occurred in the music. The din of the band gave way to a combination of sobbing violins and groaning cellos. The music, Pachelbel's Canon, floated through the air. It wafted louder and louder through the hall until it drowned out all other sounds. Then the lights dimmed. Siri saw nothing else but her dance partner who took her two hands into his own and began to whirl her to the longing melody of a classic waltz. Siri was surprised to see that Christian had been replaced by a figure of a young man cloaked in a black cape with a band of black silk tied behind his head to mask his green eyes. His strength and sureness of footing as he twirled Siri under the arch of his arm, or pulled her forwards and backwards to the tempo of the romantic waltz, made Siri feel light-headed and dizzy. But despite how she felt, Siri looked steadily into the green eyes of the stranger who in turn looked at her deeply as if completely absorbed by her appearance.

"You're him," Siri said. It took some effort for her to speak. "You're Mister Silent."

"Are you afraid?" The stranger asked, his voice no more than a whisper.

"Yes," Siri replied. She couldn't take her eyes off of her shadowy partner as he led her in the dance. "I mean…no."

"Then why do you shiver in my arms?"

Siri didn't know what to say. She continued to stare into her partner's green eyes that glimmered and flashed behind the black mask.

"I know why you're here," she finally said.

"Do you?"

"You want the clock."

"You were very foolish to take it."

"If I didn't, I never would have discovered its secret."

The stranger feigned a smile.

"The parchment," he replied. "Give it to me."

"Why do you want it so badly?"

"That is none of your concern."

"It must be very important. If you tell me, maybe I'll give it to you."

"You wouldn't understand."

"It's a secret formula, isn't it?"

"You try my patience."

"I'm just trying to figure it all out."

"Don't force me to take it."

"You don't know where it is," Siri replied.

"I can make you tell me."

"I doubt you'll try that here," Siri smiled.

"That remains to be seen."

Siri's eyes widened. She tried to pull away.

"Let go of me," she gasped. "Who are you?"

Siri could feel the arm of the dark stranger tighten around her waist as he led her in the dance, his eyes boring into hers. He began to whirl Siri faster and faster around the dance floor until a kaleidoscope of colored lights and vague images surrounded her. His voice echoed and re-echoed in her ears.

"I'll tell you who I am. I wax and wan like the moon, but I'm always at your side. I AM YOUR SHADOW!"

With those words spoken Siri's masked partner released her and backed into an envelope of darkness that cloaked around him. Suddenly Pachelbel's Canon was gone. The strobes flared and the agitating din of the Idle Bones brought Siri back to reality. She found herself standing alone amidst a throng of dancing partygoers, strobe lights flashing around her as she stood under a flickering disco ball. Siri stood momentarily stunned by the transition. Then something dawned on her. Siri grew alarmed and pushed through the dance floor to a far corner. She felt her nylon stocking. What she feared and tried to prevent had happened. The parchment she concealed there was gone. She looked over at Mallory, Cedric, and Fletcher by the punch bowl. They were gone too. Siri scanned the dance floor for Christian. He also was nowhere to be seen.

Siri flew out of a rear exit and followed a winding flight of stairs. Her footsteps resounded through the dimly lit hall like gunshots. She burst through a door and suddenly found herself standing in a wash of blue moonlight before the vaulted entrance of Windward High's sculpture garden and hedge maze. There was no sign of Mallory and Christian. The utter stillness of the garden with its chirping crickets was in marked contrast to the deafening gymnasium she had just left.

"Mallory!" Siri called, but there was no answer.

What Siri did next surprised even her. She entered the maze at night and alone. She had always wanted to go in the maze, but for some reason or another never did. At every turn a face, either hewn from white marble or molded in concrete, regarded her with blank, soulless eyes – some classical, others grotesquely Gothic. The pedestals she passed supported Grecian gods or austere Roman matrons. Other figures she dared not look at directly, for they were like gargoyles, ogling or baying, baring fangs or thrusting out clawed paws as if to tear and rend. Siri quickened her pace, moving down one aisle of hedges hemming her in on both sides, to another. She had a vision of herself looking down from above, running headlong down a gallery, finding herself confronted by a dead end and then backtracking. She began to feel like a laboratory mouse being tested for intelligence, trying to find its way to the cheese. Clearly the place was getting on her nerves.

"Mallory!" Siri shouted into the frigid night air. "Christian!"

Siri turned a corner and saw a statue of Pan. He stood on one hoof upon his simple pedestal, sarcastically playing his pipes.

"What are you doing out here?" a voice asked, abruptly.

Siri turned and confronted Constance Nash. Constance's question went right past Siri who did her best not to appear as shocked as she was by the girl's sudden appearance.

"You're missing the buffet," Constance said, coldly. She looked at Siri with an expression as stony as the garden statues. "Come back with me now."

Constance took Siri by the elbow and led her down a gallery of hedges out of the maze. Siri didn't say a word. She couldn't think of one.

# CHAPTER 26: The Search

Siri was never the type to get even, at least she never thought she was, but Mister Whispers, as Siri now dubbed Mister Silent, had changed all that. How he had gotten hold of the parchment Siri could only guess. "It must have been hypnosis," she thought. "That's how he did it. Maybe even mesmerism and autosuggestion?" It was all the same. At any rate the parchment was gone and that was a bone of contention. Siri wanted it back.

Siri decided to visit the attic trunk the next morning. She sifted through a stack of old letters, hoping that something she might have overlooked before would seem relevant now. Crows cawing outside beyond an array of louver board slats of a window helped to conjure in Siri's mind visions of her grandmother, her great grandmother, and her great aunts, all in their austere world of crepe and crinoline and sepia and silver halide – like people depicted in old photographs. Siri saw these women in a stilted half-dream that she tried to pass off as fatigue, but somehow it didn't feel that way. As Siri poured through the old letters she saw herself among her female ancestors, posing by the butter churn, or the spinning wheel, or seated in a group by a millpond. It was a weird daydream, even by Siri's standards, and the cawing of the crows seemed to have a part in it, for their screeches and cackles grew louder as more of the black birds massed just outside. Their cacophony made Siri's head reel. She almost thought she heard them call her name.

Suddenly Siri's eyes fell upon a letter she had unconsciously drew from a stack of others. The cursive penmanship was cramped and difficult to read, but it was a few lines that caught her eye and drew her face towards them. An aunt of Siri's remote past had had a flirtation with an admirer in an age of prim and proper standards, and had, it seemed, decided to arrange a meeting, or so Siri figured. It was a single entry in a journal written in Salem a century and a half ago.

Siri read from it.

*"I have grown weary of guessing, and I do not like men who make great secrets of themselves. I seem to see him everyday now, but I do not wish him away. My head says no, but my heart! Oh, this heart of mine will be my own undoing. But my honor is precious, and I must be careful. I will advertise in the gazette, and arrange a meeting, so I can, at a distance, look him over, and then I will decide..."*

Siri pocketed the letter, wondering what it all meant. It seemed her ancestor had her own Mister Whispers to contend with. Siri picked up the Highland Mantle Clock and turned the minute hand forwards and backwards until the hidden panel below the clock face popped open revealing a secret compartment. It was then Siri got a brilliant idea!

# CHAPTER 27: The Witch Curse Museum

The "Live Slow Cafe" was humming with the usual late afternoon customers, business people getting off from work at Pickering Wharf, or students kicking back. Siri hardly sipped her double tall mochachino. It was 4:30 P.M. and Siri had prearranged to meet Mallory at the "Live Slow" that afternoon, but Mallory was nowhere in sight. She hadn't even return Siri's text messages. Siri waited in their usual place by the window drumming her fingers on the table. She wanted to know what all that strange talk was about between Mallory, Cedric, and Principal Fletcher at the party the night before. Siri also had her own story to tell about Mister Whispers. But that was only the half of it. Siri had been pretty busy that day. She unfolded a copy of the ad she placed in the personals that afternoon. It was the same one she posted on a local on-line bulletin board. Siri read from it.

*"Dear Mister Whispers (you know who you are): If you think you have everything from the clock, think again. Like the saying goes, there's more where that came from. You know how to reach me if you want to know what you're missing. — SB"*

Siri tucked the ad away. Her plan was a long shot, but it was the only way she could think of to get the parchment back. She had to make Mister Whispers think there was more to the clock than just the piece of paper. Hopefully he didn't know he already had the entire formula. If Mister Whispers saw her ad and took the bait, Siri would put her next plan into action.

Suddenly Siri spotted Mallory through the café window. She was standing at a street corner waiting for the traffic light to change. Siri detected someone else on the street too. She could hardly believe her eyes. There he was – Mister Whispers! He stood in the shadow of the Immaculate Conception Church just across the way and seemed to be waiting for Mallory to cross the street. Even in dark sunglasses Siri recognized him. The traffic light changed. Mallory started crossing the street. Mister Whispers made his move. Siri got up out of her seat. Suddenly Siri watched as Mister Whispers sidled up to Mallory and took her by the arm. Siri wanted to run out the door right then and there and help Mallory, but then Siri saw something she just couldn't believe. Mister Whispers spoke to Mallory and Mallory spoke back, like she knew him. There was no shock and awe, just plain conversation. Siri was beside herself. Mallory knew Mister Whispers! She knew him all along!

Suddenly a church bell tolled. Siri watched as Mallory and Mister Whispers turned their heads and walked across town in the direction of the sound.

**GONG! GONG! GONG! GONG! GONG! GONG! GONG!**

The tolling bell caught Siri's interest. It sounded much farther away than the bell tower of the Immaculate Conception Church visible above the trees, which reminded Siri of a big witch's hat. As the tolling bell continued to resonate, Siri watched Mister Whispers lead Mallory up Hawthorne Boulevard, away from the café and out of sight.

The traffic light was still green when Siri dashed out of the "Live Slow" and darted across the street. She rushed up Hawthorne Boulevard, passing the Immaculate Conception Church and a row of old houses. Siri could still see Mister Whispers leading Mallory through a throng of pedestrians while the tolling bell echoed and re-echoed in the air. Siri ran to the next corner and stopped to catch her breath. She searched the intersection and spotted Mister Whispers and Mallory passing beneath an imposing bronze statue of Salem's famous founder, Roger Conant, grim-faced and cloaked, brooding over all who passed under him.

Siri made a diagonal lunge across the intersection. Siri thought it was strange that here the tolling grew so loud it hurt her ears. She had to cover them with her hands as she ran, but nobody else seemed to notice it. She rushed under the statue of Roger Conant and made one last dash across traffic only to see Mister Whispers lead Mallory inside a looming, brick edifice architecturally reminiscent of a church. But the arched, red windows and gold lettering branded over the entrance described it otherwise.

"The Witch's Curse Museum," Siri muttered.

She rushed towards the imposing, Gothic entrance of the church-like building and cautiously reached for the handle to a heavy, hobnailed door. Suddenly the tolling bell stopped, as if snapped off by a switch.

The shadowy room Siri found herself in was adorned with rusted manacles, chains, and framed trial testimonies yellowed with age and penned in crammed, Puritan-era long hand. For a moment she mused over the artifacts that hinted of the attraction beyond. Then muffled voices behind another door caught Siri's ear. She cautiously pushed it open a crack. Inside was a darkened theater where a lecture was going on. Although her eyes weren't adjusted to the darkness, Siri could plainly see a red spotlight shining upon a figure. It was a mannequin of a wigged, Puritan magistrate garbed in black robes and seated behind a high desk. Another spotlight lit up a mockup of a gallows tree complete with a row of mannequins dressed as condemned men and women dangling by the neck. Siri searched the dimly lit faces gathered around the macabre displays, but there was no sign of Mallory and Mister Whispers. As she turned from the door, Siri was at a loss of what to do next. Her already heightened feelings of alarm reached a climax.

Siri stepped back out into the bright afternoon sunlight and retraced her steps across the street. She tried to attach a logical explanation to everything she had seen and heard. She wandered around a bit, not knowing what to do. Then she spotted an occult shop that advertised psychic readings. A black, high-peaked gambrel house stood near the busy intersection and like a magnet drew Siri towards it. Above the purple-trimmed threshold a signboard read, *"Magic Circle Witch Emporium, Kaelyn Skye Proprietor."*

# CHAPTER 28: The Witch of Salem

The crystal ball distorted Siri's reflection like a funhouse mirror. She looked like a big beach ball with little arms and legs. Siri smiled, amused at her appearance. Siri had been in witchy shops before, but nothing like this. The emporium was dark, the only light coming from little votive candles that cast everything in a flickering, amber glow. Then there was the incense. Whether it was frankincense or myrrh, Siri couldn't tell. She only knew it was strong and made her feel like sneezing. As Siri surveyed the floor-to-ceiling shelves, she felt like she had stepped straight into a tale by the Brothers Grimm. All around her were bottles and jars containing every conceivable herb, mushroom, and root. In nooks and crannies were cauldrons, broomsticks, and bottles of potions. Tucked here or piled there were old leather-bound books on topics such as lycanthropy, vampirism, and invisibility. There was even a full-size human skeleton. It was suspended from an overhead beam, its cavernous eyes and grinning yellow teeth made Siri's skin crawl. It was plastic of course; at least Siri hoped it was as it dangled before her in the dim light. Siri didn't know why she was in the occult shop. Perhaps it was the sign advertising psychic readings or the tolling bell that nobody else seemed to hear, except Mallory and Mister Whispers. Siri was alone in the little shop as far as she could tell. Suddenly a soft voice caught Siri's ear. It was coming from a back room, its entrance covered with a black, beaded curtain. She casually stepped towards it and feigned an interest in some colorful crystals as she tried to listen in.

"Yes, you heard me correctly...Four Aconitum plants...I understand the level of toxicity...No, the oil will be distilled and added to a chemical solution...As soon as you can deliver them...I know it's also called Wolfbane...I'm sorry, that's confidential."

Siri heard Kaelyn huff. Then her voice sounded more desperate. Finally the witch sighed and hung up. Apparently she wasn't getting the Aconitum plants. Siri was beginning to have second thoughts about being in the shop. She was about to leave when Kaelyn parted the curtain and saw her.

"Hello," Kaelyn said, her blue eyes sparkling. "I thought I was alone."

"Actually, I was just leaving," Siri replied.

"You can stay if you want," smiled Kaelyn. "There's a lot to look at, and I don't close for another hour. Can I help you find something?"

"No thanks," Siri said, turning to leave. "I should get going."

Siri was halfway out the door when Kaelyn spoke again.

"You heard the tolling bell, didn't you?"

Siri stopped dead in her tracks.

# CHAPTER 29: Sisters of the Moon

Siri sat before a round table with a large crystal ball at its center. She was in the room behind the black, beaded curtain. Across from her sat Kaelyn Skye draped in a black gown which contrasted sharply with her blonde locks and fair features. Kaelyn had the honor of being the official witch of Massachusetts, a title granted to her by the governor and one she took quite seriously.

"Everyone has an aura, Siri," said Kaelyn. "In fact, all living matter in the universe have auras. Our deepest thoughts and feelings are just cosmic vibrations. Certain individuals can see these vibrations as bright rays of color. No two auras are alike and all have different hues and intensities, which can mean different things, like if you're an honest person or not."

"What color is my aura?" Siri asked.

"Pink," Kaelyn replied. "And that is very rare. A pink aura means you're very loving and close to your spiritual nature."

"Why can't I see it or feel it?"

"You will, in time."

"Is that how you knew I heard the tolling bell?"

"Yes. Only those with brightly colored auras can hear it, so I've learned."

"My best friend Mallory heard it," Siri said. "So did someone else – a dark young man who's been following me. He took my friend into the Witch Curse Museum. The tolling came from

91

its towers."

"Who is this dark, young man?"

"Mister Whispers," Siri replied. "That's what I call him. Don't ask me who he is though because I don't know. All I know he has been following me. Mallory knew him. I followed them inside the museum and lost them. She's still in there. I know it. There's something strange about that place."

Kaelyn looked deeply at Siri and chose her words carefully.

"Not everything in Salem is ordinary, Siri," spoke the witch.

"There is magic at work in this city, both good and bad. I have felt an undercurrent of unease for some time, as you must have, due to your special nature."

Siri nodded.

"I've had to learn to live in Salem with certain 'unusual' types about," Kaelyn continued. The witch suddenly smiled. "I know. It's strange to hear a witch say such a thing."

Salem's official witch leaned forward and whispered. "There are some people in Salem who don't have an aura, which goes against cosmic nature."

"Do you know why?" Siri asked.

Kaelyn paused. Then she answered.

"Let's just say that even here, in the witch capital of the world, it's sometimes best for neo-pagans to mind their own business."

"I saw you at the Halloween party last night," said Siri. "You were talking to Mayor Atwill and Principal Fletcher."

"You don't miss much, do you?"

"I need to know what you were talking to them about." Siri pressed.

Kaelyn hesitated. She drew a breath and then spoke.

"I suppose there's no harm in telling you," Kaelyn said, half facing away. "Principal Fletcher needed some rare plants for the school's botany lab. The mayor had to approve the purchase since he's on the appropriations committee. But I'm afraid I wasn't much help in getting them. I know what you're thinking. Principal Fletcher's aura is gold, which means he's motivated by the highest good."

"Miss Skye," Siri said. "What is the tolling bell? And why can only certain people hear it?"

"I wish I knew," Kaleyn replied.

"You're a witch," said Siri. "Can't you use your magic to stop it?"

"I'm Wiccan," Kaleyn replied. "Although we neo-pagans believe in forces beyond nature, we cannot control these forces, even when we invite the moon and its priestess into our hearts. Although it connects us with the divine and brings us to a heightened awareness, it doesn't give us any special powers to intercede."

Siri's heart sank, which the witch immediately sensed. Kaeyln leaned forward and took Siri's hands into hers.

"Don't worry." Kaelyn smiled. "Remember, you have a wonderful gift, the ability to see future events in dreams. It's what we witches call dream scrying. What two sisters of the moon can do in such matters, who can tell? But the tolling bell with all its mystery needs silencing, and your friend must be found."

"You mean you'll help me?" Siri asked, brightening.

Kaelyn smiled gently.

"We'll help each other," she said.

# CHAPTER 30: Call for Help

Siri waited outside while Kaelyn went about closing her shop. She was glad she could confide in the witch. A ghost tour trolley rolled past on Essex Street crammed with tourists. Siri watched their expectant faces and envied their blissful unawareness. Then a thought occurred to her. She should tell Christian about Mallory and Mister Whispers. It wouldn't hurt to have more help. Siri pulled out her cell phone and pressed some buttons. The phone rang five times. Then Christian's suave voice answered clear as crystal.

"Hello?"

Christian sounded tired, but Siri didn't let that stop her.

"Christian, it's Siri."

"I know."

Siri gathered herself and continued.

"It's about Mallory," Siri said. "A strange guy took her inside the Witch Curse Museum and now she's gone."

An odd pause followed. Siri wondered if Christian was still there.

"Christian?" said Siri.

"Yes?"

"I said Mallory is gone. She's disappeared inside the museum."

The same odd pause followed again. Siri was getting annoyed.

"Christian?"

"I heard you," Christian replied, dryly.

"Well, can we talk about this?" Siri asked.

A horse trotted by pulling an old buggy with a bride and groom. The driver was wearing a black top hat and white skeleton make-up over his face. He doffed his hat to Siri as the whole turnout rambled passed.

"I can't talk now," Christian said. His voice snapped Siri's attention back.

"Don't you care about Mallory?"

"I care," replied Christian. "I just have to go, that's all."

"Christian," Siri said, changing her tone to one of concern. "Are you alright?"

"I have to go," Christian repeated. There was a strange weariness in his voice. Siri didn't know why, but it reminded her of someone losing blood, or undergoing a transfusion. Siri didn't know why Christian's voice conjured those images in her head, but it did.

"Christian…"

Suddenly Christian hung up. Siri stood looking at her phone. She didn't know what to think.

# CHAPTER 31: Delving into the Past

Siri had no doubt Luther T. Dobbs was an antiquarian, an expert on anything that was ancient, crumbling, and covered with dust. She thought he was kind of an antique himself, but as he sat before a computer monitor in a dim back room of the Salem Athenaeum, with Kaelyn Skye looking over one shoulder and Siri looking over the other, it was *"Dopey"* of the Seven Dwarfs that came to Siri's mind. It was the way his big ears stuck out from the sides of his shiny, bald, head. Old black and white photos of the Witch Curse Museum in its first incarnation as a non-denominational church back in the 1920's scrolled down the screen and flashed before their faces. The pictures revealed bell towers a good fifteen feet taller than they presently stood. Pictures of scaffolding followed, showing 50's deconstruction of the towers.

"Why did they shorten the bell towers?" Kaelyn asked, perplexed.

"They were considered a hazard to low-flying aircraft," Dobbs answered.

"You're kidding me," replied Kaelyn.

"Oh, no," said Dobbs, half turning towards the witch. "It's on public record. Oh, yes, on public record."

Siri scrunched her brow as she studied one picture taken from the back of the church. On the horizon rose the cooling towers of the Salem Power Station, which stood five times taller than the church's original bell towers.

"Those smoke stacks are taller than the bell towers," Siri interjected. "Why weren't they considered a flying hazard?"

Kaelyn and Dobbs scrutinized what Siri noticed.

"That's a good point," said Kaelyn. "Why?"

Dobbs stuck his tongue in his cheek and resignedly folded his hands atop his lap.

"I have no records on that."

Kaelyn hunched closer.

"Do you know what became of the stones that were removed from the bell towers?"

Dobbs brightened like a light bulb and thrust a finger in the air.

"That I can answer," he said, excitedly. "They were used to reinforce the existing walls of the church's foundation which was built upon earlier existing stonework. It's believed an ancient Viking fort once stood on that very site. I remember because my uncle Nate, twice removed, was a mason and made a formal appeal to acquire those stones, but was refused."

Siri edged closer to Dobbs. She cupped her hand around his ear and whispered.

"Mister, Dobbs," she said. "Could you get us into the cellar of the Witch Curse Museum?"

Kaelyn leaned closer and cupped her hand against his other ear.

*"Tonight."*

Dobb's eyes brightened.

# CHAPTER 32: Waiting for Mister Whispers

"I confess! I killed her! Isn't there anyone in the whole world who will prosecute me? Hanging's too good for me. I demand a firing squad for what I did to her!"

"There goes Mister Preston again," Siri thought. She was lying awake in her bed waiting for Mister Whispers to reply to her postings, but it was just wind, crickets, and Mister Preston. He lived at 13 Wicks End, a tall, colonial with a flat roof and a kind of railed widow's walk. Mister Preston was 78 and lived alone. The running rumor was that he murdered his wife with a pick ax. The circulator of the vile rumor was Mister Preston himself, and he perpetuated it. Everyone knew that his wife ran off with his twin brother, decades ago. But to Mister Preston his wife was dead, dead by his own hand. So every Thursday night at midnight, the day and time his wife left him, Mr. Preston would stand on the top of his roof, beat the railing with his fists, and yell out to the cold stars his confession. Then he would brush his two hands together, straighten himself, and descend back into his house, where everyone on Wicks End would wait until the next week to hear his public confession.

Siri looked at her cell phone again, this time checking for messages from Mallory. The girl just dropped off the face of the Earth as far as Siri was concerned. Even Aunt Tilly, Mallory's legal guardian, didn't know where she was when Siri called her. It was so weird how her aunt didn't even sound worried. Siri wrestled with the notion of telling her dad what happened at the museum that day, but stopped short of his bedroom door and turned around, not really knowing why. Siri huffed. She looked at her clock. It was time to go.

Siri unplugged her nightlight and drew down the window shade. Siri wanted her room as dark as possible. Her dad usually popped his head in the middle of the night and Siri wanted to be ready. She had prepared the dummy just after she got home and tucked it under her bed. Siri didn't have to get dressed. She already was. After stuffing her jacket with her cell phone, flashlight, and her Swiss Army Knife, Siri pulled the dummy out and put it in her place under the covers. It was just a big pillow she dressed in a T-shirt, but with the blankets tossed over it and in the dark, Siri was betting her dad wouldn't know the difference. Now came the hard part. Siri had to get outside without detection. She opened her bedroom window, frightening some roosting bats that were just outside, and figured she would attempt the cliché of clichés, since it always worked in the movies. She had tied two long bed sheets together, and with one tied to the radiator she tossed the other end over the sill. It reached all the way to the ground. Siri climbed over the sill and looked down. It was cold outside and the ground was a long way down. Siri took a breath, steeled herself for her grand exit, and held on for dear life. Several bats flapped frenziedly around her as she shut the window and let herself down, one hand under the other, as if she were climbing down a rope. Before Siri knew it she was on the ground, the cold ground. Siri looked down. She was in her stocking feet.

Siri huffed and quickly climbed up the bed sheets again. She tried to open her bedroom window but it was stuck. She could see the bathroom light snap on as she dangled in the air in her stocking feet. Her dad must have woken up. No matter how hard Siri struggled to get the window open, it wouldn't budge. She just kept twirling and pushing, but to no avail. Suddenly she remembered her Swiss Army Knife. Pulling it open with her teeth, she pried the blade around the jamb and gave it another shove upwards. It worked. Siri folded the knife away and climbed back over the sill and dropped into her bedroom. As she caught her breath Siri heard footsteps in the hall. She jumped into bed just as her dad gave the door a gentle nudge. The loud snores that came from Siri's blankets satisfied him so he closed the door and went back to his room. Siri got up and stood listening in the doorway. Her dad was soon asleep again. The coast was clear. Siri slipped on her sneakers.

# CHAPTER 33: The Hidden Door

Siri rarely rode her blue cruiser bicycle. It had a white seat, handgrips, and big beach-bike tires with chrome steel fenders, which gave it that classic look. Siri pedaled for all she was worth, south down North Street, east on Essex, and north on Route 1A. The road was bumpy in places with exposed cobblestones, but to Siri the old Victorian-style street lamps seemed to fly by. At Washington Square she saw the Salem Common, a rectangular expanse of parkland, and the brick bulk of the Witch Curse Museum beyond. The cold air invigorated her and she hoped she wasn't late for the planned rendezvous. Siri gazed up at the silver moonlight shining through the bare trees, which cast twisted shadows along the edge of the park. Things were happening in Salem, deep dark things, and Siri felt an odd mixture of exhilaration and dread at the prospect of an adventure in the making.

Under the shadow of a huge elm, the wrought iron fence next to the Witch Curse Museum was the perfect place for Siri to leave her bicycle. She gave the street a quick look around to make sure no one was watching. Pale moonlight was shining down upon the bronze statue of Roger Conant, Salem's pilgrim founder, but otherwise the streets were empty. Turning to the iron fence, Siri hoisted herself over, throwing one leg over followed by the other. Before she knew it, she was standing on a patch of crab grass under a tangled cover of hedges. Crouching down, Siri cautiously made her way towards the back of the dark, church-like building, eyeing the twin bell towers that loomed over her like the turrets of a medieval castle. Siri snapped on her cell phone light, preferring its dim, blue wash to the conspicuous glare of her flashlight. There was a row of flagstones that provided a simple path to the rendezvous. Siri felt she was doing the right thing leaving the house, and the museum had a part to play in Mallory's and Mister Whisper's whereabouts. The lowering of the turrets in the museum's past had some meaning beyond being a flight hazard, and moving the excess stones to the basement conveyed intentional concealment of something.

Siri found the rear door to the museum. It was a simple windowless door with flaking red paint framed by an arch of stonework. Siri suddenly heard footsteps behind her and snapped off her phone light. She instinctively ducked behind a shrub. The footsteps sounded cautious, but pronounced, like a man's footfalls in dress shoes. As Siri listened in the shadows, the footsteps seemed to advance and then recede, as though someone was walking back and forth along the flagstones and studying the edifice. Suddenly Siri overheard some soft mutterings coming up the path in front of her, and was relieved to see Kaelyn Skye and Luther T. Dobbs following the faint beam of a penlight along the flagstones.

"Am I glad to see you two," said Siri, coming out from behind the bush.

"I thought we missed you," Kaelyn replied.

Dobbs stood before the rear door and fumbled along a large key ring he carried in the glow of Kaelyn's penlight.

"It's here somewhere," said Dobbs. "I used to be on the museum's board some years ago. I never did return the key. It's a skeleton key. That's why I kept it. This door is nearly a century old, and is so solid that I doubt a stout man with a fire ax could chop his way through it without some difficulty, but here's the key…"

Dobbs inserted the skeleton key and turned the latch back with a pronounced *"click."*

"There," said Dobbs. "Ladies first."

As Dobbs pushed the door open, the first thing Siri noticed was the mustiness of the air. She withdrew her flashlight and snapped it on. The ray revealed a flight of old, wooden steps flanked by cobblestone walls. Siri took one step down, then another. She was the first one in, followed by Kaelyn, and then Dobbs. Siri's eyes were as wide as saucers. She kept searching the walls for a light switch, but couldn't find one.

"There should be a light cord hanging from the ceiling," said Dobbs. "At least that's what I remember."

Siri cast her beam upwards on the stairwell ceiling and saw the unmistakable signs that a light fixture had been removed in relatively recent times. There were two holes for screws and a cut wire leading from an adjoining wall.

"That's curious," said Dobbs looking upwards. "Why would anyone want to remove a light down here?"

"Why indeed?" Kaelyn added.

Siri took a few more steps downwards and was soon standing on a dusty concrete floor. She flashed her light around and saw they were now in a kind of nave with Gothic style vaulting overhead, reminiscent of a church. At the far end was a stained glass window curiously boarded up long ago judging from the accumulation of cobwebs. There were some old dusty pews and other relics common in a house of worship – stacks of hymn books, chalices, some gossamer-festooned boxes, and an antiquated oil tank and furnace.

"Is this all there is?" Siri asked.

"There is a subcellar," said Dobbs. "It's not on any city plans."

"Can you show us?" Kaelyn pressed.

Dobbs stepped forward. Siri followed with Kaelyn close behind. Everywhere it seemed dust-covered treasures abounded. Dobbs rolled his eyes over a nineteenth century lectern and then steered them toward a round wooden disk on the floor the size of a manhole cover. The large iron ring at its center gave it all the earmarks of a trap door. Dobbs bent down and grabbed hold of the ring and pulled hard. Siri and Kaelyn saw how heavy it was and grabbed hold of the ring too. Siri pulled with all her might. Together they hoisted the hefty cover upwards and over. With a resounding thud it stirred up a cloud of dust.

"I see some steps," said Siri, shining her light into the hole.

She took a step downwards.

"Wait!" Kaelyn ordered. "Let me go first."

The witch pulled up the folds of her cloak and descended several steps. Dobbs placed one foot forward, but suddenly stopped.

"I don't think I can go on," he moaned.

"What's the matter?" asked Kaelyn.

"I'm claustrophobic," answered Dobbs. "I have a terrible fear of tight spaces."

Kaelyn backed up a step and took hold of Dobbs. Siri huffed impatiently.

"You better take him outside," she said.

"You're coming too," said Kaelyn, steering Dobbs towards the cellar stairs.

The witch looked at Dobbs. He was pale as a ghost.

"You should have told us about this sooner."

"The last time this happened I was in the cupola of the Old Custom House," Dobbs groaned. "I also suffer from acrophobia – fear of heights, you know."

"You'll be fine once we get you outside," said Kaelyn.

Dobbs dabbed his brow with a handkerchief as Kaelyn helped him up the dark cellar steps. She was about to call out to Siri when footsteps outside caught her ear. Fearing discovery, the witch quickly led Dobbs back into the cellar and behind the furnace with its radiating duct work resembling octopus tentacles. She hoped Siri would have the sense to hide too.

Siri was glad to be on her own. She had to seize the opportunity while she was so close to possibly solving a mystery. She cautiously followed her light down a short flight of stone steps that corkscrewed down into an extensive vault with a low ceiling. Siri was careful not to bump her head. The place was built of old ballast brick with a rough cobblestone floor that was damp and slimy in places. Siri cringed as her flashlight beam revealed a large, hairy spider darting across the uneven floor near her feet. She brushed away a veil of cobwebs and cast the beam around her, peeling from the gloom four walls composed of ancient, rose-colored blocks. An evenly spaced arrangement of deep indentations in the walls extending from ceiling to floor showed a primitive, but effective effort at buttressing. Clearly the vault was built ages before the museum.

Siri cautiously walked around the stifling room shining her light this way and that. She didn't know what she was looking for, but she'd know it when she saw it. And then she did. Of the four walls in the subcellar three wore the same dim, grimy aspect of age. Only the eastward facing wall appeared slightly different. Siri approached it and examined the stones in the light. She gave one a scratch. They were clean of grime. As Siri backed away she could see a vertical arrangement of stones about the size and height of a door. Incised above them were a series of crude symbols that appeared Nordic in design, including a strange hieroglyphic that seemed out of place. Siri recognized it immediately. She had seen something like it at the Black Ram Inn. It was a Wedjat, an ancient Egyptian symbol of the Eye of Horus, the familiar mascara-lined eye common to the ancient temples, pillars, and obelisks of the upper Nile. It appeared to be deeply carved in the center stone above her.

"Now why carve an Egyptian symbol there?" Siri muttered.

Siri was about to reach up and touch it when a series of footsteps descending into the dark space caused her to snap off her light and press herself into one of the nearest nooks arrayed about the chamber. Siri did this instinctively, for they weren't the light footfalls of Kaelyn Skye, who she expected, but the determined advance of someone heavier. Siri watched as a lance of light shown into the vault and behind it resounded a series of stealthy footsteps. Siri peeked out from behind a buttress and beheld a dark outline of a man brandishing a flashlight standing in the darkness.

Siri flattened herself against the wall as she watched the man consult a plan or map with his flashlight. He then aimed his light at the wall and Siri dodged the beam just in time. The stranger approached the wall and stood within feet of Siri as he regarded it in the ray. Siri held her breath. She was thankful for the darkness and the deepness of the crevice that shielded her, but just barely. Siri wondered who the man was. Clearly she was onto something.

Siri pressed her head sideways against the blocks, flattening herself as much as possible. She could see the stranger feeling along a row at eye level towards her, touching stones here and there with his fingers. Siri grimaced and shrunk back when the hand reached a hair's breadth away and tested a stone directly above her head.

After consulting his map once more, the stranger removed something from around his neck and pressed it against the Egyptian symbol incised atop the center-most stone. Siri heard a resounding *"click"* and suddenly found herself whirling around as the whole section of wall pivoted like so many of those secret revolving panels seen in old movies. Siri found herself on the other side of the wall staring into the cold blackness of a catacomb. Lit by the flashlight of the stranger as he entered, this subterranean gallery was the clue Siri was looking for that connected the old building with Mallory's disappearance. But Siri had barely a moment to glimpse this hidden realm when a snicker of satisfaction escaped the lips of the mystery man.

Suddenly Siri heard another *"click"* and with a whoosh, the entire wall revolved again, returning Siri and the satisfied stranger to the confines of the subcellar. Siri watched as the man folded his map into his breast pocket and followed his flashlight beam back up the stone stairwell. Siri could breathe again. She blew a lock of hair from her face and sunk in relief against the stones. It was time to get out of there.

Siri couldn't wait to tell Kaelyn and Dobbs about the secret panel and the catacomb she had accidentally discovered, and about the mysterious stranger whose identity she now suspected. She popped her head out of the trapdoor, and just when she was about to whisper into the darkness, two hands suddenly clamped down on her shoulders and hoisted her upwards.

"Now what's a nice girl like you doing in a place like this?" a man's voice hissed.

Seized with terror, Siri struggled against the vice-like grip of the stranger. He grasped her by the hair with one hand and withdrew his flashlight from his coat with the other.

"You shouldn't have left the trap door open, most untidy. Now to get a look at you."

Suddenly a **CONK** resounded in the dark. Siri felt the man's grip loosen. Then a thud followed, which told her the stranger had hit the floor. Suddenly a light flicked on and Siri saw Dobb's face peering out from behind the furnace and Kaelyn standing before her with a flashlight in one hand and a purple velvet sack in the other.

"Whew," Siri sighed. "Thanks. What did you hit him with?"

From the sack the witch withdrew a crystal ball, which she displayed in the amber light.

"I carry it with me everywhere," Kaelyn smiled with satisfaction.

"But how could you see him in the dark?" Siri asked.

"I could see his aura," Kaelyn replied. "He was radiating indigo. It's a sign of failure to find self-truth and an obsession with the occult. Now let's see who it is."

The witch swung the light towards the stranger and aimed the beam squarely on his face. What Siri saw confirmed her suspicions, for lying face-up and appearing quite knocked out, was Dent, and hanging from his neck – the silver *Eye of Horus!*

# CHAPTER 34: The Message

Siri pedaled her bike fast and hard – so fast her legs were a blur. Siri was the only thing moving on the road at that late hour on the dark, Salem streets, and that worried her. If a patrol car happened by she might have some explaining to do, for the cops knew her. Her well-meant tips to Scarpetti to be on the alert for this or that ensured her face would be recognized, and then her dad would get the call. So Siri wanted to get home quickly and without detection. She turned down one street and then another, her gears rattling on patches of bumpy, exposed cobblestone. Although it was quite cold, she could feel herself sweating under her jacket. The events of the night rolled over in Siri's mind. She had never seen someone get knocked out cold before, except in the movies. The hollow thud Kaelyn's crystal ball made when it struck Dent's cranium replayed in her ears. Siri regretted leaving Dent unconscious, but she didn't have any choice. She hoped Dent wasn't hurt too badly, and then consoled herself that his head did sound pretty hard. At least he didn't see her face. Siri felt some exhilaration in fleeing a crime scene. She had compounded a felony – two in one night: breaking and entering, and assault and battery. It would be messy trying to explain or get out of it. So Siri just put it out of her mind, like her stealing of the Highland Mantel Clock. They were necessary evils in her pursuit of a higher cause.

Siri rode up alongside the back of her house. Rather than risk entry through the front door, she shimmied her way up her makeshift rope of bed sheets, huffing and puffing until she reached the windowsill. Siri struggled with the weight of the sash and then shoved it up. In one motion she pulled herself up and tumbled onto her bedroom floor. Then, suddenly, while still on the floor catching her breath, Siri heard her dad's bedroom door creak open. Siri pulled up the knotted sheets, hurled herself into bed, and threw the covers over her. Several footsteps sounded in the hall on the way to the bathroom and stopped outside her door. Siri closed her eyes and started to imitate her best snores ever. Finally she heard her dad return to his room. It was another close call, Siri thought. Too close. It was at that moment Siri's cell phone beeped on her night table. Siri picked it up and read an incoming text message on the screen. "MEET ME AT CHARTER STREET BURIAL GROUND TOMORROW NIGHT AT MIDNIGHT. BRING CLOCK. DO NOT FAIL ME!!!"

# CHAPTER 35: A Mysterious Illness

There were a lot of phrases to describe what Siri was doing, and Siri knew them all. There was "getting in over her head" and "biting off more than she could chew." Then there was "playing with fire." But Siri wanted the parchment back and the bait she had planted had been taken. Siri did her best to pay attention in geometry class, but she kept staring at the classroom clock over the front blackboard. Her lanky math teacher, Mr. Blackburn, wrote out equations in chalk that kept shooting off tiny pieces from his enthusiastic strokes. His writing arm was a prosthetic, composed of titanium steel that culminated in a claw – like metallic crab nippers. There was no end to the rumors of how Mr. Blackburn lost his arm. Some said he lost it in a shark attack off Cape Cod. Others said it got caught in a head and gutting machine on a Gloucester fishing trawler. He never talked about his artificial limb, and also never hesitated to use it to knock sense into inattentive students by a sudden rap upon their desk. It was twenty minutes before noon and all the other students appeared quite attentive, except for one boy who watched through his eyelids. Mr. Blackburn's claw slammed down upon his open math book, impaled twenty pages in one stroke, and instantly returned the student to attention. Mallory was absent of course and that bothered Siri. She knew she had hit pay dirt with the discovery of the secret passage the night before. Siri was onto something deeply mysterious and menacing under the quaint, cobblestoned streets of Salem.

Siri still wasn't ready to tell her dad or Detective Scarpetti. She wanted this plum for herself. Besides she earned it. Siri planned to follow the subterranean passage to its conclusion with the help of Kaelyn and Dobbs, at least that was the plan.

Siri's stomach grumbled. She wished she had eaten breakfast that morning. Twenty minutes before lunchtime seemed like forever. Siri peeked inside her blue lunch box. Glinting back at her was Dent's Eye of Horus pendant. The silvery ornament was tucked beside a tuna fish sandwich and a big red apple. It was as safe a place as any, Siri figured. She had taken the pendant from Dent while he lay unconscious on the cellar floor. She had to. It was the key to the secret passage. It looked very old, much older than the door it was made to open.

How the artifact came into Dent's possession Siri could only guess at. Why was Dent at the Witch Curse Museum? How did he know about the secret passage? These were all questions begging answers. Dent played a roll in what was going on in Salem lately. That much Siri was certain. He had just as much a part to play as Mister Whispers, and Siri had a score to settle with him.

As Siri sat at her desk, she recalled how during her study period she went across the street to a phone booth and gave the police an anonymous tip about the stolen Highland Mantel Clock. It was a pack of lies of course. Mister Whispers didn't steal the clock from the Museum of Antiquities. She did. But framing him for the crime was the only way she could think of to regain possession of the parchment. It was a foolproof plan, she hoped.

As Siri thought about her next steps, she felt a pair of eyes watching her. She turned and noticed Christian Fletcher looking intently in her direction. Siri was about to turn away. She was still annoyed with Christian's reaction on the phone the other day, when suddenly he winced in pain. Siri looked quizzically at him as he reached for his shoulder and rubbed it. Christian then stood and walked to the door at the front of the classroom.

"Where are you going, Christian?" Mr. Blackburn inquired.

"I need some air," Christian replied.

The teacher surveyed Christian as if silently deliberating whether or not to excuse him.

"Make it quick," he finally said, and returned his attention to the blackboard. Siri suddenly raised her hand and spoke out.

"Mr. Blackburn, I need to go to the bathroom."

The classroom broke out in a chuckle that caused Siri to blush. Mr. Blackburn looked at Siri and nodded his approval. "Now class, let's talk about René Descartes and his contribution to analytical geometry," he announced.

Siri got up and quickly left the room, but Christian was way ahead of her down the hall.

"Christian!" Siri called out.

Ignoring Siri's shout, Christian quickened his pace. Suddenly Christian stopped as if a sudden pain overtook him. He turned towards Siri as she drew nearer. Siri could see that he was deathly pale.

"My father," he gasped. "Take me to him."

Siri helped Christian down the hall towards the principal's office. Just outside the door Christian grimaced and fell back. He tore open the upper half of his shirt in a fit of intense agony. Siri shrieked at what she saw. It was a human eye, a hideous human eye – large, liquid and swiveling this way and that, and protruding from Christian's skin between the collarbone and shoulder. Christian hollered in pain. Siri covered her mouth with her hands. Christian clawed and clutched at the walls. Siri moved towards him and half held him up in her fright. Suddenly the office door flew open and out stepped Principal Bramwell Fletcher. Christian turned and glared up him, his face wrenching and twisting in torment.

"Father, what's happening to me?"

Fletcher abruptly took Christian into his arms and ushered him into his office. The principal cast a stern expression at Siri as she stood wide-eyed and bewildered in the hall. Siri was at a loss for words when Principal Fletcher slammed the door, practically in her face. Siri took a deep breath, gathered up some nerve, and knocked forcefully on the closed door.

"Principal Fletcher!" Siri called out. "Open the door please!"

Siri tried the doorknob, but it was locked. Several students walking down the hall looked at her strangely while she pushed and pushed at the door. Suddenly Siri heard another interior door, one within Principal Fletcher's office, open and slam shut. Then a car engine turned over. Siri rushed out of a side entrance and flew down some steps. She ran towards the back of the school in time to see Principal Fletcher help Christian into the back seat of a dark sedan that quickly sped off in a cloud of exhaust. Siri caught a glimpse of the driver's face under a fedora. It was Alex Cedric!

# CHAPTER 36: The Burial Ground

Siri knew the drop off spot. She had cased the Charter Street Burial Ground right after school that day during a sunny afternoon when the sunlight filtered through the autumnal foliage of flaming reds, brilliant oranges, and screaming yellows. Tourists were milling about the ancient slate gravestones, some even trying their hand at the old art of gravestone rubbing with paper and colored wax wedges. The graveyard was a pleasant place then, quiet, leisurely, even if a little public, but that was during the tranquil afternoon. Now it was well after dark. The graveyard assumed a gloomy, melancholy appearance with stretches of deep, dark shadows and forbidding oaks that swelled grotesquely. Siri paused by the black gate on Charter Street as she surveyed this railed acre of darkness she was about to enter. She took a breath that did little to steady her nerves. Then she opened the gate. The old wrought iron squealed sickly on its weathered hinges. Siri pushed the gate wide open and cautiously walked up the grassy path overgrown with weeds and horribly shaded by those wide, twisting oaks. Oblong granite sepulchers, some crumbling with age, lined the walkway along with slate gravestones shaped like headboards, some tilting forwards or backwards or sideways like crooked teeth, while others were almost sunken entirely into the ground as if swallowed in quicksand. Siri had heard the Charter Street Burial Ground was

115

the oldest cemetery in Salem and the second oldest in the country. Established in 1637 and located on Charter Street, across from the Museum of Antiquities, the burial ground contained such notable tenants as John Hathorne, the infamous Judge in the Salem Witch Trials, Captain Richard More, a passenger on the Mayflower, and Samuel McIntire, Salem's renowned eighteenth-century architect, as well as other intriguing historical figures. But Siri didn't care about any of that now.

Siri passed tombstone after tombstone, each carved with its own grim death-head, skull and crossbones, hourglass, or lonely urn. Finally Siri found her perch. It was in the fork branch of the center-most oak of the cemetery overlooking the drop off spot. Siri shimmied up the tree and clambered into her little roost. Once settled she got her binoculars out equipped with night vision capability. Siri took a piece of bubble gum and put it in her mouth as she raised her binoculars to her eyes. Through the range finder she saw the burial ground aglow in unearthly green tints and highlights. If so much as a mouse darted across the grass she would see it. Siri casually chewed her grape-flavored gum while shifting her night vision on one section of the graveyard and then veering it over toward another. Siri was at first a little apprehensive about what she was doing, but now that she was doing it, she felt a little giddy with anticipation, like a hunter might while waiting in a blind for a leopard to appear and take the bait set out for it. It was an intoxicating feeling in the cold darkness, and Siri liked it.

The tree Siri had chose for her nocturnal vigil was situated next to a spooky old house that abutted the cemetery, its entrance covered in vines, its windows all darkened save but one. It was rumored the old place was haunted by Nathaniel Hawthorne's wife, Sophia Amelia Peabody Hawthorne, but it wasn't the looming house that was getting on Siri's nerves. It was the colony of Whippoorwills nesting in the cemetery trees drowning out every other sound with their haunting, ethereal song, *whip-poor-will, whip-poor-will, whip-poor-will!*

Now that the graveyard was cloaked in darkness, Siri had

the opportunity to place the Highland Mantel Clock bedside the gravestone of Judge John Hathorne, the pick-up spot she designated. Now she waited. It was five minutes before midnight and Siri felt a little guilty sneaking out of the house again by way of her knotted bedsheets, but she had to stay on mission, at least that's what she told herself. The events at the Witch Curse Museum and that bizarre incident with Christian, that still made her cringe with repulsion just to think about it, had left Siri in an abstract daze. Did she really see what she thought she saw, a human eye swiveling between Christian's bare neck and shoulder? What in the world is going on? Now Siri added Christian to her growing tally of concerns. Siri let out a shiver. It was getting cold up in that tree. Siri sucked the last bit of flavor out of her gum and spit it out. She pulled a chocolate bar from her pocket, tore off the wrapper, bit off a hunk of chocolate, and scanned the graveyard again with her night vision. Then, while surveying the landscape, she took a bigger bite. Something had to happen soon, Siri thought. Her anticipation was mounting, and her candy bar was shrinking. Siri resisted looking at the time on her cell phone. Its blue glow would certainly be spotted from the ground. Suddenly Siri heard the midnight toll of the Immaculate Conception Church bell tower drifting eerily though the night. She could hear it above the din of the Whippoorwills, loud as they were. *Gong! Gong! Gong! Gong!* The bell tower sounded twelve times. Suddenly Siri heard something else – the squeal of a rusty gate!

Siri held her breath. Through her night vision goggles she watched a solitary figure cloaked in gloom walk the grassy path towards her lofty vantage. It was Mister Whispers, with all his mystery, wrapped in a long black coat that almost brushed the ground. Siri watched his every step, like a sniper trained on his target. Mister Whispers surveyed the rows of slate gravestones in the shadows of the oaks and maples. So far there was no sign of Scarpetti. It was just Siri and Mister Whispers among the tenants of the graveyard. Suddenly Siri froze. Mister Whispers walked over to Siri's tree and stood directly under her perch. He panted frosty breaths beneath her dangling sneakers. Siri didn't move a muscle. She sat as quiet and still as a mushroom with a piece of chocolate sticking out of her mouth until her graveyard companion moved on towards some crumbling oblong sepulchers and a patch of darkness beyond. It was then Siri breathed a sigh of relief and devoured the rest of her candy bar.

Suddenly a bright spotlight snapped on from somewhere within the graveyard. It shined upon Mister Whispers who threw up one hand before his chalk white face, shielding it from the ray's intensity. His other hand held the Highland Mantel clock Siri had hidden behind Judge Hathorne's gravestone.

"You, in the cemetery," a gruff voice rang out. "This is the Salem Police. Place the clock on the ground and come out with your hands high over your head!"

Siri knew that voice anywhere. It was Detective Scarpetti's. He stood behind the fieldstone wall that separated the burial ground from the witchcraft victim's memorial park. Siri could hear the wailing sirens of approaching squad cars. Suddenly a flashlight snapped on behind Mister Whispers and two more in front by the cemetery gate. Siri watched as Mister Whispers, clutching the clock, turned one way and then the other, like a cornered fox in the glaring lights searching for a way of escape.

"Put the clock down and your hands up!" Scarpetti ordered again. "And come out quietly!"

Siri switched her binoculars from Scarpetti to Mister Whispers, who sprang atop a granite sepulcher like a cat, and using it as a springboard, leaped over the heads of two approaching police officers, the folds of his long, black coat flying about him like a hovering storm cloud. The two officers turned in time to see him hurtle the wrought iron fence in a single bound and then disappear across Charter Street. Scarpetti shouted into his handset.

"All units. All units. This is Scarpetti. Priority. Establish a cordon around Charter and Front Streets. I want a lockdown, a K-9 unit. The works. Over!"

At once the vicinity around the old burial ground became a kaleidoscope of motion and sound. Siri shimmied down the tree and dropped to the ground. It appeared the entire Salem police force was out. All around her sirens blared, blue lights strobed, radios crackled, and officers converged on the scene from every direction engaging in a desperate foot chase. Siri found her bicycle where she had hidden it, in some bushes by the railed entrance, and hopped on. She needed to get home, and fast. Her work that night was done. Scarpetti would catch Mister Whispers and somehow she'd get the parchment back. She needed to see Mister Whispers on her terms, not his, and Scarpetti would help out with that, unwittingly. Siri turned her bike onto Charter Street, and pedaled for all she was worth.

Siri didn't want to be spotted by the police, busy as they were. She rode down Charter Street behind the brick bulk of the Museum of Antiquities. There she could see police officers massing, their flashlights lancing the dark in all directions as they focused their search in a back alley. Siri looked up and saw Mister Whispers in the sporadic rays of flashlights as he led officers in a frenzied foot chase along gambrel rooftops. He leapt from building to building, and weaved about the chimney pots, all the while clutching the singular clock. Siri pedaled with all her might catching upward glimpses of the fleeting, black form of Mister Whispers peeled from the pitch gloom of the night sky by spotlights aimed from squad cars below. Both she and Mister Whispers were traveling the same parallel course it seemed, with him being four stories above her, and with a knot of police on his heels.

Siri made a sharp turn onto Washington Street. Her bike rattled over storm grates and exposed cobbles. The avenue was empty except for a K-9 unit and several squad cars parked at odd angles by an old bank building. The police dogs could do little from the ground except bark and buck against their tethers while the action unfolded above the streets. Siri swerved around a mailbox and jumped a curve. Another upward glance revealed a yawning gap between the bank and a series of flat rooftops. Mister Whispers cleared the expansive gap between the buildings, and landed cat-like on the other side. Siri just wanted to get home now, but wherever she went she found herself in the center of the action. It was following her like a shadow.

Siri skidded onto Essex Street and shifted gears. She pumped the bike pedals until her legs hurt. She huffed and puffed shooting glances behind herself. Suddenly something black and sleek dropped onto the glistening street in front of her. It was Mister Whispers. He rose from a shock-absorbing squat, still holding the clock, and stared ominously in her direction with eyes that reflected the light. Siri jammed on her brakes and slid to a halt before him. Suddenly several squad cars careened from around a corner behind her. Mister Whispers reached for Siri, but she pulled away and pedaled. Events forced them both to join in a desperate dash down the cobbled avenue. Siri knew what it felt like to be a fugitive now. Mister Whispers flashed a stern glance at her as he ran alongside her and she flashed one back. They were both out of breath and couldn't shout what they thought of each other, even if they wanted to. At one point they were traveling neck and neck, like dueling racers, when Mister Whispers suddenly closed the gap and forced Siri to jump the curve and negotiate the narrow sidewalk, barely avoiding fire hydrants and trash cans.

The menacing Witch House with its high-peaked roof breaking the skyline ahead told Siri she was nearing North Street. It was there that Mister Whispers surprised her again. In one motion he leaped from the street and onto a series of parked cars that separated them both and was sprinting over their hoods and trunks, the precious clock clutched at his side, his eyes catching the fitfull gleams of lamp posts. Siri knew she was in big trouble and didn't dare stop her bike. There was something uncanny about her running adversary that gave Siri the creeps. She could hear the crush of metal as it buckled under the weight of Mister Whisper's boots as he wildly leaped from car to car, his black coat tails flapping crazily behind him.

Siri careened and skidded onto North Street and came face to face with a roadblock of converging squad cars. Siri skidded again, her bike sliding beneath her and making a big half-arc of burnt rubber on the asphalt and cobbles before going down on its side and taking her with it. When she looked up she saw Mister Whispers launch into the air and cover the distance of several police cruisers in an effortless single jump. Searchlights following his airborne course separated him from the inky blackness and prevented him from finding the anonymity of darkness.

Mister Whispers landed before the Witch House, the only house in Salem with direct ties to the witch hysteria of 1692. Two German Shepherds broke their restraints and bounded towards him, despite shouted commands to stop. To avoid the police dogs, Mister Whispers hurled himself against the side of the ancient landmark, and spreading out his hands, executed a side-winding crawl all the way up the side of the house, his black coat spreading over his back and giving him the appearance of a bat. In a moment he surmounted the peaked roof. Hardened police officers drew back when their suspect rose to his feet atop the roof, turned, and revealed a livid face from which two glaring eyes reflected back the light of their spotlights. The agitated dogs circled around the house barking and growling. Mister Whispers sneered down at them, his white face wrinkling in a ghastly way. He clutched the clock to his chest as if his very life depended on it. Siri felt a surge of pity as she watched the scene unfold. She had no idea her plan would turn out like this.

"Take him!" Scarpetti shouted, as an officer with a rifle stepped forward.

The policeman approached the Witch House and aimed his rifle. Mister Whispers stood defiantly in the crosshairs, half turned at them, the wind wrapping the excess folds of his black coat around him as he clutched the clock.

"No!" Siri exclaimed. "Don't shoot him!"

Suddenly a gunshot followed by a hiss punctuated the night. Siri gasped. Mister Whispers lurched, hit in the shoulder. Then, as the narcotic administered by the dart took effect, he shuddered and staggered. In less than a minute he lay sprawled on his back, breathing and heaving like a bellows, the clock still clutched to his side. The cloaked body then went limp and began to slide down along the roof. Only one hand clutched at the roof, but the weight it bore proved too much and the tenuous grip began to fail, leaving five ragged furrows along the wooden roof tiles.

Mister Whispers fell to the ground taking the clock with him. He landed upon the grass with a dull thud. Two officers rushed in and pulled off the police dogs tearing at his coat. Siri watched spellbound as Mister Whispers was turned over and cuffed. She suddenly felt a heavy hand plant atop her shoulder. Siri turned and looked up into Detective Scarpetti's brooding, pit-bull face.

# CHAPTER 37 : Hot Seat

For a big guy Scarpetti sure had a small office, Siri thought. Even Mister Chaney, Windward High School's janitor, had a bigger office. And that was a broom closet. There wasn't even enough room for a couch to lie down on, and Siri wanted to lie down. She was that tired. Siri noticed Scarpetti's expression as he dialed her home telephone number. It was a big smile, like the Grinch's, when he got a Grinchy Grinch of an idea. The smile stretched from ear to shining ear. Siri sat in a wooden chair next to the detective's desk. The seat was really hard and uncomfortable, and Siri was squirming in it. Siri heard some commotion just beyond Scarpetti's office door, which was slightly ajar. She realized that a police precinct is a busy place at night. Siri watched police officers escorting Salem's assorted drunks and burglars down the hall to be processed. She thought of Mister Whispers and all the company he was going to have.

Siri's conscience bothered her a little that night. She was feeling guilty about how she framed Mister Whispers. It was pretty low-ball stuff. But she had no choice, or so she kept telling herself. It was the only way to get the parchment back and find Mallory. Siri hoped Mister Whispers was going to be okay after being shot by an anesthetizing dart. Getting the flu shot hurt enough, so she couldn't even imagine what he went through. Who Mister Whispers was and why he wanted the parchment were questions Siri kept thinking about. Siri knew there would be a lot of questions for her to answer too. She wondered how her dad would react to being woken from a sound sleep at 1:30 in the morning to come down to the police station to get her.

"Braddock," Scarpetti said over the phone after about half a dozen rings. "Guess who? ... That's right. Did I wake you? ... Good. Do you know where your daughter is? ... No? ... She's not in her bedroom. Guess again. ... That's right. She's right here in my office. I'm holding her as a material witness to felony theft, and if I want to, I can make her more than that. How does an accessory sound to you? ... Now that's not the way to talk to a public servant, Braddock. ... Now that's better. ... I'll be right here waiting."

Scarpetti placed the phone back on the hook and looked at Siri. He was still wearing that big, Grinchy smile.

"Your dad's on his way down," Scarpetti said. "Now what do you have to say for yourself young lady? I'm waiting…"

Siri didn't say a word. Her face turned sullen and pale. Then she bent over and threw up.

# CHAPTER 38: The Man in the Hallway

Siri sat in the hall just outside Scarpetti's door while the janitor mopped up the detective's floor. Her dad had arrived. He was having a closed-door session with Scarpetti – a loud one. The janitor came out with his mop and pail and shook his head as he closed the door behind him. He was tall and grizzle-headed. He took one look at Siri and shook his downy head again, while walking down the hall.

Siri preferred the chair in the hall to the one inside Scarpetti's confining office. At least it had a padded seat. The ginger ale she sipped made her stomach feel much better too. The excitement of the night must have gotten to her, Siri thought. It was nice of Officer Mace to bring her a glass of ginger ale from the precinct kitchen. When her dad arrived Mace was right there and directed him into Scarpetti's office, so he didn't have a chance to give her a piece of his mind. Mace was a big fellow, square-headed, brawny, like a grizzly bear, but nice as can be once you got to know him. A voice over the intercom suddenly called Mace to the precinct's front desk so Siri sat by herself. There was a sudden lull in hallway activity, and it gave Siri an idea. She drank up the last of her ginger ale, sat back against the wall, and held the empty glass against it. Then she put her ear to the bottom of the glass. Siri strained to catch words. She was surprised by how much she caught.

"I can't prove your daughter knew the suspect," Siri overheard

Scarpetti say, "but she was there at the take down. And it was no coincidence. There's a connection there. I haven't questioned her yet. That's why I wanted you down here."

"You're grasping at straws, Scarpetti," Siri overheard her dad say. "How could Siri know anything about your suspect? She's just a kid."

"My gut tells me she knows something about this guy. He's confessed to stealing the clock and mentioned your daughter by name before he lost consciousness.

"You have nothing to hold her on," Siri's dad said. "Release her. Come on."

"My gut also tells me I've got the perpetrator behind all the missing persons cases that have been piling up. Not to mention the case of the stolen mummies."

"That's a lot to hang on one suspect," Siri's dad returned. "I think you're barking up the wrong tree,"

"You wouldn't say that if you saw him," Scarpetti huffed. "He's right out of a nightmare."

"I say the asylum is the place to go looking for your answers," Siri heard her dad say.

"You still on that asylum kick?" Scarpetti interrupted. "You got a one-track mind, Braddock. I tell you there's nothing up there. We've been all over that place. It's clean."

"Where's your suspect now?"

"We've got him out back," Scarpetti said. "We're taking him over to the old Salem jail. He's giving the winos here more shivers than they can handle."

Suddenly Siri overheard someone talking while coming around a corner. She hid the glass and sat down. It was two police officers – Officer Dwight and Pantano. They passed by talking to each other and didn't even notice her as they hastened down the hallway towards the back entrance.

"You gotta see this guy before they take him away," Officer Dwight said to Pantano. "He's got crazy hands and weird eyes. Salem has all kinds, but this guy…!"

Siri watched Dwight and Pantano disappear around a corner.

She looked at the closed office door. Scarpetti and her dad were still talking, or arguing rather. She got up from the chair and quickly followed the two officers. She passed the booking room and saw a toothless old man getting fingerprinted.

"Hey girly," he hollered. "What are ya in for, stealing Teddy Bears?"

When Siri reached the back entrance, she paused and peered around a corner. Officer Dwight and Pantano were standing at a delivery bay. They watched a black police van being loaded with someone strapped to a gurney, his face covered by an oxygen mask. It was Mister Whispers, and he was unconscious. His eyes were open, but vacant-looking. Siri's heart sank as she watched two men close the back doors to the van and signal it to drive off.

Siri walked back down the hall and returned to her chair, but didn't feel like sitting anymore. Instead she started pacing the floor, wishing her dad and Scarpetti would finish up. It was then she spotted Officer Mace seated behind the front desk talking to an old gentleman wearing a Fedora and tweed overcoat. Whoever he was, he seemed bent on finding out about one of the police suspects, the one who was being taken away in the van. Mace politely shook his head, silenced by some confidentiality rule. The gentleman turned his head toward Siri. Siri quickly ducked out of sight. It was Alex Cedric!

# CHAPTER 39: The Room of Relics

Whenever something strange happened or someone disappeared, Alex Cedric seemed to pop up, like a bad penny. His house was easy to find. A quick search on the Danvers town website told Siri where the archivist lived. Siri suspected Cedric knew something about Mallory and Christian, and even Mister Whispers. Siri figured if she confronted him, plain and straight out, he might be caught off his guard and might let something important slip out. Siri had no real plan. She decided to just wing it, like she did the previous night when Scarpetti fired all those questions at her about why she was there at the exact place the strange suspect was apprehended. She had a dream about it the night before, Siri told Scarpetti with her dad looking on, and was just checking to see if her dream was right. And it was. It was a pack of lies of course, but it got her off the hook.

Siri didn't want to look too conspicuous loitering outside Cedric's home, the old Nathaniel Silsbee Mansion. She had rung the doorbell, but there was no answer. So she went around back. There was a Knights of Columbus hall downstairs, but the bulk of the old Federal-style building seemed to be a residence. Siri followed a brick walkway towards a rear door accented with a stained glass window and a rose motif at its center. She reached for the doorknob, but before she touched it, a breeze pushed the door ajar. It was open. Siri took a deep breath, mustered her courage, and entered the house.

"Mister Cedric," Siri spoke out, looking up from the bottom of a back stairwell, a grand curving affair. She swallowed nervously and spoke out again. "Hello. I'm Siri Braddock. You don't know me, but I'd like to speak with you if I may?" The house was deathly still, too still, but something about it drew Siri's hand upwards along the dark, mahogany banister. The walls were white plaster, cracked in places with old gas lamp fixtures that were long past use.

"Mister Cedric, are you there?" Siri spoke out again.

Siri wound her way passed framed black and white photographs depicting Egyptian expeditions to the Upper Nile dating back to the 1920s. They were lined in rows, yellowing pictures showing native diggers in white linen robes with European scholars donned in pith helmets and khakis. Looming behind them was the great pyramid-shaped rock of Al-Qurn of the Valley of the Kings in the Theban Necropolis. Siri noticed some of the pictures had white lettering saying, "KV14 Field Force 1921," or "KV11 1922," which she figured meant Kings Valley, tombs fourteen and eleven, whatever they were. There was also a curious, time-yellowed corner of paper sticking out from behind one of the photographs, hidden between the glass and the backing. Siri plucked it out a little until she revealed a folded newspaper clipping. She unfolded it and saw that it was from the Boston Crier, dated September 20th, 1927. It read: *Boston Museum Robbed! Egyptian Statue Stolen along with Several Golden Treasures.* The article was accompanied by a black and white photograph of the falcon-headed statue of Horus. Siri wanted to read more, but the article was lengthy and time was pressing on her. Siri put the article in her pocket. Daylight streamed in from some upper room. It beckoned Siri upwards. A strange, lingering smell in the air, like burning incense, caused her nose to crinkle.

An antique Ottoman couch, a relic from some Turkish bazaar at the top landing, didn't prepare her for what was to come. Siri stood awestruck. She stood at the entrance of a spacious gallery dedicated solely to the science of Egyptology. Everywhere her eyes roamed, relics of the pharaohs abounded. Siri knew them all from Mrs. Breath's ancient history class. Immense statues of hawk-headed Horus, the sky god, and Jackal-headed Anubis, the god of mummification, carved of pink Aswan granite, adorned two opposing corners, and Sobek, the crocodile-headed god, stood in between. Two upright gilt cedar sarcophagi with their lids half pulled aside lay against one wall decorated with inlaid Turkish daggers and curved scimitars. Ancient papyruses crammed with hieroglyphics encased in glass attested to the scholarly pursuits of their owner. Everywhere the grandeur of Ancient Egypt stared down at her from blank faces carved of basalt, limestone, or alabaster. There were scarabs carved from beryl and jasper, amulets of Amethyst from Abu Simbel, and stringed beads of Sinai Turquoise.

As Siri surveyed the great room she had to remind herself that this was the home of Alex Cedric, and not an annex of some museum. The only ghastly object to meet her eye was a mummy partly unwrapped, laying full length upon a table. The chest cavity had been opened for some sort of pathology, judging from the collection of post-mortem knives to the side along with some test tubes.

"This must be one of the stolen mummies," Siri guessed to herself.

Suddenly a hand reached out and clutched Siri's shoulder, swinging her around. Siri gasped. It was Alex Cedric! His eyes were wide and glaring.

"What are you doing here?" Cedric snapped, clasping Siri by both shoulders.

Siri tried to stammer out something to say when stealthy footsteps coming up the stairs compelled Cedric to shove Siri backwards in the direction of an upright sarcophagus standing in the middle of the room. Siri couldn't believe what was happening and was about to yell when Cedric covered her mouth with his hand.

"Shhhh!" Cedric said. "Be quiet or they'll hear you. Now just stay in there and don't make a sound and you will be left out of all this. If you don't, then Heaven itself won't be able to help you. Now be quiet!"

Cedric tucked Siri into the upright sarcophagus and sealed the lid over her. No sooner had he done so two swarthy men entered the room followed by one of light complexion. Siri peeked out from the musty sarcophagus. She could see only a slice of the room, and the entrance. Siri couldn't believe her eyes. There was Dent walking into view! He was wearing a dark overcoat and standing alongside him was the bearded man donned in a red Fez with tassel and beside him was a big Mongolian whose Cheshire Cat grin looked all too familiar. Then it dawned on her. It was the fried dough guy she saw outside the Museum of Antiquities!

"I told you I don't have it," Cedric said to Dent. "I lost it years ago in Thebes. I must insist that you leave my house."

"Now that's not very polite," Dent said as he inspected the room with an arcing glance. "We're partners you and I. Remember? I don't believe you would lose so valuable an art object. You'd lose your own right arm first."

"The Osiris Key is more than an art object," Cedric said.

"So right," Dent corrected himself. "It's a treasure of incalculable value – in the right hands. And there are only two in the entire world. And to be of use they must be used in concert – together. I lost my Osiris Key very uncomfortably I might say." Dent said, holding the back of his head. "I knew only you possessed its twin. But you tell me it's lost. Want to know what I believe?"

Dent now stood toe-to-toe with Cedric.

"I believe you're working with someone else – a girl no less. I ran into her the other night. So you had stooped that low to involve a child – this artful dodger. Don't worry. I'll find her. And I'll find the Osiris Keys. I believe they're somewhere in this house – in this fabulous temple to your reigning passion – and my own – Egyptology. Perhaps they are in this very room?"

"I don't have them and I'm not working with any girl," Cedric said firmly. "That's the truth." He opened a cigar box, put a cigar in his mouth, and lit it up. "If you don't believe me, search. Search all you want."

Dent nodded to his henchmen. Then he raised an authoritative finger.

"But don't damage any relics. I have a tender and foolish heart toward relics, especially Egyptian relics."

As Dent's confederates began rummaging around the room, searching display cases and going through desk drawers, Dent picked up a small alabaster statuette of Thutmose IV carved in the pose of taking a stately step with a regal staff in hand. Dent smiled upon the figurine and turned it about in his hand, examining it from all sides.

"Exquisite!" Dent said. "Nineteenth Dynasty?"

"Eighteenth." Cedric clarified.

"Of course. How stupid of me," Dent admitted. "So solid, heavy, yet so fragile and irreplaceable. It would be terrible to damage such a precious thing."

Dent palmed the alabaster rendition of the great Thutmose.

"You acquired this from the Egyptian Museum." Dent said.

"It was the British Museum," Cedric corrected. He took the cigar from his mouth and puffed a ring of aromatic smoke skywards. "Now please put it down."

"You want me to put this down?"

"Yes."

Dent smiled and returned the statuette to its place on a stand. He walked over to where the disemboweled mummy lay full-length upon a table amidst an array of post mortem knives and laboratory reagents.

"I see you're interested in the alchemy of embalming," Dent said.

"You mean the chemistry," Cedric said.

"Oh, I mean alchemy," Dent stressed, taking up a test tube in his fingers and examining its contents of gray dust through the window light.

"What are you talking about?" Cedric asked.

"If you come with me, I'll show you," Dent said.

"I'm not going anywhere," Cedric stated.

Dent's henchmen approached.

"The place is clean," the big Mongolian said. "No keys."

"Are you sure?" Dent asked. "The study and the bedroom. Did you search them?"

132

"We've found nothing," the bearded man spoke.

"There," Cedric said. "Satisfied? Now get out of my house."

"Take him to the car," Dent ordered.

"Keep away from me!" Cedric exclaimed, two strongmen approaching him from each side. They set their meaty hands upon his shoulders, and wrestled him out of the room.

"But don't damage him," Dent said. "Not just yet. He's sort of a relic himself. And you know how I feel about relics."

Dent was about to turn and leave the room himself when his eye caught a glimpse of the upright sarcophagus secretly giving cover to Siri shining in golden splendor in the afternoon sunlight. He approached it suspiciously, his hands thrust in the pockets of his overcoat. For a moment Dent roamed his eyes over the sarcophagus, up one side and down the other. Siri held her breath.

"I see you looking at me," Dent finally spoke. "You and your prying eyes. Staring. Ever watching. Eyes that never close. You dead Egyptian. Forty centuries look down on me. Isn't that what Napoleon said upon viewing your dusty pyramids? Forty centuries?" Dent snickered as he eyed the carven face of a king the great upright box was fashioned after. "Your pyramids are NOTHING compared to the power behind the Osiris Keys!"

Dent extended a foot and kicked over the upright sarcophagus with a great bang. Dent sneered again at the great, toppled coffin as it lay on the floor, painted eyes aimed upwards. Then he walked out of the room.

Siri didn't move until she heard a car start up outside and speed away. Then she pried off the heavy wooden gilt lid and pushed it aside. Siri crawled out of the great box holding her aching back and wincing. She stood up, staggered a bit, and then shook her head, regaining her bearings.

"Wow!" Siri said to herself. "That was close. What did all that mean?"

Suddenly Siri felt something in her pocket. She reached in and withdrew a silver amulet depicting the now familiar Eye of Horus, exactly like the one she had taken off of Dent. Siri remembered she had carried that amulet in her other pocket. She reached in and withdrew the counterpart of the relic she held in her other hand. They were perfect twins – glinting and dazzling in the slanting rays of the late afternoon sun. Siri realized with the darkest of apprehensions that she was holding in her hands what Dent desired most, the twin Osiris Keys! Their purpose still a mystery! Their value, incalculable! One she had surreptitiously taken from Dent. The other Cedric must have slipped into her pocket!

It was then Siri was struck by something else, something that caught her attention on a supporting wall. It was a photograph, another from the early 1920's. Siri scrutinized the picture. It was of the Kings Valley again, this time outside of a newly excavated tomb labeled in white lettering KV62. Standing outside of the descending shaft were three figures, two of whom Siri recognized from her history lessons. One was a stuffy looking Lord Carnarvon, financier of the dig, the other was a debonair Howard Carter, the discoverer of the tomb, and in between stood another familiar figure, Alex Cedric – Alex Cedric not young in years, but as Siri knew him, bearded and sixtyish. The tomb they stood before was equally familiar to anyone who had cracked open a history book. It was the tomb of the boy king, Tutankhamun, the most famous discovery made in the Valley of the Kings, the most famous tomb of all, and here it was, photographed newly discovered in 1922 with Alex Cedric of Salem, Massachusetts on hand, and looking like time never touched him. Siri stood astonished.

# CHAPTER 40: Narrow Escape

Siri walked out of Cedric's house as if in a fog. She couldn't believe she had witnessed a kidnapping. She didn't know what to do next. It was a lovely fall afternoon and all the maples hemming the Salem Common were ablaze with vivid crimson and orange. Siri walked slowly with her head bowed and hands thrust deep into her jacket pockets. She felt the cold silver of the Osiris Keys. She paid no attention to children laughing and playing on a nearby swing set or to an old woman crossing her path while walking a pair of greyhounds. Siri ambled toward the Grand Gazebo, which was the bandstand and centerpiece of the park. For some reason she was drawn toward it. Siri approached the landmark and then ascended its several steps. The elevated vantage gave her a good view of the Witch Curse Museum on the opposite side of the field. Siri stared at the church-like building for a few minutes. She reflected on the uncanny picture she had seen, the one of Cedric in Egypt. That picture was taken way back in 1922. Was it real? Siri asked herself. It sure looked authentic. And if it was, how could Cedric still look the same after all those years? It was uncanny. That was the word alright – uncanny!

Siri wondered what Cedric's role was in all that was happening. Why did he slip her his Osiris Key – to keep it out of Dent's hands? And what was Dent all about? Mallory had vanished. Christian had been whisked away. The Salem police had a stable of missing person's cases to deal with, and Halloween was coming. And then there was

Mister Whispers. Why did he confess to stealing the clock? What was the significance of the formula on the parchment? Why did Mister Whispers want it so badly?

As Siri leaned over the railing of the Gazebo she mused over the scene before her. The Witch Curse Museum appeared unusually quiet for the time of year. There were no tourists entering or exiting the building. It was 3:30 P.M. on a Saturday afternoon and the place seemed quite dead. Siri studied the two front bell towers. She knew what had become of the extracted stones. She had seen them. They had found a secret use to cover a hidden passageway beneath the edifice. But Siri consoled herself with the fact that she had the keys to open that clandestine passage – if she dared. Siri left the gazebo, crossed against traffic, and walked toward the looming museum with its twin turrets and crimson stained-glass window shaped like the arched grating of a cemetery gate.

Siri then noticed a sign printed in bold, black letters. It was attached to the front door of the museum and plain enough to see from the sidewalk.

*"Closed For Renovation!"*

Siri stepped back and looked the place over from the bell towers to the foundation. The place had no activity and there wasn't scaffolding or a workman in sight. It struck her as odd that the museum would undergo renovations during peak season.

Siri took a quick look around. Except for road traffic no one was on her side of the street. Siri walked toward the railed fence and leaned over to see if she could see anything, but there was only the flagstone walk leading towards the back. It was the same section of wrought iron fence she scaled before and for a moment she entertained the notion of scaling it again.

Siri lifted her boot in hope of making a quick hurdle and received an eyeful of gnashing canines and wrinkled snouts. She shrieked and fell back upon the sidewalk. Three Doberman Pinchers had dashed down the walkway straight at her. The pointy-eared, black dogs struggled to leap the fence, their paws rending the air as they furiously tugged against chains that gave them just enough range to cover the yard, but no more. The autumn air resounded with their vicious snarls and barks. Startled, Siri quickly regained her feet and continued along the sidewalk as inconspicuously as she could under the circumstances. She had a fright, and a good one too. As she looked back, Siri could see the dogs still straining against their tethers, barking savagely. She hated to think of what might have happened if she had made it over the fence. The dogs were clearly trained for a purpose it chilled her to think about.

Siri followed a cloud of rust-colored leaves at her feet carried by a gust down Howard Street. She kicked a small pile here and there and figured she would walk around the block to try to clear her head, then go straight home. Siri suddenly stopped in her tracks where the Howard Street Cemetery abuts the Old Salem Jail. Her dad's roadster was parked at the back of the dingy, brick jail with its single stovepipe smokestack and Gothic turrets. Suddenly a rear door opened. Siri was surprised to see her dad walking out the back with Detective Scarpetti. The two men stopped and stood talking in the biting afternoon air. They didn't see Siri. She ducked quickly behind a nearby gravestone. It was a gray slate slab engraved with a skull and cross bones. Siri gave a brief double take at the inscription: *"As you are, so were we. As we are, you shall be. Thomas Hardy, born 1698. Died 1747."* The caw of a crow overhead startled Siri. She skulked over to another gravestone that was closer to her dad and the detective. Siri came face-to-face with another skull only this one had angel wings sticking out from the sides. *"Praises on tombs are titles vainly spent. Man's good name is his best monument. John Shipton. Born 1701. Died 1734."* Siri crouched down, gathered her nerve, and peeked out from behind the withered slate as discreetly as possible. She strained to hear the conversation passing between her dad and the detective. Her dad's voice was difficult to hear, for he was speaking very low. Scarpetti, on the other hand, was no problem.

"So, do you still think I'm barking up the wrong tree, Braddock?"

"You've got to get him to talk," Collin replied.

"He'll talk," said Scarpetti. "Maybe he can shed light on who's behind these vitamin heists. Another pharmacy was broken into last night. Nothing was taken except bottles of vitamins. The cash and prescription drugs weren't even touched. Now that's weird, just like our pale-faced, possum-eyed friend in the cell."

Siri perked up and listened. They were talking about Mister Whispers and he was in the old jail. Siri suddenly saw her dad take out his cell phone and thumb the scroll button. Siri's own ring tone startled her. She had forgotten she had changed it to Latin salsa so when the rapid, tinny beats pulsed from her jacket pocket she fumbled for her phone like it was a hot potato.

"Hi," Siri answered, breathless.

She thought she had given herself away, but a quick glance from behind the gravestone confirmed she was undiscovered.

"What's up?'

"Where are you?" Collin's voice rang over the phone.

"Just hanging around in the park," answered Siri. She cringed at the lie.

"Stay there and I'll pick you up in twenty minutes," said Collin. "We'll get some burgers."

"That sounds great, dad. Bye."

Siri tucked her phone away and watched from her graveyard vantage as her dad and Scarpetti walked into an adjacent brick building that was the old jail-keeper's house. As soon as they were out of sight, Siri stood up, eyed the old jail, and bit into her lower lip as if hatching an idea – a real gem.

# CHAPTER 41: The Prisoner

Siri made her move. She figured if she hesitated, she would lose her nerve. There was no one around the old jail and no surveillance cameras. The place was practically abandoned. Built in 1813, the jail and adjacent keeper's house were listed on the National Register of Historic Places and were rumored to be haunted. The Salem police used the buildings to archive old evidence records before deeming them worthy of disposal. Siri climbed over the century-old retaining wall that separated the property from the graveyard. She gave the back iron door a sturdy rap with her fist and then hid behind a nearby dumpster. After a brief pause, Siri heard a metal latch unfasten and the door swing open with a perceptible squeal. Siri saw her chance and threw a stone into a nearby row of sumac bushes. Peering out from her hiding place, she saw a tall, lanky, police officer walk away from the door to investigate. It was Officer Dwight, looking a little uneasy. Her moment had come. Siri slinked around the corner, and while the officer's back was towards her, she slipped into the jail. Siri instinctively knew the basement held what she was after, so she made a beeline towards a flight of dusty, concrete stairs.

The stairwell was gloomy, lit by one naked light bulb. It was musty too. Siri crinkled her nose at the odor of old, moldy cardboard. At the bottom of the stairs was a long, whitewashed corridor with rows of dark prison cells lining both sides. Siri heard Officer Dwight return to his post upstairs and flap open a newspaper. Siri stepped quietly, advancing slowly along the corridor. She turned to the first cell on her right and cupped her hands against her eyes. She saw nothing but darkness. Then she turned to the cell on her left and did the same, still nothing.

Siri progressed down the corridor looking into one jail cell and then another. She didn't see anything of Mister Whispers. Siri began to feel like she goofed up. She hated to think of what might happen to her if she got caught. For a brief moment she saw herself taking front and profile shots for her first booking for breaking and entering – a jail. And since she was still a minor, she saw herself shipped off to some correctional home for wayward girls tucked in the Berkshires or Upstate New York or Lord knows where.

Siri was just about to give up when she thought she heard a noise coming from a dark cell she had just passed. Siri stopped, took a step back, and peered inside. What she saw was a white blur of a face half turned away at the extreme back of the cell. It seemed to hover in the darkness about six feet off the ground, at least that's how black the rest of the figure appeared. Except for a pale hand clutching a bar stapled to the wall the occupant seemed wrapped in a cloud of shadow.

*"Yooou,"* the figure whispered.

Siri got up the courage to stammer out a response.

"My name is Siri," she said quietly, "but I suppose you already know that."

There was a moment of silence.

"Do you have a name?" Siri asked. She stepped closer to the cell. "I asked you what your name is. Can't you tell me?"

The figure within the cell maintained his silence.

"Look," Siri said. "I don't have all day. Can't you say something to me?"

"You've come for the parchment," the prisoner suddenly spoke. His voice was raspy and still a whisper.

Now she was getting somewhere, Siri thought to herself.

"Yes," Siri answered. "It belongs to me. Do you still have it?"

The prisoner turned towards the dim light so his eyes reflected the dull radiance like two, brilliant green gems. The sight of the figure's eyes startled Siri.

"What ussssssssse could you posssssssibly have for it?" he hissed.

"I know that it's very important," Siri replied. "Otherwise you wouldn't have stolen it from me."

"It never belonged to you," the prisoner spoke, lowering his head, his long black hair framing his face.

Siri listened to some footsteps walking above her. They went back and forth, and then back again. She returned her attention to the dim-faced prisoner.

"Tell me why you confessed to stealing the clock?" Siri asked.

"Can you not be content with the path I cleared for you?" The prisoner asked. "You needn't involve yourself any more in this. Now leave me!"

"Not until you tell me what has happened to Mallory," Siri said. "I saw you take her into the Witch Curse Museum."

The prisoner turned his face away so Siri could only see it in profile, the broad white forehead, the aquiline nose, the jutting, noble jaw.

"Tell me where Mallory is!" Siri insisted, half placing her face between the iron bars of the dank cell.

"He's coming," the prisoner said, turning toward Siri and listening. "The bailiff!"

"Tell me where Mallory is," Siri demanded. She scrutinized the inmate who, though strangely pale, was not unhandsome. "Who are you and why do you want the parchment?"

The prisoner clutched the bars and shook his head. He then backed away into the deeper shadows of the cell while extending a white hand with fingers that tapered off into points, warding off his visitor.

"Go now," he said. "Depart!"

Suddenly a thought occurred to Siri. She reached into her pocket and withdrew the Osiris Keys. She then held them up against the bars.

"Do you know what these are?" Siri asked.

The prisoner's glimmering eyes became riveted at what he beheld shimmering in the dim light.

"Where did you get them?" he demanded.

"That's what you'd like to know," Siri replied. "The important thing is that I have them."

"Give them to me," the inmate said. He approached the bars in slow, stealthful steps.

"No," Siri replied.

The inmate extended his white hand, palm upwards. His eyes fixed on Siri like two gleaming pole stars.

"Give them to me now," he insisted. "You know that you must. You have no choice. You must do what I say."

"You can't pull any of your tricks with me now," Siri snapped. "You can't hypnotize me like you did the last time. I'm onto you."

"Is that so?"

The prisoner made a sudden lunge at the bars. There was something so panther-like in the movement, so sinuous and abrupt that it sobered Siri into rearing away just in time as the prisoner tried to snatch the Osiris Keys from her grasp. Siri put her hand to her heart and caught her breath.

"You don't know what purpose they serve," the prisoner sneered, straining to reach the keys through the bars. "Give them to me!"

"No!" Siri replied. She held the keys close to her chest. "If you won't help me then I'll just have to help myself. I know what door these keys open and I also know they open something else that's even more important. Maybe you should stay in that crummy old jail cell for a month or even a whole year! It will give you time to think. Anyways, I'm going."

"No!" The prisoner said.

Siri turned to leave.

"Forget it," she huffed. "I've made up my mind."

The prisoner's thin, pointed fingers clutched the bars.

"Please, stay!"

He sank upon his knees and bowed his ashen face, so that Siri saw only the white line defining the part of his long, shoulder-length hair.

"If you go through that door, you go to oblivion! I do not want that. Not for you." The prisoner lifted his pale countenance and looked deeply at Siri, his strange eyes dazzling her with their luster. She felt a tremble course through her, not caused by fear, but by something softer. Suddenly Siri heard footsteps descending the stairwell. She spied an opposite flight of steps leading from the other end of the corridor. She took one last look at Mister Whispers sunk before the bars.

"I have to go," Siri said. Then she hurriedly ascended the steps, and exited the building.

# CHAPTER 42: The Invitation

Siri had burgers and onion rings with her dad in the "Pig's Ear Tavern." She sipped a root beer from a straw. Her dad drank a beer. It was a quiet, out of the way joint to eat in. Hardly anyone was in the place – just a bartender standing behind the bar wiping glasses and a gaunt, crinkle-haired waitress taking orders from the few patrons. Boston sports were amply represented with hanging caps and jerseys. A football game was playing on a television hanging over the bar. Siri and her dad didn't talk much. They each munched their burgers from opposite ends of a table they shared by a cheery fireside hearth. Siri and her dad were good at putting up fronts. Collin kept the conversation on homework while biting into a cheeseburger. Siri played along, sipping her root beer from the straw and chomping on fries like a woodchuck. Both had weighty issues on their minds, but this was father and daughter time, and they made a go of it.

"Dad, do you believe people can come back from the dead?" Siri asked.

"What kind of question is that?" Collin returned.

"The ancient Egyptians thought they could," Siri replied.

"Well they can't."

"Some people come back during séances."

"Harry Houdini debunked a lot of that stuff back in the twenties," said Collin.

"Harry who?"

144

"Never mind."

"I wish I could talk to mom," Siri spoke, sipping her root beer.

"Me too," Collin replied. "But she's in Heaven. Now finish your burger."

The ride home through Salem's narrow streets was quiet between Siri and her dad. Collin drove while Siri listened to classical music over the radio, occasionally looking over at her dad. Her mother was in Heaven, she thought. And she and her dad missed her.

Once in the driveway Siri threw open the car door and bolted for the mailbox. Siri liked getting the mail first because her dad always tossed out the junk mail. Siri liked junk mail. It was better than bills. Siri shuffled though the stack quickly – gas bill, electric bill, water bill. Then she found something interesting. It was an envelope addressed to both her and her dad. The paper was thin, crinkly parchment that had an aged look, which appealed to Siri. She quickly opened it. Inside was a Halloween card depicting a haggard witch with a crooked jaw and a single tooth. She was flying on a broom with a cross-eyed black cat arching its back atop the broom handle. The style was reminiscent of the 1930's, conjuring up images of Betty Boop, Steamboat Willie, and laughing cows with xylophone teeth and crankshaft tails. When Siri opened it she saw an invitation gleaming up under the light of the lamp post.

*"You are cordially invited to attend our annual autumn séance here at the Black Ram Inn, Tuesday night at nine o'clock sharp. Please come and bring your positive vibrations with you. Signed, Amy and Dody Putnam (and Bernie)."*

Siri called to her dad as he was putting the key in the front door.

"Hey," she said, waving the invitation. "Look what we've got!"

Siri heard a car approaching and turned. It was her neighbor, Tom Mash, undertaker and proprietor of Mash Memorials and Funeral Parlor, driving by in his long, black hearse. He smiled at Siri as he drove by and parked at 38 Wicks End. Tom Mash wasn't very old, only 50ish. He took the business over from his dad who was an avid cyclist at the time of his death. Tom Mash embalmed his dad and mounted him on a bicycle at his wake. Not many people came.

Since that day business had been slow. Tom Mash walked over and handed Siri his business card, tipping his hat as he did so. Then he turned and walked back toward his house. Collin didn't give the man a second thought. Siri looked at the card and shook her head. It read: *"Mash Final Parlor and Plots: Tom Mash Proprietor. Making final arrangements memorable since 1941."*

# CHAPTER 43: The Séance

It was Tuesday night. Amy and Dody, in their best ruffle collar dresses, cheerfully welcomed guests into the candle-lit parlor of the Black Ram Inn. Siri never attended a real séance before, so she was a little nervous and a bit uncomfortable in a dress. Collin didn't accompany Siri. He had other things planned and he kept her in the dark about them. Siri gave her dad a quick peck on the cheek as she got out of the MG. She didn't ask any questions as he drove off. Siri stood before the Black Ram Inn and looked at her invitation. Then she tucked it back in her purse next to the Osiris Keys and Tom Mash's business card, which she kept. Siri knew she was delving into Salem's darkest secrets and who knew what the future held for her.

When Siri walked in, she was glad to find Kaelyn and Dobbs standing in the front parlor of the Inn. Siri gave Kaelyn a smile and Dobbs too. Kaelyn smiled back and Dobbs nodded. It was no coincidence that they were there. Kaelyn regularly attended séances at the Black Ram, and Dobbs was her guest that night. Kaelyn was dressed in her Wiccan finery and Dobbs was wearing a baggy grey suit. Siri milled around, took a teacake from a silver caddy, and sidled up to Kaelyn.

"Dent's suppose to be staying here," Siri whispered, expecting to see him sitting like a spider in the middle of a web, "but I don't see him anywhere."

"Me either," Kaelyn added.

"What happens now?" Siri asked.

Suddenly Bernie took Siri by the arm.

"Hey," he said. "I was hoping you'd come tonight."

"Will I see any ghosts?"

"You might," Bernie winked.

Other visitors had just arrived. Bernie excused himself and took their coats. There were the Armstrongs from Danvers, the Pinkstons from Marblehead, the elderly Melon sisters, twins Honey and Dew, and the medium, Tegan Faye, who ushered all toward a round, mahogany table centered in the antique appointed room. Siri followed the others in and took her seat among them.

"We must all hold hands to form the linking circle," said Tegan, layered in turquoise beads and wrapped in a colorful woolen poncho. She looked at everyone present, observed every sitter clasping hands with their neighbor, and then said, "It is important that all be of open mind and quiet heart to make the spirits receptive. We may ask what is relevant. That is all. If you ask something foolish, the spirit will not answer. I request a moment of silence to prepare."

The medium gently closed her long-lashed eyes. Everyone in the room sat in silence. Siri looked around her. The faces at the table were all so serious. Siri fought an impulse to chuckle. This was business, she told herself. Everyone seemed focused on a tall copper cone in the middle of the table. For several minutes nothing stirred. Then Amy and Dody started to sing, raising their tremulous voices in unison. Siri almost jumped out of her seat.

Siri glanced around the table as Bernie's aunts sang. It was an old ballad about a woman named Rose who was poisoned and stabbed by her lover, who was eventually hanged for her murder. Suddenly a placid, uncharacteristic smile spread across Tegan's lips. With her eyes still closed, she took a deep breath and then let it out. The medium reared her head high and arched her back disturbingly, like she had been poked in the spine with a broomstick. All eyes fastened on Tegan when suddenly she slumped forward, her head resting on the table, exhausted. Then, she slowly lifted her head. Her face assumed the mellow, ruddy composure of one who had long-indulged in hard liquor. With a lower jaw cranked askew, which cast her in a more masculine guise, Tegan set a steely eye upon every person at the table. As she absorbed her surroundings, Dent emerged from the shadows garbed in a white Nehru suit.

"Is this a private séance, or can anyone join in?"

The group was taken by surprise by Dent's sudden arrival. Aunt Dody turned towards Dent and stammered.

"Well, this is rather unusual."

She looked at Tegan who stared quietly ahead.

"Since the medium doesn't seem to mind, I don't see why you can't join us. Do you Amy?" Dody asked, looking to her sister.

"No, I don't see why not," answered Amy. "Come sit down and join the circle Mr. Dent. Uncle Joe has just come through for us. We can tell it's Uncle Joe because his face always got red after he knocked a few whiskey sours back."

"Splendid," said Dent. He pulled up a chair, seated himself down beside Siri, and paid her a quaint, neighborly smile. Siri smiled back, halfheartedly. "Just Dent," he said, turning towards the circle of sitters. Dobbs glanced towards Kaelyn and swallowed. Dent looked at her also, but his glance was keener, with a touch of gravity. Kaelyn smiled politely and then quickly suppressed it.

Aunt Dody turned to Siri.

"You know, Siri. Our Uncle Joe was once a merchant marine," she said. "He got swept overboard during a gale off Singapore. Before he went down to Davy Jones he brought us back such wonderful gifts: conch shells, shrunken heads, and ivory carvings of Genesh, the Hindu elephant god. They never did recover his body."

"Shhhhh," whispered Amy. "You'll disturb the trance."

Dobbs was about to reach for a handkerchief to wipe his brow when Tegan's hand suddenly lashed out and seized him by the wrist. She turned to Dobbs and scowled.

"I know you," she said, in a husky man's voice. "You're Roger Dobb's boy. I caught you peeing in my boat!"

Dobbs was startled at the strength of the medium's grip, her changed voice, and the embarrassing accusation.

"I'm, I'm very sorry," he stammered. "You see, I was doing an errand for my mother and...."

Tegan's wandering eyes then fixed on Bernie and his two aunts.

"Hello, my dearies."

"Hello Uncle Joe," Amy and Dody said together.

"It's good to see young Bernie being useful."

Bernie forced a smile.

"Thanks Uncle Joe. I'm getting better at it."

Tegan turned her gaze to Siri and Dent. She paused and narrowed her eyes upon them.

"These sitters I haven't met before."

"You wouldn't know me, Uncle Joe," spoke Dent.

Dent reached boldly across the table and shook the medium's hand.

"The name is Dent."

"Pleased to meet you, Mr. Dent," said Uncle Joe.

"Just Dent."

Siri hesitated. Then she spoke.

"My name is Siri."

"Pleased to meet you, young lady," the medium said, jaw hanging askew. "Fair weather we're having."

"You know," said Dent, as he looked about the table. "I've just returned from Cairo where they believe the gods of ancient Egypt are always present, waiting to be invoked. Even here in New England they can supposedly be reached. Would any of you object if I were to put this to a test?"

Bernie looked at his aunts who in turn looked at each other equally baffled.

"No? Good," said Dent. He then leaned forward, looked directly at the medium, and after a moment of concentration, clamped his eyes shut. He spoke in a low voice.

"Amun-Ra," Dent intoned. "God of creation and guardian of Karnak, send forth your servant Imhotep, who now resides with Anubis, the protector of the dead. I, who am unworthy in your eyes, humbly ask of his noble presence here tonight."

Dent opened his crystal green eyes and kept them riveted straight ahead to an image forming in his mind. Several moments passed. The medium, seated stiffly in her chair, suddenly punctuated the room with a gasp, and sunk her head in a swoon upon the table. Mr. Pinkston stood up to check on her. Mr. Armstrong did the same. Siri, Dobbs, and Kaelyn kept their gaze fixed on Dent who calmly regarded all around the table and asked everyone to return to their seats.

"There's no need for alarm," he said. "Let's concentrate on the task at hand."

Everyone uncomfortably acquiesced. Dent closed his eyes once more.

"Imhotep, builder of Egypt and ender of droughts, if you are indeed among us, then reveal yourself. The shaper of monuments surely cannot be quelled by the mear incident of mortal death. Reveal yourself. Reveal yourself to me, your servant."

Suddenly the cone on the table started to wobble. Dent opened his eyes and observed its vacillation. Dobbs looked on in amazement.

"It appears the gods of ancient Egypt are at our very elbow," said Dent. "But I suppose we should make certain that it is indeed Imhotep and not some ethereal imposter."

Dent closed his eyes once more and spoke.

"When I was a boy my mother and I made a ferry crossing while vacationing in Luxor. The year was 1970. I remember leaning over the railing and dropping a souvenir Napoleon into the Nile's dark waters and watching it sink into oblivion. If Imhotep really is among us, then you will know this. Go to the bottom of the Nile River, the life's blood of your great land, and bring me back the coin."

The copper cone ceased to wobble. Dent extended his upturned palm into the middle of the table. A gold coin then dropped from the ceiling into his hand, wet with water. He displayed it to everyone at the table. The front bore the stamped profile of Napoleon. The back bore an engraved date, 1970. Dent passed the coin to Siri to examine. She then passed it to Kaelyn who gazed inquisitively upon its gleaming surface.

"This is proving to be a night of revelations," said Dent. "I recently mislaid a very precious object, lately of Egypt, and I would like nothing better than to have it back."

Dent looked at Siri seated beside him and smiled.

"I wonder," he continued, talking out loud to the empty air, "if I dare ask the whereabouts of this object. It is in the form of an amulet, of pure silver, and bears the unmistakable motif of an eye, the Eye of Horus. I invoke Imhotep's name once more to return to my possession this most precious of objects, so lately of Egypt, and so rudely appropriated from me in a manner embarrassing to recount."

Suddenly the cone wobbled and fell over. Siri stiffened. Then, right before her eyes the table rose several inches, oscillated, returned to the floor, and began to vibrate as if there was an earthquake underfoot. The tremors infected the room, and then the china hutch rattled with all the crockery within. The back door blew open and then slammed shut with a startling bang. The copper cone levitated into the air before all seated before it. Siri stared wide-eyed as the object flew around the air over their heads, like it was being pulled and jerked around by invisible hands. Then, just as suddenly as the cone ascended, it quietly returned to its place on the table, settling down as gently as ever. Just as Siri and everyone else began to calm down the lights went out and a rush of wind whirled about the interior shadows, rustling everyone's hair and gowns, and stealing their breath away. Amy and Dody looked around the room, which whooshed with violent gusts.

"This is far from usual, Amy," Dody shouted above the roar of the whirlwind.

"I quite agree, Dody. We should ask Uncle Joe to step in and put a stop to it, just like the way he used to break up the fights on the quarter deck of his ship by banging sailors heads together."

Bernie rose from his seat, and might have stood up had not his aunts on either side of him held him in place. Mr. Armstrong cleared his throat.

"Perhaps this has gone far enough?"

"I quite agree," said his wife. "I don't like this. I want to talk with my son, Edward."

Dent lifted his face toward the ceiling and cried out to the colliding winds:

"RETURN TO ME THE OSIRIS KEYS! RETURN THEM TO ME! RETURN THEM TO ME, GREAT GUARDIAN SPIRIT OF KARNAK!!!"

Suddenly a crack of thunder shook the whole house to its foundation. It was like a detonation. Siri shrieked. She looked at Kaelyn who wore an expression of fear. Dobbs sat like he could catch a fly in his mouth. Suddenly the wind died and all became quiet and still.

"Miss Faye doesn't look well," said Kaelyn. "Perhaps we should stop."

"Someone please wake up the medium," said Mrs. Pinkston with alarm.

"No," said Dody. "It's dangerous to wake a medium from a trance."

"Is she dead?" asked one of the Melon sisters.

"She's quite alright," answered Dent, lowering his gaze and relaxing his stern demeanor. "Apparently what I wish returned to me is a lot more difficult than dragging a coin from the bottom of the Nile. I could almost swear another force was at work. Here. Let me prove our medium is unharmed and quite alive."

Dent turned to Siri.

"There's a hand mirror on the window seat, young lady. Please hold it under Miss Faye's nose and mouth to show everyone that she's still a tenant of this world."

Siri reluctantly got up from her seat, stepped across the darkened room, and retrieved the hand mirror. She carefully placed it under the unconscious medium's mouth. Siri was the only one at the table who could see in the oval glass mirror. She saw the reflection of the medium's parted lips, her warm breath fogging the mirror's surface, along with something else. Siri could see in the mirror a collection of objects working their way like grey caterpillars up the medium's throat, over her tongue and past the open mouth. They were the gray, bandaged fingers of a mummy's hand that ultimately birthed from the very gullet of the unconscious medium! The startling appendage moved tarantula-like over the medium's chin and attempted to snatch Siri's purse, which was draped over her shoulder. The terrible reflection caused Siri to suddenly drop the mirror, shattering its glass. Mr. Pinkston stood and switched on the light.

Tegan's eyes fluttered opened. Most sat dumb struck, except for Dobbs, who helped the medium regain consciousness with the aid of some brandy. He quickly poured a glass for himself, quickly drank it down, and then poured himself another. Siri stood alone by the windowsill, bewildered. Kaelyn asked her what she saw in the mirror. Siri looked at Dent who was still seated and gazing knowingly at her.

"It was nothing," she replied. "I guess I'm just tired."

# CHAPTER 44: Wake of the Witches

Siri stood in the back room of Kaelyn's witch shop. The place was so cozy with throw pillows and books and occult knickknacks that it felt like a second home. Siri placed the Osiris Keys on the table beside one of Kaelyn's crystal balls. The Witch of Salem, draped in her purple robe, marking her as high priestess of her Wiccan chapter, tossed back her broad hood as she took a seat beside Siri and gazed upon the silvery surfaces of the twin amulets shimmering back at her. Siri had told her everything that had happened in the last few days: Christian Fletcher and his horrible affliction, Alex Cedric's strange abduction, the vicious Dobermans at the Witch Curse Museum, the mysterious prisoner in the old Salem jail, and Mallory was still missing. Kaelyn looked at Siri and then returned her large, blue eyes to the amulets.

"I've never seen anything like them," Kaelyn said. "Yes, they are the traditional Eye of Horus, but the craftsmanship, the metal work, the inlaid details within the pupils of the eye. It's all so...."

Suddenly the little bells over the shops door rang out. *Ting-A-ling-A-ling! Ting-A-ling-A-ling! Ting-A-ling-A-ling!*

Siri turned and looked through a part in the black curtain that separated the back room from the rest of the occult shop. She could see tourists picking through little packets of potions, admiring gemstones in cases or musing over shelves of books about pyramid power, crystal power, and just about every kind of power. Siri eyed the girl at the cash register. Her name was Wren and she was in Siri's chemistry class. Wren always dressed in black tank tops, combat fatigues and boots. The bangs of her cute Dutch clip were dyed a bright pink and were the only specks of color about her. The two glanced at each other for a moment. Siri smiled, but Wren just shook her head and rang up a customer. Siri drew back the curtain and returned her attention to the amulets.

"All I know is that they're keys of some sort," Siri said, "Keys to the underground passage – and something else."

"I think I need to consult the cards," Kaelyn said. "Sometimes when I'm stumped or indecisive, the cards help."

The witch placed Tarot cards around the Osiris Keys, the major arcana of The Emperor, The Empress, The Lovers, The Hermit, The Wheel of Fortune, and The Fool.

Siri hated bothering Kaelyn when she was so busy, but the witch didn't seem to mind. Kaelyn sat back in her chair, looked at the cards she had dealt, and then poured Siri and herself a cup of tea.

"Why are you troubling yourself with tea?" Siri asked.

"I'm thirsty," Kaelyn replied. "No. Really the tea leaves tell me things as well as the cards. I'm using a double whammy today."

Kaelyn stirred her tea around with a little movement of her wrist. Then she drank down the contents. Siri looked quizzically at the empty cup Kaelyn suddenly placed in her hands. There were things floating in the little bit of tea left, bits of soft, bark-like stuff that churned around each other in the bottom of her cup and settled into the unmistakable shape of an eye. Kaelyn turned over the cards she had spread out. She turned one over, then another, and as she went the rounds turning over the cards the expression on her face grew graver and graver.

"This man, Dent, is dangerous," Kaelyn spoke. "The cards tell me he is a shaper of his destiny. He rules – like the Emperor. But he can be cunning – like the Fool. He spins the Wheel of Fortune, and the result is Death, but not his death, the death of things we take for granted. He's a game changer, this Dent. He can summon disincarnate entities to do his bidding – restless, evil spirits. His power is very old and very potent. We must be on our guard."

"But the secret passage?" said Siri. "And the Osiris Keys?"

"I know," said Kaelyn, interrupting. "But fools rush in where angels fear to tread. We must be careful now. Dent is no fool. He suspects something. And he will make his move. We must be vigilant about how we go about things now, for we may find ourselves being watched. The atmosphere is thick and heavy. I feel a sense of oppression, of conspiracy. There are bad signs everywhere."

Kaelyn veered her brilliant, blue eyes from Siri and gazed into space as though witnessing something terrible in her mind's eye.

"A false move, a careless step, could cost us our own eternity."

Siri looked at her teacup and put it down. Kaelyn snapped out of her reverie and placed a comforting hand over Siri's.

"It won't be all bad news, Siri. Don't worry. There's a lot on our side. We won't be alone in our quest to find Mallory or in dealing with Dent. You're experiencing many new and strange things, but remember. You possess a rare gift. Salem has a long and strange history of people with such gifts, and I believe your gift of dream scrying will help us more than anything. So don't be afraid to use it."

Kaelyn paused for a moment and stood. She walked over to the little statue of Isis on a nearby mantle, her mug of tea cupped between her hands. Then she turned towards Siri.

"This stranger in the old jail," Kaelyn said. "He might be someone we could bring to our side."

"I think you're right," said Siri. "The more I think about him, the more I think he can help us,"

"See," Kaelyn said. "Already you are using your gift. You're learning, girl!"

"Thanks," Siri replied.

"I need to see his aura," said Kaelyn.

"I wish I could see auras," Siri remarked.

For a moment the witch stood silent, as if giving what she was about to say much thought.

"Siri," Kaelyn finally spoke, turning. "I want you to attend our

Drawing Down ceremony tonight."

"Drawing Down?" Siri asked.

"Yes," said Kaelyn. She resumed her seat next to Siri. "It is our Drawing Down of the Moon. It is the most important and most beautiful rite in our neo-pagan faith. Each year near Samhain our sisterhood makes a pilgrimage to Gallows Hill. There, we convene and commune with The Goddess, the Great Mother of all things. In our Drawing Down of the Moon we all become one with her. I want you to join us, Siri. Will you come?"

Siri looked at Kaelyn in all earnest.

"You bet I will," Siri replied.

Kaelyn then gazed off into space again.

"Perhaps if we entreat her solemnly, and with belief, the Great Goddess might guide us in our quest."

# CHAPTER 45: Drawing Down the Moon

Another full moon was on the rise. It was bitter cold, close to freezing. Siri met Kaelyn's pea green VW Bug on the corner of Howard and Brown Street. Hugging her sides Siri couldn't wait to get inside a warm car, but was sorely disappointed.

"Sorry, the heater's busted," announced Kaelyn, donned in a blue parker. She handed Siri a spill-proof cup of cocoa freshly poured from a thermos bottle. "I've been meaning to get it fixed."

Siri was wearing a black, commando-style knit cap, leather jacket, gloves, jeans, and boots. She had on a wool sweater under it all, but still the cold got through. Siri looked in the back and saw a bundle of dark, heavy woolen ceremonial robes that appeared to warm her just by the sight of them.

"Sorry for the wait," said Kaelyn. She pulled the VW away from the curb.

"That's okay," answered Siri. "Where are the others?"

"At Gallows Hill Park," answered Kaelyn as she negotiated a corner. "We'll meet them there."

Siri glanced at the digital clock on the dashboard. 10:05 P.M. Even though she successfully snuck out again, she felt a little guilty. The conversation that passed between her and the witch as they wound their way through the little narrow streets was basically instructional for Siri's benefit. Kaelyn explained simply what she knew about neo-pagan faith, its roots in the development of ancient man, from dim pre-history to the present day. In ancient times, Thessalian witches were believed to hold the moon in place and stand still the day. Modern neo-pagans Draw Down the Moon to commune with the Great Mother Goddess. Through the high priestess she would speak with her devotees and give them insight and wisdom. Many times Kaelyn had fallen into a trance and became one with the Great Mother Goddess. It was a temporary union, she told Siri, but one so overpowering and beautiful that it was utterly beyond words to describe. Such was the brief introduction Siri received, but it was enough to fill up the short time during the drive across town to Gallows Hill Park where a tragedy had occurred over three hundred years earlier in 1692, the execution of 19 innocent people as witches.

As Kaelyn's VW pulled into the parking lot, Siri noticed other cars parked there as well, about twenty in all. The lot was off to the side near a baseball field. To the southwest, on the very edge of the ballpark, loomed the dark eminence of Gallows Hill. As Siri stepped out of the vehicle she saw teenage girls like herself, as well as middle-aged and senior women. All donned ceremonial scarlet robes and lit little purple candles held in votive glass. Kaelyn removed her parker and drew on her purple vestments, throwing her cowl over her head in the process. She handed Siri her robe of simple white, denoting her as a novice of the sisterhood. The other women convened around Kaelyn, kissing her cheeks and taking her hand. Siri stood back and watched this simple and beautiful show of respect to Kaelyn's office. Siri put on her robe and hood. It was woolen homespun, heavy, but quite warm. After some small talk, Kaelyn took the lead and directed the group in a silent, candlelit procession up a well-worn dirt path inclining up the dark, grass grown hill. As a novice, Siri was instructed to walk directly behind Kaelyn. Siri carried a white candle in a threading line of purple ones.

The crest of the hill was bathed in a wash of blue moonlight, the lights of Salem spreading out in a grid below with the dark band of the Atlantic shimmering like black satin on the horizon. From under her hood Siri saw that the hill was crowned with a patch of leafless oaks on one side. On the other, a water tower loomed with an emblem of

Salem's famous witch riding a broomstick. The night was quite cold and clear, but after the climb Siri felt quite cozy in her vestments. She enjoyed Kaelyn's friendship. Somehow the witch filled a void left by Mallory's disappearance.

Once atop the hill's highest point the robed congregation formed a circle with Siri and Kaelyn at its center. Kaelyn composed herself before a ceremonial brazier prepared by two robed sisters of the temple. A small fire soon glowed and it was into this that Kaelyn tossed a powdered concoction that sparkled in the moonlight. A green flame rose from the bowl, burning brightly. The weird, vernal light illuminated everyone in a way that was both haunting and beautiful. Kaelyn gestured over the bowl again and a dazzling eruption of scarlet fire threw a ring of long shadows back upon the grass. Siri gazed wide-eyed, her face under her hood flaring with crimson brightness. The fire died, and in the midst of twinkling candles Kaelyn raised her hands to the night sky so that her broad sleeves fell to her elbows revealing her long, white arms. This was the Goddess Pose, shaping herself in a Y preparatory to Drawing Down the Moon Goddess into her body. Uplifting her palms she called out in a loud voice that nearly startled Siri.

"Sister Moon, we worship you!"

The conclave refrained.

*"We worship you."*

"Sister Stars," Kaelyn cried out. "We worship you!"

The gathering repeated the chorus.

*"We worship you."*

"Mother Earth," Kaelyn called. "We worship you!"

*"We worship you."*

"Great Goddess. You. Mother of all things, we worship you!"

*"We worship you."*

Siri didn't quite know what to make of the proceedings. Suddenly the robed women began to move in a slow, clockwise direction around Kaelyn. Carrying their candles, they reminded Siri of a spiral constellation, rotating in the void. Their movements were solemn and silent. With her arms raised and palms uplifted to the midnight heavens Kaelyn bowed her head. Siri could see that she had her eyes tightly closed.

"Great Mother Goddess," Kaelyn spoke. "My body is yours. My mouth is yours. Use this vessel to work the good and to allay the bad. Fill it with your wisdom and kindness. Nurture it with knowledge so that it chooses the right path when the way is tangled and unclear and clouded. Come down from heaven and dwell amongst us mortals, frail and unsure as we are. Come, Great Goddess. Come. We entreat. We implore. Draw down from heaven and become one with us. Become one with us now!"

Siri watched spellbound. The coven circled, droning a kind of singsong chant that was barely a murmur. She couldn't make out the words, only a low, vocal hum, as one might hear in a monastic enclave. Kaelyn stood immobile, arms raised, eyes closed, like a statue. Siri couldn't even see her breathe. Suddenly Kaelyn lowered her arms and held them relaxed at her side. A placid smile spread over her face, her shoulders softened, and her eyes opened in a glazed, dreamy reverie. Then she spoke.

"I am among you, my children," Kaelyn said, as gently as a mother would to a newborn. "Fret not, for I am here." Then she turned to Siri.

"There is one among you who sees much, but understands little, who dreams realities and whose realities are not unlike dreams. There is much danger for her, and for those who help her. But if she is steadfast, and stumbles not upon that path of her choosing, many whose days have been nights, will at last see light. Walk toward the North, my child. There you will see high over the town the lost and the found and the blood on the ground. Leave us and see. Leave us now!"

Kaelyn's eyes rolled back and her whole slender form collapsed in a swoon upon the grass. The circle immediately closed around her. One of the sisterhood cradled Kaelyn while others rubbed her hands in an effort to bring her back to consciousness. Siri took the opportunity to steal away toward the northern end of the hill. She shed her cloak and ran across the bluish, moonlit crest. Siri felt a sense of urgency she didn't understand. She instinctively knew she had to hurry. Siri approached a veil of stunted briars. Then she saw something up ahead. It was a dark shape moving through a grove of leafless, gnarled oaks on the north side of Gallows Hill. Siri stopped and crouched down behind a bare shrub shivering in the evening breeze.

Siri couldn't see the figure well in the dark. She needed to get closer. Siri crept like a commando, on her elbows, pushing herself forward with her knees through the grass. She kept her head low trying her best to view the shape. No use. She still had to get closer. Somewhere below a dog barked. Another bark echoed across town. Siri kept her eyes fixed on the figure as she crept closer. She felt like a hunter stalking its prey. Siri stopped by a fallen branch and peeked over the limb just enough for her to see.

Finally, she saw the thing plainly. It was a human shape, all covered over in a black hooded cloak or cape. It was doing something to a very wide and very ancient looking tree. The trunk was exceedingly broad, like a bridge pillar, and its rough bark deeply furrowed. Its branches were leafless, huge and spread tentacle-like in every direction. It was a patriarch of trees.

Suddenly a dull tapping noise caught Siri's ear. She could see the glint of a dagger as the figure repeatedly stabbed into the trunk. Siri watched transfixed. The figure then placed an antique copper vessel under the cut in the bark, and caught what appeared to be a black, clumpish liquid that began to spill from the wound in the tree. Siri could hear it drip into the receptacle. Worse yet, she could see it glistening in the moonlight. Although Siri didn't know why, the sound made her squeamish. Soon the drips slowed and the vein in the tree ceased to run altogether. Siri estimated that enough sap had poured from the old oak to fill two big orange mugs at the "Live Slow Cafe."

She watched as the figure hid the dagger amongst the folds of its robes and prepared to bear the vessel away, but before it turned to the shadows, the figure revealed itself in the moonlight. Siri's heart nearly stopped when she recognized the plain, austere face of Constance Nash peering cautiously out from under the hood, and then becoming lost to darkness as she quickly disappeared into the briars.

Siri waited until she was certain her presence wouldn't be detected. Now quite alone, Siri got up off the ground and approached the tree. She had to know what had flowed from its ancient, corrugated bark. A sweet, sickly odor seemed to cling to the surrounding area. It almost repelled Siri, but still she drew nearer. Siri snapped on her LED penlight and roamed its small, blue beam over the trunk. There wasn't a trace of any wound or fissure.

Suddenly Siri noticed a brackish droplet staining a broad upturned root at her feet. She bent and couldn't resist touching it with her finger. She rubbed her thumb against it and then in one sudden motion quickly wiped it off with a stroke against the grass. Siri couldn't believe it – *it was a crimson drop of blood!*

# CHAPTER 46: The Clone

When Siri left for school that morning her dad was fast asleep on the couch. As she got ready she tried to be as quiet as possible and not wake him. She had a bowl of cereal and some juice and had her plan for the day, which didn't include school. She didn't sleep well after visiting Gallows Hill. She kept seeing the face of Constance Nash in her dreams, dreams that were vivid and wild and seemed to be a jumble of strange, ancient people and ancient places in an ancient time when Salem hanged accused witches. Now Siri was up and had to strike while the proverbial metal was hot. She was glad her dad was out like a light. Before Siri left, she wrote a note saying she had left for school on her own and not to worry. Then, as she quietly stepped towards the front door, she noticed her dad's key ring on the coffee table next to the couch. One key was new. It was brass, thick, and important-looking, like it belonged to a security door. Siri carefully picked up the keys, trying not to jangle them. She took them into the kitchen and studied the new one carefully. The key tab read: "SJ 10501 DO NOT DUPLICATE." SJ, Siri thought, could mean only one thing: SALEM JAIL. A beauty of an idea hatched in her mind.

Siri opened one of the kitchen draws that had old odds and ends and took out an egg of fun putty. She peeled a hunk of it out of the little container and spread it on the kitchen table. Then she went to work, pressing the key, once for each side, deep into the putty creating a perfect mold. Siri then returned her dad's keys to the coffee table, and after taking a parting glance of him sleeping, left the house.

Siri showed up at Mrs. Breath's history class for first period, and then excused herself for feeling sick. It was a good acting job on Siri's part. In the lady's room she spun around until she got dizzy, just to give her face that pale "I'm not kidding, I'm gonna be sick" look. The ploy worked. Mrs. Breath excused Siri without a hint of suspicion. At the school nurse's office where Siri had to sign out as "sick" for the day, she noticed Constance Nash listed as absent, having called from home. Siri looked across the dim, wood-paneled hall at the door of principal Fletcher. There was an index card taped on it saying: "Principal Fletcher out this week."

"Something's up," Siri thought. "Just where does Constance Nash live anyway?"

Siri knew Constance was up to something, and felt that she played a part in everything that was going on. Siri wasn't going to waste this day. This day she was determined to find out a lot of things.

At Kaelyn's shop, Siri updated her witch friend about her new suspicions; namely, about Constance's roll in the weird affair of the night before. Kaelyn was noticeably placid and serene in her consulting room that morning, a usual after-effect from her communion with the Goddess, like she had been on a restful vacation. She was sitting in her purple robe with her eyes closed on her wicker chair and stroking her black cat, Grimalkin. It took a little nagging from Siri to prod Kaelyn out of the relaxed state she was in. Kaelyn took several deep breaths, blinked her eyes, and although refreshed, wore a grim aspect of one who had no choice but to get back to dire business.

Kaelyn had a friend who made jewelry, primarily Celtic and Nordic rings, amulets, and pendants. It wasn't long before Siri and Kaelyn stood in her little corner shop across town watching the artisan donned in a leather apron pouring a gray, molten liquid from a metal ladle into the putty mold Siri had made of the key she found on her dad's keyring. The artist was a woman of around sixty with short-cropped gray hair and a plain face with a pug nose that had a big metal ring through both nostrils, like a South Pacific cannibal of

Captain Cook's time. Her sinewy arms were heavily tattooed with a tangle of roses and thorns, but she was able-bodied, judging from the array of hammers, rasps, and crimping pliers laying about the cluttered workroom. The woman worked mainly with pewter and silver, and some amalgams. The metal she employed for this work was of the latter. It had a low melting point, but was firm enough upon cooling to be used as a key, providing not too much pressure wasn't exerted on it. Siri watched amazed as the gray, smoking liquid filled her mold and began to harden before her eyes. The warning on the key not to duplicate didn't hinder the operation. The artist went to work breaking the new key from its mold, cooling it in a beaker of water, and filing it down on a grinding wheel as if it was just another one of her superb creations. When it was over Siri held in her hand a grayish clone of SJ 10501 DO NOT DUPLICATE.

# CHAPTER 47 : Heavy Persuasion

"No. No. No-no-no," said Dobbs. "Ladies, I'll have no part in it!"

Dobbs leaned back in his chair in the rear office at the Salem Athenaeum. His arms were folded resolutely behind his bald head, which he kept turning sharply from side to side.

"What you propose is highly illegal and I won't do it. No!"

Kaelyn and Siri flanked Dobbs like interrogators trying to crack a suspect into spilling all he knew, but this nut wasn't cracking. They each half sat on his cluttered desk and looked at each other, trying to think of ways to sweeten the offer. What they had in mind was bold and criminal, but they saw no other way. All they needed was a hiding place, and for that they needed to rely on Dobb's participation, and he wasn't budging.

"What you're suggesting is breaking and entering, abduction, interfering with a police witness, aiding and abetting, conspiracy and a half dozen other felonies."

Dobbs turned from Siri to Kaelyn then back to Siri, his large, winking eyes giving him the appearance of a newly hatched chick.

"I could lose my job," he said. "This library would become a shambles without me."

Dobbs kept turning to them even after he stopped talking, like his head was on automatic. Then Siri hit on it. She smiled at Dobbs, leaned forward and whispered.

"Mister Dobbs," said Siri. "I bet this guy in the old jail knows secrets about Salem, big secrets. He could tell you things about this town that even you don't know about. Think of what you'll learn from him – all the dirty laundry in this city and who's behind it all. That kind of information could be really useful in certain situations. And all you'd need to do is leave your back door unlocked. Now what do you say?"

Siri glanced towards Kaelyn who now stood back, letting Siri take the lime light. Siri was stretching the truth like a politician on election night, but her words seemed to have an effect on Dobbs. His large, round eyes narrowed and his mouth puckered like he was sucking a sour ball. Siri could almost see the wheels turning in his shiny head.

"Well, Mister Dobbs?" Siri pressed.

"All I need to do is leave the door unlocked?" Dobbs asked, quizzically.

"And hide him in the library basement for the night," Siri added.

Siri noticed an old book on the corner of Dobb's desk that resembled an ancient tome judging from its thickness, brown leather binding, and yellowed pages. It was open to a huge title page framed in a Romanesque arch of brownish, iron gall ink: ***"The Wonders of the Invisible World**, written in the Time of the Late Wars, Corrected and Amended with Several Additions and Annotations. London, Printed, and are to be Sold by Nathaniel Sacket at the Atlas in Cornhill."* Cotton Mather. 1693.*

"Think of the wonders you'll learn," Siri added, putting the emphasis on the word *'wonders.'* She closed Dobb's book.

Dobbs veered his eyes toward the ancient tome.

"Wonders?"

"Wonders," Siri replied, nodding.

Dobbs bent towards her.

"I'll do it!"

Siri and Kaelyn turned to each other and breathed a sigh of relief.

# CHAPTER 48: The Search for Constance Nash

Siri crouched down in the passenger seat of Kaelyn's VW Bug parked across the street from Windward High School. It was a gray, windy day and dead leaves were blowing all over the place and gathering in little, swirling piles. Siri eyed the old Gothic campus at the same time taking care not to be noticed. She was bent on getting her ducks in order that afternoon. She was devising her plan as she went along. As she watched students idling about the front steps she was checking things off her list in her mind: the duplicate jail key – done, the hiding place in the Athenaeum basement – done, springing the prisoner – she'll get it done, one way or another. The harder parts, like getting past the Dobermans, breaking into The Witch Curse Museum, and getting the prisoner to guide her and Kaelyn into that subterranean labyrinth to find Mallory and to root out deeper, darker secrets, she'll have to take in steps. But right now she had to follow up on something that was nagging at her, and she needed Kaelyn's help to do it. And a "no" from the Official Witch wasn't an option.

"I can't believe I let you talk me into this," said Kaelyn. She was sitting in the driver's seat slipping on a gray wig and donning dark glasses. Then she wrapped an old black shawl around her shoulders.

"It's the only way," Siri replied.

"I don't think I can pull this off," Kaelyn returned, looking at herself in the rearview mirror.

"Yes you can," said Siri. "Just stick to the plan."

"Here goes nothing, then," the witch replied.

"Remember," said Siri, keeping down. "Room 102."

"I got it," Kaelyn said, getting out of the car and looking in at Siri. "You owe me."

"Get going!" Siri said, urging the witch with a thrust of her hands.

Kaelyn got into character, and walked up the old granite steps to the school, slowly and slightly bent over. She kept peering over the tops of her sunglasses to make sure no one recognized her. She entered the foyer and went straight to room 102, the school administration office. There, Kaelyn coughed a couple of times and attracted the attention of a young woman behind a desk. The witch spoke in a weak voice announcing she was Constance Nash's aunt and wanted to update her emergency contacts file. The young woman went promptly to the file drawer and withdrew a file with Constance Nash's name printed on a label. She opened it before Kaelyn and withdrew a form that bore the student's name and address: *"Constance Nash, 302 Becket Street."* Kaelyn tipped her sunglasses down upon her nose and made sure she memorized the information. Then she smiled at the young woman.

"Just put your name, address, and telephone number here," the young woman pointed on the form, "and your relation to the student."

"Thank you, my dear," Kaelyn's voice cracked.

As Kaelyn updated the form, she noticed the young woman looking at her curiously. Kaelyn began to get nervous. She bent more and gathered her shawl about her throat.

"So you're Constance's aunt?" The woman inquired, almost skeptically.

"Yes," answered Kaelyn, shakily.

Kaelyn tried hard not to make eye contact with the attendant. The young woman studied Kaelyn's quivering hand and illegible writing.

"Funny," said the young clerk. "I thought Constance was a ward of her uncle, her only living relative."

"You know how families can be," Kaelyn stammered hoarsely. "They never mention the black sheep."

"Would you like to sit down," inquired the young woman, noticing the tremors in the old woman before her, "or have a glass of water?"

"No, my dear," Kaelyn answered. "But you're so kind to ask."

The woman grinned. Kaelyn finished her paperwork, thanked her attendant, and turned away. Kaelyn couldn't get out of the school fast enough. She shimmied across the foyer, hurried down the steps, and dashed across the street. She opened the car door, her hand upon her heart and breathless.

"Did you get it?" Siri asked, shooting up in her seat.

"Got it," Kaelyn gasped. "Three-O-two Becket."

Kaelyn got in, started the car, and pulled away from the curb. About half way down the street she pulled the gray wig off her head and threw it on the dash.

"The things I do for you. I'm glad you're not twins."

Kaelyn turned onto Derby Street on the Salem waterfront. Driving past Derby Wharf with its spacious view of Salem Harbor and the old Custom House, Siri kept her eyes on the cross streets. With her cell phone she searched an on-line street map, but nothing came up under that street number. 302 Becket was a blank and Siri wanted to know why. She watched as they drove down Turner Street, with its famous "House of the Seven Gables," and then down nondescript Carlton Street. Finally they arrived at Becket.

"It's a one way street," Siri said, spotting the red "Do Not Enter" sign. "You had better park here. I'm getting out."

Siri hopped out of the VW and read the house numbers on the south-facing side of Becket Street. Becket was a narrow lane lined with old saltbox type houses and some colonials with gambrel roofs. Kaelyn followed close behind. Siri read off the house numbers as she past them. Siri stood dumbfounded. There was no 302, just a vacant lot between two houses overgrown with weeds and brambles. There were signs of a brick foundation resembling an old cellar hole and a weathered, stone door stoop. Siri waded through the tall, amber grass and discovered some cobblestones shaped in the form of an ancient well. As Siri drew closer she saw that there was a rusted iron disk covering it.

"Help me," Siri called to Kaelyn

Together the two shoved with all their might, but they couldn't get the lid to budge. They combined their efforts again. Finally the iron lid slid off and fell from its stone base upon the ground. Siri stood frozen. Kaelyn didn't know what to say as she stood looking into the well. Inside they saw broken, Puritan-era, slate gravestones piled on a bed of musty brown earth choking the opening. One bore a name Algernon, born 1675, died 1721. The other – Abigail, born 1676, died 1698. *They both bore the surname, NASH!*

# CHAPTER 49: Stake Out

It was amazing how long Siri and Kaelyn watched the back entrance to the Old Salem Jail from the vantage of Kaelyn's parked VW. Siri was dressed in her black stocking cap and fatigues and watching the door through her dad's night-vision binoculars. Kaelyn sat with her driver's seat all the way back. The dashboard clock read 11:30 P.M. and the hour was beginning to tell on the witch. Siri on the other hand was wide-awake, like a kid on Christmas Eve.

"I just don't get it," said Siri. "Why would Constance Nash hide her ancestor's gravestones in a well on purpose? It just doesn't make any sense."

"Heck if I know," Kaelyn remarked. "I'd just like to know where the girl sleeps at night. It's certainly not in that abandoned lot."

"I wish I could have seen her aura," Siri continued. "It might have told us more about her and that drop of blood I found. I bet she even knows where Mallory is."

"Nothing would surprise me at this point," said Kaelyn.

Siri wiped condensation off the passenger side window. Suddenly her eyes widened.

"I think they're leaving!"

"Hooray," Kaelyn yawned.

Kaelyn's VW was parked in the shadow of graveyard trees about fifty yards from the Old Jail's parking lot. Siri brought the binoculars to her eyes again and watched four men walk out the back door of the jail and gather in conversation. Two appeared to be doctors because they wore long, black, woolen overcoats, and carried black, doctor-like cases. They were talking to Detective Scarpetti and Siri's dad.

"Hey, my dad's there," Siri huffed. "He's supposed to be at home."

"And he thinks you're in bed," said Kaelyn. "Boy, does he mind the store."

Siri rolled the window down a crack and snaked out a long boom microphone. Then she slipped a pair of earphones over her black stocking hat, fitting them over her ears.

"Where did that all come from?" Kaelyn asked, in surprise.

"Quiet," said Siri, adjusting the dials to a little red control box. "I got this for my birthday two years ago. It really works!"

"Did you get a decoder ring and bubble gum with it?"

"Shhhh!"

Suddenly a crackle of voices coming in over the receiver caused Kaelyn to perk up. They were faint, but audible. Siri and Kaelyn listened breathlessly.

"We'll begin at eight in the morning," said one of the doctor types. "The subject must fast until then. No food. No water, the usual pre-general anesthesia protocol."

"The procedure will take most of the day," spoke the other doctor type. "While he's sedated we'll obtain tissue and DNA samples, perform MRI and CT scans, we'll also assess brain pattern activity and so on. A police escort will only attract attention, so will an ambulance. Can you provide an unmarked van for transport to our facility?"

"That can be arranged," Scarpetti spoke.

"They're gonna dissect him," whispered Siri.

"Don't exaggerate," Kaelyn replied. "It sounds like they just want to examine him. I think."

"Whatever they're planning," said Siri, adjusting her earphones, "I don't like it. And I don't like my dad being involved."

She watched the four men part company and leave in separate cars, their taillights disappearing out of the dimly lit parking lot. Collin left in Scarpetti's sedan, which turned in the direction of Wicks End. Siri reached for the door handle.

"We have to work fast."

"We're already guilty of breaking and entering," Kaelyn remarked. "What else do we add to our rap sheet?"

Siri held up the grayish clone of SJ 10501 DO NOT DUPLICATE. "It's time to aid and abet."

## CHAPTER 50: Jail Break

Siri remembered the security office was to the right. She quietly inserted the key into the lock and gave it a turn. The bolt unlocked. Siri opened the door a crack and peered inside. She could see Officer Dwight talking on the phone through an open door, his back towards them. There was no time to lose. Siri tiptoed inside and beckoned Kaelyn to follow. Once in the hall they crept downstairs. Siri could see the corridor of the sub-cellar ahead of her illumined by a row of naked ceiling lights. This was familiar territory for Siri, but Kaelyn looked around bewildered. Dark, vacant jail cells lined either side of the corridor. The witch had never been in a jail before and for a moment imagined how horrible imprisonment must have been for those accused of witchcraft back in 1692. She also began to wonder if they were doing the right thing. Finally, Siri located the cell containing the jail's sole prisoner. He was seated on a bench, head bowed, his black duster coat enveloping him.

"Hey," Siri whispered. "It's me again."

The imprisoned figure rose to his feet. Kaelyn scrutinized the inmate standing in the shadows, his pale face framed by two shoulder-length sheets of jet-black hair. She swallowed nervously.

"You're sure he's not dangerous?" the witch whispered.

The prisoner advanced towards the bars, his eyes, like embers, burning with light.

"Can you not see my life-field?" the inmate whispered back, "you, with your inner sight?"

Kaelyn was caught off guard by the prisoner's telling remark. But he was right. She could see waving bands of light, greenish in color, much like the Aurora, shimmering all around the prisoner's frame. The color had a duel significance of dedication and secretiveness, which still left the witch in some doubt. She then looked to the lock on the cell door. It was old fashioned and rusty.

"How are you going to open it?" Kaelyn asked Siri.

Siri reached into her jacket and produced a glass vial containing a clear liquid.

"I'm going to use this."

"What's that?" the witch inquired with alarm. "Not nitro, I hope!"

"Hydrochloric acid," Siri answered. "I borrowed it from our chemistry lab."

Siri unsealed the vial and extracted several drops with a glass syringe. She carefully placed the tip of the syringe over the door lock and let the drops flow into the keyhole. It began to smoke immediately.

"What's happening?" Kaelyn asked.

"Watch," Siri replied.

The prisoner stepped back from the smoking bars. In a matter of seconds the antiquated mechanisms of the lock corroded into uselessness. The cell door opened. Siri felt a tinge of apprehension as she stood before the inmate with no bars between them.

"You can trust us," Siri said, as reassuringly as she could. "We're going to take you someplace safe."

Mister Whispers stepped out of the cell. For a moment he assessed Siri with a look of curiosity and wonder.

"How do you know I won't just escape?" he asked.

"I just know, that's all," Siri answered.

"Let's go," Kaelyn whispered.

"Come." Siri said to the inmate. Before she realized it, Siri had taken Mister Whispers by the hand and led him up the stairs into the frigid night, and as she did, she felt that she had entered a new and even stranger world.

# CHAPTER 51: The Hidden Room

Dobbs was snoozing in a back room at the Salem Athenaeum when a rap at the rear door roused him from his chair. He didn't mean to nod off, but his favorite author, Cotton Mather, whose Puritanical oaths and maledictions did much to send many an accused witch to the gallows, could numb any reader into insensibility.

"What?" Dobbs said, springing up. "Who's there?"

The rap sounded again. Dobbs checked a clock on the wall and saw that it was the appointed hour. He recalled his midnight bargain, and as he made his way into a narrow hall past old filing cabinets and a bulky old typewriter toward the back door, he regretted the agreement. He put his ear to the door first and whispered.

"Who is it?"

"It's me, Siri," said a voice from the other side. "Open up."

Dobbs hastily unfastened two chain locks and a dead bolt and cracked open the door. He saw Siri's blue eye and brown eye twinkling back at him in the faint hall light. He then opened the door all the way and saw Kaelyn in her cloak. In between was something tall and dark with a pale face covered in a black, scarf-like wrap. But it was the eyes of the stranger that arrested Dobbs, for they glared at him like two drops of fire. He stepped back and allowed them in, his mouth open in bewilderment.

"This is Mister Dobbs," Siri told her dark companion. "You can trust him too."

Dobbs nodded and swallowed nervously. His Adam's apple bobbed up and down like a balloon trying to land.

"Mister Dobbs," Mister Whispers returned, brushing passed the librarian.

Dobbs closed the door. He took the precaution to quickly set the chain locks and turn the dead bolt. Despite the coldness of the night, he wiped perspiration from his forehead with a handkerchief he pulled from the back pocket of his trousers. Dobbs led Siri, Kaelyn, and his mysterious guest down a flight of creaky stairs. Then he guided them through a labyrinth of basement bookstacks. He kept looking back at the dark stranger in their midst, fighting the urge to run for the hills.

"It's just over here," said Dobbs, stopping before a tall bookcase, which he swung ajar with ease. His motion revealed a hidden room, small, but quite cozy and equipped with a cot, table, chair, and a paraffin lamp, which Dobbs struck a match to light.

"I have it all ready. He'll be quite comfortable."

The stranger sat down before the lamp, absorbed by its luster. He pulled the scarf from his face allowing its folds to fall over the shoulders of his long, black coat. Siri, Kaelyn, and Dobbs gathered around the table to gain a better view of their strange companion. Siri studied Mister Whispers' face now that he had plainly revealed it. True, there was enough of the unusual that would have made him an outcast, but it was far from ugly. The pale, youthful features possessed a strong brow ridge and sharply angled cheekbones, and the mouth was sensitively molded. But it was the eyes that captivated Siri, the eyes with their strange, reflective quality as they surveyed the room and its occupants.

"Now that you see who is in your midst, do you still wish to harbor me?" Mister Whispers spoke, shifting his striking eyes to each of his hosts, especially Siri.

Siri moved toward Mister Whispers, so that she was just a few feet away.

"What's your name?"

Mister Whispers hesitated. Then he spoke.

"Ash," he replied, hoarsely. "I am called Ash. Is it not fitting? Look upon me. What you see before you is a remnant – a cinder – an ash."

Siri, Kaelyn, and Dobbs glanced at each other. Siri looked at the time on her cell phone. It was well past midnight and she knew she would have a lot of explaining to do. Kaelyn needed to get her home, but Siri felt compelled to spend more time with Ash. There was a lot she had to find out. A faint cry of a police siren hurrying past from outside told her that things were cooking at the old jail.

"Are you hungry, Ash?" Siri asked.

Ash shook his head no. He looked at Siri and whispered.

"You risked much bringing me here. For that I thank you. But I must leave now, and with the Osiris Keys. Please give them to me."

"I can't," Siri replied. "I need them."

"You don't know what you possess," Ash said.

"I have a rough idea," Siri returned.

"Stay out of all this," Ash advised.

"It's too late for that now," Siri said. "I need to find Mallory. Now I know you were with her on the day she disappeared. Please tell me what happened to her. I also want to know about the parchment and why it's so important."

Ash stared at Siri, his eyes shimmering like sunlight on water. She could see him struggling with his answer. Suddenly Ash reached out a pale hand and clutched Siri by the chin, rising as he did so. Kaelyn and Dobbs drew closer out of alarm, but Siri remained still.

"I will not haggle with you like a seller of melons in a market stall," Ash gritted. "I mean to leave, and with the Osiris Keys."

"You're not going anywhere," Siri said, lifting Ash's hand from her face. She gazed into Ash's eyes. "The police will only capture you again. They're looking for you right now. Hear them? Hear their sirens? Like it or not you have to trust me. We need to help each other. Now tell me what I want to know."

Ash ground his jaw. He took a deep breath and then exhaled. He veered his opalescent eyes towards Kaelyn and Dobbs. He then turned to Siri and slowly closed the gap between them, wrinkling his brow as he did so. Siri took a deep breath too and stared into Ash's pupils, which were like two phosphorescent green pools. Maybe it was the late hour telling on Siri, or it might have been that the adrenaline rush, which had driven her most of the night, had worn off, but she felt weightless, like she was going to float away. Then she closed her eyes and opened them. Finally, her eyes rolled up and she collapsed backwards. Ash was quick to grab Siri and hold her on her feet. He regarded her limp form as she lay back in his arms, like she was melting.

"What have you done to her?" Kaelyn asked in alarm. She took Siri and seated her in the chair.

"She is unharmed," Ash answered.

"You did something to her," Kaelyn insisted, studying Siri's face.

"She now has the answers she seeks," Ash said.

Siri stirred as her head lay on the table. Then she lifted it as though she was just waking up from a dream. She looked at Dobbs across from her, Kaelyn standing by her side, and finally Ash, gazing at her deeply from the wall.

"Did I pass out?" Siri asked.

"Are you alright?" Kaelyn pressed.

"Yes," answered Siri. "I think so."

"You're exhausted, dear," said Kaelyn, helping Siri to her feet. "It's time I got you home."

Siri placed a hand on her forehead and gazed over at Ash standing in the glow of the paraffin lamp. The look they shared at that moment was like a tranquil sunrise and a gaze into the caldera of a lava-belching volcano. Then she allowed Kaelyn to lead her up the stairs.

Dobbs appeared hesitant to remain alone with his singular guest. From the look on his face one would have thought he was being marooned on a desert island. He turned towards Ash standing silently before him, regarding him intently, and then smiled.

"I'll put on a pot of coffee. Are you percolated or drip?"

# CHAPTER 52: The Nightmare

Collin pulled up to the house just as Siri was putting the key in the door with Kaelyn at her side. It was 1:15 A.M.

"What's going on here?" Collin asked, coming up the steps. "Sprout, what are you doing out? Why aren't you in bed?"

Siri opened the front door and looked back at her dad.

"Not now, dad," she pleaded.

"We were at my place," Kaelyn remarked, as she walked Siri inside. "We lost track of time."

"Lost track of time?" Collin returned, raising his voice. "She shouldn't have been out in the first place."

Siri went straight upstairs. She could hear her dad and Kaelyn having something like an argument on the front porch, but she couldn't bother with it now. Siri just wanted to go to sleep. She opened her bedroom door, closed it behind herself, and went to sleep.

An hourglass floated in the darkness. It turned over and over, but the fine, white sand inside spilled upwards instead of downwards. Siri could see the sand poring in reverse. It came closer and closer until it was right before her eyes. She threw her arm over her face, and then threw it down again on her blanket. She tossed in her sleep, flinging her head left and right and left again. The flowing sands of time were running backward, never stopping, until the top bulb of the hourglass filled and shattered, causing sand to pour out everywhere. Siri, by the alchemy of her dreams, stepped onto it.

The sand was hot. The glaring sun above it was the cause. Siri had to shield her eyes it was so bright. In the distance she could see a great pyramid-shaped hill in the distance. It was Al-Qurn, dominating the dusty, desert valley. Siri had a good idea where she was – Egypt, more specifically – the Valley of the Kings.

All around her dark-skinned native diggers in linen headdresses and long, white, dirty robes were hustling about, rushing this way and that, some hauling rickety wooden carts laden with bundles of supplies. Others were carrying clay water jugs on their heads. A hand-cranked Victrola on a table by a pile of quarried stone squawked a tinny musical number by Cole Porter, but was hardly discernable, for a babble of excitement seemed to electrify the place.

Nothing was standing still or keeping quiet, except Siri and Al-Qurn. Something important seemed to be happening. A European man sporting a trim mustache and dressed in a loose shirt and dark trousers hurried past. He was wearing a plain hat, which he threw down from his head in excitement as he ran while being led by a barefoot boy in a ragged striped robe and turban. Siri could hear the gasps of the man as he hastened in the heat. He appeared desperate.

The man followed the boy to a knot of native diggers and pushed past them, his eager eyes following the boy's pointing finger. The man got down on his knees and used his hand for a brush. His effort revealed a carved step, a single stone step buried for eons, and a wipe of a hand confirmed it. Siri knew when and where she was from her history class: November 4th, 1922. The man was Englishman Howard Carter. And he had just discovered the tomb of the boy king, Tutankhamun.

Siri was used to having vivid dreams, but nothing like this. It seemed so real, she felt like she was really there. She breathed the oppressive arid air and felt the burning sun on her back. Even the chalky grit that seemed to lay over everything in the valley was palpable. It was on her clothes and skin and she coughed it out too. Siri knew that Ash had done something to make this dream seem so real. It was like she was put on an amusement ride, and could do nothing but wait for it to stop.

Suddenly the sand beneath her feet began to swirl in a vortex and rise from the ground, enveloping her like a dust devil. Siri covered her eyes with her hands, and when she uncovered them, she was amazed at what she saw. She found herself standing in a vault of cool limestone. It was dark, but not so dark that she couldn't see. A glare of work lights up ahead had shed stray beams her way. She could hear the echo of a hammer and a chisel, and muted voices.

Siri walked toward the voices while feeling the cool, smooth, limestone wall. When her fingertips felt ridges she stopped and examined them.

Finely incised hieroglyphics ran the length of the wall from ceiling to floor, row upon row. Siri recognized the symbols of jackal-headed Anubis and Sobek, the crocodile god. She saw images of scarabs and papyrus reeds, lotus flowers and funeral boats.

Siri finally entered the chamber and saw two men crouching over a shimmering sarcophagus all sheathed in gold, its one-ton lid suspended in mid-air by a network of ropes and pulleys. Siri drew nearer, passing a great marble statue of the hawk-headed god, Horus, crowned with the Aten disk representing the sun.

The two men didn't notice her though she was plainly visible under the glare of work lights. One was Howard Carter, the famous archaeologist, the other – Alex Cedric! As Siri stepped closer, she looked into the sarcophagus. Within the extravagant coffin lay another coffin, also of molded gold. The great receptacle was inlaid with jasper, lapis and turquoise, and bore the recumbent image of the dead king, Tutankhamun – his arms crossed upon his chest, his golden hands holding the striped crook and flail, his eyes open patiently awaiting eternity. It was the treasure of the ages, finally revealed.

Suddenly Carter excused himself and left Cedric alone in the chamber. Cedric appeared to take advantage of the opportunity. He picked up a small, alabaster box tucked in a corner and yet to be tagged and catalogued. He opened it and removed two silver amulets that Siri immediately recognized. They were the Osiris Keys. Together with the amulets, Cedric also removed a scroll of crisp papyrus, which was set between them. Siri watched the archivist quickly apply the amulets to matching motifs at the base of the Horus statue which stood against the wall. Immediately there was a *click* and a hidden compartment budged ajar. Cedric aimed a pocket lamp inside it and grinned at the secret drawer he discovered. At the sound of approaching footsteps, Cedric tucked the scroll into the alabaster box and placed it into the aperture. He then pressed the hidden compartment shut so that not a seam showed. Cedric quickly pocketed the amulets and composed himself upon the return of his fellow archeologist, assuming the same, studious expression over the coffin as when Howard Carter first left him.

"You stole them!" Siri said loudly, her voice echoing in the ancient vault. "You stole the Osiris Keys!"

But neither Carter nor Cedric could hear her. Siri rushed over to the statue and felt all over the base. She pushed and pulled, but the hidden draw wouldn't open.

"And the secret scroll!" Siri continued. "You hid that in this statue!"

Siri wanted to snatch the Osiris Keys from Cedric's pocket and test how much of the vision was a dream. How the man was able to be there in 1922 and in Siri's own time, and in such vim and vigor, as if he defied the ravages of age, was a mystery. Siri looked about her. Ebony statues of pharaoh's soldiers holding spears glared at her out of the murk. Suddenly Siri found herself embraced by their elongating shadows, as if by some trick of the light they were coming to life.

Siri ran blindly through the darkness. She wanted to wake up and find herself snug and warm in her bed. Suddenly out of the gloom, rooms began to appear on either side of her. Siri turned from one to the other. These weren't Egyptian tombs and galleries. They were great recesses, lighting up one after the other and then growing dark again. They were living displays like bizarre pantomimes in a nightmare theater. Siri couldn't understand how they fitted into recent events. It all seemed so important, like pieces to a puzzle falling into place one at a time.

Siri had no time to think. She saw a laboratory where glass beakers bubbled and strange machines winked in dark corners. Suddenly, the shadowy form of a woman emerged wearing the trim whites and hair cap of a clinical nurse. Siri immediately recognized her sauntering walk. It was Mallory! She was carrying a rack of test tubes over to a gurney whose unconscious occupant was strapped down. Siri recognized that shadowy figure too. It was Christian Fletcher. And standing over him was a masked and gloved surgeon who was about to inject a syringe full of green liquid into his arm.

"Mallory!" Siri shouted as her friend passed within feet of her, but Siri's words had no effect on Mallory, who just stood watching the delicate procedure.

"Mallory, can you hear me?" Siri spoke again, trying to be heard. "It's me, Siri!"

Siri tried to reach out and touch Mallory's shoulder, but the gallery faded into oblivion and in its place another chamber appeared. There, within, Siri saw a slender girl dressed in Puritan homespun ringing a bell-pull at the base of a stone tower. Siri could have sworn it was Constance Nash standing in the murk. Then, as the gallery melted into darkness, another came into light and a bearded man with spectacles appeared. He stood in the gloom before an upright glass sarcophagus that held something sleeping – or dead. Then Siri saw two silvery amulets shaped like heavily-mascaraed eyes staring at her in the dark, and beyond them was something towering and menacing, which reached out stiffly towards her with bandaged arms and fingers as if it would take hold of her and crush her!

Siri woke up like a shot to the sun shining in her eyes. She looked at her bedside clock. It was 9:00 A.M. She was drenched in sweat and her pajamas could practically be wrung out. When she remembered it was Saturday she was relieved, but when she remembered it was also Halloween morning, she threw her bed covers to the side and hurried to take a shower. There was no time to waste. She had to see Ash. Siri could smell ham and eggs cooking in the kitchen as she came down the stairs rubbing her wet hair with a towel. She leaned over the banister and saw her dad in the kitchen. Siri could remember him making breakfast for her only twice before. The first time was when he discovered that she was steaming open and reading his mail, and the second time was when he found out that she had not only steamed open his mail and read it, but answered it on his behalf.

Siri sat down at the table and took a bite of toast as Collin sat opposite her. She smiled at him, enjoying her hot breakfast. Collin smiled back. Then he put his key ring on the table. Collin took particular care to make sure key SJ 10501 DO NOT DUPLICATE stood out. Siri stopped smiling.

# CHAPTER 53: Shadowy Confrontation

Kaelyn was already standing outside the Salem Athenaeum waiting for Collin and Siri to show up, driven by Scarpetti. Siri had never ridden in a police car before. She sat in the back of Scarpetti's black, unmarked sedan behind the shotgun rack. There was no siren and no handcuffs. Siri could see Kaelyn standing in the cold morning air, breath puffing from her lips. She was wearing her formal purple vestments under a sable hooded cloak. Siri could tell the witch was nervous. Collin sat in the passenger seat beside Scarpetti. Siri had told him everything. She didn't mean to at first, but when confronted with the key to the old jail, she had no choice. For the moment the detective was going to play the maverick and give Siri a day in his court, Kaelyn and Dobbs too. When Siri saw Emma and Bernie pull up in Emma's pick-up and get out with Simon, Bernie's dog, bounding onto the sidewalk, she thought Scarpetti was going to blow his cork, but interesting enough, the detective merely muttered "Namaste," and pulled his car against the curb.

"What's going on?" Emma asked, walking up to Collin.

"You'll see," Collin answered.

"I hope this won't take long," Bernie said. "We're hosting a big conference tonight."

"You have time for this," Scarpetti remarked.

He knocked on the back door of the athenaeum. All waited with bated breath as the door creaked open a crack. In the space a sheepish face appeared. It was Dobbs.

"Salem Police," said Scarpetti. "Please open the door."

Dobbs looked to all the faces confronting him on the porch. When he saw Siri's he gazed at her quizzically. She just shrugged.

"I hear you have a roommate," Scarpetti quipped. "Introduce me."

Dobbs guided his troop of visitors downstairs into the archives. He could feel Scarpetti walking close behind, almost breathing down his neck. Once or twice Siri looked at Dobbs and Dobbs looked back at Siri. He led them down a main aisle of book stacks, then around the corner past some old microfilm machines. When Dobbs arrived at a wall of empty bookshelves, he turned meekly to Scarpetti, practically bumping into him.

"Perhaps I should announce you," he stammered.

"Just open it," ordered Scarpetti, pointing to the wall.

Dobbs swallowed and pulled open the bookshelf that doubled for a secret door.

"This was built during Prohibition," Dobbs said. "Back then the library doubled as a speak-easy."

"Never mind the history lesson," Scarpetti said. "Open it up."

Dobbs swung the hatch open.

"Hey, that's cool!" Bernie exclaimed.

Inside the only items were: a lit paraffin lamp, a half loaf of French bread, and two empty mugs. Cotton Mather's moldy tome was open on one side of the table along with several scraps of paper with notes scribbled in pencil.

"Well, Mr. Dobbs," said Scarpetti, as everyone entered the room. "It seems your guest isn't here."

"I can't understand it," Dobbs said. "He was here a moment ago."

"I've seen enough," Scarpetti said, clearly annoyed. "You're all going down to the station house with me where some formal charges will be awaiting you – aiding and abetting a felon for starters."

Siri was speechless. Suddenly the flame of the paraffin lamp on the table began to flicker and dim. For a moment everyone stood silent watching the quivering flame reduce itself, expanding the darkness, until it became nothing more than a glowing red wick in a void. Suddenly a rush of wind filled the tiny room, scattering notepapers like leaves in a November gale. All at once the turbulent atmosphere filled with the chatter of voices, all talking at once, until in the gibberish, distinct voices stood out, some modern, others in foregone accents of America's colonial age.

*"Start at twelve, turn twice passed three, then back to nine, to open thee,"* a woman's voice rang out, assailing their ears.

Then the voice of a man called out in the darkness.

*"Molly! Why must we be apart? Why must we be forsaken?"*

Suddenly the voices of two men in hot argument rang out, but they didn't belong to any of the men in the room.

*"No snake on Earth lies lower than you, John Pitcher!"*

*"And you have looked in wonder at your last dawn!"*

Suddenly what seemed to be the clanging of swords rang out. The tolling of clashing blades shrilled in Siri's ears. She gasped and hugged Kaelyn. Collin stepped forward to relight the lamp, but a cold, pale hand knocked the match from him.

Two twinkling green specks appeared in the darkness, one beside the other, looking down from above the region of the ceiling. They blinked and glimmered upon each of the room's occupants. From their uncanny position above, it seemed the owner possessed a power to defy gravity. The eyes gradually descended.

A chair groaned with the weight of someone taking a seat. Scarpetti produced a pocket light and flashed it across the room. The ray revealed Ash standing in the doorway, draped in his long coat, composed like a statue. The light also shown on Dobbs seated back in a chair, in a total faint.

"Put that away," Ash spoke, turning his face from the beam and stepping into the chamber. "I am not accustomed to the light." Ash lifted a gray-white hand to shield his pale face, his thin fingers spread like claws.

"Who are you?" Scarpetti pressed, maintaining the beam.

"The light," Ash repeated, turning his back to the detective. Ash turned left and right, desperately seeking the anonymity of the shadows, but the beam held steady on him. "Turn off that beastly light!"

"Tell me you who are." Scarpetti said, in a commanding tone.

"My name is of no consequence," Ash replied, his face half turned toward the detective as his back absorbed the brunt of the beam. "But if I must have a name you may call me wanderer, castaway, or better yet, star with no sky. That is who I am."

"Not exactly Shakespeare," Scarpetti said.

"His name is Ash," Siri declared.

The detective looked at Siri. He snapped off his flashlight and struck a match, lighting the paraffin lamp. The room warmed and brightened with its expanding glow. Ash turned and faced his visitors with his dazzling eyes. He looked at Scarpetti who had his hand on his gun.

"You need no weapon here," Ash said. "I could have fled, and yet, here I stand amongst you. Is that testament enough of my good will?"

Scarpetti let go of his weapon. He looked at the fugitive, and then the others, and scratched his bald head.

"Okay," said the detective. "I'm listening. Now if it's not too much trouble, will someone please tell me what in blazes is going on?"

Siri presented herself squarely before the detective.

"Detective Scarpetti," she began. "Ash is only a small part of your problem right now. Dent is the one you should be concentrating on. Like I told you before, I saw him kidnap Alex Cedric. And I believe he's behind all your missing persons too, not to mention the stolen mummies."

"That's fine bold talk, young lady," Scarpetti said, sizing Siri up. "But I can't arrest Dent without proof. A public defender would have him out in no time."

"I can get you proof," Siri said.

Scarpetti smirked. "What do you have in mind?"

Siri slunk back beside Ash and smiled at the outlandish scheme she was about to hatch. Kaelyn, Emma, Bernie and Dobbs all looked at each other and then at Siri. They circled around her, and Collin and Scarpetti too. Then Siri told them her plan…

# CHAPTER 54: A Strange Incident

Amy and Dody were amazed at the celebrity-like status of some of the newest arrivals to the Black Ram Inn that afternoon. Amy lifted a curtain in the parlor and peered out at the assortment of gleaming limousines lining up on Hardy Street. She was excited to see a squad of velvet-jacketed valets, hired by Dent, bustling back and forth. The two women wondered how on earth they were all going to fit on the tiny street, never mind in the parking lot. It had been a brilliant, autumn afternoon. In a few hours it would be Halloween night, and the weather was perfect for trick-or-treaters.

Several of Dent's tuxedoed minions greeted the new arrivals as they strolled into the main hall. Some guests entered alone, while others walked arm-in-arm with their partners. Most were attired in black tie or in elegant gowns bedecked with jewelry and other accessories. They seemed to represent every culture on the planet, with some even dressed in the colorful regalia of their native countries. A maitre d' hired for the occasion conducted the flow of attendees down a flight of stairs.

Amy pulled herself away from the window only to be confronted by a tall man with a narrow mustache speaking with an Austrian accent.

"Guten Nacht!" he uttered with a half civil nod.

"Oh, hello," Amy said, a little surprised by his sudden presence. "Can I help you?"

"May I see?"

The Austrian gestured to a ceramic haunted house model complete with a domed observatory and a mad scientist's laboratory proudly displayed on a side table. His attempt at English was labored, as if he was chewing the words. He then proceeded to remove a quaint, handcrafted ornament of a black cat arching its back from atop a miniature gabled roof. He curiously regarded it as he turned it about in his hands

"I made it myself," Amy added. "It's porcelain."

The guest smiled and took care to insert the figure into the laboratory of the mad scientist. He promptly wheeled about and followed the other guests downstairs. Curious to see why the man didn't return the figure to the roof, Amy stood before the display and peered over her bifocals into the little laboratory. Suddenly her lighthearted expression turned to dismay. A strange alteration had occurred. Instead of the whimsical feline she created, Amy looked upon a figurine of a cat-headed human body, the cat face subtly altered in the image of Dent, head-dressed and robed like a pharaoh and seated upon a golden throne. Amy removed the figurine and hid it in her apron pocket when she saw her sister hang up the phone and leave the front desk and approach her.

"That was Bernie," Dody said, in a low voice. "He said to go on without him and that he and Emma will show up later."

"They're probably quarreling again." Amy said.

One of Dent's tuxedoed henchmen cocked his head in her direction from his station in the hallway.

"Something very strange is going on," whispered Dody.

Amy placed her hand in her apron pocket.

"You can say that again."

# CHAPTER 55: All Hallows' Eve

Siri sat in the back of Scarpetti's unmarked sedan on the corner of Derby and Hardy Street. She was watching all the cars filing down the avenue and pulling up to the Black Ram Inn. Several trick-or-treaters accompanied by their parents walked by the detective's car. Siri eyed them enviously as they rang the doorbell of a nearby house.

"I ought to have my head examined," Scarpetti muttered, watching all the cars heading for the inn. "That scarecrow we left back at the library belongs in a jail cell, not waiting for us to return from a wild goose chase. I don't know any more about him now than I did at the time of his arrest, except that he's probably a skilled magician. There better be something to this Dent fellow or Commissioner Brooks will have my..."

"Here's Emma and Bernie," interrupted Siri, pointing from the back.

"Good, they're on time," mumbled Scarpetti, glancing at his watch.

It was 5:00 P.M. Emma and Bernie drove down Hardy Street in Emma's pick-up and turned into the inn's driveway. Scarpetti glanced at his watch again. Collin did the same. Siri checked the time on her cell phone and watched as more trick-or-treaters strolled past on the narrow lane. Halloween was here and tonight she was going to miss it. Her big plan was about to go into full swing and her timing had to be exact. Scarpetti and her dad didn't like it one bit. The plan she concocted was dangerous, but it was the only way to obtain evidence against Dent. The spotlight was on her.

"Ten past five," Siri said, looking to her watch. "It's time."

"I'm calling it off," Collin said, turning in his seat.

"No way, dad!" Siri exclaimed. "We've been through all this. I'm going!"

Siri opened her jacket and revealed a small transmitter duct-taped to her waist and a thin wire running up her side.

"Plus I'm all wired up. You'll know if I need help."

"Remember to record everything on video," said Scarpetti. "And shoot straight. We'll need that footage for evidence. Good luck."

Siri nodded and hurriedly kissed Collin on the cheek and left the car. He watched her dash down an alley between two houses, climb a chain link fence, and disappear from view.

"That kid of yours sure has guts," Scarpetti said, turning to Collin.

"That's what worries me," Collin returned.

# CHAPTER 56: The Conclave

The Black Ram's function hall was licensed to accommodate one hundred and fifty people and on Halloween night it was at full capacity. During colonial days, the rum cellar was used for storing gunpowder, some of which was used to fight the redcoats in Lexington and Concord. The British Colonel, Leslie, once dared to invade Salem to seek out the secreted powder stores, but was stopped without a shot fired by defiant colonials who barred his passage across the North Bridge that spanned the Salem River. A portrait commemorating "Leslie's Retreat" hung over the entrance of the function hall, which was garlanded with rusty autumn leaves and acorns.

The room hummed with conversation passing between guests. Finally the last arrivals filed into the recess and found their seats, and the room's large double doors were swung closed by two sallow-faced men who stood outside the chamber. The dull roar died to a murmur and then to complete silence.

Paneled in white pine the function room exuded a cozy ambience. The lighting, provided by electrical fixtures in the shapes of candlesticks, were set to their lowest setting. All guests faced a small rostrum and podium. A figure emerged from an alcove. He was robed and head-dressed like a royal pharaoh of old. He advanced in stately steps in sandaled feet and looked upon his audience with stern eyes emboldened with black mascara. His face was cleanly shaven except for a protuberant beard meshed in golden thread, and he held the golden crook and flail folded across his chest. Then, with artful swiftness, the great lord of Egypt peeled the beard from his face to an eruption of applause. Dent shed the folds of his pharaonic attire and flung it into the wings. He presented himself open-armed to the assemblage with all the ego and eccentricity of a rock star. The white of his Neru suit was humble compared to the rich attire of those seated around him. Dent motioned for silence and stood before the podium.

Watching the proceeding, Siri looked down from above behind the grill of a ceiling air duct. Dent's men were everywhere. The only way into the inn was through the old coal chute which Bernie unlocked at precisely 5:20 P.M. according to the plan. Security was very tight, so he had to fake a problem with the thermostat to get into the basement. Siri had to make a mad dash through some holly bushes to get to the chute, but she made it undetected. Once down the chute, Siri followed Bernie's map of the cellar to the air vents. The main air exchanger was new and made of light aluminum. One bang against it and it would sound like a tin drum through the entire building. Siri opened the filter system and slithered through the network of ducts, following Bernie's map with her penlight. There was no time to breathe relief now. She took out her video camera and got ready to work. Dent's voice seeped up from below, clear and loud.

"Welcome to Salem, Massachusetts" announced Dent, his voice unaided by amplification. "I hope you're all feeling like Egyptian kings and queens this evening. Now I know most of you have come a long way and could probably eat a camel. So let the banquet begin! There'll be time for speeches later. You know, we are getting better at this occult technique of astral-physical projection. Here we are altogether hailing from every part of the globe and not one of us had to bother with a plane ticket! A couple of hundred years ago and these provincials would have burned us at the stake as, should I say it, witches! There's nothing that our minds linked in one communal chant can't accomplish. After we work out some bugs, I think next year we should hold our conference on the French Riviera. What do you say to that?"

"Here! Here!" replied a chorus of voices amid thunderous applause!

Siri watched through her viewfinder as the assembly continued with their enthusiastic applause. She was growing uncomfortable in the tight confines of the duct. She shifted a little to keep the blood circulating while aiming the lens through the grill.

Suddenly the maitre d' entered from a side room ahead of a troupe of caterers wheeling carts bearing oversized, covered platters and great carafes of wine. A troupe of female dancers wearing golden headbands and draped in flowing white robes, with gold waist sashes, skipped and leaped to the playing of flutes and cymbals, accompanied by fire-eaters and jugglers.

Strains once heard in the royal courts of the upper Nile reverberated through the great room as caterers set down platters and uncovered their steaming dishes. The platters were the finest examples of weird, culinary cuisine – each one representing a sign of the Egyptian Zodiac. Siri couldn't believe some of the dishes, like the whole roasted boar with King Khafra's head substituted for its own, molded in beeswax. There were also heaping plates of smoked ram's tongue, deep-fried scorpions, and lotus flowers stuffed with lamb's eyes. The centerpiece of the platter was a clod of green sod surmounted by a large honeycomb, dripping with honey, and tenanted by unborn drones. Table settings, napkins and eating utensils were conspicuously missing from the wretched affair. The lack of implements posed no obstacle to the banqueters who commenced to eat with their fingers and drink straight from the carafes never minding the spills and stains on their clothing as if all was routine. A blend of strange aromas wafted through the chamber. Dent walked among the guests with a carafe of wassail and sampled the various dishes. At one station a regally dressed woman popped a lamb's eye into her mouth. Siri cringed. She withdrew her cell phone and typed a quick text message.

"IN DUCT. EXECUTING PLAN. KEEP U POSTED."

Siri hit the send button and blew a lock of hair from her eyes. In two seconds she got a return message, which she knew was from her dad.

"B K-FUL!!!"

Siri smiled, tucked her phone away, and continued recording. She watched through the little viewfinder.

Dent was true to form – a master showman. He resumed his place on the platform. With a wave of his hand he drew the attention of his audience to a partition off to the side of the stage. The curtain parted revealing a man seated in a chair – his hands bound behind him, his head covered by a black sack.

"Ladies and gentleman," Dent said. "If I may interrupt you for a moment, I'd like to introduce you to someone who shares our passion for antiquities, as well as our love of ancient Egypt. In the past he was a trusted colleague and friend, letting nothing hinder his own acquisition of strange and rare archaeological finds. I'm sure he would like nothing more than to be spelunking in some Neolithic cave or delving into a long-forgotten desert tomb. Today you can see he's a little tied up at the moment, but I'm sure he can spare some time for us. Let's find out, shall we?"

Dent took three steps over to the seated figure, and in a stroke, pulled the sack off his head. Siri, her eyes fixed to the viewfinder, stifled a gasp. It was Alex Cedric, gagged with a kerchief, his head tilted to one side, his spectacles barely clinging to his nose. He appeared dazed, and blinked rapidly as his eyes adjusted to light again. Dent pulled the gag off Cedric's mouth.

"What's going on here, Dent?" Cedric gasped. He looked out on all the faces observing him. "And who are all these people? I demand you release me at once or you'll wreak the consequences!"

"Now one demand at a time," Dent replied, matter-of-factly. "You're here as my guest, of sorts. I'm about to conduct a little experiment and I value the observations of a colleague. These wonderful people you see here before you are my followers. They see the world as I see it, and want the same thing I want. What's this here?"

Dent reached into Cedric's breast pocket and withdrew a brownish slip of paper that was half protruding. He unfurled it and held it up to the light.

"Give that back, Dent!" Cedric huffed.

"Hold your tongue," Dent said, reading the scrawled writing to himself. Siri zoomed in on the paper Dent held and her jaw dropped. It was the parchment she had been searching for. How Cedric got a hold of it she could only wonder. Ash, for some reason or another, had given it to him. It was the only conclusion Siri could draw. Siri watched the viewfinder intently and bit into her lower lip.

"You've taken something that belongs to me," Dent said to Cedric. "It's only fair that I take something from you. Tell me where the Osiris Keys are and I will give you back your precious paper, whatever it is."

"I told you before," Cedric said, struggling against his bonds, "I never took the one from you. The other key is no longer in my possession."

"Then whose possession are they in?" Dent smirked.

"I don't know," Cedric replied, curtly.

"Come now, Alex," Dent said. "You're a man after my own heart. You know the value of those keys. You wouldn't lose them any more than you would lose your own head. To whom did you pass them?"

Cedric remained stubbornly mute. Dent smiled and studied the parchment.

"This looks like a recipe for fruitcake," Dent quipped. "Tell me, what's so important about this list of ingredients?"

"It's of no value," Cedric stated.

"It must have some importance to warrant your outburst," Dent said. "Why won't you share it with us all?"

"The Devil take you and your followers, Dent," Cedric snapped.

Dent grinned and turned to his audience.

"Not for some considerable time, I trust," he said to a room that replied with a dull roar of courteous laughs and chuckles.

Dent returned his attention to the parchment clutched in his right hand.

"This certainly looks like a recipe for fruitcake. And I hardly think the world needs another one of those. I don't know anyone who doesn't just toss their fruitcake in the garbage upon getting a tin of it from their old Aunt Agnes on the holidays. I know I do." Dent turned toward his members. "What say all of you, shall we rid the world of another recipe of Aunt Agnes's fruitcake?"

"HERE! HERE!" A chorus of voices rung out.

Dent withdrew a lighter from his pocket and flicked it on. He raised the little flame towards a corner of the ancient parchment.

"You're out-voted, Alex. Tell me where the Osiris Keys are and I will return this little piece of paper to you, intact. If not, I will spare the world of another fruitcake recipe right here and now. So which will it be?"

Siri watched from above, her eyes wide open and her jaw even wider.

"Please don't destroy it," Cedric pleaded. "I beg you. As a fellow archaeologist, I beg you! You don't know what you have in your hands!"

"Then enlighten me," Dent replied. "Enlighten all of us."

"I can't," said Cedric.

"You are a stubborn clam," Dent replied. "Very well, have it your own way." With that Dent set the parchment alight. Siri gasped out loud. She just couldn't help it, but Cedric's frantic protests drowned her out. Dent held the parchment while watching the flickering flame grow along the paper's edge until the entire crinkled sheet became a curling mass of ash. Dent dropped what was left at Cedric's feet, which wasn't much. Cedric quickly reached out a foot and stamped the flame out.

Siri clamped her eyes shut. She couldn't believe she had just seen the parchment go up in smoke.

"Dent!" Cedric gasped. "You're no archeologist, no scientist. You're nothing but a cheap, fairground trickster!"

"Sticks and stones, Alex," Dent said, wiping his hands together. "Now that that's over with, it's time to get on with the business at hand. It's time for you to put your scientific faith to the test. Let's see if it's a match for my own."

Dent gestured to a door beside the partition. It swung open. A sheeted figure rolled in on a gurney wheeled by the big Mongolian. The sight of it captivated Dent's audience and Siri watching from above. Bright arc lights, promptly wheeled beside it, switched on.

The radiance made the sheeted figure spectral-looking and glaring.

Dent tore the sheet from the figure with the adeptness of a magician doing a table trick. Cedric stared at the spectacle Dent unveiled. Siri did a double take from her cramped confines. It was a mummy – an Egyptian mummy! The body, swathed in linen wrappings, was gray and dusty. Despite its very human shape, it reminded Siri of an old, papery, wasp hive. Even in the ceiling duct she could smell the sickly, sweet odor of camphor wood and scented gums used for embalming wafting up from the chamber below. Semi-precious stones cut in the shape of scarab beetles and cobras adorned a golden collar surrounding the neck of the mummy. Their sheen under the lights dazzled Siri.

But it was the face of the thing that made her feel queasy. Although the head was bound with wrappings, the face was entirely exposed, framed by prominent cheekbones and fine white teeth, but otherwise completely shriveled.

Dent uncovered a table. It was equipped with a rack of test tubes, scissors, a syringe, and a green liquid in a clear, glass flask. This liquid was being heated over an alcohol burner, but not quite to a boil.

"Excellent," said Dent, donning a surgical gown, mask, and snapping on a pair of rubber gloves, "We're ready to begin." He turned to the assemblage, speaking through his surgical mask like an instructor to a roomful of medical students.

"What you see before you is a mummy dating back to the Old Kingdom, Fourth Dynasty, about forty-five hundred years ago. It is a man about thirty, and one of high rank I might add. His name was Ptah. You might also say he's as dead as can be. No doubt you are all wondering why I chose to hold our annual meeting here in Salem, Massachusetts. I tell you the selection was not a random one.

"I have gathered you all here because the time is right for us, we practitioners of the occult, and what better place than the witchcraft capital of the world? My friends, our movement has been up until now a psychic one. True, we can cast spells, summon spirits, and astral project ourselves. But we are mortal and being so are prone to mortal weaknesses. The specter of Grim Death will one day have his sway over us. That is about to change.

"The Egyptians were great preservers of bodies. On that score we can all agree. But only a few are aware that they were on the verge of preserving the vitality of life itself! YES! LIFE! ETERNAL LIFE! A transcript of a formula scribed by a high priest known as Menmaatre Thoth has eluded mankind for forty-two centuries. Simply stated, this Scroll of Thoth contains the secret of life and death.

"That is why I seek the Osiris Keys, for they unlock a small sarcophagus, which contains this holy of holies. Though I have been cheated of the Osiris Keys, I dare say by trial and error, I have prepared enough of this ancient formula to prove much of what I have said.

"But with this announcement comes a warning. There will be a reaction, but I caution you it will be an imperfect one without the Osiris Keys to lead me to the apotheosis of perfection. LIFE ETERNAL! LIFE WITHOUT END! So what happens next I cannot predict. Too much of this solution and I may raise a soulless demon bent on our destruction. Too little and this dry husk will remain forever incapable of movement. I will now begin the procedure of RESURRECTION!"

# CHAPTER 57 : The Mummy

Dent took up a scissors. He carefully snipped some wrapping off of the neck of the mummy, just below the left ear. He then loaded the syringe with the green fluid, and after studying its dose with minute care, inserted the needle into the gray, crust-like skin.

"Ladies and gentleman," announced Dent, his eyes fixed on the body of the Egyptian as he slowly forced the green liquid with the pressure of his thumb into the husk-like body, "you will be interested to know that there are over one hundred and fifty-three compounds to this ancient formula, some so common, like ammonia, you will find under any kitchen sink. Others, like potassium hydroxide, needs to be distilled from potassium carbonate. This solution helps provide a nucleophilic base to attack polar bonds in organic and inorganic matter. Here I am using a half grade solution, or 50 cc's in combination with 100 cc's of epinephrine – adrenaline, and levoamphetamine – a neural stimulant. Life began in a soup of amino acids and proteins. What you are witnessing with the introduction of this solution is an artificial abiogenesis or chemical evolution, which should bring to our Egyptian friend here, a semblance of life!"

Dent gazed down at the prostrate mummy and checked his wristwatch. Cedric watched with rapt attention from his chair to the point where he ceased twisting in his bonds. Siri stared down from above, overcome with curiosity herself. Dent was either a madman or a genius, and she wanted to find out which. Dent turned to Cedric and whispered.

"Make no mistake, old friend. I will find the Osiris Keys and the Scroll of Thoth. Both are wondrous and beyond price, and deserving to be in the possession of my conclave, The Osirin Legion of Horus."

Dent returned his attention to the mummy.

"We only have to wait a moment or two, my friends," Dent said under the great glare of the arc light, his gaze riveted on his dusty, bandaged subject. He waited for the result with measured patience. "Any moment now…"

Siri didn't know what to do next. There was certainly enough evidence against Dent. She was about to contact Scarpetti and her dad when suddenly it happened – the mummified corpse below her heaved. Suddenly the whole torso arched off and on and off the gurney, like a fish flopping on the deck of a boat. It was a terrible thing to watch. It was as if an electric shock of devastating potency shooting through the long dead frame was exciting nerve endings long dormant and struggling to reconcile the phenomenon of life again.

Siri grimaced at the horrid sight. The arms, folded across the chest, shivered and writhed as if in the throes of a fit, and the jaw distended wide to the point of unhinging itself. Then the whole figure shook, like a dog shaking off water, rapidly turning its body one way, and then the other.

The audience watched the spectacle with rapt attention. Some stood up from their seats, absorbed by the turn the experiment was taking. Dent stood back, smiling smugly through his mask. The mummy's arms unfolded and reached upwards toward the air, fingers straightening and bending, clawing at vacant space. A hiss of air escaped the region of its mouth. Then the chest cavity swelled and expanded, and shrunk again. The head bent upwards, lifting off its slab. Then, in a quick motion, the body sat up into a sitting position. Finally, the head turned, slowly, as if on a rusted hinge, until the withered face aimed towards the audience.

Siri stared down through the grating and felt like pinching herself to prove she wasn't having a nightmare in daytime. Cedric twisted and wrestled with his bonds. Sitting next to a mummy coming to life wasn't a good thing.

Dent slowly approached the mummy. He bent his head and studied the wrinkled, slit-like eyes.

"Can you hear me?" Dent asked through his mask.

The mummy sat immobile. Dent spoke again.

"The ancient gods of Egypt have bestowed upon you the means to understand my colloquial tongue. I repeat. Do you hear me?"

The mummy's head jerked in Dent's direction. Then it slowly nodded up and down.

"Do you feel any pain?" Dent continued.

The mummy cracked open its slit-like eyes, which caused some particles of dust to fall from the lids. The dark eyes that were revealed emitted a glimmer of rejuvenated liquidity. Its head began to jerk stiffly from side to side, like a broken weathervane.

"Excellent," Dent said. "I want you to stand."

The mummy's body stiffened. Suddenly its grey fingers gripped the sides of the gurney and turned its rigid body like a dial, so that its linen-wrapped legs stuck straight out over the floor. Then, in one menacing motion, the mummy pushed itself off the gurney and stood, tottering like a tree in a wind, its arms pressed stiffly against its dingy, bandaged sides. It stood beside Dent towering and immobile in its tattered, dusty wrappings. A murmur of voices resounded from the spectators. Dent lowered his surgeon's mask and stepped to the edge of the platform, the mummy looming behind him, big as death.

"I believe it's safe to say the demonstration is a success," said Dent. "Now I must ask all of you to understand our Egyptian friend is no automaton bent to do my bidding, but a reanimated being prone to all the same inherent moral complexities found in all intelligent life. In other words he has feelings. He's a stranger in a strange land. All that he once knew has crumbled to dust or resides in the dim vaults of some museum. Imagine the shock that would befall one of us if we were to switch places with him. So do not fear him. In fact, show him that he is amongst friends and allies. Show him that we too are worshipers of the great gods of Egypt: Osiris, Anubis, and Horus. Show him the SIGN!"

"Sign?" Cedric muttered, bound in his chair.

Dent turned to Cedric and snickered.

"Yes, let's not forget our other guest here. Show him the SIGN too. Show him our pretty marks."

At Dent's request, all in the audience bowed their heads, and in a gesture of reverence, peeled off wigs and hairpieces, revealing a roomful of bald heads, white and hairless as gourds. Siri's jaw fell open in astonishment. Below her was the Eye of Horus, over a hundred and fifty of them stamped atop the dome of every scalp. There was no mistaking the staring, mascara-outlined eye, just like on the Osiris Keys. To Siri, it appeared every unwinking pupil in its pale, round orbit was regarding her tucked up in the duct, and it chilled her blood to look down at all those boldly painted, staring eyes tattooed on all those bald heads. Cedric squirmed in his chair. Dent laughed. Then he peeled his own wig off, revealing a gourd-like head crowned with a staring eye which he bent for Cedric to see so that The Eye of Horus fell full and glaring upon the archivist.

"I think the EYES have it," Dent laughed.

Dent straightened and faced the mummy towering before him on the platform. He crossed his arms over his chest, and spoke, the mummy staring off like a noble statue.

"Here, somewhere is in this town, are the Osiris Keys, the keys to the holy of holies. Ptah, I want you to find these sacred relics, and bring them to me. You will seek them out wherever they are. You are one with the keys and they are one with you. Inseparable – linked. You will find them as easily as you can find your own two hands in the dark. Go, Ptah, and find the Osiris Keys. That is why I have revived you. That is your purpose. And may the ancient gods of Egypt guide you in your task. Now go."

The mummy stood as resolute as a mountain and for a moment Dent looked at the thing quizzically, wondering if his command was understood. Suddenly the mummy raised up one of its rigid arms over its bandaged head. Then, with Dent looking on, it closed its enshrouded fingers around a ceiling beam like a vice, and with a jerk, yanked it down amidst a violent shower of plaster, gypsum dust, wood slats, and duct work.

Siri tumbled out of the venting and onto the cluttered floor holding her smarting backside. Dent didn't lose a moment in calculating. He seized Siri by her elbow while the big Mongolian, standing hard by, snatched her camera and stripped her of her listening devices. Siri shrank in horror when the mummy, suddenly before her in all its dusty, bandaged monstrousness, stretched its two arms towards her, upturned its hands, and thrust them at her, demanding she place something into them. The sound it emitted from its throat was like a thrum or throaty rattle that told of a voice box clogged with dust and just as dry.

Siri reached into her jacket. She removed the Osiris Keys and held the dazzling relics by their chains. Then, awed by the mummy glaring down at her, she lowered the amulets into the thing's gray, waiting, upturned palm where its linen-wrapped fingers closed around them. The monster turned to Dent and handed the relics to him. Dent held up the amulets, and gloated over his prize.

Siri saw that the parchment – charred and almost beyond use, still had an unscathed section where Dent had held it. It was only a remnant, but Siri slyly bent to where it fell at Cedric's feet and shoved it into her pocket. Dent was too busy displaying the Osiris Keys to his followers who, bald as market melons, rose out of their seats in wondrous awe at the sight of them. Siri snuck behind the mummy standing big as an obelisk on the stage beside Dent and worked to undo Cedric's bonds, but he was too tightly knotted. Suddenly Dent turned to her and she had to stand up, well away from Dent's other prisoner.

"Well now, my dear," said Dent, palming the Osiris Keys. "What am I going to do with you?" He took several steps towards Siri. "I certainly can't let you go. And for all the trouble you've caused me, I think you will not go unpunished."

Dent nodded to his henchmen, the big Mongolian and the bearded man with the Fez. They both smiled sinisterly and drew closer towards Siri. Siri's eyes searched the room for a way out. There was none. She backed against the dessert table arrayed with cakes and other goodies and armed herself with two custard pies. The big Mongolian grinned broadly as he and Fez Guy drew nearer.

"What are you waiting for?" Dent said to his henchmen. "Get her!"

"You big apes!" Siri exclaimed. "You asked for it!"

Siri threw her pies and achieved direct hits into the faces of her targets. Dent's henchmen wiped the gooey mess from their eyes. Dent took a step to attend to the situation himself when a double layer Dutch chocolate cake topped with maraschino cherries splattered into his face and dropped in two big clumps atop his shoulders. Dent wiped chocolate frosting from his eyes and regarded his stained Neru suit. He looked at the mummy and pointed to Siri.

"Ptah!" Dent shouted. "Seize THAT GIRL!"

The mummy took a step, but staggered from the impact of a cheesecake pasting him in the face, followed immediately by a cherry tart that splattered over that.

"Save yourself!" Cedric said to Siri. "Don't waste time on me!"

Dent's followers snarled at Siri with faces wrinkled with rage. They rose up from their chairs and closed in on Siri from all directions, approaching the platform cunningly, fingers curled into claws, as if they were wolves hemming in a woodland deer. Siri jumped over the dessert table and kept behind it. The mummy swept a rigid arm over Siri's head. Siri ducked the whooshing limb, its waving, ragged pennant of bandages brushing over her.

Siri dashed for the gurney, hoping to use it as a barricade, but the mummy shoved it off the stage with an abrupt push of his dusty arms. Siri quickly skirted over to another dessert table, but the creature overturned it in a stroke. Dent, his henchmen, and his followers – the Osirin Legion of Horus, gathered around her, cutting off her retreat, obviously preparing to pounce.

Siri took up an entire pastry tray like an artist's palate. She started throwing every dessert she could get her hands on wildly in all directions. Lemon tarts, cherry tarts, cheesecakes, cupcakes and cream puffs splattered and burst over every snarling face opposing her. The stout Austrian, hit in the eye by a cupcake, had not a moment to shake his fist when a soggy cream puff filled his mouth like a basketball does a hoop. A woman whose bald head was formerly adorned by a red hat and a peacock feather was pasted by a cream pie with devastating effect. A dark-skinned man, who was unfamiliar with apple crumble, wore a hefty dollop of it in place of his wig. And a Norwegian, doubtless of Viking blood by way of his brawn, was stopped short by the pewter tray itself, gonging like a cymbal, when it met his hairless cranium dead on. In the end, every gourd-like head stamped with the Eye of Horus, was covered in custard, blueberry filling, cherry, and or whipped cream. The walls of the room did not escape the carnage of sugary gore, which slid down the woodwork in viscous chunks and clumps. The hardwood floor was slippery with exploded cake goods to the point where it was hard for Siri, never mind the Osirin Legion of Horus, to get a good footing without sliding in the frosted mess. But for all of Siri's efforts and direct hits, the mummy was back and looming over her, its face dripping with pie filling and remnants of crust, and reaching out two menacing, bandaged hands in her direction. Siri looked up, opened her mouth, and screamed her loudest scream ever!

# CHAPTER 58: kidnapped

Collin scrambled out of Scarpetti's unmarked car and dashed toward the door of the inn. Emma and Bernie, Bernie's aunts behind them holding their hands to their mouths in alarm, met Collin at the door.

"Where's my daughter?" Collin pressed.

"In the function room," Bernie replied. "They bolted the doors. We'll have to break them down!"

"Braddock!" Scarpetti barked, half out of his car and pointing up at the sky. "Look!"

Collin, Bernie, and Emma stepped out on the stoop and looked up at where the detective was pointing. There was no missing it. A clatter of rotors dinned in their ears and a blast of down-washing air cleared the sidewalk and street of crisp, fallen autumn leaves. Collin watched horrified. A touring helicopter rose into the air from somewhere behind the inn. The big Mongolian was at the controls and grinning like his face would split. Pressed against a passenger porthole towards the back were Siri's hands framing her face – her lips mouthing a scream.

"DAD HELP ME!"

Dent peered over Siri's shoulder and grinned victoriously down at Collin and Scarpetti. Then something pulled Siri from the window and sat in her place. It leered down at Collin and then pressed its hand, wound with linen wrappings, against the glass to block his

215

view. Collin could hardly believe his own eyes.

The chopper angled its nose and hovered across the parking lot and adjacent street. Its landing rungs just cleared the high-peaked roof of the House of Seven Gables where Siri thought she glimpsed a squatting shape leap upward. The Mongolian pulled back on the joy stick control, and Siri could see the dark waters of Salem Harbor swing into view below her window dotted with little sail boats at their moorings. She was squeezed in the rear of the chopper with Fez Guy, Cedric, and the musty smelling mummy, who seemed to take the new experience of flying with a grain of salt. Dent and the Mongolian were talking closely to each other. Siri couldn't hear a word over the deafening roar of the rotors. The helicopter made a broad sweep over the harbor. Then it turned its nose sharply toward land again. Siri figured a police chopper would be on Dent's tail any moment and Dent seemed to read her thoughts.

"Don't get your hopes up, little lady," Dent said from the cockpit. "We're just leapfrogging across town. The real getaway hasn't even begun."

"My dad's gonna pound you for kidnapping me," Siri said. She glanced up at the dehydrated face of her seat partner and sneered. The mummy sneered back in return.

"What are you going to do to us?" Cedric asked.

"That's for me to know and you to find out," Dent answered.

Siri looked over at Cedric.

"That parchment you had. Who gave it to you?"

"No one, young lady," Cedric replied, curtly. "I found it. It was old and interesting. No need to make a mystery out of it."

"Didn't you know, Alex," Dent said. "Siri Braddock loves to poke her nose where it doesn't belong. Curiosity killed the cat."

"And satisfaction brought him back," Siri quipped.

Suddenly the chopper lurched violently, throwing Siri against the sickeningly soft, yet crusty side of the mummy, causing a dust puff to erupt. The mummy pushed her back. A blinking light on the front console kept the Mongolian and Dent distracted – a fuel indicator, Siri guessed. Something was wrong. The helicopter was losing altitude and speeding sideways over the tops of houses and trees. Siri was glad she was belted tightly in. She felt like she was on one of those carnival rides that dipped close to the ground only to rise up high above the trees again. Siri could hear the wail of a police siren and caught sight of Scarpetti's sedan being passed by Bernie on his speeding motorcycle. A pea-green VW bug careened around a corner and followed. Siri knew Kaelyn had joined the chase. From her aerial vantage they looked like playful squirrels chasing each other's tails. Suddenly the mummy slid open the hatch and a violent inward rushing gust made Siri scream. Dent looked back.

"Ptah!" he shouted. "Have you gone mad?"

The mummy thrust its torso halfway out the port side hatch, its bandaged arms struggling violently to swat something off the landing gear. Dent looked out of his window and Siri bent in her seat. Ash was clinging by one hand to a landing rung while warding off the mummy's lunges with the other.

"Ash!" Siri shouted. "Hang on!"

"Head for the trees," Dent ordered his pilot. "Try and brush the spider off."

The big Mongolian jerked the joystick forward and the sputtering helicopter dipped into autumn foliage. Siri could see bright orange maple leaves brush the rungs below. Ash disappeared into them.

"Ash!" Siri shouted once more.

The helicopter cleared the trees and sunk lower, passing scores of trick-or-treaters filling the streets. Siri tried to see a trace of Ash below, but the mummy pushed her back into her seat again.

"Creep!" Siri snapped, wiping a smudge of gray residue from her shoulder left by the thing's hand. Siri could see they were over North Street by the Witch House, its black, stern, Puritan architecture looming beyond the cockpit.

"Good enough," Dent said, spying a vacant yard and garden behind the old, dark mansion. "Touch down there."

# CHAPTER 59: The Witch House

Siri tried hard to bite the hand of the big Mongolian, but he was wise to the attempt, so he just held her in an armlock in the dark. Siri could see his big yellow teeth glinting in the streetlight that filtered in through the diamond-paned lattice window. He was grinning like the Cheshire Cat again. Dent had gotten them all inside the Witch House with no trouble and even had the key to the place, which surprised Siri a lot. Dent had a plan up his sleeve. He made his henchmen force his prisoners up against a corner of the old dark house and there he waited, his eyes fastened to the simple Puritan-era door.

Siri wondered what Dent's next move would be. Why the Witch House? Siri remembered the book report she did in Mrs. Breath's history class. Accused witches were brought there in 1692, and in the 1940's when North Street was widened, it was moved thirty-five feet from its original location.

Siri could hear police sirens fading in the distance and figured Dent's ploy had worked. She hoped Ash was all right. It pained her the way he just disappeared into the trees. He risked his life to save her. The mummy's dark outline shown menacingly in the moonlight. It cranked its head down in a series of short jerks, aiming its withered face down at her, and then returned its gaze to the door.

"Why don't you just let us go?" Cedric asked, restrained by Fez Guy next to Siri. "Let us go and nothing more will be said of this. You have my word."

"I never leave a game until I hold all the cards," Dent said, standing calmly in the darkness.

"My dad and Detective Scarpetti won't fall into your trap," Siri said.

"I have never gagged a young lady before," Dent quipped, "but in your case I'm willing to make an exception. Just one more word out of you, and I'll do exactly that. Understand? Ptah, if little Miss Muffet says just one peep ... take your dusty, smelly, who-knows-where-it's-been, three thousand year old hand and put it exactly over her mouth, and keep it there. Do I make myself clear?"

The mummy nodded a jerky up and down nod, which gave Siri a shudder of revulsion. Suddenly the doorknob of the old house jiggled.

"Shhhh," Dent said. "They're right on cue."

Dent motioned for his henchmen to take their positions in the dark. The big Mongolian put his finger to his lips and looked at Siri. Then he released her to obey Dent's command. The mummy stepped next to Siri in the gloom. Siri hated the way its bandaged body felt against her, like a giant, papery, icky beehive.

Suddenly Siri felt a hand cover her face and pull her into a cramped recess of even greater blackness, and neither Dent, his henchmen, or even the mummy saw her disappear from their midst.

# CHAPTER 60: The Hidden

"What makes you think they came in here, Braddock?" Scarpetti said, as Collin pushed open the front door of the Witch House.

"Call it a hunch," Collin replied. "Then there's that helicopter parked in the yard next door."

"Not to mention footprints leading this way," Bernie said, bringing up the rear.

"They came in here. I feel it," Kaelyn added, clinging to Bernie's arm.

Collin snapped on a light switch, but it didn't work.

"Allow me," Scarpetti said, snapping on a service flashlight and scanning the silent gloom of an antique parlor with its roaming halo. The pale light gave the interior of claw-footed mahogany chairs and polished tables a harsh aspect. The detective stepped into the room followed by the others.

Suddenly another flashlight snapped on and shined brightly on all of them, like a theatre spotlight.

"Step into my parlor," Dent said. "I've always wanted to say that…"

Siri watched Dent step from the shadows aiming a pistol. She was in some aperture choked with cobwebs, closed to just a sliver. Siri could hardly believe her eyes when she saw her dad, Scarpetti, Kaelyn, and Bernie with their hands in the air, forced at gunpoint into the middle of the room by Dent. The big Mongolian quickly confiscated Scarpetti's service revolver. Fez Guy bolted the door. The hand over Siri's mouth kept her from instinctively crying out. She switched her eyes in the blackness trying to see who held her. Then she heard a voice breathe in her ear.

"Remain silent if you want no harm to come to them."

Siri nodded. She felt the hand slip from her mouth. She turned to see a mist of a face in the darkness – its pale, angled contours almost made her gasp. It was Ash! Ash brought a pointed finger to his lips and directed Siri's gaze towards the center of the room, which they saw through a crack or fissure in some hidden chamber.

"You won't get away with this," said Scarpetti to Dent.

"But I am getting away with it," Dent replied. "There's a lot to be said about having a revitalized Egyptian mummy on your side."

"The girl is gone," said Fez Guy, suddenly noticing Siri's absence. Both he and the big Mongolian strode about the dim parlor, searching for her in every corner. Dent edged closer to Scarpetti and then looked directly at Collin.

"Your daughter is very resourceful. She may have evaded us for now, but no matter. I have what I need."

Dent then turned to Cedric, who smiled knowingly at Dent with twinkling grey eyes.

"Now old partner," Dent said. "You may as well wipe that smile from your face or someone here with a bad case of rigamortis will do it for you. We may not be in the sub-cellar of that tourist museum. Oh yes, I know about that hidden door of yours. I also know the secret of this house. And I know you do too. Now show me where it is."

Cedric looked Dent in the eye with an air of defiance.

"I refuse," Cedric said. "Do your worst."

Dent grinned. "Do you think you can keep me from my destiny? Think again."

Dent nodded towards the shadows. The mummy moved into the light. Scarpetti and Collin backed away. Cedric looked up into the mummy's wide eyes glowering down at him, re-thought his position, and reluctantly did what he was told. He walked to a far wall, turned and paced out thirty-five feet along the floorboards, stopping just before a lampblack portrait of a scowling Jonathan Corwin, the original owner of the Witch House and one of the magistrates who presided over the Salem Witchcraft trials. Cedric then marked an X on the floorboards with a ruby ring he wore on his left hand.

"Stand aside," Dent ordered. He gestured towards the mummy. "Ptah, you know what to do. *Negi hai kekewey.*"

The huge bulk of the Egyptian lumbered stiffly into the halo cast by Dent's flashlight. It approached the scratch mark on the floor like a tottering pillar in a wind, its weight creaking the floorboards under it. Kaelyn watched amazed as the mummy strode past her, big as death. Bernie froze as Ptah's huge shadow fell over him, like a cloud. From their vantage point in the recess Siri and Ash watched the mummy bend mechanically and yank up two ancient floor boards. The thing then rose to its full stature and climbed down into the shallow space it uncovered where it proceeded to dig up a quantity of loose earth. Finally, Ptah unearthed and swung open an ancient slab of heavy gray slate. Siri noticed that the stone bore a death's head motif, like the kind in Puritan-era graveyards all over New England. The Egyptian descended into the hole further, corkscrewing into it, until his whole, terrible form sank out of sight.

Dent gestured for his prisoners to follow the mummy with a wave of his pistol. Siri watched helplessly as her dad, Scarpetti, Kaelyn, Cedric, and Bernie, all with their hands in the air, climbed into the hole and descended beyond the level of the floorboards. They were joined by the big Mongolian, Fez Guy, and ultimately, Dent, who chuckled to himself while palming two objects as he sank beneath level ground. Siri recognized the objects – *the Osiris Keys!*

# CHAPTER 61: Flashback

"We have to follow them," Siri whispered, peeking through the crack.

Ash and Siri pushed open a brick fireplace. The whole mantle swung open from the wall revealing their secret hidey-hole. Siri walked over to the torn up section of floor. Ash moved up behind her. Siri studied the slate slab thrown to the side bearing the grim symbol of mortality, the skull and crossbones. She then directed her gaze deeper into the crater and saw a flight of stone steps leading underground, revealed by the uprooted floorboards. The stairs spiraled downward into dark, forbidden regions. Ash stood next to Siri, gazing down, and placed a hand upon her shoulder.

"I know what you want to do," he said, "but they are gone. You must reconcile yourself to their fate."

"That's easy for you to say," Siri said. She pushed Ash's hand away. "You stay here if you like, but I'm going to try and help my dad and my friends."

Suddenly Ash saw the remnant of the parchment half projecting out of Siri's jacket pocket. He took it into his white, tapering fingers and looked at its charring with an expression amounting to pain.

"Who did this?" Ash sighed, lowering his head and covering his face with one hand.

"Dent," Siri replied. "He took it from Cedric's pocket and put a match to it, the snake."

223

"He took it from the old man?" Ash asked.

"Yes," Siri replied. "You gave it to him, didn't you? You gave the parchment to Cedric after you stole it from me?"

Ash nodded with an air of dejection.

"This man Dent will pay for what he has done," Ash gritted, releasing his grasp on the remnant.

Siri took the parchment and returned it to her pocket.

"I know this old scrap of paper is important," Siri declared. She studied Ash's angular face where hardly a line or wrinkle shown. Siri could sense there was more than the appearance of youth behind his countenance. His pale, smooth visage was like a dam holding back a lot of something. "You know what the parchment means. Won't you tell me, please?"

Ash said nothing. Siri produced a penlight and took a step downward into the vault.

"Fine," she said. "Be that way. I'll find out for myself."

"Wait!" Ash insisted. He raised one hand and aimed a finger upwards.

"What is it now?" Siri asked, impatiently. "I told you I'm going down."

Ash bent his head back and gazed up towards the beamed ceiling and a dusty candelabra chandelier that harked back to an age of horse-drawn coaches and waiting footmen. Siri followed Ash's stare towards the tall white candles suspended overhead, and when she did, vivid tongues of flame erupted from their long-disused wicks and sent wax drippings raining down over her. Siri clamped her eyes shut as wax beaded her eyelashes. When she opened her eyes again, the room, which had been so dim, became aglow with amber light, which charmed the parlor, revealing fine pewter, rich tapestries and handsome portraits. A melancholy tune filled the air, played by a corner quartet of violinists in powdered periwigs and swallowtail coats, as if they had been there all along. They were playing *Pachelbel's Cannon in D Major*.

## CHAPTER 62: Molly Pitcher

Siri surveyed the richly gowned young ladies led by dapper young men in satin swallowtails and waistcoats, their powdered hair tied back in the style of the late 18th Century with a ribbon of eel skin. Her eyes followed one young lady in particular, reflected in a broad mirror gilded in gold leaf. She was being led in a minuet by an austere, chisel-cheeked young man with a wedge-like nose whose periwig headdress was overly large to the point of pompous display. He kept his eye not on his beautiful partner, but upon the chimes of a Highland Mantel Clock over a fireplace. As the couple danced, moving backwards then forwards, each dainty step timed to the fawning rhythms of the Cannon in D Major, Siri was struck with a revelation. Both her face and that of the young woman's she beheld in the mirror, her blonde hair done up in high curls reminiscent of Queen Marie Antoinette, were the same, down to their dissimilar eyes. They could very well have been twins!

Siri's mind whirled. She suddenly felt herself being carried away like a leaf on a current. Her own thoughts and memories were melting into those of someone else – someone who had never heard of smart phones, computers, or electricity.

She wasn't Siri Braddock from Wicks End anymore. Siri no longer existed. She was yet to be born. Siri had a new name now – Molly Pitcher; and even more, she was married. It was September 9,

1775, and as Molly Pitcher danced with her husband, she searched the shadows cast by flickering candles.

The old Jonathan Corwin house, once used as a meetinghouse, was now seeing an incarnation as a home for the Enfields, who were holding a ball in honor of one of Washington's recent victories over the British occupiers. The Enfields were fervent supporters of Washington, and their guests included all of Salem's notables, including the Pitchers from Marblehead.

"Your dancing is very stiff tonight, my dear," spoke John Pitcher, as he led his wife Molly in the dance. "Is something troubling you?"

"Why no, John," replied Molly. "I suppose I am just tired. Besides, my dancing suffers no more from my weariness than yours does from the attention you pay that clock on the mantelpiece."

John Pitcher regarded his wife with a cold, aloof eye.

"Sink me," he said, "if my wife is not jealous of a clock."

The violins concluded the final movement of the Canon and the couples joined in a cordial applause. John Pitcher looked upon Molly with an air of curiosity as she forced a smile, turned, and while lifting the hem of her gown, glided toward a punch bowl in the corner of the room. Molly could feel her husband's stare upon her as a gloved servant poured her a goblet of spiced punch. His approach was even more palpable. She didn't even have to turn to know he was standing right behind her.

"Would my husband care for some punch?" Molly asked, looking at her husband's fractured reflection in her fluted, crystal goblet.

"You've read my mind, my dear," John Pitcher replied.

Molly took up another goblet and offered it to her husband. He stepped closer to her and raised his goblet in a toast.

"To the moon and the globe, my dear," he announced, not taking his eyes off of Molly.

He touched his goblet against hers.

"A curious toast," Molly replied.

"Is it?" John asked. "I see it as quite fitting, for we, like those heavenly bodies are bound to each other in an eternal embrace."

"If that is so," Molly replied, "then which am I?"

"The moon of course," John answered. "It has a side I never see."

Molly responded with a smile. John managed a strained grin. He then drank down the goblet as young men courted their ladies to the punch bowl. Molly unfolded an embroidered fan and fanned her face with it.

"It is very warm inside," she said. "I think I'll go into the garden. Pray excuse me, husband."

"Of course, my dear," John replied, cordially bowing, allowing his wife to pass.

# CHAPTER 63: The Meeting Place

Once in the cool night air Molly felt relieved. The stars were winking beyond the golden leaves of the broad oak she stood under. The moon was waxing full and silvery through the canopy and its soft radiance dazzled Molly's hair and gown as she waited by a hollow in the tree. Through the diamond-paned window she could see her husband between the roving guests in the main hall, his eyes fixed to the Highland Mantel Clock, the goblet still in his hand. At any moment he would come for her, she thought, but when she saw Rodger Enfield address her husband and lead him into another room, she breathed a little easier. Suddenly rustling in some bushes caught her ear and she felt brave enough to whisper.

*"Ash?"*

A shadowy figure presented itself in the darkness. Molly's heart quivered when she saw the shape become clearer in the silver light. She rushed forward and closed the distance with an embrace – and a kiss.

"God, how I missed you," Molly breathed, her lips parting for a brief moment before pressing them against her shadowy lover's again, this time more lingeringly. Suddenly Molly regained her presence of mind, pushed herself back, and took a needed breath.

"I got your note," she whispered, her chest rising and falling. "You shouldn't have come here. It's not safe."

"Nothing in Heaven or Hell could keep me from you, Molly," said

Ash, his handsome, chiseled face bent over hers. He ran his fingers over her delicate features.

"What news do you bring?" he asked.

"I wish it were good," Molly said, lowering her head against Ash's chest. "I need more time."

Ash's eyes narrowed.

"Time," he gritted, turning away. "How many more years must pass?"

Molly took Ash by the chin and redirected his gaze towards her.

"Fret not," Molly whispered. "Before spring all will be well. I promise."

"I could almost believe you," Ash said.

"Believe then," Molly replied, "as I believe the old Wampanoag sachem whose advice I sought."

Ash gazed deeply into Molly's eyes.

"When can we be together again?"

Molly looked towards the window once more, but there was no sign of her husband.

"Here is not the place and tonight is not the time," Molly said, turning back to Ash.

"When then?" Ash pressed, impatiently.

"My husband has business in Boston tomorrow that will detain him most of the night," Molly replied, her gaze alternating between Ash and the window. "Meet me this same time at the old burial ground. I'll be waiting by the mill pond. Now go quickly before you are seen."

Suddenly a dark figure stepped into the dim light cast from a diamond-paned window. Molly gasped, but breathed easy when she recognized the shadowy features of Ash's friend and confederate, Christian Fletcher, who desperately beckoned for Ash to follow him. Molly pulled Ash towards her and hugged him tightly, bringing her full lips to his ear.

"Until the stars fall from Heaven," she whispered.

Ash hated letting Molly slip from his arms, but he reluctantly turned and followed Christian into the shadows. A rustling of bushes told of their departure. Molly took a breath, restored her composure, and turned toward the house and the gala within. The snap of a twig caught her ear. She thought she detected a movement in the moonlight, but the voice of her husband calling her from an open doorway drew her attention back toward the party. Molly smoothed her dress, adjusted the ringlets in her hair with a pat of her hands, and rejoined her husband inside – taking his hands into hers.

# CHAPTER 64: The Gift

John Pitcher's coach was a spectacle on the quaint lanes of Marblehead. The turnout was black and trimmed with gold leaf, and although not of royal birth, Pitcher had a coat of arms designed and fitted onto the door regardless. He owned a stake in a rum operation in the Caribbean and his emblem was a stalk of sugarcane framed in a shield of cobalt. As the coach wound it's way along Marblehead's narrow lanes that evening, John Pitcher took a pinch of snuff from the tiny silver box he always carried in his pocket and applied a pinch in each of his nostrils, sniffing deeply. Molly sat across from him as the coach jostled along at a leisurely pace, her eyes focused on a Highland Mantel Clock resting at her husband's side.

"Tell me, John," said Molly. "Why did Rodger Enfield give you that clock?"

"Are you still jealous, my dear?" John returned smugly.

"Please don't jest with me," Molly replied.

"Very well," John said, returning his snuffbox to his pocket. "If you must know, it's a token of his thanks for supporting General Washington. Sink me, if your turn in the garden didn't do you a world of good. Your coloring is very rosy, my dear. I'll call you my little moon flower."

Molly put a hand to her cheek. She then turned towards the window. Molly regretted her marriage and taking John Pitcher's name. Molly Good was her maiden name. Good was an old, established name in

Salem, and she missed it. She could still feel her husband's eyes upon her.

"You're very pensive this evening, my dear," John said, studying his wife. Molly turned from the window and managed a disarming smile.

"I suppose I'm just weary from the night's frolic," she replied.

"We'll be home directly," John coolly stated.

The coachman directed the turnout onto a circular drive. Steam rising from the horse's haunches in the coach lamps told of the frosty night to come. The carriage stopped before an impressive entrance to a white, colonial Georgian style home, crowned with a cupola. A wigged footman wearing epaulettes upon the shoulders of his swallowtail coat opened the door of the coach and took Molly's hand, assisting her down. A doorman in waiting opened the front door to a spacious candlelit hall, which Molly quickly disappeared into. John Pitcher stepped from the coach and stood looking towards the house.

"When is she meeting him next?" he asked the coachman.

"Tomorrow night, sir," the coachman replied. "They're meeting at the old burial ground by the millpond. Shall I take steps, sir?"

"No," John Pitcher returned dryly. "The plum is not ripe for picking. Just report to me what you see and hear. And be sure you are not seen. Understand?"

"I understand, sir."

Pitcher removed three gold sovereigns from a side pocket of his waistcoat, pressed them one after the other into the open palm of his coachman, and not giving a second thought to their conversation, he entered his grand home.

# CHAPTER 65: The Secret Room

Molly Pitcher knew the risk she was taking in concocting the potion. The stigma of witch had not entirely left 18th Century New England, even though it was an enlightened age. The cool light of science was brightening colonial minds, but in the shadows of that light superstition still dwelt. Socially it wasn't proper for a lady of the house to be familiar with the kitchen, it being the place for servants and the household cook, but Molly saw a way around that. Behind a narrow row of shelving was a long forgotten scullery, and it was there Molly and her loyal servant, Alice, prepared various herbal remedies and potions. Molly would often send Alice into the woods and fields to harvest the wild roots, seeds, and weeds for her mixtures, sometimes even joining her when her husband was away.

Molly was becoming a little famous for her draughts and teas that restored the health of ailing friends and neighbors. A hundred years before she would have been driven up Gallows Hill in an ox cart and hanged as a witch, but Molly knew what was now socially acceptable. What she was concocting would probably earn her a public dunking. Luckily, she could conduct her operations out of sight. The recipes for Molly's potions came from old books and parchments handed down from her mother and grandmother, and sometimes from Wompanoag shamans.

Molly opened one of her journals to make a notation. It was then she spied her husband and his poker-faced coachman, Sebastian Clay, through a crack in the scullery door. The two were standing in the hall whispering suspiciously. Then they disappeared into her husband's study and closed the door. Tucked under her husband's arm was the Highland Mantel Clock.

# CHAPTER 66: The Traitor

Molly approached the door to her husband's study as silently as she could. She never did trust Sebastian Clay. Why her husband kept him in his employ she could only guess. He was like a snake charmer's serpent, ever ready to be summoned from the basket to rear his ugly head. No illicit task was too wicked or beyond him. Molly took a breath and brought her ear to the door. She could hear voices inside the room. She cracked the door ajar and peeked in. The two men's backs were facing towards her before the fireplace and the elegant Highland Mantel Clock was plainly visible above the hearth. John Pitcher scratched his chin and turned the minute hand of the clock like a dial.

"Let's see if Rodger Enfield is true to his allegiance," Pitcher said to Clay. "How does it go? Oh yes. Start at twelve, turn twice passed three, then back to nine, to open thee," he said.

Suddenly Molly heard a pronounced click come from the clock, and saw a secret compartment slide open just below the face. She then heard a chuckle of satisfaction escape her husband's lips and saw him withdraw a parchment that was hidden within the clock.

"Excellent," her husband said, "absolutely splendid." He folded the paper and handed it to Clay.

"Bring this to Gage and have him send a detachment to the Black Ram Inn in Salem. The powder stores he is searching for are secreted in the cellar."

"These insolent colonials will rue the day they defied good King George," Clay huffed.

"They will indeed," Pitcher replied. "From the looks of these ragged provincials, Gage will make short work of them. It's sure to take the bloom off the rose of General Washington's recent victory to say the least."

"Will that be all, sir?" Clay asked.

Pitcher paused and thought for a moment. He turned and directed his gaze towards a life-size portrait of Molly hanging above the fireplace. His icy blue eyes studied her radiant beauty rendered in oil paint. She was depicted in an elegant French gown amidst beautiful red drapery, parted slightly to reveal a rose garden beyond. He then turned to Clay.

"As you know I'll be in Boston most of the morrow," Pitcher continued. "Once you've completed your errand, I'll need you to tend to matters here. Understood?"

"Of course, sir," Clay replied. He then turned to the door and brought a finger to his lips.

Pitcher nodded and feigned talking while Clay tiptoed towards the door, which was closed. He put his hand to the handle and with a jerk, pulled it open. He poked his head into the hall, looking one way, then the other. There was no one there. Satisfied their conversation wasn't over heard, Clay ducked his small, vulture-shaped head back into the study and closed the door.

Molly stood with her back against the grandfather clock, its brass pendulum ticking away the seconds. She had concealed herself just in the nick of time within the little hall nook where the great clock resided. Molly knew there was no time to lose.

## CHAPTER *67* : The Conspirators

Molly took full advantage of her husband's absence. He had left for Boston early that morning in his coach to take care of business matters he preferred to remain vague. Molly dismissed the maid and the footman from their duties for the day and watched them depart to the market or tavern from behind the veil of a window curtain. Only her servant, Alice, remained.

"Alice," Molly said, summoning her loyal aide to her side. "The house is ours. We have not a minute to waste."

The plan Molly and Alice formulated in the kitchen scullery over the Rumford hearth required cunning and nerve. Sebastian Clay had already left the house to perform his vital errand for his master, and time was at the essence. So it was before an iron cauldron boiling and billowing clouds of steam that Alice drew for Molly with a stick of charcoal, a rough, topographical map of the route she would have to take across Old Burial Hill in Marblehead and through the Salem Woods.

"It will be rough going, mistress," Alice said. "Not the work for a lady like yourself."

"But it's the only way to warn Greenleaf Putnam," Molly said. "The British redcoats will be on their way to the Black Ram Inn to confiscate the gunpowder stores secreted in the cellar. Our men folk will need that powder to fight."

Molly donned her riding cloak from a peg on the wall when Alice

239

intervened with a staying hand.

"Mistress, allow me to go in your stead," Alice said, pulling off her poked bonnet and taking half the riding cloak into her hand. "It will be better that way. You have much to do here, and there are those depending upon you not to fail them. You said it yourself. We have not a minute to waste, and two tasks are at hand."

Molly turned to the table in the middle of the scullery, where upon it were spread the vital ingredients: Satyrion Root, Yarrow Seed, Meadow Sweet, Mandrake Root, Wolfbane, Moonwort, Hawthorn Blossoms, and other rare herbs and compounds.

The brew they were concocting was desperately needed. That was true. This time Molly's patients were unique. Her reputation had reached even them, hidden though they were. Molly never dreamed that she would fall in love with one of them, whose affliction was the strangest she had ever heard of. In the end, Molly knew that Alice was right. She turned to her loyal servant.

"God speed to you, Alice," Molly said.

"Fear not, mistress," Alice said with a gentle smile. "You may safely rely on me. There's not a devil or a redcoat who can catch me on horseback. Greenleaf Putnam will have warning enough, mistress. Depend on that."

"Alice," Molly said, emotion catching in her slender throat. "You are the sister I never had – the partner in all my labors. Now depart before I change my mind."

"Yes, mistress."

Molly kissed Alice's cheek. Her servant slipped out the back door, cloaked in a dark riding hood and cape. A black steed waited at a hitching post, the gleam of a genuine devil in its eye. Alice quickly mounted it, and with a pull on the reins, made good her departure. Molly stood at the door, her eyes fixed with worry. As she watched the black steed gallop down the way, disappearing along a winding, tree-shaded path, her servant's riding cloak flapping about her like raven wings, she wondered about Sebastian Clay and his whereabouts.

# CHAPTER 68: Rendezvous

"I want you to leave that house tonight," Ash told Molly. He looked down into her eyes, which were like two dark pools. If he could, Ash would have waded in and disappeared into them. Instead, he held her close against his body as they stood by the sagging grey tombstones of Old Burial Hill. A waxing moon shimmered over the tranquil waters of the Atlantic just beyond, and cast the small, round hill in a blue wash of light.

"You know that's my dearest wish," Molly replied. She pressed her head against Ash's chest, as if it was a pillow. "But I need more time, my love. In that house is the means to a cure for you and the others. To flee now would risk months, perhaps years of delay to our efforts."

"But Pitcher is a traitor," said Ash, separating himself from Molly's embrace and looking her in the eye. "And he's no fool. As long as you remain under the same roof with him, you're in danger."

"I can handle my husband," Molly replied. She faced the tranquil harbor waters and watched the moonlight play. "It's that viper Clay who gives me cause for concern. He has the eyes of an owl and the ears of a bat. Both he and my husband are conspiring with the British, and I fear a greater plan is afoot than what I have discovered. I must remain there as long as I can. Already I am worried about Alice, for she hasn't returned from her vital errand when I left. She is a brave and loyal friend, and I wish to take her with us when I finally depart that troubled house."

Ash took Molly by her shoulders and turned her towards him.

"She will come with us if that is your wish," he whispered, "for if ever I had cause to believe in the existence of Heaven, it is because of you."

"And if ever I had cause to believe in a man…" Molly said, looking into Ash's sparkling eyes.

Ash and Molly gravitated towards each other, their bodies meeting and blotting out the rising yellow disk of the moon. They enveloped one another and kissed deeply in the darkness. Ash bent over Molly's small figure. Molly locked her slender arms around Ash's neck, submitting herself entirely to him. The two parted, drawing a breath, and then collided again in a lock of passion. Above the two, a bough rustled in a sea breeze. Then a nighthawk, late on the wing, screeched high overhead. And Sebastian Clay, hidden in the deep shadows of a huge, spreading elm just a few tombstones distant, saw and heard everything.

# CHAPTER 69: Confrontation

Molly paced before her oval bedroom mirror several times. Her reflection, gowned in satin, her brown hair done up in ringlets, glided back and forth before a canopy bed, its open drapery revealing a riding cloak haphazardly thrown across the silken sheets. Molly approached a window, parted a curtain, and looked out into the night. The narrow riding path into the woods was dark, but moonbeams penetrated the tangled branches of trees in places. There was no sign of Alice. It was past midnight and she still had not returned. Molly suddenly heard voices downstairs. They belonged to her husband and Sebastian Clay. Molly opened the bedroom door and listened. The voices, before loud, now sounded hushed and calculating.

Molly lifted the hem of her gown and descended the wide, curving staircase. The flickering candles on the crystal chandelier above threw strange, refracting colors over the walls, which were papered and stenciled with ferns and flowers, the French fashion of the times. As she suspected, Molly found her husband and Clay in the parlor before the roaring hearth. They were lifting goblets in a toast. Molly wanted to make her presence known, just to see their reaction. Pitcher and Clay turned to Molly as she entered, their faces stamped with suppressed amusement.

"I thought you had retired to bed, my dear," said Pitcher, lowering his goblet. "What a nice surprise." He turned to Clay. "Isn't it my good fellow?"

"It is indeed, sir," Clay replied, smiling before the brim of his glass.

Molly studied the two men standing smugly before the licking flames of the fireplace, goblets clutched in their ruddy hands. She raised an eyebrow.

"It is the dead of night, John," said Molly. "It is a curious time to be making a toast."

"We were toasting you, my dear," Pitcher said, raising his goblet, and gesturing towards Molly's portrait above the mantle.

"On such a chilly night as this, your beauty and radiance warms us by the sight of it, and justly deserves a glass raised in its appreciation." Pitcher turned to Clay.

"Isn't that so?"

"As you say, sir," Clay replied dryly.

Pitcher turned to Molly.

"And what brings you to us, my dear, on such a late hour? Surely you should be in bed dreaming of satin dresses, rose gardens, and knights-errant performing heroic deeds in the names of their ladies."

"I am concerned for Alice," Molly replied. "She went out this afternoon and hasn't returned."

Pitcher drank down the contents of his goblet and studied his wife before him.

"Perhaps she's eloped with some village Lothario," he said. "She always was a romantic little thing."

"It's not like her to be late," said Molly.

"Perhaps she's been delayed at the tavern," Clay added, "over a potation of rum. I've never known a scullery wench to turn down a bumper of West Indies rum, or a waggish kiss. And Alice was never too particular what she drank or who she drank with – or who she kissed."

"You lying devil!" Molly exclaimed, taking up a fireplace poker and lashing out at Clay with it, just missing his ear.

Pitcher and Clay burst into a volley of laughter at Molly's rash act. Molly stood before them red and fuming, her eyes looking from one to the other. Finally, in a climax of rage, she flung the poker at her own portrait, splitting it. Then she took up the hem of her gown and hurried out of the room.

Pitcher poured out a decanter and filled their goblets until wine overflowed all over the polished floor. Then he raised a boasting toast to his wife in absentia.

"Here's to my Molly – who has more courage in her than any man I know."

Pitcher then took his goblet and threw it at the divided portrait of Molly hanging over the mantel, splashing red wine across it and the wallpaper.

"Keep watching her, Clay," Pitcher said, thoughtfully, eyeing the splattered wine as it trailed long streaks down the wall and dripped upon the Highland Mantel Clock like fresh blood. "In time, all will be finished."

# CHAPTER 70: Discovery in the Kitchen

John Pitcher entered the dark kitchen lit only by the ruddy glow of embers in the Rumford hearth. He left his clay pipe beside the high-back Moroccan chair he kept by the fireside of his parlor where he had been staring into the leaping flames. Molly had gone to bed. She hadn't spoken to him in months. She blamed him and his coachman Clay for Alice's disappearance, but never outwardly accused them of abduction or worse, but there was more on Pitcher's mind other than treachery and conspiring with the British. Molly was now with child, and Pitcher displayed great reserve on his expectant fatherhood. He never did bother to remind Molly that a bout with small pox rendered him incapable of producing children.

From Clay's reports, Pitcher learned not only of the secret meeting place of his wife and her lover, but also that his wife's skill with the mortar and pestle were also being sought in these nocturnal meetings. It seemed she had prepared a special draught to be taken by both her admirer and a band of his confederates, on a night when the moon was at its fullest, and for reasons he couldn't fathom. Pitcher knew Molly couldn't do this work in the open. There had to be a secret scullery or hidey-hole where she performed her alchemy.

Pitcher went quietly about the darkened kitchen, tugging on bricks and pulling at crevices in the woodwork. He spied a cupboard with its collection of fine pewter and crockery built into the wall and studied it up and down. He approached it, and wrapping his hands around a raised corner, pulled on it. To Pitcher's surprise the whole cupboard swung open with ease, as if on a concealed hinge. Pitcher smiled slyly at what he discovered. He was standing before a dark recess and staring into utter blackness. It was a room he never knew about, and in his own house. He took up a taper and lit it causing its soft glow to bathe the little chamber in amber light. Pitcher stepped into the hidden room and looked upon its strange contents which met his eager eyes at every turn. Arranged on shelves were colorful bottles containing dried herbs, powders, or dark liquids. There were pieces of bone, a crow's wing, and several dried toads strewn on a cutting board along with remnants of crushed berries. Garlands of garlic and other medicinal plants hung from the ceiling, and stacks of parchments and old leather-bound books were arrayed neatly beside clay vessels emblazoned with strange designs. Pitcher spied a little glass vial suspended on a series of strings and examined the brackish liquid within. He picked it up and held it against the light.

"What is the little witch up to?" he whispered.

# CHAPTER 71: The Hag of Screeching Lady Beach

It was a nocturnal meeting John Pitcher had arranged through Clay his coachman. The little hovel he was driven to sat on a windswept crag by an open beach in Marblehead. Called "Screeching Lady Beach" by the superstitious locals because of a ghost of a women murdered by pirates said to haunt the place, John Pitcher regarded the grim location and the dark, roaring Atlantic beyond with a rigid expression. The woman he sought was noted for her skills with potions, though her concoctions brought her fear, not fame. Her name was Meara and to the more generous Marblehead locals she was considered mad. The woman's ramshackle house by the sea was constructed mostly of driftwood and was avoided by small boys and stray dogs. She went by the name of Miss Meara, or Sorceress Meara, or Witch Meara, depending on the visitor. One thing was sure. No one ever went to see her on an errand that was honest or good.

John Pitcher's business with Meara was private. He bid his coachman to wait by the road as he entered the shack. It was a dim, ill-smelling place crammed with garlands of strange herbs and seaweed hanging from rafters and a great, spiny puffer fish suspended from a central beam. Pills were half rolled out on a table, no doubt some love potion in the making or an agent to speed someone into eternity. A rude, stuffed Osprey or sea eagle in a corner glared at

Pitcher upon his closing the door. The lady of the house, a hunched creature shrouded in rags, was busily filtering a solution in a far corner by a hearth fire that cast crazy shadows about the place. She beckoned her visitor closer without bothering to turn around, a huge bundle of keys jangling at her side, apparently for the many padlocked chests stacked in the shadows amongst discarded oyster and mussel shells. Pitcher advanced, cautiously, passing eels, octopi, and other lesser-known marine life preserved in jars, and burying his nose in a handkerchief.

"It's not exactly a flower garden, is it?" commented the owner.

She turned slightly so that Pitcher could see only a corner of her face, which was wrinkled, but not unsightly, except for one eye that was filmed over.

"I have your fee," stated Pitcher, producing a small money pouch.

"Good evening, John Pitcher," spoke the hag. "I have your order just about ready."

"Will it do what you said?" Pitcher stammered, with a rare weakness in his voice.

"That and more, sir," replied the crone.

The old lady corked her concoction in a small, glass vial and approached her customer in short, feeble steps. A glossy sea otter bounded clumsily out of a corner and squirmed up the woman's robes to rest upon her shoulder where she petted and caressed its sleek fir. Meara handed the vial to Pitcher after an exchange of money. Pitcher then held the vial of dark liquid up against the dim light of the room and inspected it.

"It looks like ink."

"Believe me, sir," spoke the crone. "That little bottle holds more wildness than the heathen village of Dog Town. One dram of that and he'll change, and not for the good."

"He'd better or I'll be back with a horse whip."

"Miss Meara never failed in her art yet, John Pitcher. You'll be satisfied."

Pitcher reached into his pocket and tipped the woman an extra gold sovereign, which she accepted with a gracious bow. Then he turned and left.

A rising wind shivered the branches of trees and drove curtains of clouds across the face of a waxing moon as John Pitcher's coach jostled along the ruts back towards his grand home. The hint of a smile was stamped on his otherwise immobile face.

# CHAPTER 72: The Grotto

Bain put everything out of his mind, except the portrait he was painting. It was of Constance Nash, who sat patiently modeling for him. Bain reached over and adjusted her chin, aiming it towards the torchlight.

"Now don't move an inch," he said.

Constance watched Bain draw back by his easel. She admired his talent and unkempt locks that curled over his ears and shoulders. His hair was jet black and wild as a storm. Christian Fletcher emerged from the shadows and into the firelight. The sunken grotto had been made their *sanctum sanctorum* from the changing world above. It had a broad pool fed from the sea and dancing green water reflected the firelight upon stalactites that served for pillars in their subterranean world.

"The way you two flitter about heedless of our condition astounds me," Christian remarked. "I don't know whether to be envious or cross."

Bain didn't stir from his work. He gestured with his brush towards a wine barrel half covered by a large tapestry that served for a wall. The makeshift partition depicted a wolf hunt and the beast's ultimate dispatch by a horseman with a lance.

"Over there you will find some very excellent port. Go drown your impatience."

251

Mallory suppressed a smile as Christian shook his head in bewilderment. She was tending a cooking pot suspended from a tripod of wooden poles. Through the curtain of smoke she saw Ash enter the cavern, passing others like themselves without the slightest notice. Mallory watched him sit upon a great chair that would have served as a judge's seat. Beside him a candelabra flickered, revealing a shining end table where rested a Stradivarius violin. Ash appeared solemn and engrossed in thought. The artifacts surrounding him were grim reminders of how time can play its cruel hand. A Viking long boat half rotted, but still intact, supported a crew of complete skeletons clad in long-rusted armor and horned helmets. There were other treasures nearby, some glittering, others fashioned from exotic woods into rich furnishings, but in these Ash saw no value. His treasure lay above him in the fresh air and sunshine.

"Ash," said Christian, pouring wine into a goblet. "You brood too loudly."

Ash lifted his eyes from his thoughts. He rose from his chair and walked over to where the water lapped at his boots. He looked down into his own reflection, which was wrapped in a dark cassock, making him appear like a great, black bat. Soon other reflections joined his in the pool, but these appeared to be from another time and place. Whether it was the past or the future, Ash could only guess.

"Molly," Ash whispered. "Do not fail us."

# CHAPTER 73: The Potion

Molly Pitcher had heard of the new sciences. She knew the moon controlled the tides, but didn't understand how. She also knew the moon at its fullest would endow the elixir she prepared with the potency it needed, but still she didn't understand how. She only knew that on that night she had to deliver it to Ash. She had made enough only for one. The others would have to wait their turn. More than anything Molly wanted to liberate Ash from his affliction so that they could live out their lives together and raise the child that was soon to arrive. She wouldn't even bother to seek a divorce from her husband. She just planned to run away with her beloved to another one of the thirteen colonies, perhaps New Hampshire.

Molly's mind was in a whirl as she put the little glass vile in a leather pouch and set it on the counter. She was relieved her husband had business in neighboring Salem. At least she could move about freely. Molly leaned her face against the frosted kitchen window and beheld a full moon rising like a great silver shield over a bank of trees. In a matter of days she would know motherhood. She smiled down at her own roundness and caressed it. Molly did have a nagging doubt about the paternity of the child she carried. In the beginning of this whole affair it was Christian she first met and thought she loved. Christian – wild and dashing, Christian. Then came Ash, and in the end it was he who captured her heart.

Molly quickly shook off the doubt. She had to get ready. She untied her apron and set it next to the pouch. Then, before she went upstairs to prepare for her nocturnal meeting, Molly took all of her medicinal notes and books on potions and remedies, and tossed them into the Rumford hearth, where she watched them ignite into a towering blaze before her eyes and curl into crumbling grey ash. The only thing she saved of her labors was a formula written on a sheet of parchment paper, which she folded and held tightly in her hand. She knew a safe place to keep it.

Molly swept into the candlelit parlor and approached her little writing desk. She took up a quill pen, dipped it in an inkwell, and tore from a writing tablet a scrap of paper. Composing herself, Molly sat and hurriedly wrote out the combination to the Highland Mantel Clock. Then she rose, took the timepiece down from the mantel, and with her delicate finger turned the minute hand several times forwards, then backwards, then forwards again. Sebastian Clay watched every movement Molly made through his spy hole bored under the hall stairs. He then watched Molly open a little drawer in her desk and remove a needle, a spool of thread, and a scissors. He held in his hand a corked vial containing a special fluid prepared by Meara, the hag of "Screeching Lady Beach."

# CHAPTER 74: Desperate Struggle

Molly was in no condition to do what she did – harness two black stallions to her husband's coach, but she accomplished the task without much struggle. The horses neighs and whinnies told of their nervousness. Molly stroked and patted their shiny necks, soothing them. Then she finished hitching them up in the courtyard. Molly surveyed the darkness from under her riding hood and mounted the front of the carriage. Once seated, she gave the reins a tug. Nestled at her side was the Highland Mantel Clock with all its mystery.

The tree-shadowed road was long and winding. It was the same road Alice took to warn Greenleaf Putnam of the Black Ram Inn. Molly wondered about Alice every day, her dearest friend and accomplice. Molly knew Alice was dead. She could feel it. Like one feels a severed limb that is no longer there, she could feel the presence of her ghost. Several times Molly even thought she heard Alice's voice calling to her from downstairs while she was in bed.

*"MOLLLLYYYY,"* the voice would call, softly and sweetly, in the small dark hours. *"MOLLLLYYYY. WE MUST HELP THEM. HEAR ME, MOLLLYYY. HEAR YOUR SWEET ALICE...WE MUST HELP THEM COME HOME."*

Molly would sometimes get up and go down into the kitchen, for that was where the voice always came from, but no one was ever there, just darkness and the ticking of the Highland Mantel Clock in the parlor. Molly sighed as she rode. She knew she would never see Alice again. She deeply regretted her decision to let her friend go to Salem in her place. She knew she would regret it for the rest of her life.

Molly tugged on the reins to make the horses go faster. That was when she spied two bone-white hands emerging from the shadows behind her. They were reaching for the Highland Mantel Clock!

Molly shrieked and tugged harder at the reins. The horses bolted down the narrow, rutted road. Clay fell back by the jostling, but righted himself quickly enough to make another desperate lunge for the clock. Molly hugged it against her side and warded off the coachman with a lash of her riding crop.

"I will have that clock, witch!" Clay shouted, fending off the blow, appearing out of the gloom like a phantom.

"I will rather see thee dead," Molly shouted, striking out again and again with her crop.

"I will not ask again!" Clay insisted, lunging at Molly.

"Keep off me, you devil!" Molly shouted, striking the coachman back.

"The CLOCK, WITCH!" Clay shouted, his face branded with a stinging red cut.

He drew from his cloak a pistol, and cocked it. "Give me the clock NOW!"

Suddenly the coach lurched upon a sharp curve. Molly pushed Clay's pistol away. The gun discharged in a sparking burst. Startled, the horses whinnied and broke into an open clearing that took the speeding coach along a path close to rocky cliffs. Molly turned expecting to see Clay in the shadows, anticipating another assault, but he was nowhere in sight. Molly held the Highland Mantel Clock tightly and turned to the winding road that hugged the cliff and the churning white surf below.

Suddenly Molly saw Clay thrust his wrinkled, determined face down at her from above the cab. He grabbed the reins, and wrenched them from her grasp. The coach lurched sharply. Then the whole carriage overturned, throwing Molly deep into the back of the cab. The way she was being jostled about, Molly feared for the child she carried. It was certain death for both if she remained. Above her Molly saw her only hope – the door of the coach. She reached up for the handle as the cab lurched and rocked violently. Then, in one desperate motion, Molly threw open the hatch like one does a trapdoor. The coach rocked and side-winded along the rutted road, but Molly managed to poke her head out, only to choke on dust and gravel that flew into her face. Molly gasped for breath as she crawled out of the coach and clung desperately to the side of the carriage using any handhold she could find. Suddenly Molly felt something grasp her riding boot. She looked back and saw Clay holding onto her foot, threatening to pull her to her death.

Molly kicked and kicked at Clay's boney white hand. Suddenly the coach, traveling crazily on its side, lurched and struck a boulder, shattering the elegant trim and sending a rain of splinters and wooden missiles over Molly's head. When she looked back at Clay he was still holding on, the spoke of a wheel jutting through his throat. He gurgled something as he glared at her. Molly gave him one last battery of kicks. Clay's grasp weakened and he tumbled down the side of the cliff into the raging surf below.

"There's your due, Sebastian Clay," Molly muttered under her breath. "You will tell no more tales of me, or of Alice."

Molly turned to the horses. She could sense them tiring as she held on. What remained of the coach was starting to slow down.

# CHAPTER 75: The Meeting Place

The millpond ice was starting to break. Ash waited in his usual spot at the brink of the icy pool, his hand resting on the hilt of his sword. Fallen logs, half submerged, resembled lurking alligators in the moonlight. The boding cry of a tree toad caught Ash's ear. The seasons were changing, the snow melting, which glistened in white, ghostly patches on the ground and at the bases of leafless trees. Ash was impatient. He strained his eyes, attempting to catch the first shadow of Molly's approach in the moonlight. She usually wore her cloak and cowl. Her approach was always an endearing sight. Ash knew the risks she took for him, and for the others like him, and he loved her all the more for her bravery.

"We envy you," spoke a dark figure emerging from the shadows. It was Christian.

"You are to be the first," said Constance, stepping out from behind a tree surrounded by slate gravestones, the folds of a riding cloak twisted around her.

Mallory appeared next, wrapped in a fur-trimmed hood and cloak. Then other darker figures stood further back, a colony to themselves.

"I wonder what it will be like," Mallory whispered. She cast her sparkling eyes up at Christian. He looked at her, not fully understanding.

"To share a mortal life together," Mallory finished.

Christian smiled. He placed an arm around her and held her

tightly. Mallory turned and reached out, pulling by the hand a young man with dark eyes and black, shoulder-length hair. It was Bain. He emerged into the starlight and stood beside Mallory and Christian.

"Bain, dear cousin," Mallory said. "Please show Ash your gift."

Bain withdrew from his cloak a small object that reflected the moonlight. He handed it to Ash with care. Ash studied its delicate, shimmering molding. It was a little gold locket suspended on a sliver of golden chain.

"Open it," Bain urged.

Ash found the clasp, sprung it, and opening the tiny hinge, beheld a sight that made his face tremble with emotion. It was a miniature portrait of Molly in all her radiance and promise, rendered in hand-painted porcelain.

"I painted it with all my skill," said Bain. He turned towards Constance, whose silent gaze met his. "Give it to her from all of us."

Ash's eyes welled. He placed a thankful hand on Bain's shoulder. Suddenly a sound caused Ash to turn towards the darkened woods before him. When he looked back at his companions, they were gone, swift as shadows. Only the sagging slates of gravestones stood behind him in the gloom.

# CHAPTER 76: Cry for Help

The coach incident tired Molly as she hurried along the wooded path that led to the burial ground. Her delicate condition was also beginning to exhaust her. Molly had managed to unharness one of the horses and ride it through the dense wood, but only so far. Now she was on foot. She carried the Highland Mantel Clock close by her side. The howl of a distant dog and the screech of an owl momentarily stole Molly's breath, but her heart beat with anticipation. She wanted to see Ash, but more than anything she wanted to see him drink her remedy. The cure she carried was tucked in a leather pouch tied to her cloak. Her riding boots quickly became damp and mud-caked during the journey. Suddenly she slipped while crossing a bridge of mossy stones over a deep brook, and found herself almost up to her knees in water. She prevented another slip by supporting herself against a large boulder while clutching the Highland Mantel Clock. Molly struggled to get back onto dry ground, but another step found her waist deep in the icy brook.

"Ash," Molly gasped, shuddering with cold.

Ash stood alone by the millpond. His senses were keen when it came to Molly, and he felt deeply that something was wrong. It was unlike her to be so late. Ash quickly abandoned his post and hastened through the woods. His pace soon became a chase. Something happened to Molly, he could feel it. The horrible sensation stung like a dagger. A large trunk of a fallen oak crossed his path, which he leaped in one bound. Ash landed catlike and sprinted through the darkness like a creature of instinct and purpose.

"Molly!" he shouted.

Ash's sharp ears suddenly detected a faint splashing sound.

"Molly!" he cried again.

This time Ash heard his name being called weakly in the darkness ahead. When he arrived at the brook he could scarcely believe his eyes. Without hesitating he waded into the icy water and lifted Molly up like a shivering bundle and carried her out.

"The clock," Molly spoke weakly. "Save the clock."

Ash picked up the Highland Mantel Clock which was half submerged between two stones, and carried both it and Molly through the woods.

"I must get you warm," he said, his breath puffing before him.

"Do not take me home," Molly insisted, her face pressed into Ash's neck.

"I know a place," Ash replied. "It is not far."

Early labor pains surprised Ash and frightened Molly. Ash carried Molly back toward the millpond. He soon spied what he was looking for – a little lighted window nestled behind a slope, which guided them like a beacon.

# CHAPTER 77 : The Midwife

The Widow Redd, skilled as a midwife, administered to the birth in her cottage by Redd's Pond. Named for the widow's grandmother, Wilmont Redd or "Mammy Redd" as she was better known, who was hanged as a witch in 1692, the pond was an ideal place for those seeking solitude. Against the decorum of the day, Ash was present during the birth. He held Molly's hand, which closed around his with such tightness that it almost made them one. Molly never cried out, but instead gasped when she felt pain. Finally the child arrived with a cry and the Widow Redd wrapped it in a blanket and placed it in her mother's arms. It was a baby girl. Molly cradled her newborn daughter as Ash wiped Molly's forehead with a damp cloth. Molly smiled at the little, pursed face of her baby and then up at Ash, whose soft eyes glistened with affection.

"She looks like her mother," Ash said, his voice almost cracking.

"I will call her, Ashley," said Molly, weakly.

Molly's eyes strayed over to a frosted, lattice window and a full moon beyond.

"It is time," Molly said softly, so as not to disturb her snuggling baby. "You must take the potion by moonlight."

Ash stroked Molly's cheek as she and her baby lay bundled in Widow Redd's best bed. Ash rose and retrieved the vial from the pouch. The silence that enveloped the candlelit room was palpable. Even the squirming infant was quiet. Molly reached out to Ash. Ash

263

knelt at her bedside once more, took Molly's soft hand into his, and kissed it.

"Go quickly," Molly said, gathering her strength. "When I see you next you will be free, and soon we will waltz, as man and wife."

Ash sunk his head upon Molly's breast as she stroked his hair.

"Now go, my dearest," Molly whispered, "and when you return, I'll tell you a story about that clock you saved and a certain gown. I know it will amuse you."

Ash rose with purpose. He closed his hand around the vial and walked to the door. He glanced back at Molly smiling at him from the bed.

"Until the stars fall from Heaven," Ash whispered. Then he strode out into the night.

# CHAPTER 78: The Duellists

Redd's Pond was still frozen over at the edges. Ash trudged through patches of snow on his way to the summit of the Old Burial Hill where rays of blue moonlight washed over looming oaks and sagging headstones. As Ash neared the crown he was imagining a normal life with Molly and their child. No longer would he have to endure another century, to eternally witness man's cruelty to his fellow man, and the effects of disease and war.

Ash finally reached the dome of the hill and stood by the sagging slates of Minister's Row, where a cluster of gravestones wore the epitaphs of parsons from the First Congregational Church of Marblehead.

Ash withdrew the vial from his cloak and held it against the moonlight. He drew a breath, uncorked the bottle, and held it high as if toasting the new existence it promised. Ash then brought the vial to his lips. It tasted bitter at first and then turned strangely sweet. Ash looked to the moon and let its light fall full upon his face. Eagerly he awaited the effects of the elixir. Suddenly Ash began to feel something. Although it was cold, he began to feel warm, and then almost feverish. Then his throat began to tighten. He gripped his windpipe and staggered back from the rows of slates and deaths-heads that surrounded him at the crown of the hill. He began to feel dizzy, and then a strange shiver went through his upper body. Ash knew that something had gone terribly wrong. He dashed down the slope of the hill. He was frightened out of his wits and more than anything wanted to be with Molly. Upon reaching the frozen edge of the pond, Ash stumbled. Quickly, he crawled forward seeking his reflection in the ice, where in the bright moonlight he saw a change happen. His face was altering before his eyes. Muscles realigned themselves and congealed into a sight that chilled his blood. Ash smashed the ice with his fist and buried his face in his hands, which had also transformed, for they were hideously knobbed at the knuckles and covered with filaments of hair.

"There," spoke a voice from a grove of nearby oaks. "Justice is served."

Ash turned to see John Pitcher standing in the shadows.

"You!" Ash groaned.

"What you drank was not my wife's handiwork," said Pitcher, "but something I had prepared especially for you."

Pitcher let out a chuckle.

"You chose to behave as a wolf. Then be a wolf," he said.

"Molly," Ash gasped as his thoughts returned to her and the baby.

"Even she wouldn't want you now," said Pitcher, advancing, "and I have plans for her too. My footman, Stafford, is now attending to that."

John Pitcher drew his sword from his scabbard.

***"NOOOOOOOOOOOOOOOOOOOOOHHH!!!"***

Ash was astounded by the sound of his own voice, for it was deep and guttural, like that of a woodland beast. He then realized his vocal organs had suffered a change as well. Pitcher snickered as he raised his weapon.

"Now it is time for a gentleman to slay the wolf."

The mottled shadows of tree branches passed over Pitcher, until finally in the open, moonlight shown along his brandished blade. Ash read the fatal meaning in Pitcher's serpent smile. He turned towards the widow's house when a sword slash across his back spun him around to face his attacker. Ash drew his own saber from under his cloak and stood gasping. He could feel warm blood soaking his back. Pitcher made two quick revolutions with his blade in the air, spoiling for a duel. He extended his weapon, bent his knees, and raised his rear arm so that it appeared like a scorpion's tail cocked to strike.

"Turn your back on me again, wolf, and I'll cleave you in two!" Pitcher sneered.

Ash took the jealous husband at his word. Every second counted now, for some horrible fate was in store for Molly. Ash lashed out with his blade. The slice meant for Pitcher's throat was parried by Pitcher's blade. The peal of clashing steel rang through the quiet graveyard. Pitcher lunged forward for a quick stab. Ash countered with a slice of his saber. Pitcher swung his sword at Ash, but it whooshed through empty air. Ash rolled behind a series of gravestones. Pitcher beat the slates, moving from one to the other as though he was swinging a scythe, sparks and flashes flying. Pitcher laughed like a mad butcher.

"Take my wife from me, will you?" he shouted, whipping his sword back and forth. "I'll lay you both in your graves! Let the earth be your adulterous bed!"

Pitcher stabbed deep behind a stone he was certain concealed his enemy, but buried his point in the ground instead. Pitcher suddenly felt a sting across the side of his face. When he reached for his ear, he found that it was gone, just a river of blood running down the side of his neck. Ash leaped from the shadows roaring like a leopard. He swung his sword over his head as though he was wielding a club. Pitcher blocked the blow with his saber just inches from his face, but Ash brought his full weight upon Pitcher, forcing him backward over a sagging headstone. Confronted with the snarling face of his adversary, Pitcher shrunk back. He was no longer combating a man, but something less in the chain of creation. Pitcher lifted the heel of his riding boot and kicked the heaving monster from him. Ash flew back against a gnarled oak. An animal's bellow escaped his lips. Pitcher's anger welled up again, and like a cocked spring, he struck out with his saber. Ash dodged the blow that hacked a shower of oak splinters into the air.

"Let me do you a favor and kill you?" Pitcher shouted as he held the side of his bloody face. "Already she is lost to you!"

Ash answered with a volley of sword strokes. Pitcher met his blade with his own, stroke for stroke. The clashing of steel clanged through the midnight air like the hammerings of a forge. Locked in mortal combat, the duelists moved unconsciously through the burial ground, heedless of the grim memorials. Each matched the other in skill and endurance and looked for some opportunity to deliver the decisive blow. Ash hardly knew his own soul. Goaded by the jeers and taunts of his enemy his heart filled with hate, which only a short while ago welled another emotion. Pitcher was consumed by a desire to stamp out the adversary who had stained his perfect existence. At times sure of their footing, sometimes slipping on the snowy patches dotting the slope, Ash and Pitcher arrived upon the crest of Old Burial Hill where the moonbeams caused the tolling sabers to flash and glitter like lightning.

Pitcher hacked away, flailing this way and that, as though his weapon was a whip. Ash deflected each stroke, the clashing blades crisscrossing in a burst of sparks, like striking flints. Exhausted, Pitcher summoned a reserve of strength and lunged forward stabbing Ash through the shoulder. Ash groaned like a wounded animal. Pitcher struck again at Ash's head, but his stroke clipped off the corner rosette of a gravestone in a brilliant flash. Ash saw an opening, but Pitcher avoided it causing Ash to divide the air between Pitcher's remaining ear and another stone marker. He then swung his weapon laterally. The blade met flesh this time, slicing clean through Pitcher's coat and cutting his arm. Pitcher spun out behind the cover of the headstone, blood pouring out of the ruff of his sleeve like wine out of a bottle. He began to stagger from exhaustion and loss of blood.

"By now she is lost to us both," Pitcher stated breathlessly, holding his bleeding arm with his sword hand, one side of his face awash with gore.

Something in Pitcher's words struck a chord in Ash. His fury faded, he discovered that he could no longer fight. Ash backed away amongst the graves, lowered his bloodstained sword, and opened his shirt. Without uttering a word he presented his opponent an easy target – his bared chest. In the glow of the moon Pitcher saw his opportunity. He lunged forward and leveled the point of his saber into the breastbone of his adversary, and as a victorious grin spread across his lips, he pushed the weapon deeper with all his remaining strength. Ash grimaced as the weapon plunged through his torso. He could feel the razor sawing through his insides and burrowing out through his back. Pitcher wasn't satisfied until he drove the blade up to the hilt so that the silvery point shot out and glinted red in the blue wash of light. Ash stood expressionless, impaled on the weapon, staring into Pitcher's grinning face.

"Now die, wolf!" Pitcher exclaimed. "For you have nothing to live for!"

A tear ran down Ash's altered cheek. Pitcher felt satisfaction upon seeing his enemy's hopeless position, but Pitcher soon felt something wasn't right. The smile shrank from his face. Ash was still standing and looking at him, keenly, mockingly, despite two feet of razor edged steel jabbed through his body. Pitcher abandoned his weapon where he had driven it and backed away, astonishment branding his face.

"What in God's name are you?" Pitcher gasped.

"What I am has nothing to do with God," Ash replied.

Ash lifted his hand, gripped the hilt, and in one long, smooth movement withdrew the saber from his chest. Ash stepped toward Pitcher, and as he did, the lines and muscles of his face bunched up into wrinkles of animal fury. He approached Pitcher until only a foot of space stood between them. Pitcher remained frozen in place, as if turned to stone from beholding the petrifying gaze of the storied Gorgon.

No one ever knew what became of John Pitcher. He was never seen or heard from again, although it was told that a young boy fished up a severed human skull out of the still, black waters of Redd's Pond a year later. Ash had greater matters to deal with other than the deed he had just committed. He ran wildly around the wind-worn tombstones of Old Burial Hill until he had reached the open threshold of Widow Redd's cottage. The sight that greeted his eyes caused a bellow to erupt from his throat, a wild cry which startled every sleeping colonial in the neighborhood out of his snug bed. Ash staggered as though in a daze toward where Molly Pitcher lay white as soap tangled in bedclothes. The midwife, the newborn baby, and the Highland Mantel Clock were gone. Ash took up Molly in his arms, and stroked her lovely, lifeless face.

# CHAPTER 79: The Weird Chamber

Whether it was hours or minutes that passed before Siri woke up she couldn't tell. She was coming around and was glad she wasn't dreaming anymore. Or was it all a dream? Everything she experienced seemed so real. The last thing Siri remembered she was with Ash in the Witch House. Then something strange happened to her. She felt like she wasn't herself anymore, but someone else in a different age. Siri opened her eyes, but discovered that she couldn't see. Everything was black. She couldn't move either. She was tied up. Then Siri realized her head was covered over by a black sack. How it got there she hadn't a clue, but her first order of business was to get it off. Siri tried to use her teeth to tug the covering from her head. At first things didn't look promising, but soon Siri felt it slipping off a little at a time as she chewed on a section of burlap. Finally, with a few shakes of her head, the sack slipped from her face.

"Yuk!" Siri blurted, spitting out some bad tasting fibers.

She squinted until her eyes adjusted to the brightness of her new surroundings. She felt groggy as if she had been drugged. Siri turned her head from side to side, but Ash was nowhere in sight. As far as she could tell she was alone. Something had happened to her and Ash, but Siri couldn't remember a thing about it. Surely Ash wasn't responsible for her predicament. She trusted him, or thought she could. Siri's eyes focused on a whitewashed, cinder block chamber illuminated by a brilliant arc light. The room reminded her of an old hospital

273

basement as tables arrayed with racks of test tubes, Bunsen burners, and compressed gas cylinders all came into view. Siri crinkled her nose from the smell of alcohol and chemicals. Somewhere off in an adjoining room she could hear tinny, jazz-age lyrics about a paper moon and a cardboard sea buzzing over a phonograph or radio.

Siri only became aware of her own situation when she tried to move. Strapped to an upright gurney, a leather band across her chest, the other across her feet, and with a white sheet covering her, Siri felt like she was about to undergo some terrible surgery. Siri knew better than to make noise. Whoever tied her down didn't account for her wriggling powers. Siri wriggled this way and that, pulling and twisting her limbs until at last she was able to free one hand and then the other. Once she could move her hands Siri lost no time unfastening her legs. As the music droned on Siri tiptoed her way towards another adjoining room, darker than the one she was in.

Siri was wide-awake now as she peeked into the shadows. She had a feeling that her dad and friends weren't far off. The chamber looked like some kind of shipping room judging from the bales of packing straw and the many upright boxes resembling coffins standing along the mildewed walls. Shelves lined with chemical bottles and strange laboratory apparatus, together with a huge forklift in the middle of the floor, captured Siri's eager eyes. A great curtain hanging from the ceiling partitioned off the other half of the strange chamber.

Siri stole around the blind to see what it concealed. Her jaw nearly fell open in astonishment. Arrayed upon the floor were twenty Egyptian sarcophagi spaced neatly apart in rows. Composed of wood and painted to resemble their tenants, it was plain to Siri that these were the stolen mummies. The smell of cedar and camphor wood, and the sweet scent of aromatic gums and natron used in mummification permeated the room. Of the twenty sarcophagi, four were wide open and empty.

Siri then saw why. Before her, strapped to its own surgical table, were four mummies swathed head to foot in grey bandages, some with their arms still bound before them or held at their sides as if waiting their turn for some outlandish procedure. Nearby loomed rows of shelves stacked with linen, dressings, and other medical supplies. One large box on a top shelf caught Siri's attention, for it was boldly labeled "CLOTH BANDAGES." Siri quickly switched her attention to the discarded lids of the open sarcophagi and examined the painted likenesses of their contents. Staring back at her with wide, soulful eyes were the faded faces of three men and one woman, their black hair trimmed in ringlets. Siri returned her gaze to the four mummies lying like eerie cadavers in a morgue and noticed one was a foot shorter than the rest, about her size, Siri thought. Then a twinkle came to her dissimilar eyes.

# CHAPTER 80: A Strange Disguise

Siri quickly put her plan into action. There was no time for second thoughts. Her captors would be checking on her and she had to have everything in place before they arrived. There were more than enough linen rolls on hand. Siri took one and wound the bandages around and around her body. She could hear another scratchy song echoing from some distant chamber, this time about seeing someone in old familiar places.

Siri tried to keep her mind on her bandaging as the old fashioned music went on. She wondered who was playing it. Finally she reviewed her appearance in a full-length mirror on the wall, turning one way and then the other, like a lady in a dress shop. Siri looked like an accident victim, or a mummy. She was bandaged entirely from head to toe with just a slit for her eyes. The second part of her plan required a strong stomach. Touching the stiff, dusty thing was bad enough, but pulling the slight, mummified figure off the gurney and dragging it across the floor, and then putting her own clothes on it was something that had to be seen to be believed, but Siri tucked it up nicely on the surgical table in her place, threw the sack over its head, and was proud of her dead ringer.

Siri overheard footsteps approaching. She shuffled across the floor over to the gurney, stumbling once when a loose roll of linen tangled about her foot. Siri hoisted herself upon the table and laid flat down, crossing her arms across her chest. Suddenly she could hear two men commenting on her hooded double in the next room.

"She sleeps like a stiff," said the first.

"We'll come back for her later," said the second. "Let's get this over with."

Suddenly two men pushed back the broad curtain and entered the room. They wore thick, round goggles and were garbed in white linen surgical caps, masks, and tunics with rows of buttons that fastened down the side from the shoulder. Their attire seemed like hospital wear from another era and Siri vaguely recalled seeing something similar on a Bugs Bunny cartoon when Bugs was about to go under the knife. Siri closed her eyes and froze as stiff as she could as she felt their gaze on her. She overheard a piece of paper being unfolded.

"This is the one – MOFA 12," said one of the men.

Siri could only wonder what MOFA meant. Then it hit her: Museum of Fine Arts.

"Here's the other one – METNY 13," spoke the other. "Let's wheel them out."

"Metropolitan Museum of Art in New York," Siri thought to herself.

Siri felt a wheel brake being released and then an uneasy sense of motion. Siri breached her eyes just a crack and saw row after row of dim ceiling bulbs pass by overhead as she was wheeled along a corridor partitioned by a series of concrete arches. Siri had no idea where she was when all of the sudden the thought hit her. She was somewhere under the Danvers Asylum. She had to be. Her instincts told her she was probably in some long-forgotten sub-basement the police never searched, but that didn't matter now. What the two men planned to do with her did. So Siri just kept still. Suddenly from out of some deep recess Siri could hear a scratchy recording of a woman singing about "not getting a kick from champagne," and other things, but getting a kick out of someone. Her powerful, piercing voice boomed through the murky corridor.

Siri could see specimen METNY 13 being wheeled beside her through the corner of her eye. The feet, legs, torso and then the head progressed past her down the corridor. It resembled a giant bowling pin wrapped in linen strips as it rolled by. Siri's gurney began to gain on it. It was as if they were drag racing. Some grand scheme was afoot and whatever it was Siri knew she was in the middle of it.

Siri was growing anxious. Things were getting too crazy. She tried to calm herself by telling herself to stay on mission. She was confident that if there was any way to find her dad, her friends, and Ash, then this was it. The brassy song about someone not getting their kicks was growing louder and clearer as she got nearer to the source. Siri saw that the hall suddenly became very dark and then light again, as if she were being wheeled into regions where overhead lighting was sporadic. She became aware of potted date palms common to Libya and Morocco lined in rows on either side of her. Their long, green pinnate leaves reached out from their trunks like peacock feathers on a bad hair day. Even though she was covered in bandages, Siri's nose was sensitive and she could smell a cornucopia of strange chemicals. She then heard the grinding of a motor. It was obviously an electric generator of some kind. Siri felt like she was about to enter a very unpleasant place. For an old abandoned insane asylum, it was anything but abandoned, Siri thought.

# CHAPTER 81: The Secret Laboratory

As Siri rolled along she watched the corridor ceiling yawn into an open cave of sorts so that lighting was now provided by evenly spaced work lights set on stands, like the kind used on construction sites. The floor was still smooth tile beneath the wheels of her gurney, and the impression Siri got from obliterated stonework moving passed her was that someone had taken great pains to knock down dividing walls to create a vast open space. She felt a weird vibration, like being dangerously close to a high voltage line. It gave Siri a tingly feeling all over.

Suddenly the gurney came to an abrupt stop in what appeared to be a great, gray dungeon-like chamber. Siri's eyes widened. From her limited vantage she could see long black tables with glass beakers boiling on burners with strange liquids gurgling from one glass bulb into another with strange glass rods in-between. Racks of test tubes caught her eye; they were filled with green, red, and yellow fluids that seemed viscous and bubbly, like honey with too much air in it. A large, box-like machine with three tapering stacks of metal disks on top reminded Siri of transformers used on utility poles.

Then Siri saw a strange control panel with dozens of dials, switches, and gauges, all festooned with heavy black cable overhead. The sight of it all gave Siri the sinking feeling that taking the mummy's place wasn't such a great idea after all. Suddenly the crackle of a high voltage arc startled her. It sounded like a bed sheet tearing. All around

Siri vivid bursts of bright blue light flashed casting a wild menagerie of shadows. As Siri switched her eyes around, she could see the flares playing upon the brass surface of a huge Chinese gong suspended from a wooden frame. Then a great statue gaped at her out of the murk, which looked strangely familiar. It was the hawk-headed god, Horus, its smoothly formed, human body carved from pink marble. Two rows of stone, lotus-shaped columns suddenly directed Siri's gaze upon a great black and white wall mural framed at the end of the strange gallery.

Siri's eyes widened even more. The gilt mural depicted a middle-aged American man and a pretty young woman posing before the Great Sphinx of Giza. It looked like an old Kodak snapshot blown up into a big painting. The man wore a white turban and the woman, a fashionable headscarf tied to one side. They looked quite happy together, Siri thought, but then she found herself focusing on the man with his laughing eyes and dashing smile. At first glance one could have mistaken him for the silent film legend, Rudolph Valentino. Although young and without oval glasses and a trim beard, Siri recognized him. He had come to her science class to give a lecture on the sun. He was Emil Adelman, Professor *Emeritus* of Molecular Biology and Astrophysics from the Massachusetts Institute of Technology!

The sporadic blasts of light suddenly caught the motions of human shapes, their movement's strobing like actors from the silent film era. One shape caught Siri's attention and when she recognized it, it took all of her willpower to suppress a jubilant shout. It was Mallory! She was dressed in a trim, white nurse's outfit, and was carrying a rack of test tubes from one table to another. Her blue eyes were riveted straight ahead and her movements appeared slavish and mechanical, as if she was sleepwalking while awake. Christian Fletcher and Constance Nash were lying unconscious on gurneys, covered in white sheets up to their necks. On a table beside them was a young man with shoulder-length hair. Siri recognized him from the dream state Ash placed her under before he disappeared. It was Bain, the painter from the grotto, and Mallory's cousin. Other young people were reclined on planks suspended from the vaulted ceiling by cable wires at various heights, their limp arms hanging in the air.

"It's the missing teenagers!" Siri thought.

Then the orderly who rolled her into the room positioned a dolly topped with surgical instruments next to her gurney. Siri didn't like how things were going, particularly when Mallory took up a scalpel from one of the trays and divided a sheet of onionskin paper in half with barely a stroke to test its sharpness. Siri was wondering if things could get any worse when all of the sudden the scratchy music abruptly stopped. Then a wizened, trim-bearded face bent over her garbed in a surgical gown and cap. It was Emil Adelman. He held out his hand to Mallory who was acting as his assistant.

"Scalpel," he said. "I'll remove the head. I have no use for it."

"I advise making the incision between the Atlas C1 and Axis C2," offered Mallory dryly. "The sternocleidomastoid should pose no difficulty."

Doctor Adelman nodded.

"Yes. I agree," he said.

"Adelman, see reason!" shouted a voice from the shadows. Siri knew at once who it was – Alex Cedric!

"We pledged to help these unfortunate souls," Cedric continued. "Not experiment on them. They trusted us! Don't betray that trust now!"

Adelman lowered the scalpel. Siri trained her eyes on the glinting, razor-edged implement as it narrowly passed her eyes and ear as Adelman, distracted, put it down upon the gurney close beside her head. Siri suddenly overheard Adelman mumble. "Vitamin D, not enough Vitamin D, poor fellow. To paraphrase the bard, all the world should be in love with Vitamin D, and pay no heed to garish Vitamin C."

Siri watched Adelman impatiently beckon to both orderlies and walk over to a section in the room from where she had heard Cedric's voice, the folds of his surgical gown trailing behind him. With Adelman and the orderlies out of sight Siri decided to take a desperate gamble. She raised her head a little and saw to her astonishment her dad, Scarpetti, Kaelyn, Bernie, Cedric, Dent, Fez Guy, the big

Mongolian, and even her school principal, Bramwell Fletcher. They were chained in a row along a section of whitewashed wall fitted with iron staples once used to secure the criminally insane. Even Dent's mummy was incarcerated, tucked away in a corner and bound in a cocoon of iron chains so that only his head was visible. The thing looked so dejected that even as a resurrected mummy it appeared to have given up the ghost. Siri saw that her only hope lay in Mallory!

"Pssst!" Siri said, raising her head a little more and pulling down a portion of bandages to reveal her face. "Mallory, it's me, Siri. Don't you know me? Snap out of it!"

Siri noticed a little silver Ankh amulet glinting at the base of Mallory's throat suspended on a chain. It also gave her an idea. When no one was watching Siri reached out and snatched it, chain and all. Mallory showed no change in expression and just kept staring into space.

Adelman opened a great glass cabinet that had once stored medicines to treat the demented. Its shelves were crammed with factory fresh, plastic bottles of Vitamin D. Adelman took a bottle and walked over to where Cedric was manacled to the wall, his two orderlies accompanying him. One carried a glass pitcher of water and a stack of paper cups, the other – a German Luger pistol.

"Emil," Cedric called out, straining at his jangling chains. "You're a great scientist. Think of what you're doing!"

Adelman took a large, white tablet from the bottle and pressed it against Cedric's lips. Cedric tried to turn away, but a nudge from the barrel of the German Luger held against his head returned Cedric's attention to the pill.

"My good friend, Alex," Adelman smiled. "You're displaying all the classic symptoms of Vitamin D deficiency: nervous behavior, erratic outbursts. Withdrawal will soon follow without an intervention. Just one tablet of Vitamin D will remedy all this. Now be good and open your mouth."

Cedric reluctantly did as he was told. Adelman popped the tablet in and his orderly followed with a cup of water.

"Emil," Cedric gasped after swallowing. "Please, let us go."

"Calm yourself," Adelman interrupted.

He then raised both hands as if concentrating on a reverent thought.

"Soon the glorifying and revivifying effects of Vitamin D, the sunshine pill, will take effect. Akhenaten, the greatest and wisest Pharaoh of Egypt, was right when he insisted all Egyptians worship the sun, bringer of warmth and life. And he ordered his priests to distill from the sun its life-giving properties, because Akhenaten wanted above all things to be like the sun, and have eternal life. They called him a heretic for this and tore down his statues and defaced his name from monuments. But the secret of eternal life written down in the Scroll of Thoth they never destroyed. That Akhenaten gave to his son, Tutankhamun, and Tutankhamun had his father's secret buried with him until your grandfather discovered the Osiris Keys of Imhotep. IMHOTEP! Master artisan and high priest – clever contriver of the impregnable vault that hid the Scroll of Thoth under Howard Carter's very nose!"

"Adelman!"

Cedric tried to cut in, but Adelman rattled on, his eyes and hands still raised, his extreme concentration unbroken.

"Your grandfather stole the Osiris Keys together with the statue of Horus that hid them, until someone unsuspected by your grandfather stole one of the Osiris Keys from him. But lo! Imhotep was no fool. One Osiris Key is worthless without the other, for to open the statue of Horus both Osiris Keys must be used in concert. Together! How it must have agonized your grandfather when he discovered this, for above all things he wanted eternal life too! So to safeguard the statue of Horus and the Scroll of Thoth it contained, your grandfather removed that statue to Salem to an old smuggler's tunnel to buy him the time and the secrecy to try and crack Imhotep's vault. But when the Witch House was relocated over that entryway, your grandfather sought out another access. This posed no problem, because beneath the streets of Salem are warrens of tunnels. The subcellar of the Witch Curse Museum provided the answer. Sadly, your grandfather lost his race against time. But he left a journal, and following where he left off, you stumbled upon these unfortunate young people locked in time, afflicted with the yoke of a life unending leveled on them by a gallows curse..."

"But Adelman!" Cedric blurted.

Adelman was carried away by his own open floodgates of thought.

"Yes. These poor, underground Salem souls. Their plight aroused your pity, a sentiment which surprised even you. From them you learned of a legendary parchment scribed during the time of the Revolution which contained in its precious writing a formula that could dispel their affliction, but the trail to this last scrap of hope had long grown cold and the parchment forever lost. But your passion to help these young people was infectious. You recruited others to your cause to help them. I was one of them. You sought out a place for us to work. This abandoned asylum proved most suitable. Then it occurred to your scientific brain. If the compounds written on the Scroll of Thoth were reversed perhaps you could bring an end to the suffering of these poor, subterranean souls, their problem of immortality. You long suspected Dent's grandfather, the Right Honorable Lord Chase, of acquiring the twin Osiris Key from your grandfather. You lured Dent to Salem with a promise of scholarly fame in Egyptology knowing full well he knew you meant unlocking the Scroll of Thoth, and that he would bring the long lost Osiris Key undoubtedly bequeathed to him by his notable grand-dad. You hoped to get your hands on that key, for with the Scroll of Thoth at last unlocked and its secrets combined with the legendary elixir these underground worthies vainly sought for centuries, yes, yes, with that too in our cabinet of miracles, we might apply one in reverse, and the other to accelerate the effect, and dispel the endless, looping life cycle that entraps the souls of these unfortunate young people in undying bodies. You hoped to get your hands on his Osiris Key. But then I had the revelation! The great, wonderful day! The Scroll of Thoth, giver of life and taker of life, could restore life! YES! LIFE! THE RESTORATION OF LIFE TO THOSE WITHOUT LIFE!"

Adelman's hands and eyes were raised, his concentration riveted to a rapturous vision nailed like a Time Square billboard in his brain. He turned sharply towards Cedric.

"It is no mere accident that we are here, on the brink of another great discovery. It is divine providence! And after this great, wonderful day, we will do as we had originally pledged. Keep up the good work, dear friend. You'll be as great as Carter one day."

Adelman lowered his hands to his side and smiled at Cedric who could say little after listening to the scientist's raving.

# CHAPTER 82: The Mad Scientist

Siri sat up on her gurney. She was trying, vainly in seemed, to snap Mallory out of her trance by swaying the silver Ankh amulet back and forth before her eyes.

"Mallory," Siri whispered while keeping an eye on Adelman and his orderlies. "Concentrate. You see only the amulet. You hear only my voice. Try to forget everything you've heard before and hear only my voice. It's Siri, Mallory. I'm your best friend. Try and remember."

Siri watched the Ankh sparkle in Mallory's blue eyes. Mallory's eyelashes blinked once. Encouraged, Siri kept at it.

Adelman moved over to where Collin stood fastened to the wall. Collin gave his wrist manacles a vigorous tug, but seeing how useless his struggles were, he simply resigned himself to Adelman's pill and water. He swallowed it all down with a look of glaring defiance.

"Ah, Mister Braddock," Adelman said with satisfaction. "I see that I was just in time with a booster dose of Vitamin D. It will reduce the drag effect of your grief. I understand you too have suffered the loss of a loved one, a dear companion in life, as I have. I am not your enemy, but your friend. I understand what loneliness is, what it is like to live in the dark, to talk with shadows on the wall. Savor her memory, her smile in the morning and her kiss at night. I wish I could do more for you, my boy."

Adelman patted Collin on the shoulder and moved past Scarpetti who simply looked at him in bewilderment as he and his orderlies went by.

"Never mind the policeman," Adelman said. "Vitamin D can never help policemen."

Adelman passed Dent's dejected looking mummy tucked in a corner. At the sight of Adelman the creature raised its head, stiffened, and mustered all of its power to wrestle off the cocoon of chains it was secured in. Then it sort of gave up and sunk its head down again.

"We'll let him cool off," Adelman spoke, as he strode past the bound Egyptian.

Adelman stopped before Dent.

"Professor Adelman," Dent said earnestly, trying to gain his captor's confidence. "You are a great scientist in search of a secret that has dogged mankind since the world began. I too am a seeker and a scientist. I know what you're trying to do. Let me help you, for as you can see, I've had some success. You and I, we are not ordinary men. We are giants in a world of Lilliputians. Certainly we can make some sort of arrangement. I have many rich followers."

"Administer two tablets of Vitamin D to this one," Adelman said, with a disgusted huff. He then moved over to where Bramwell Fletcher stood chained to the wall.

Confronted by Adelman, Fletcher smirked, as if predicting the sermon he was about to receive.

"Well, well. What have we here?" Adelman's voice assumed a tone both haughty and indignant. "Could this be the noted hematologist Doctor Bramwell Fletcher of Queens College, Cambridge England and Nobel Laureate, discoverer of the Alpha Protein? You might remember me. I once corresponded to you under the name of Francis Lorre and tried to secure a fellowship in your lab to further my study of the Beta Protein. You denounced my theory as a joust for windmills. I tell you the Beta Protein is the bond that holds all other proteins together. Vitamin D unlocks its potential and propels it to the forefront of all other proteins. Without Beta, there would be no life. Akhenaten knew this in his own way. Now you come to Salem, summoned by Alex Cedric and posing as a school principal, in the hopes of putting your knowledge to work freeing these unfortunate immortals from the shackles of eternal life."

Adelman widened his eyes and raised an authoritative finger in the air.

"Without Vitamin D, all your efforts are doomed to fail!"

Adelman looked over to where Christian unconsciously lay covered in a white sheet up to his neck. Adelman bent his head to Bramwell's and spoke into his ear.

"One of your experiments backfired with hideous results. That poor boy you hypnotized and tried to cure has no memory of who he is. He even believes you're his father. Thanks to a heavy infusion of Vitamin D, I was able to reverse the horrid effects your blind groping set into motion."

Adelman folded his arms before him and momentarily studied Fletcher.

"But I suppose I should give you some credit. Your mastery of hypnotism, gained under Professor Falconer of Edinburgh, who could mesmerize entire stadiums of people with the toll of a gong, you put to good use here in Salem when you tuned the bell of that tourist attraction to summon our singular patients to therapy. You even tried to hypnotize me to stop me from my glorious work in Vitamin D extraction. But don't let my praise go to your head. Stick to hypnotism and leave science to me, Doctor Bramwell Fletcher! Doctor, huh!"

Fletcher looked earnestly at Adelman.

"At least I now know what to buy you for your birthday – one room and ten rolls of rubber wallpaper."

"Be grateful I already had three tablets of Vitamin D after breakfast," Adelman replied. "Otherwise, I would have Clive here deal with that remark. He's impetuous and has an itchy trigger finger. What more, like me, he has no patience for those who don't take their vitamins seriously."

Adelman poured out three tablets from the bottle and forced them one after the other past Fletcher's lips.

"That should take care of you." Adelman grinned. "Be grateful I was in time to save you."

Siri desperately swung the amulet back and forth before Mallory's eyes. Mallory's dilated pupils seemed to react to the reflections that danced over her placid face.

"Come on, Mallory," Siri said, urgently. "It's me, Siri. You've got to snap out of it. We're all in great danger!"

Then a thought occurred to Siri. She leaned forward and whispered into Mallory's ear.

*"Mallory, you've got a run in your stocking."*

Suddenly a hand came out of nowhere and snatched the amulet from Siri's grasp. Siri gasped and turned. It was one of Adelman's orderlies, and he caught Siri red handed.

"Look what I found," he announced, dangling the amulet and aiming his Luger at Siri. "A mummy with a little kick still left in it."

"Here's a kick for you!" Siri exclaimed. She struck out with her foot.

Adelman appeared indifferent to the sight of his crony crumpling to the floor.

"Deal with it, Clive," he said, while administering pills to the big Mongolian and Fez Guy. "Can't you see I'm busy?"

Kaelyn, Bernie, and Scarpetti couldn't believe their eyes. Neither could Collin. There was his daughter dressed as a mummy, kicking the Luger into a floor grate and dodging the lunges of the second orderly. He wanted to shout out to Siri, but didn't want to call Adelman's attention to her either.

Siri's petite figure sidewinding around the chamber, ducking behind machinery, and skidding along the tile floor in narrow escapes caught the eye of Dent's mummy and roused him to attention. His dark eyes followed Siri through his bandages.

In all the confusion, Mallory blinked, finally coming to her senses. Siri skirted right in front of her followed by Adelman's assistant. The sight of Siri's plight snapped Mallory awake. She checked her stocking, grabbed a loaded syringe, and injected it into the orderly's rump as he passed by. The orderly, stung but not deterred, cornered Siri between two, tall electrical machines, their dials winking like traffic beacons, their circuits buzzing deafeningly, like a hive with a billion bees. Siri had nowhere to go. She turned her head to the right, and then to the left. The orderly, satisfied and grinning, closed in. His hands reached out for Siri menacingly. Then, suddenly, his eyes upturned. He felt the air with wiggling fingers, and collapsed backwards upon the floor.

Siri was overjoyed that Mallory was back to her old self. Mallory, seeing Siri wrapped to her neck in bandages, begged questions, but this was no time for long tales or celebration. They both stole behind the looming statue of Horus and watched the mad scientist at work in his laboratory.

Adelman appeared relieved with the distraction gone and the return to quiet. He re-approached Fletcher. "In science there is no passion, no mercy," Adelman declared, his head bent slightly to the side, as if Fletcher was some curiosity. "Without passion there is no life. I am a man of passion. My blood is hot as a desert wind. And my late wife, Vera, was the object of my passion. It puzzles me why she took her own life thirty years ago while we were vacationing in Thebes. I made sure she was well fortified with Vitamin D and that she never hid herself from the restorative rays of the sun. I fawned over her every need. Wherever she turned I was there to greet her, my arms burning with passion. I supplied her lips with red-hot smooches, and poured her glasses of warm milk fortified with Vitamin D. With my own hand I spoon-fed her daily doses of even more Vitamin D. My voice never ceased to sing her praises. The music I played for her on the Victrola spoke of my unbridled, furious, glorious love! She was my Cleopatra, my Nefertiri, my Pookie. I never knew of the gun she hid under her pillow that morning, as I prepared her breakfast of Vitamin D. How could I? Surely I was not to blame for the fatal step she took against herself. Oh, those days in Egypt! They were a special time for us. Mars was in conjunction with Jupiter. And for a moment, in the night sky, they went backwards, just for a moment, to meet and embrace, as we embraced the night before she left me."

"You believe the planets can go backwards?" Fletcher scoffed.

"But they do go backwards," Adelman said dryly. "At least that is how they appear. It is what we astronomers call retrograde motion. And tonight, Mars once again will be in conjunction with Jupiter, as it was over Thebes on that night so long ago. And like those divine satellites, once again we will embrace!"

# CHAPTER 83: The Woman in White

Siri smiled at Mallory, glad to have her friend back. Mallory smiled in return, apparently reading Siri's thoughts. From their vantage point behind the statue they could see the whole crazy chamber. It was half dungeon, half insane asylum, half Egyptian temple, and half mad scientist's laboratory all rolled into one. Adelman walked over to Siri's empty gurney, ignoring his fallen assistants. He scratched his beard and then turned his attention to the remaining mummy specimen, the bulk of which was blocked from Siri and Mallory's view by bubbling glass beakers. Siri watched with rapt attention as Adelman took up a scalpel, and apparently worked it around the neck of the mummy, and judging from the squeamish expressions of Kaelyn and Bernie, he was removing the head. He then took a kind of barbed probe and withdrew some gray matter that resembled a dust bunny to Siri. Siri and Mallory looked at each other in bewilderment and then looked at Adelman. The scientist tucked the specimen into a test tube and then poured a few drops of a bluish liquid into it.

"What's he doing?" Siri whispered to Mallory.

Mallory moved closer to Siri and whispered back.

"For over a year now Cedric, Fletcher, and Doctor Adelman have been trying to cure us of a curse that was put on us long ago and reverse its anti-aging effects. I know it sounds cliché, but it's true. Christian volunteered to be the first to undergo these experiments. At first things looked promising, but then came setbacks. He forgot who he was, who I was. Christian assumed the identity Doctor Fletcher had given him, that he was the principal's son, and the doctor helped Christian to blend back into this modern world of yours. But a hideous side effect soon followed. Fletcher was at a loss of what to do until Doctor Adelman used the Vitamin D gathered from the balsams of mummies to stabilize the vaccine. It worked, but only for a short time, until Fletcher came upon the idea to bond Adelman's reagent with a certain xylitol, tree sap, mixed with a vial of Christian's own blood. It was a three-stage process that concluded just last night. Constance knew the tree to use."

"I think I saw that," Siri said.

"Then about a month ago Adelman snapped. His mind just went to pieces. He saw us all as guinea pigs for a new kind of experiment. Instead of helping Fletcher and Cedric get us back to leading normal life spans, Adelman and his henchmen began a campaign of obtaining live blood donors for experiments in Vitamin D extraction. When we all protested, he forced Fletcher to hypnotize us all and wipe that fact from our minds. The only one he couldn't hypnotize was Ash. Ash went into hiding until he saw you one day, and when he did, he remembered the Highland Mantel Clock and its importance. So he kept a watch on you. Somehow Ash knew you were our one and only hope."

Siri was astonished at what she was hearing. For once Mallory sounded brilliant, like she was the recipient of a brain transplant, and not the dim blonde she was use to hearing.

"Where's Ash?" Siri pressed.

"I don't know," Mallory replied. "The last thing I remember is Adelman forcing Fletcher to place me under hypnosis at gunpoint. Everything in the last two hours is a blank. Adelman's completely mad about immortality!"

Mallory quickly brought a finger to her lips.

"Shhhhhhhhhhh," she whispered, keeping an eye on the doctor.

Siri and Mallory watched as Adelman placed the blue test tube on a rack.

"He's really gone," Mallory remarked.

Adelman then reached into the neckline of his surgical scrubs and produced twin amulets which bore the Eye of Horus motif Siri recognized only too well. They were the Osiris Keys. Adelman removed the ornaments from their chains, held them face out, and approached the looming, hawk-headed statue of Horus in reverent steps as a priest might in some holy shrine.

Siri's eyes widened as Adelman in his scrubs converged upon her and Mallory's hiding place. The scientist regarded the great statue with a wild-eyed stare which to Siri hadn't one scrap of sanity left in it. Siri backed up slowly into a dark recess directly behind the statue. Mallory did the same. Suddenly Siri bumped up against what felt like an upright glass box, like a phone booth. It instantly lit up. Both Siri and Mallory turned and looked. Their eyes widened in disbelief. There it stood as white as soap, silent and still in the surreal light of footlights as if on a stage – the slender form of a woman. Her brunette hair was done up in a bun with little ringlets gracing her temples like a Grecian maiden – one pale shoulder exposed. The rest of her figure was draped in a white, shimmering gown that ran down to the very floor of the booth. She looked like the Venus De Milo or some Aegean queen, like Helen of Troy. Her eyes were closed and her long lashes were black with mascara, her lips – red and voluptuous. She appeared as if she was in the midst of a deep sleep with her arms at her side, but Siri could see that the sealed woman was quite dead, preserved by a method that would be crude to call embalming. The display caused Siri to squirm and she wondered what sort of mind could take such pains to make a dead woman so beautiful, so lifelike, and put her in a glass box like a department store window display. Siri had read about glass coffins in fairy tales, but to be confronted with one in real life made her cringe.

As unnerved as Siri was, she still had the presence of mind to find out what Adelman was doing at the front of the statue. She dared not peek just then, but instead pressed her ear to the sculpture and listened as Adelman made contact with the Osiris Keys somewhere on the pedestal. Siri heard a sharp *"click"* and then the sound of stone sliding on stone, as if some secret compartment in the base of the statue was opening by the release of a hidden spring or counter weight. Siri then peered around the corner of the statue. Mallory peeked around the other side. They watched Adelman back away from the carved figure reverently bearing a white, alabaster box between his hands. He turned solemnly and returned to his work table in the center of the great chamber. His orderlies were moaning into consciousness.

"Clive, Kettering," Adelman declared with authority. "Get up off the floor. I didn't summon you junior faculty from the institute here to nap. We have great work to do."

Adelman set the box upon the table and raised his palms slightly off the top as if feeling some energy from it.

"At last," he said, "the great, wonderful day!"

Hieroglyphics carved onto the lid of the box captured Adelman's attention. As his orderlies attended his side, he read from the inscription.

*"Life and death, the flower and mould of existence, needn't be our masters. The sparrow that falls will one day rise as a falcon unto the sun. The opener of this casket has no reason to fear life and death, for he is the conqueror of both."*

Adelman's eyes assumed a luster at the finish of the translation. He wiped his palms on his smock and lifted the cover off the box – what lay inside struck him with emotion. With quivering hands he reached into the chest and withdrew a simple rolled scroll of brown papyrus. It was bound with a leather strap, which upon touching quickly broke away into dusty fragments. Adelman carefully unrolled the scroll and read from it silently, his lips moving, sometimes shivering with the importance of the words he translated for himself. He appeared as a man half enthralled, half afraid. He then lowered the scroll, rolled it back up and placed it on the table, his eyes fixed straight ahead of him, as though he was witness to something both terrible and sublime.

"Bring HER to me," Adelman said half dazed.

At the approach of the orderlies, Siri and Mallory abandoned their hiding place behind the statue and slipped behind a bank of machinery. Adelman's assistants took hold of the glass coffin and wheeled it upright into the center of the chamber. As they moved it from its niche, the top of the case caught on a curtain that blocked off an observation window used in times past to observe innovative therapies for the violently insane.

Siri could hardly believe her eyes when she saw Ash behind the glass. He was strapped to an upright surgical table, secured by the neck, wrists, and legs, beside a Jacuzzi-type tank, evidently once used in the process of water curing or hydrotherapy. Clear, rising liquid blown by jets swirled about the bath like a whirlpool and from its viscous and sticky bubbles Siri could see it wasn't water. Then another orderly stepped into view behind the glass and checked several temperature dials. Even in profile and wearing scrubs Siri recognized her. It was the head barista from the "Live Slow Café!"

Adelman proceeded to take a blood sample from Christian, and then busied himself with mixing it with a final batch of chemicals in a glass beaker, incorporating the contents of the blue test tube. He was completely distracted by his work and seemed to be in a world of his own. A plea from Kaelyn and a shout from Collin both failed to get his attention. Siri took the opportunity to slip closer to the observation window. Ash appeared unconscious, but more alarming was the sign on the steel door: "Vitamin D Tissue Preservation Trial, Phase 1: Efficacy Experiment." Siri tried to enter the room, but discovered it was locked!

# CHAPTER 84: Mad Love

The sight of the encased woman in the foot lights startled Adelman's prisoners to silence. There was no doubt she was a corpse. Kaelyn had to turn away. Bernie swallowed hard. Adelman, bearing the beaker in his hands, approached the case with awe, conscious of every step he took, as if he was in the audience of royalty. He stood before the woman with upward cast eyes, and for several moments stood as silent and still as the vision of beauty he gazed upon. Suddenly Adelman bent and opened an aperture at the base of the glass coffin. He carefully poured in the contents of the beaker. Almost immediately a misty cloud arose within the case. It became thick and milky as it rose and completely enveloped the figure of the woman, shrouding her from everyone's view. Adelman then walked over to an old Victrola and gave its handle a few cranks. He then placed the needle on the spinning record and a strain of music filled the air. It was an old song that had some kind effect on the scientist, for his eyes turned glassy and red. Adelman began to mouth the words silently at first. Then he slowly stepped around a table and began serenading the gas-shrouded woman within the glass case, singing about pyramids along the Nile, and sunrises on tropic isles, and that she'll always belong to him…

As the song doled on, the front door of the glass case swung gently open. The vapor inside poured out and spread upon the floor – followed by a woman's foot. Adelman stepped back in wonder.

His eyes widened and a smile of rapture split his face. A murky shape sauntered out of a cloud towards him, its milky-white arms outstretched, its two soap-white hands reaching for him. In a supreme display of his success Adelman tore his scrubs from his body in one motion. He was arrayed in the white headdress and robes of a desert prince with a huge, flashing crescent of a scimitar stuck in his belt, and appeared like Rudolph Valentino or Lawrence of Arabia.

"Vera!" Adelman exclaimed. "At last! Come to me! Come to your SHEIK!"

Adelman stared pie-eyed when his resurrected wife drew nearer to him, the hollows of her face partly visible in the dispelling mist. The scientist beamed with rapture as he felt her touch. As her ivory fingers traced along his temples, one could have sworn there was a hint of disdain in the woman's hypnotic stare. Adelman laughed out loud.

"HA! HA! HA! HA! VERA! YOU HAVE ALWAYS BEEN MY ONE AND ONLY LOVE!"

Then Adelman's expression turned to wide-eyed surprise when he felt his late wife's slender hands wrap around his throat with a vice-like grip, which bore him to the floor in a series of drawn out gurgles and gasps. One orderly fled from the room in panic.

"Mallory!" Siri shouted. "Get the keys!"

Mallory stuck out a foot just as the orderly dashed passed her. When he hit the floor face first she snatched a key ring from his belt. The second orderly went to stop her, but in an abrupt motion Dent's mummy head-butted him into unconsciousness upon the tiles. Suddenly there was a pronounced *"click"* and the door to the observation room opened. Siri saw the barista in her scrubs peer out in curiosity. Siri then saw Ash in the room behind her. Hardly thinking, Siri picked up a Bunsen burner, cranked up the flame, and grabbed the barista by the collar.

"Release my friend!" Siri ordered, brandishing the burner. "Or I'll melt your face!"

The barista turned and looked back with astonishment, but not at Siri or the Bunsen burner with its roaring jet of blue flame aimed at her. She was looking past them, and as she did she backed up, her jaw dropping open in a fit of stifled awe. Siri turned sharply and saw Adelman's wife, white as a marble statue, eyes glassy cold, alabaster arms reaching out, lumbering towards her with a suspicious, lingering trace of a morbid smile on her lips.

Adelman raised his head from the tiled floor just as the silken train of his wife's gown swept over him like a death shroud. The record spent itself, scratching and skipping on the phonograph player. As it scratched away, Adelman lifted his eyes toward heaven and choked out:

"Too – much – Vitamin – D! Too...much...Vitamin... DEEEeeeeeeee...!"

Then he fell back dead, eyes aimed forever upwards. At his side lay the ancient papyrus scroll crumpled into useless fragments upon the floor, its secret of eternal life and death lost forever.

"The blue vial," Fletcher shouted to Siri, jutting his chin in that direction.

"Whatever happens, she mustn't get it!"

Siri spied the blue vial in a test tube rack two steps away. The walking cadaver of Adelman's precious Vera toppled violently upon the rack of tubes, its two alabaster arms extended in a desperate reach that terminated into stiff, tapering fingers shaped into claws. Its awkward, graceless motion, no doubt owing to the onset of rigor mortis, obliterated half the contents of the table, mostly bubbling beakers, but it failed to obtain what it sought.

Siri quickly snatched up the vial, holding it close. The animated cadaver straightened, and turned mechanically towards Siri. Then throwing out its smooth, bloodless arms, it lurched at Siri with a mouth opened to a wide square as if drawn by invisible wires. The sound that came from the parted lips was like the guttural squawk a long coffin nail makes when wrenched from splitting pine.

"Run Sprout!" Collin shouted. He struggled in his chains while Mallory desperately tried working the padlock. "Get out of here!"

Siri backed into the further recesses of the chamber and saw her only route to safety. She dashed towards the observation room, followed by the barista. Once through the threshold she closed the metal door and threw the bolt. A terrible pounding ensued from the other end. Through the peep slot in the door Siri could see the wide, cold, dark eyes of Vera glaring in at her. In her flight, Siri must have dropped the Bunsen burner. Its flame must have ignited the white, silken fabric of Vera's gown. It must have. For what else could explain the terrible pillar of fire that shot up before the gaping eyes of Adelman's precious Vera on the other side of the observation window, a fire that swayed and hammered at the metal door with a glaring horror for a face, a face that was fast being consumed by flames?

# CHAPTER 85: The Terror

Siri didn't like the look of Ash strapped upright and unconscious on the inclined surgical table. He was covered over in a sheet up to his neck and strapped down at the chest and legs, but he looked like he was past help. His eyes were closed and his chin was resting on his chest, and that sent a surge of emotion through Siri.

"Bring him out of it!" Siri ordered the barista over Vera's incessant pounding, "and no tricks! Get me?"

To Siri it sounded like Adelman's living-dead widow was using a wrecking ball against the door. Black smoke was seeping through the peephole in the vault-like panel along with a nasty, acrid smell of burning flesh and embalming compound. Siri towed the barista by her elbow over towards Ash.

"Bring him out of it now, or so help me..." Siri yelled.

The barista pulled off her surgical cap and shook her short cropped, brunette hair free so that it poofed into a fuzz-ball about her head. She regarded the assortment of beakers and chemicals arrayed on a metal counter before her.

"I never brought anyone out of it before," she said. "I only put them under."

Siri gritted her teeth.

"Well you're gonna do it now."

The barista selected a syringe, and quickly loaded it with a bright orange fluid.

"What's that stuff?" Siri asked.

"It's the antidote," replied the barista. "Now no more questions. This is delicate work."

"No tricks, remember?" Siri said. "Or you'll be on that table."

The barista injected the contents of the syringe into the carotid artery just below Ash's ear.

"He should come around in a moment," the barista said, stepping away.

Siri studied Ash's sharply angled features for a reaction. Suddenly his broad chest heaved as he drew a breath. Then Ash's eyelids cracked open as he stirred in his restraints.

"He'll be fine in no time," the barista said, watching Ash's response. She narrowed her eyes at Siri. "But I wish I could say the same for you."

Siri turned. She had just a split second to catch the hand swooping a scalpel down at her own neck.

"Doctor Adelman was a great scientist," the barista growled, forcing the deadly, glinting implement closer towards Siri's face. "He saw in me more than just a double mocha swirl with a biscotti on the side and a tramp stamp. Now he lies lifeless in the next room. Because of you I'll have to study for the SAT, when Adelman could have given me all the answers!"

Siri applied all her strength in her effort to force the weapon back. Suddenly she switched her attention from the razor-sharp scalpel closing in on her nose to something moving towards them that was quite the attention-getter.

"You better look behind you," Siri remarked. She resisted the increasing pressure of the barista's determined thrust as best as she could, but she knew she couldn't hold out for long.

"You expect me to fall for that old trick?" The barista smiled, fiendishly. "That's the oldest one in the book. I'm gonna slice and dice you like an onion in a Vego-Meat-Oh-Matic for $9.99 minus the shipping!"

Siri's eyes widened.

"Really, I'm not kidding. Look behind you!"

"You must think my head zips up the back."

"Please! Look," Siri exclaimed, "before it's too late for the both of us!"

The barista turned out of curiosity. Then she screamed, and screamed, and screamed again, dropping the scalpel. Siri backed away at the sight of the thing emerging into the light from an umbra of shadow and smoke. She could hardly believe what she saw. Into a cone of dull yellow glare cast from an overhead light fixture walked a faceless pillar of blackened human framework. A charred skull surmounting a rocking, smoking skeleton bedecked in a gown reduced to ashen, smoky rags stalked into clear, unmistakable view. It was Vera, or what the ravages of the flames failed to claim of her. She rose to level height, reaching out her left and right arms scorched of all recognizable flesh that wafted ceiling-ward curling tendrils of grey smoke. The barista quickly joined Siri's side, and both backed against the humming, Jacuzzi-type tank and its whirlpool of viscous and sticky bubbles.

"Sh...Sh...She's still coming!" The barista stammered to Siri. "What do we do?"

Siri looked at Ash. He raised his head, regaining his bearings, shaking off his drug-induced daze. The last thing Siri wanted was for him to fall victim to the reanimated creature that was once Adelman's wife. Siri turned to Vera with her blackened, eyeless sockets and the smoldering pile of articulated bones beneath, the whole figure advancing and swaying, to an fro, like a drunkard along an alley. Siri could hardly believe that this tottering column of bones and rags could possess living strength, but it did. When the thing encountered a sturdy wood table piled with flasks and beakers forming the only obstacle, a skeletal arm swept it away with a stroke that overturned it as though it was nothing.

"Somehow we've got to distract it," said Siri.

"Distract that? You're joking," replied the barista, her eyes wide as saucers.

"It only wants the blue vial," Siri added, clutching the test tube.

"Then give it to her for crying out loud," the barista replied. "What are you waiting for?"

Siri spied another door at the opposite end of the chamber. A sign on the wall next to it read "GENERATOR ROOM."

"No. I've got a better idea," said Siri.

Ash let out a groan. Siri turned to him as he struggled in his straps.

"Ash!" Siri shouted. "Don't move!"

Siri eyed the door and tugged the barista by the arm.

"Come on!"

## CHAPTER 86: The Torrent and the Turbines

The desperate tone in Siri's voice alerted Ash into greater wakefulness. In a supreme application of animal power he sucked in a long breath that swelled his chest beneath the sheet until the strain of his inflated torso became too much for the leather manacle to resist. The belt burst and went flying from him with the sound of a cracking whip. Ash then wrenched the leather straps that bound his wrists, first the left, then the right, ripping them out entirely.

The generator room's grotesque vaulted arches had a chilling effect on Siri and the barista. The arrangement of three, great, churning paddle wheels over a slimy stonework sluice also caught them by surprise. Siri was expecting to find a turbine generator, the kind found in electric power plants. Her hope was to lure Adelman's late wife close enough to a transformer and electrocute her to ashes, at least that's how it worked on Saturday afternoon Creature Features. But instead Siri saw a gaping, brick-lined channel of water rushing past banks of machinery bolted in stages over the drab walls, powered by the paddle wheels and the foaming torrent.

"We need to go to plan B," said Siri.

"I didn't know we had a plan A," the barista returned.

Siri looked around the gloomy sanctum. She needed a moment to think. Suddenly the generator room door burst open and Vera lurched out of the shadows.

"Here she comes again!" the poofy-haired barista shouted.

"Give her the vial!"

"No," Siri replied.

Siri pulled the barista out of harms way and under some vaulted brickwork, while Vera, quick as a rat and grinning rows of ivory teeth, glided across the chamber to confront them eyes to eye sockets, barring any chance for escape.

"Hey, bone head," Siri shouted. "You want this?"

Siri then did a foolish thing even by her standards. She held the vial aloft between her finger and thumb. Suddenly Vera, like a marionette dropped by invisible cords, bowed her rickety frame and approached Siri like a beggar beseeching a morsel. The horror then extended its two ghoulish arms and opened and closed its gruesome, articulated finger bones in a ghastly, if not pitiful, display of need.

"Come and get it," Siri said.

"Are you nuts?" shouted the barista.

Siri cautiously crept from the sanctuary of the arch and moved towards the gushing torrent that hissed incessantly in the middle of the ancient, generator room. Vera followed determinedly, arms inclined outward, sauntering and swaying, like a tipsy barfly hypnotized by the promise of another tumbler of gin. Siri turned to the barista.

"I know what I'm doing. I hope."

In the split second that Siri took her eyes off her, Vera had snatched the blue vial from her grasp and uncorked it with speed and artfulness.

"That's not good," said Siri, standing dumbfounded.

Vera tilted back her skeletal head and raised the cobalt blue life-ever-after fluid to her hideous jawbone, which fell wide open. Siri's eyes bulged. She couldn't believe she blew it.

Suddenly a dark blur swept passed Siri with bat-like speed. Ash emerged from the shadows and seized the tower of blackened bones bodily. His abrupt entrance upon the scene knocked the vial to the floor, shattering it. Vera's cavernous eye sockets aimed down upon the destroyed container. Somehow the creature must have sensed all hope for eternal existence was now futile, for the thing, roused to unmitigated rage, suddenly broke Ash's hold.

"Leave here!" Ash shouted to Siri.

"Not without you!" Siri shouted back.

Turning to Ash, the skeletal horror, which was once Adelman's precious spouse, converged upon him with malignant purpose. It reached out two fleshless claws for a deadly, impending grasp. Ash, glancing at the foaming current, read the monster's fatal intent, and made his move first. He rushed at Adelman's one and only Vera, and in a nightmarish struggle, both plunged head first into the gushing torrent.

"Ash!" Siri shouted, rushing over to the brink and looking down into its foaming depths.

Siri could see Ash and Vera locked in a deadly embrace, each pushing the other's head under the water. Ash popped up and gasped for air. His arm reached for Siri. Siri reached down to take Ash's hand, but Vera's charred head bobbed up again and her bony grip pulled his hand away. Ash and the skeletal horror disappeared under the froth and were flushed away in the surging waters channeling into the slimy, brick arched tunnel. Suddenly in the frothing, stewing current Siri detected a movement, and saw Ash surface again, but further down. He was anchored only by a tenuous grip on a slippery hunk of brick.

"Hold on!" Siri shouted. She moved into position, fell upon her knees and held out her hand to him.

Ash wiped a veil of water from his face and drew a needed breath. The barista, seeing the desperateness of the situation, rushed up behind Siri and hung onto her waist, so she didn't fall in.

"I've got you!" The barista shouted. "Try to grab onto him!"

"I'm trying!" Siri cried. "I'm trying!"

Ash reached up, straining every fiber of his arm to force his own fingertips to meet Siri's.

"Come on, Ash!" Siri shouted, leaning out over the foaming current as far as she could, the barista clinging onto her. "You can do it! You can do it!"

"It has me by the legs!" Ash gasped, struggling in the swirling froth. "It's pulling me under!"

Siri turned to the barista. "I'm going to try something! Don't let go!"

"Don't worry! I won't!" The barista shot back.

Siri quickly unwrapped her arm bandages and tossed out a strand to Ash, using it as a lifeline. He snatched it up and held on.

"Now pull me back!" Siri shouted to the barista. "We'll reel him in, just like a tuna!"

"Okay, I'm pulling!" The barista returned, yanking Siri backwards with all her might. "Start reeling!"

The barista pulled and pulled at Siri. Siri reeled and reeled her bandages. By the looks of things, the idea appeared to be working. Ash was getting nearer to the channel's edge. Adelman's one and only love must have let him go and was washed downstream. When Ash finally gripped the wet stonework, Siri bent down to help him to safety.

"You did it!" Siri exclaimed, reaching out to Ash, her fingertips almost touching his. "Thank goodness!"

No sooner did Siri say the words, a terrible, skeletal hand burst out of the churning water, severed the bandage lifeline with its dripping claws, and clamping its bony fingers over Ash's face, dragged him under the raging current and out of sight.

**"NO!"** Siri screamed, her face petrified by the cruel reality of what she had just witnessed. **"NO, PLEASE NO!"** Then followed a moment in which Siri could say nothing, only breathe and gaze. Finally, Siri uttered something, but in a voice softened with choking emotion, her gaze still fixed on the place where Ash had vanished from her sight.

*"Ash."*

Then she bowed her head.

# CHAPTER 87 : Silent Reflections

Siri had no appetite. She usually ate like a horse, or so her dad told her, but in the three days she last saw Ash disappear within the raging current of an underground stream, she had hardly touched a thing. It was almost midnight and Siri was sitting at her desk in her bedroom that overlooked the old gas-style street lamps of Wicks End. A crescent moon was rising over a line of jagged rooftops and bare trees. The night was remarkably cold for early November, and black as black with twinkling stars scattered here and there, like sugar on velvet.

Siri was watching Miss Sinclair, the spinster who lived in 29 Wicks End, the Gothic, three-story house next door. Miss Sinclair was setting out her snares again. Her whole front yard was arrayed with booby traps of every kind. She was one hundred and two, and believed that the blood of small animals kept her trim and sprightly, and quick with her wit. The side of her house facing away from the street was tacked with squirrel and raccoon pelts drying in the sun, not to mention the occasional stray cat. Even in the darkness Siri could see Miss Sinclair in her favorite sun hat, decorated with the little dried head of a squirrel peeking over the brim.

"That will be me some day," Siri said to herself.

Siri unfolded a piece of paper and flattened it on top of her desk. It was the parchment she rescued from the Black Ram Inn. The last time Siri looked at it she was with Ash. If only she knew then how terribly that night would end, maybe she would have done things differently. But the night did end, and there was no going back. Siri remembered the brickwork of the Danvers Asylum bathed in the blue and red bursts of emergency police lights when she finally stepped outside.

Scarpetti had closed a rear door to a squad car on Dent handcuffed in the backseat behind a wire grill. The big Mongolian, Fez Guy, and Adelman's orderlies (including the poofy-haired barista), were similarly secured in squad cars parked immediately behind. Dent's mummy, conveyed on a stretcher, was carried passed Siri as she stood beside her dad and Mallory. Bound in chains, it paused from its struggles, its dark eyes regarding Siri with a twinkling token of friendship. She was still wearing her mummy bandages under a policeman's coat. Cedric stepped in and helped two EMTs lift the Egyptian into a waiting police van, and as the doors closed on the mummy it raised its bandaged head to gain one last glimpse of his rescuer. Scarpetti strode over to where Siri stood with her dad and Mallory.

"You should be very proud of yourself, young lady," Scarpetti said to her. "That was the best police work I ever saw."

Scarpetti turned to her dad.

"By the way, Dwight and Pantano led a SWAT team into the Black Ram. It was like a whole bakery exploded in there. They found nothing, not a trace of Dent's followers. Emma and Bernie's Aunts are busy as we speak cleaning up quite a mess."

"You'll never find the rest of my followers," Dent bragged from the squad car. "Communal astral projection is a concept your narrow policeman's brain will never get its closed mind around. I won't be in custody for long. You'll see, Detective Vincenzo Artoro Scarpetti. Mark my words..."

A police officer entering the squad car closed the door on Dent's rant. Scarpetti turned again to Siri and patted her on the shoulder.

"Yes, little lady. That was quite a bit of police work you did."

"Yeah, right," Siri muttered at her desk. "Some police work."

Siri wrapped her bathrobe tighter around herself. She felt cold, despite the thermostat being turned up. She turned to the charred parchment and focused on the scrawled writing that was still legible. It was definitely a formula of some kind, an important one, judging from Ash's reaction to it almost being completely destroyed. Ash never did tell her in words what the formula was for, but Siri did have a notion. The pictures he made flash behind her eyelids in the Witch House told her something, a story of sorts, a story she was now part of, but it was far from a fairy tale. Suddenly Siri heard a floorboard creak behind her.

A sudden chill ran up Siri's spine – a chill of no degrees Fahrenheit, but a draining of blood from her vital senses. Siri suddenly felt scared. She didn't want to turn around. The reflection in her bedroom window told her why, for it was black and clear, like looking into the still waters of a millpond. The tingly sensations of small hairs standing on the back of Siri's neck added to her unease. She could see everything behind her, her whole room in fact. Siri saw her own reflection at her desk, especially her frizzy, tangled hair outlined by a nightlight. And then there were the others things she saw – the dark, silent, figures of women emerging from the thin air directly behind her, some bedecked in dresses with frilly collars and puffy shoulders, others in carriage bonnets of a by-gone pattern, and still others in black, high collar crinoline gowns, their hair done up in buns, all standing in a cluster behind her.

Siri couldn't see their faces, for they were something like shadows thrown upon a wall, but they were there all the same, drawing nearer and nearer. Siri felt a surge of panic, but maintained her courage and control. Then she felt something touch her and she no longer felt afraid. Nor did she feel the cold anymore.

Siri turned slightly, and when she did, she saw a soft, soap-white hand resting upon her shoulder as if to comfort her. Siri recognized the smooth, tapered fingers and the blue sapphire ring on the ring finger, twinkling like a pole star in the dim light, for it was her mom's birthstone. Siri also recognized the gentle voice whispering softly in her ear, sounding like music.

*"H e l p   t h e m."*

Siri finally summoned the courage to turn around, and when she did, she found herself alone.

# CHAPTER 88: Letter from Molly

Siri felt compelled to climb the attic stairs a few days after the bedroom incident. It was twilight and she had a flashlight with her. Siri had found a letter nestled in the bottom of her mom's trunk, which she started to read. It was strange how legible this letter was compared to all the others she had sifted through. There was a shine in the writing that was unmistakable.

*"I have come to an understanding,"* the letter read. Siri continued reading it in the glow of her flashlight.

*"No one is born without purpose, whose discovery is the quest of every living soul. We are like storm-tossed mariners desperately searching for this guiding star. I am thankful that I have come to know my purpose, although my path is beset with countless difficulties. If I falter, then another must take up the gauntlet, for we are all prisoners of time and there never seems to be enough of it. Yet if what we strive for is noble and good then the results will transcend this insurmountable of barriers. To whoever reads these words be comforted. You will find your way. – Molly Pitcher. February 27, 1775.*

Siri placed the letter down and sat thoughtfully for a moment. Then she overheard her dad calling from downstairs.

"Sprout? It's time to go!"

# CHAPTER 89: Guest of Honor

The last place Siri wanted to be was standing before a big microphone in front of lots of people, but that's where she was. She was in the grand atrium of the Museum of Antiquities with its soaring skylight, standing at a podium. The museum was celebrating the return of the stolen mummies and Siri was their guest of honor. Siri had never spoken into a microphone before. Of all the horrors she had been through, the big microphone, made all the bigger with its black sound cushion, scared her the most. Siri was wearing a downy vest over a black turtleneck and blue jeans. She could see her dad and Detective Scarpetti sitting in the front row of metal folding chairs. Kaelyn Skye and Bramwell Fletcher joined them. Dobbs took a seat in the opposite row and fanned himself with a museum brochure. Emma and Bernie were there seated two rows behind him. Bernie gave Siri a wink. She smiled back. There had to be over a hundred people filing into the museum. Siri wondered if there were enough chairs. Even Mayor Atwill was there, along with other Salem dignitaries. Old heating pipes hissed and clanged amidst the din of people settling into their seats.

Siri took something from her vest pocket and stole a peek at it. It was a picture postcard airmailed to her from Cairo, Egypt. It showed Cedric and Dent's mummy, both in khakis and wearing pith helmets, mounted on camels posing before the sun-drenched Great Pyramid of

Giza. Siri felt silly about mistaking Cedric's grandfather for Cedric himself back in 1922, as if he discovered a secret revitalizing formula. A note below the photograph read:

*"Both doing well. Getting close to locating Ptah's nearest (living) relative. According to a little-known custom it's his next of kin's duty to take our preserved friend in."*

There were also some hieroglyphics on the card written by a hand not used to pens, and evidently translated by Cedric. They read: *"Wish you were here, kid!"*

Siri looked around. She saw Mallory sitting with Christian. Both were fashionably dressed in matching black leather. Siri smiled when she noticed his hand was gently holding hers. Constance Nash was there too – seated next to Bain, Mallory's cousin. And for the first time Constance looked truly happy.

Suddenly the lights dimmed and the atrium hushed into silence. A spotlight snapped on Siri. She squinted uncomfortably in the glare. A cordial applause welcomed her after a brief introduction by Mister Pew, the museum's aged and hunched-over curator. Siri cleared her throat and started reading from a poem printed on a little sheet of paper she held in her hand.

"Acquainted With The Night," by Robert Frost," spoke Siri, the sound of her echoing voice startling her. She stepped back a little from the microphone and continued to read the poem about a lonely wanderer walking an empty street at night, without a friend in the world. When she finished reading, Siri raised her head. She swallowed nervously and cleared her throat again.

"Good evening, everyone," she said. "My name is Siri Braddock. I'm a sophomore at Windward High School. A month ago that poem wouldn't have meant that much to me. But it sure does now. I've learned a lot about myself in that time and about Salem. I've discovered Salem is not your average city. Hey, where else can one meet a witch, discover a secret stairway, and have a great latte, all in one day? Sure, Salem is known the world over as the "Witch City" because of its tragic past. But I think it's time for Salem to be known for something else. Don't you? Salem doesn't persecute people anymore. It welcomes them, especially people who are different. Salem should be known for its acceptance and tolerance, not just for its witches. Salem should be known as a sanctuary from prejudice and hatred, a place where everyone can reach for the stars. I bet it was tough being a teenager three hundred years ago. It's even tougher now. Trust me. Believe it or not, I'm standing at this microphone because I found some stolen mummies. It was very nice of Mister Pew to invite me here for that reason. But I also lost something too, someone very dear to me. I realize now you never really know where you'll find that special someone. It could be in the unlikeliest place or at the unlikeliest time. That special someone can't be here with us tonight. So I'd like to dedicate this piece of music to him. It was always special to me, and I think in some way, special to him. For like the lonely wanderer in Frost's poem, he was truly acquainted with the night."

Siri looked at her dad. She could see him raising a questioning eyebrow. She leaned back towards the microphone.

"Thanks for having me."

Siri stepped away from the microphone as enthusiastic applause filled the vast room. She made a beeline to a corner pillar as a spotlight fell upon a string quartet. Principal Fletcher stood and introduced two sophomore girls and two senior boys from Windward High School seated on stools. They were uniformly dressed in white shirts and black pants. The girls tucked their violins under their chins and struck their bows, the boys played their cellos. The forlorn strains of Pachelbel's Canon in D Major floated through the atrium like a spell, riveting every eye and stilling every breath, Siri's most of all.

As Siri listened in the corner, she felt her youth slipping away. She thought of her childhood, her departed mom, and the passing of the seasons. Siri began to see things too – shapes floating and revolving in the air. As the somber chords of the Canon in D Major rose and fell away, Siri felt her own emotions welling and subsiding. The swirling figures she saw merged into two distinct forms. They were like suspended ghosts gowned and fitted in the fashion of another age enjoying an eternal waltz before a millpond. One looked like Siri, the other – Ash. Siri remembered how she felt when Ash disappeared that night back at the asylum. She looked over at Mallory sitting with Christian, and Constance sitting next to Bain. It was then she slipped out of the atrium.

# CHAPTER 90: Night Gallery

Siri wound her way up the dimly lit stairwell that led to the second floor of the museum. She didn't know where she was going. She just felt she needed to get away from everyone. Siri turned down a corridor, passing display cases containing Polynesian war clubs, some lined with razor-sharp shark teeth. She paused at the threshold of a dark gallery. As Siri peered into the dimly lit room, she could still hear the haunting, somber cords of the Canon in D Major drifting up from the atrium below. Somehow she felt drawn to this gallery. Siri entered it, and as her eyes adjusted to the low light, she saw that it was a room she had entered before. A rhythmic tick-tock sound told her she was right.

Siri turned in the direction of the ticking sound and saw the Highland Mantel Clock displayed over a colonial-style hearth. The clock looked as good as new, considering all it had been through. This was where it had all started, Siri remembered, as she stared at the elegant clock face. It was strange how much better she felt standing near it, like it was an old friend who knew her deepest secrets. Siri knew the clock's secret too.

Above the hearth was a big mirror gilded in gold leaf and something in its reflection caught Siri's eye. It was on the opposite wall hanging directly across from her so that its reflection was caught in the mirror. Siri turned – and took a breath. She couldn't believe her eyes. She found herself gazing upon a life size portrait of a young woman donned in a shimmering ball gown, her hair done up in ringlets, her smooth, alert face looking so familiar.

"Why it's me!" Siri whispered to herself.

She stepped towards the portrait while gazing upon the wide, blue and brown eyes, which seemed to gaze back at her. Siri looked to the base of the portrait. Judging from a little brass plaque at the bottom, which listed the artist and subject as unknown, it was a recently restored painting from the 1700's. Siri brushed a lock of hair from her eyes as she studied her own likeness, and when she did, she heard a name being whispered in her ear, a name out of the darkness – *"Molly."* Siri felt a sudden chill run up her spine. It was weird to look so much like someone else, someone who lived long ago. She could still hear the Canon in D Major drifting from the atrium below.

Suddenly the already dim gallery got darker, as if light from the corridor was abruptly blotted out. Siri turned towards the doorway and her eyes widened. Standing in the threshold was a dark figure with shoulder-length hair and a ground-sweeping great coat of a bygone fashion. It was like a living shadow and for a moment it stood tall and silent as it regarded Siri in the gloom. Then in measured steps it advanced towards her. Several times Siri blinked for she thought she was dreaming. She even wondered if she was losing her grip on reality.

As the Canon in D Major continued to drift from below, Siri could have sworn time was moving backwards and forwards and then backwards again, like the two figures she saw in an eternal waltz. She felt her mind slipping away, and found herself in a shimmering ball gown while being led in a dance with a handsome young man who she thought was lost to her forever. Siri didn't want to wake up if she was dreaming. It was night, with it twinkling stars and shining moon hurtling through the blackness of space. It was when Siri felt most alive – when her senses were awakened. It was the time for dreams and fantasy. And where such notions end and reality begins, who can tell? It may have been minutes, hours, or days that passed, when Siri found herself standing next to Ash under an old, gas-style lamppost at the corner of Wicks End, and relishing her beautiful nightmare.

# The End

Join Siri of Wicks End in her next Salem Mystery

# "The Phantom of Winter Island."

Cutting From The SALEM TIMES, 11 November.
*(pasted to the bulletin board of the Salem Harbor Master's Office)*

A strange, tall, veiled, inordinately thin woman walked into the office of Jack Wall, assistant Harbor Master, around midnight last night inquiring on the latitudinal and longitudinal map bearing of the Egyptian Museum in Cairo on the Nile Delta. Mr. Wall, a stolid maritime sort, thought the request too out of the ordinary to take seriously at first, but when the woman advanced on Mr. Wall, pressing her inquiry, Mr. Wall got out his maritime atlas and obliged his visitor with the map reference of Cairo, Egypt. When Mr. Wall asked the woman whose face he could not see clearly on account of her heavy veil, why she wanted the information, she replied it was a *"matter of life or death."* With this announcement Mr. Wall inquired the name of the woman, but she turned and left the office before anymore could be learned of her. It was later reported by one Walter Sullivan of Salem that while walking his dog down by Salem Willows after midnight that same night he saw a tall, thin woman covered in a veil walk eastward into the sea and disappear under the waves.

# Siri's letter to Ptah

Siri Braddock  
7 Wicks End  
Salem, Massachusetts 01970  
USA

November 27, 20--

Ptah Ptahhotep  
Hotel Sakkara  
13 Ahmed Ragheb Street  
Cairo Old City, Egypt

(Hello, Mister Cedric. Please translate this into hieratic, Old Kingdom. Thanks, Siri.)

Dear Ptah,

Thank you for the postcard. You and Cedric make a good team on camelback. I hope I get a chance to visit Egypt one day. I'd like to see the pyramids and sail along the Nile. What an amazing experience it must be for you to be back home, but it must be bewildering too, for the sands of Egypt have covered over everything you knew and loved for thousands of years. The world has changed so much since the days of the pharaohs. You must miss your friends and family a lot.

Want to know something, Ptah? I've come to realize that Salem and Egypt are a lot alike. They both have a long history and places that attract tourists from all over the world. You and I aren't so different from each other either. We're both unique, and that makes us special, at least that's what my dad says. I've also learned that fate has a way of bringing people together and giving us friends. We meet them at the most unlikeliest times and places. So let's consider each other friends. Good luck with finding your living relatives and a place to stay. It's going to happen soon, I feel it. And if you're ever in Salem again, please drop by for a visit. It would be great to see you. Well, that's all for now. Until next time!

Yours friend always,  
Siri

P.S. If you're ever short on rolls of linen bandages, just let me know and I'll send some over - Express!

# Salem Survival Kit

- [ ] Graveyard Map of Charter Street Burial Ground *(know where the important bodies are buried)*
- [ ] Map of Salem's haunted houses *(helpful when detecting gloating faces staring out from windows – you'll know when to run)*
- [ ] Binoculars *(no need to get too close to that haunted house)*
- [ ] Swiss Army Knife *(you never know when you need to open your own bedroom window from the outside)*
- [ ] Compass *(know where your latte is)*
- [ ] Bubble gum. Grape flavored *(to pass the time during graveyard stakeouts)*
- [ ] Chocolate bar *(you can't eat bubble gum)*
- [ ] Museum pass *(you never know when you need to duck out of sight)*
- [ ] Black knit commando cap *(keep your head warm on cold nights)*
- [ ] The business card of a Salem psychic *(you never know when you'll need good advice)*

## Some Do's and Don'ts

- Don't ever stare at witches *(it's not polite)*
- Know the directions to Gallows Hill *(because a tourist will ask you where it is, and you'll want to look smart)*
- Read Nathaniel Hawthorne's "The House of the Seven Gables." *(because if you go there one of the tour guides will ask if you read the novel, and believe me, they will)*
- Know what a Salem Gibralta is *(No. It's not a big rock)*
- Pick up your feet when you walk Essex Street *(you don't want to trip on a cobblestone)*
- Buy a love potion *(because we all could use some help in that department)*
- Believe everything you see and hear in Salem. *It's part of the magic!*

# About the Authors

Don't look for John and Vincent DiGianni on the road well traveled, for they are drawn to byways less frequented. Their shrines are the haunted spots and twilight places of Salem and Marblehead, the desolate lighthouse islands off Manchester by the Sea and Rockport, or the broken mausoleums in remote and misty graveyards.

John enjoys oil painting and his artwork has been displayed in many North Shore art galleries. He likes rambles in the countryside or along wind swept beaches, and has an interest in astronomy and paleontology.

Vincent is a reader of esoteric books. He enjoys ancient history and classical literature, particularly the works of Edgar Allen Poe and Washington Irving.

In writing this novel the authors invite the reader to glimpse a specter behind every curtained window, find a secret panel in every living room, or a mysterious trapdoor in the basement – if they dare. Shadowy, hidden realms are all around us, waiting to be explored. "Shadow Over Siri" is an expedition to such a place, and its name is WICKS END.

21877049R00190

Made in the USA
Middletown, DE
14 July 2015